To my dau...
Hope you enjoy.
Bob

WhipSw

Robert L. Hecker

Hard Shell Word Factory

© 2003 Robert L. Hecker
ISBN: 0-7599-4036-3
Trade Paperback
Published August 2003

eBook ISBN: 0-7599-4035-5
Published June 2003

Hard Shell Word Factory
PO Box 161
Amherst Jct. WI 54407
Books@hardshell.com
http://www.hardshell.com
Cover art © 2003 Dirk A. Wolf
Printed in the U.S.A.

Chapter One

IT WAS NEARING one o'clock in the morning. DEA Assistant Supervisor Jim Hendrix of Group 4, Los Angeles District Office, stood on the sidewalk two blocks from the hamburger stand at Beverly and Rampart trying to put aside the thought he might not live to see the sun come up.

Beside him, his partner, Agent Marc Duval, leaned cross-legged against the front fender of Frankie Rodriquez's Cadillac Brougham cleaning his nails with a small pen knife. Hendrix was probably the only one in the group who knew Duval's nonchalance was an act. He was just as antsy as any of them; it was just that experience had taught him to hide it better.

Jim Hendrix looked at the other three agents standing close by. "Frankie says this dude is mean, so watch yourself."

He turned to Frankie sitting behind the wheel of his Caddy. They were using Frankie's car because his three hundred-plus pounds didn't fit well in the type of unmarked cars the DEA generally used.

"That right, Frankie?"

Fat Frankie bent his thick neck into what passed for a nod. "Yeah. *Muy macho.*"

Frankie had changed a lot in the five years since his army hitch with Hendrix and Duval. For one thing, he'd picked up more than 100 pounds and the nickname of 'Fat' Frankie. His thick hair was just as black, but his close-cropped beard and mustache, designed to concealed heavy jowls, was shot with gray. He wore an expensive Italian suit tailored to conceal at least part of his bulk.

The collar of his silk shirt was open, both because he could not get a necktie comfortably around his neck and because it allowed a gold cross and a heavy gold medallion to be seen. He touched the cross with stubby fingers festooned with a wide variety of rings, all flashing precious stones.

"Yeah," he repeated. "He's one bad *hombre.* You guys watch yourself."

"You guys got all your gear for a change?" Hendrix asked. "Including your cuffs?" Agents were forever going out on a bust, and after it was all over and the defendants were in custody, they found that nobody had brought handcuffs. It was embarrassing to take a prisoner to county jail with his hands secured by shoelaces.

The agents nodded.

"Okay. Everybody got vests on?" Hendrix was referring to the lightweight body armor, sometimes erroneously referred to as bulletproof vests, that most agents had issued to them.

Some agents preferred raid jackets that had body armor sewn inside the fabric of the dark blue, nylon windbreaker itself. These jackets had a gold cloth 'DEA' badge on the front left panel. Across the back in large gold letters was the word 'POLICE' with 'US AGENT', also in gold, beneath it. Some agents wore jackets which were identical, but didn't have armor sewn inside. Generally, the first two or three agents to go through a door on a raid wore the armor. Tonight, there'd be no doors. They'd be in the open so everybody was supposed to wear his armor except Hendrix who would be making contact with the suspect.

"Sandy," Hendrix said. "You got the portable?"

Sandy Tate held up the small PT-200 radio. "Sure. Got it."

Sandy Tate matched Hendrix's six-foot height, but where Hendrix was a German police dog, Tate was a Doberman. He looked fast and was—both physically and in his life style. He was relaxed, but reliable. He had a way of strolling into the office at ten or eleven in the morning that caused the blood pressure of their supervisor, John Hodges, to skyrocket.

But the way Sandy looked at it, their hours were flexible. Management said nine o'clock was the start of the work day. They forgot, however, to pin down a quitting time. Everybody liked Sandy; he came through when it counted.

The other agents were Arturo 'Arty' Hernandez and Bob Dansen. They could not have been more different. Arty was five-foot nine with a medium build. He spoke fluent Spanish which made him particularly valuable as an undercover agent in LA. Basically, Arty was a quiet man who went about his job with a cool precision.

Bob Dansen was also quiet, but there the resemblance ended. Dansen was six-two and weighed twice what Arty did. He'd been with the DEA for ten years. Dansen never, never did any undercover work. He claimed that the undercover role was unnecessary, but most members of the group sensed the truth: Dansen was scared shitless of working undercover. On top of that, he was lazy, doing exactly what he was told and no more. Nobody thought they could trust Dansen if the going got rough. Hendrix generally assigned him to a surveillance team, which was just fine with Dansen.

"What about the shotgun?" Duval asked Hendrix.

"Arty," Duval said, "you take it. We'd better not have it in

Frankie's car."

Taking a shotgun on a bust had to be authorized by the supervisor. It was the most powerful weapon an agent carried. Hearing the sound of a shotgun shell being jacked into a chamber had kept more than one crook from going for his gun.

"Okay," Arty said. "But I hope to hell we don't need it."

You don't hope any more than I do, Hendrix thought. Maybe he was getting too old for these busts. They was always hard on the nerves. You had no way of knowing what the asshole you were trying to bust would do. He might be high himself. And, nowadays, just about all dealers carried guns and were willing to use them. At the same time, more and more rules were being laid on the agents, making it increasingly difficult to get the job done without getting your ass in a sling. Hell, these days it might be the agent who ended up in court while the trafficker was living it up and laughing his head off.

Hendrix sighed and looked at his watch. "Okay. The guy's supposed to show in forty-five minutes. We'll try to make the bust in the burger stand parking lot. If I've got to go with the guy someplace, Marc'll let you know. Don't forget your radio codes. Watch for my signals.

"You know the deal. When I see the dope, I'll go around to the back of Frankie's car and open the trunk. If I take out the money in the brown paper bag—" He picked up the bag. "—this bag, it's just a flash and not a bust. You got that?"

Everyone nodded.

" Good. If I take the scales out of the trunk, that's the bust signal and you make your move. Okay?"

Duval didn't look up from digging at his nails. "What if it's a rip?"

"If it's a rip, you'll probably hear guns and cussing and screaming. That'll be me."

Everyone laughed nervously. As usual, the agents were on edge before a bust. Hendrix might have been joking, but what he said about a rip was true. The only indication the surveillance team would have that something had gone wrong was either the sound of shots or some other ominous noise. Anything other than the expected was never good.

Marc Duval leaned down to look inside Frankie's Caddy. "When it goes down, Frankie, get the fuck out of the way."

Frankie looked offended. "What'd you want me to do? Run?"

The idea of Fat Frankie running broke them up, nerves or not, even though there was a good chance that if Carlos Garcia, the guy they planned to bust, was suspicious, Frankie might be the first person shot. Garcia would know instantly it was Frankie who'd set him up. But

Frankie knew the risks. It wasn't the first time he'd helped out the DEA.

Frankie wasn't a snitch. A snitch would never be allowed to hang around the office. He was an informant. There was a big difference. An informant helped because he wanted to. A snitch only helped to save his own hide. Either cooperate or else. And if the snitch did cooperate, everybody figured he was a son-of-a-bitch who'd rather sell out a buddy than take his medicine. You could never trust a snitch. If they turned on their friends, they sure-as-shit wouldn't have any compunctions about turning on their enemies.

Frankie wasn't like that. He'd even go along on a bust, like tonight, to help set up the deal. This guy, Garcia, knew Frankie and trusted him. So far Garcia had bought it. So far.

"Okay, guys," Hendrix said. "Let's get this show on the road. And keep your ears on."

The other agents returned to their cars and Hendrix put the bag in the Caddy's open trunk. He slammed the truck lid, making Frankie flinch, then climbed into the passenger seat.

"You don't have to slam it," Frankie said. "It closes itself."

"Yeah. Just like my fifty-year old Chevy."

Frankie snorted. "You got the extra key?"

Hendrix felt in his pocket. "Yeah."

Frankie reaching for the Caddy's ignition key and Hendrix said, "Wait a minute. Don't go in yet. Let this guy get there first."

Frankie frowned. "You want me to drive around? This mother eats gas like a damn buzzard."

"You can afford it, Frankie. Christ, if I had your money I'd be on a beach in Acapulco or someplace."

"Too dull. What's more exciting than this?"

"You've got a point," Hendrix admitted. "Just park across the street from the hamburger stand where we can see."

Frankie started the car and drove the two blocks to the hamburger stand. He had to go around the block before he could find a parking space across from the hamburger stand. From their location, they had a good view of the parking area and they settled down to wait. It shouldn't be long. Dope dealers were usually on time. If they were smart they arrived early, like the DEA agents, watching the movement of cars and people for a while before they made their move.

Hendrix twisted around so he could keep an eye behind them through the back window.

"Want a drink?" Frankie asked after a minute.

"Nah," Hendrix answered. "Maybe after the deal." He made it a point not to drink on duty, unless, of course, he was undercover at a bar. Then you almost had to drink something. But generally he stayed away from booze. He didn't want his reactions slowed by alcohol if something happened.

"Then get me a glass of *tequila*, will you, *amigo?*"

Hendrix leaned back over the seat to open the car's built-in bar. He selected a bottle of Jose Cuervo Premium Gold Special from the well-stocked cabinet and a large shot glass. Settling back in his seat, he opened the bottle and poured the glass three-quarters full. He handed the glass to Frankie and the big man swallowed half its contents in one quick gulp. He grimaced and said, "Man, that's good. You sure you don't want a hit?"

Hendrix was back looking out the windows. "Nah. That shit rots your insides."

"Not if you eat Mexican chili. Your stomach is immune."

"Yeah. It probably thinks tequila is medicine."

"You got that right." Fat Frankie took another swallow. "You know, you cops miss out on a lot of fun. There's nothing like a good woman, good tequila and good *musica*."

"Oh, it isn't all bad. We do all right with the women. And speaking of women, if Carmen catches you with a broad, you'll wish you'd stayed with the booze and *musica*."

Frankie laughed. "*Tiene razon*. You got that right. And don't forget Maria. She's still trying to get me in church. Shit. I couldn't even get through the door."

In more ways than one, Hendrix thought. He knew that Frankie was no saint. When their army unit had been stationed in the Middle East, Frankie'd had his share of women even though he was married.

But he probably wasn't lying about Maria. He'd always talked more about his daughter than his wife, Carmen. When he had new pictures to show around, they were always of Maria; never of Carmen. Through the pictures, Hendrix had watched Frankie's daughter grow from a chubby teenager into a beautiful woman of twenty-two. The latest pictures were easy to take. Maria had developed into a remarkably beautiful woman considering she was Frankie's daughter. Of course, Carmen had the looks to be a movie star. Frankie must have looked *muy quapo* when he was young.

Hendrix shook his head and concentrated on watching the hamburger stand and the street. Frankie'd said that Garcia drove a flashy Pontiac Firebird with a giant Mexican eagle painted on the hood. If Garcia wasn't stupid, he'd cruise past a couple of times to look the situation over before he pulled into the lot.

Sure enough, five minutes before he was due, Garcia's car appeared. He drove by the stand slowly, taking a good long look at the hamburger stand. He didn't think to look in their direction across the street.

Hendrix shook his head. How could a guy in one of the world's most dangerous professions be so careless? Maybe it was that lack of gray matter that got him in the profession in the first place.

On Garcia's second pass, he pulled into the hamburger stand's parking area and parked near the back of the lot where there was the least light.

Hendrix picked up his radio and clicked on the microphone. "Fourteen-oh-one to surveillance units," he said. "He's here."

"Ten-four," each of the two units responded.

"We're moving in. Follow us, but not too close."

"Ten-four."

Hendrix clicked off the radio and told Frankie, "Let's go."

Frankie started the car and made a U-turn, wheeling into the hamburger stand's parking lot. Hendrix checked the .38 Colt automatic he had strapped to his right ankle. He wasn't wearing his belt gun in case Garcia asked him to pull up his jacket for a look.

"Pull up on his left side so I'm next to him," Hendrix said. "Not too close. I want to get the door all the way open."

"You think I'm going to the other side, you're fuckin' crazy," Frankie said.

Hendrix's was a little surprised to discover his heart was pounding hard. He might be able to fool his head into thinking that this was going to be an easy bust, but his heart didn't believe it. Maybe that was good. It would put more adrenaline in his blood.

Frankie slowly pulled in next to Garcia's Firebird and stopped. Hendrix didn't move. Both he and Garcia had their windows down, and Hendrix gave the dealer plenty of time to look them over.

Across the street, Sandy Tate eased his car to a stop. He and Marc Duval took their revolvers from belt holsters and checked to make sure they were loaded. Then Duval retrieved a pair of handcuffs from a briefcase at his feet, the shiny metal gleaming in the dim light. He secured the cuffs in his belt opposite his gun, one cuff down inside his jeans and the other hanging outside where he could reach it easily. He took a brown leather pouch from the briefcase and placed it in the pocket of his jacket. It contained six rounds of extra ammunition in a speed loader.

Sandy gave the speed loader a nervous look. "You think we'll need that?"

"I'd rather not need it and have it than need it and not have it."

Actually, Duval hoped he wouldn't have to use any of the rounds in his gun. Since Jim Hendrix had talked him into joining up with the

DEA five years ago, he'd been on scores of busts and they always played hell with his nerves. Unlike regular cops or even FBI agents, every time they made a bust, DEA agents almost always faced a guy with a gun. That was one thing Hendrix had failed to tell him during his recruitment pitch. Fortunately, he hadn't been forced to kill anyone—yet. He hoped this wasn't going to be the night.

He didn't like having passing traffic between him and Hendrix so he said, "Pull into the lot. Get up close to the stand like we're buying hamburgers."

Sandy expertly swung the car into a position where they could get out fast. Duval slumped down in the seat so he could observe without being obvious. He wondered where Arty and Dansen were. Thank God, Arty was driving. He would get in a good position to move in.

The thought took him back to a time right after he'd become an agent. One day, his senior partner at that time had taken him on a tour of the DEA parking facility with no explanation except "there's something I want to show you."

He'd made Marc look inside every DEA car parked in the garage. When they had finished, he asked Marc what he'd noticed in the cars. Marc couldn't really think of anything and said so. His partner told him to go back and count the cars with a book or newspaper in the front seat. Marc did so, counting seven cars with either item.

"What does that tell you?" his partner asked.

Marc didn't know.

The man stared at him, then said slowly, "That tells you those are guys you don't want covering your ass on a deal. When something happens and you need help, they won't see it. They'll be reading a book or working a fucking crossword puzzle."

The subject was never mentioned again, but Duval never forgot. He made sure that on surveillance he was always alert. When things happened, they happened fast.

He saw movement at Frankie's Cadillac and nudged Sandy. "He's getting out."

They watched as Hendrix leaned down to talk to Garcia. Then he walked around to the passenger side of the Firebird and got in.

Marc didn't like that. "What's he doing? We can't see him."

"I hope the shit he knows what he's doing," Sandy muttered.

"He knows," Duval answered. But he still didn't like it. What the hell was Hendrix thinking? He was supposed to stay in sight.

On the other hand, if Garcia insisted on driving to his pad to make the deal, Hendrix would have to go in with him. Then he'd really be out of sight. And behind a locked door. They had damn well better make the bust here.

They waited, eyes glued to the Firebird, breathing shallow.

"Damn," Sandy Tate muttered. "They gonna talk all night?"

The intense staring was hard on the eyes. Afraid to look away even for a second, even afraid to blink, caused their eyes to burn with fatigue.

The doors of the Firebird opened.

"He's coming out," Sandy's voice came out on a breath of relief.

"I see him."

"Good. They're both getting out."

Garcia and Hendrix walked around to the back of Frankie's Cadillac and Hendrix fished a key out of his pocket.

"Be ready," Duval cautioned, knowing his words were unnecessary. Every agent would be clinching his toes.

Hendrix motioned to Garcia to stand where he could watch him.

"That's right," Marc muttered. "Don't let the bastard get behind you."

Hendrix unlocked the trunk and raised the lid. He stepped back and motioned Garcia over with his left hand. Garcia walked to the trunk and bent over, Hendrix at his side. Duval knew Hendrix was showing him the money. But he wouldn't give it to Garcia. Getting the money and the dope in the same car at this stage was not a hell of a good idea. But both men knew that.

There was a ritual to dope dealing with a stranger that was as precise as a ballet. Professionals knew the procedure and respected it. So Garcia didn't object when Hendrix left the money in the trunk of Frankie's car and took out a pair of balance beam scales before he closed the trunk.

Sandy reached for the ignition key. "That's it. It's a bust."

"Wait'll Garcia gets back in the car so he can't see us," Duval cautioned. He hoped to hell that Arty and Dansen didn't jump the gun.

They watched Garcia and Hendrix get in the Firebird and close the doors. Duval opened his car door. "Wait'll I'm almost there, then block him off." As Duval got out of the car, he added, "Watch out for Frankie. He might bail."

"Gottcha," Sandy said. He started the car and put it in reverse, his foot holding down the brake.

Duval closed the door softly and began walking what seemed like a mile toward the Firebird, his hands empty. He kept slightly to the side so Garcia couldn't see him in his rear view mirror. From the corner of his eye he saw Arty begin walking toward the Firebird from the other side of the lot, the shotgun held unobtrusively down by his side.

When he was ten feet from the Firebird, the engine of the Cadillac suddenly sprang to life and the big car squealed backward to fast it almost hit Duval. He leaped aside as Fat Frankie, shifting gears like a stunt man, burned rubber hauling ass out of the lot.

"Christ," Duval snarled. He sprinted the last few feet to the Firebird, yanking his gun from his belt, coming up on the driver's side. Through the open car window he saw Hendrix trying to claw his gun from his ankle holster. Garcia, stupidly, carried his gun in his belt on the right side and he was trying to reach it with his left hand while he tried to turn the ignition key with his right.

"Freeze!" Duval's gun plowed a furrow under Garcia's ear. At the same time, Hendrix gave up trying to get his gun. Instead, he yanked Garcia's right hand away from the car's ignition so he couldn't start the car.

Garcia made a scream like a cornered mountain lion and slammed open the car door so fast Duval was knocked to the ground. He managed to hang onto his gun and when Garcia scrambled out of the Firebird, he had a clear shot at his back. He didn't fire. Visions of endless investigations and reams of bad publicity made him hold his fire. Better to let the small time dealer get away than suffer the consequences of shooting him in the back.

An instant later, he knew he'd made a bad mistake.

Arty had come up on the other side of the Firebird. He was followed at a safe distance by Bob Dansen who didn't even have his gun out. As Garcia sprinted around the back of his car, Arty brought the shotgun up. But he couldn't fire. Too many hamburger customers in the line of fire.

Duval was on his feet and he took off after Garcia who was running hard with his head turned toward the shotgun, his eyes wide with fear. Garcia did not see Dansen and he smashed into the lumbering agent.

Dansen grunted as though he'd been hit by a demolition ball and both men fell in a tangle of arms and legs. Except that one of the arms was Garcia's and now his hand gripped a gun.

Reacting with the speed of terror, Garcia put his gun to Dansen's temple and screamed at the agents closing in on him. "Back off! I'll kill 'im! Back off!"

The agents stopped. Garcia was on the edge of losing it. Except for a fine sense of self-preservation, he would probably already have taken out Dansen and started pumping shots at all of them. The agents stood staring at Garcia and Dansen, their guns at their sides, afraid to move.

Garcia dragged Dansen to his feet and moved behind him. He looped his left arm around Dansen's neck while he pressed his gun against the agent's right temple. Dansen's eyes were popping, and his mouth opened and closed like a fish sucking air.

Hendrix, his gun in his hand, walked slowly toward the group, saying, "Easy guys. Easy."

Hendrix continued walking and Garcia pushed his gun so hard against Dansen's head that Hendrix was afraid he would accidentally pull the trigger.

"Back off!" Garcia screamed. "Back off!"

Hendrix stopped. "We can't do that, man. You know the rules."

"I'll kill 'im! I'll kill 'im!" The brief standoff had given Garcia the seconds he needed to get his cool back and his voice had lost some of its terror. But, in a way, his hate-filled snarl was even more menacing, and Dansen's eyes rolled so far back in his head Hendrix thought he was going to faint.

Hendrix said, "Look, Garcia. You're doing it all wrong. This isn't going to get you a damn thing."

"Fuck you, man," Garcia rasped. "You guys back off or I off 'im."

Hendrix shook his head. "Now that would really be stupid. You see all these guns. Arty's even got a shotgun. Show him, Arty."

Arty jacked another shell into the chamber, ejecting the unfired round onto the ground. The sound gave Hendrix a chill and the shotgun wasn't even pointed at him.

Garcia licked his lips. His eyes locked on the round hole in the barrel of the shotgun that was pointed at his head. "Fuck you, man," he repeated, but a lot of the machismo had gone out of his voice.

"Look at it this way," Hendrix said. "If you shoot him, then we'll all have to shoot you."

Garcia's eyes swiveled back to look at Hendrix, and Hendrix grinned.

"Now, what I'm going to do is walk over there and you're going to give me your gun, and we all go home happy. Except you, of course. You go to jail. But shit, you'll be out in a couple of months. That's better'n being dead. *Verdad?*"

Hendrix again started walking toward the two men and Garcia dragged Dansen back a couple of feet. "Hold it, damn it!" he gritted. "I walk or I kill 'im."

Hendrix, still smiling, continued walking, his eyes locked on Garcia's. "Ah, come on, man." His voice was slow, soothing. He held his gun at his side. He hoped Dansen wouldn't screw things up by fainting. "I just want to talk. You can keep your gun on him."

Now he was next to Garcia, and he lifted his gun and placed the muzzle under Garcia's chin. "Bingo," he said.

Garcia's chin came up and he glared down his nose at Hendrix.

"What the fuck?" he rasped. "What the fuck?"

"It's like this," Hendrix said. He brought his mouth close to Garcia's ear. "I'm going to count to three, then I'm going to blow your fucking head off. One!"

"I'll kill 'im." Fear had returned to Garcia's voice. "You kill me, my finger's gonna go."

"Maybe not. My shot's gonna splatter your brain. You might not be able to pull the trigger. Two!"

"Yes, it will!" Garcia's voice had climbed to a scream.

"You might be right. But you'll never know, will you? Th—"

Garcia yanked his gun away from Dansen's head. "No! No! All right!"

Hendrix reached across with his left hand and took Garcia's gun. Garcia released his grip from around Dansen's neck and the other agents leap forward. Duval yanked his cuffs from his belt, twisted Garcia's arms behind his back and clamped on the steel.

Hendrix lowered his gun and slipped it back in his ankle holster. "You okay?" he said to Dansen.

Dansen couldn't talk. He nodded. Sweat dripped off his chin and his lips quivered.

"Good," Hendrix said. "Arty, take Bob to his house."

"You mean to the station," Arty said.

"No. Take him home. I think he needs a change of underwear."

Nobody laughed. Each one wondered how he'd have reacted if a guy who might be high on dope and was certainly crazy with fear held a gun at his head. They might need a change of underwear, too.

Hendrix turned to face people who had gathered. "All right," he said. "It's all over. Get back to your burgers."

Marc Duval walked beside Hendrix while Sandy hustled Garcia toward their car, reciting his Miranda rights as he walked.

"That fuckin' Frankie," Duval said. "He damn near got somebody killed."

"Aw, you can't blame Frankie. He did his part. It was a good bust. That's another one we owe him."

"I hope we don't owe him any more like this."

Hendrix chuckled. "Me, too. You'd better bring in the Firebird. I'll see you back at the station."

"Okay." Duval started to turn away, then hesitated. "Hey, would you have shot the guy?"

Hendrix thought a second. "I don't know. You've got to put it in context. Now, I could say no way. But then...I was pretty high. As they say, you hadda be there."

"Don't shit me. I'm not internal affairs. Would you have shot him?"

"Naah. I just wanted Dansen to shit his pants."

Chapter Two

IT WAS NINE o'clock the next morning when a call from Miami came in to the DEA's District Office. Most of the Group Four agents were at their desks filling out paper work—much of it from the Garcia bust. Group Supervisor John Hodges, a big African-American wearing a dark gray pin-striped suit, took the Miami call in his office.

Many of the agents around the country knew each other, especially on the supervisor level, so Hodges knew Jerry Bennington in Miami. Hell, everybody knew Bennington. With Miami and Southern Florida one of the principle point of entry into the U.S. for cocaine and marijuana, agents around the country spent a lot of time talking to Jerry Bennington. Hodges figured it was another semi-routine call asking for information on some dude or about ship or plane movements. But his face was ashen when he hung up a few minutes later and motioned Hendrix and Duval to come into his office.

When Hendrix saw Hodges' expression, he could tell whatever Hodges was going to say was going to be bad. He glanced at Duval who made a tiny shrug. He, too, knew they were not going to hear anything good.

Hodges motioned to them to take seats and they eased into chairs, sitting on the front edges. Hodges stood beside his desk fiddling with a letter opener shaped like a stiletto. "I just got a call from Miami," he began. "We've got one hell of a problem."

So what else is new, Hendrix thought.

"They made a bust out there last night," Hodges continued. "You probably know the dealer. He's from L.A.—Guillermo Trespalacios."

Hendrix and Duval both nodded. "Yeah," Hendrix said. "Small time. He works for somebody out here."

"That's the point. They talked to him last night. He's had two falls already so they were able to put a lot of pressure on him. He agreed to snitch."

The two agents sat up straighter. Hell, this wasn't bad news. "He name his boss?" Duval asked.

Hodges nodded, his face grim. "Yeah."

"Maybe it's the big guy we've been looking for," Hendrix said.

"Bennington thinks it is. So do I."

"So, who?"

"That's the problem. He says the guy is one of the biggest on the

West Coast. But here's where the shit hit the fan. This Trespalacios says his man has been able to work real safe because he's friendly with most of the narcs in town—especially the feds."

"What's that supposed to mean?" Hendrix asked. "How could he know them all?"

"Because he's an informant. Has been for years. Shit, he's practically got the run of the place."

Hendrix felt his mouth go dry. "Frankie? Fat Frankie?"

Hodges nodded without looking at them. "You got it."

Duval bend his head into his hands. "Oh, shit."

Hendrix was silent, stunned. Frankie? Impossible. And yet—the pieces fit. Frankie was the only civilian who had the run of the place. He usually knew when a bust would take place, and where. The busts he'd set up for them had been small, so they could've been designed by Frankie to establish his credibility. Or, more likely, to get rid of somebody on his shit list. But Fat Frankie? My God, it was hard to believe.

"Are you sure?" he asked Hodges. "He could mean somebody else."

Hodges shook his head. "The snitch said his man got into the business when he was soldiering in the Middle East. Frankie was in Turkey."

"Yeah," Duval said. "So were we."

"Yeah, but his guy used his dope money to buy a restaurant and a gym." Hodges stopped, letting the impact of his statement sink in. Duval and Hendrix were silent as they desperately tried to think of someplace where the snitch might have slipped up in his identification.

"I called you guys in because you know Frankie better than anybody. What do you think? Could it be true? Or did this guy pull a name out of a hat?"

How well did he know Frankie? Hendrix thought back to when they'd first met. Duval, Frankie, and he had been assigned to support for the Air Force's Air Mobility Command. Their job had been to provide protection for Air Force transports picking up weapons and supplies from an army depot in Pakistan and flying them to Uzabekistan or Tajikistan where they were hauled by horses and mules over the mountains to Afghanistan's Northern Alliance forces fighting the Taliban. It would have been easy for Frankie to hook up with dope dealers in Pakistan.

After they were discharged, Hendrix had returned to his old job in the DEA. He'd talked Duval into becoming an agent.

But Frankie had bigger ideas. If he had hooked up with some traffickers, it would explain where he got the money so quickly to purchase a nice restaurant and bar at Sunset Boulevard and Alvarado. The restaurant proved to be a real money maker, and a couple of years later, Frankie bought an old candy factory in East LA and remodeled it into one of the country's best gyms for fighters and body builders.

Frankie had gotten into the habit of hanging out with his old army buddies at DEA headquarters. Then, a couple of years after opening his restaurant, he told Hendrix he picked up a lot of information at his restaurant and gym, and he might be able to give the DEA some leads on drug dealers.

Hendrix had jumped at the opportunity. Leads were hard to develop and Frankie offered inside connections that would take years to set up on their own.

Since then Frankie had come through with several deals that had resulted in good busts. Nothing real big, but enough to put a dent in the local trade like the one last night. Carlos Garcia wasn't a heavy hitter, but still they'd been after him a long time.

Hendrix glanced at Duval. "Shit, I don't know. I sure as hell don't want to believe it. What do you think, Marc?"

Duval's eyes were clouded, sick. "I sure as hell don't want to believe it, but...it could be."

Hendrix stood up. He couldn't remain seated when he was so upset. "When you think about it, it fits. Frankie's in a perfect spot to be the man. He's even got that restaurant and the gym to launder money."

"And the boxing," Duval added. "He promotes fights all over the fucking world."

Frankie's Gym had gained a reputation as a center for bodybuilding. But Frankie's main love was boxing. He'd been a fighter himself when he was younger, or until his desire for food proved greater than his desire to impress the girls.

"Bodybuilding competitions, too," Hendrix added.

"Yeah. He moves a lot of money around. But all we've got is the word of the snitch. He might have coughed up a name—any name— just to save his own hide."

"True," Hodges admitted. "Everybody knows Frankie."

"Damn right," Duval said, reaching for hope. "He could've named you or me or anybody. The mayor even. What the hell? That doesn't mean it's true."

"It doesn't matter who he named," Hodges pointed out. "We've got to move on this."

"Why don't you let me and Duval work this out? If Frankie's in the clear, nobody gets hurt," Hendrix said.

"Right," Duval added. "And this way, if he turns out to be dirty, L.A.'ll get credit for the bust."

"Well, I'd like to give Frankie every benefit of the doubt," Hodges said slowly. Mention of credits had started him thinking like a politician. "But we're not talking weeks here. We're talking months. I'm sure he's got to have himself covered from all angles. That's why we've never made him."

"If he's guilty," Duval said.

"Either way, it's going to take a hell of a lot of time and effort to build a good case."

"So," Duval said, "how the hell are we going to smoke him out without tipping him off?"

Hendrix said, "I've got an idea." He had his emotions under control now and he was beginning to think like an agent instead of somebody who'd just been kicked in the balls.

"So?" Hodges said.

"What we need," Hendrix said, "is somebody on the inside."

Duval nodded. "You got it. It's our only chance."

"How the hell are we going to do that?" Hodges snapped. "Frankie knows practically every agent in town."

"We have to assume he knows every agent in the DEA. At one time or another, just about all of them have been to L.A."

"We could borrow an LAPD narc," Hodges said.

"He knows most of them, too," Hendrix countered. "Beside, you want them to get credit for the bust if he's the man?"

Hodges shook his head. "Shit, no. Washington is already trying to do us in." He was referring to efforts in Washington to amalgamate the DEA and the FBI.

"We have to find somebody he doesn't know," Duval said. "Maybe a rookie out of NTI."

Hodges looked skeptical. "A rookie? Frankie'd eat him alive."

"Yeah," Duval admitted. "But where else are we going to find somebody we can be sure he doesn't know or even heard of?"

Hendrix said slowly. "It'd be better if he did know him."

Hodges wrinkled his forehead. "Come again?"

"Look, if Frankie is the man, he'll be too smart to let a stranger get close to him. It should be somebody he knows."

"If you're thinking about bringing in a civilian..."

Hendrix lifted his hand. "No. He'd have to be an agent or we'd never make a case that'd stick."

Hodges threw up his hands. "You're not making sense. Where are we going to get somebody Frankie'll let in his organization?"

"Somebody from his past," Hendrix said. He looked at Duval. "Somebody who was in the army with him. Somebody he thought a lot of."

Duval grunted as the idea penetrated. "The kid?"

Hendrix grinned at Duval. "You got it. Brent Thomas."

"Who?" Hodges said. "Never heard of him."

"He won't want to be an agent," Duval said.

"Neither did you until I started bending your ear."

"Who," Hodges asked, "is Brent Thomas?"

Duval smiled and nodded. "Yeah. How old is he now? Twenty-five?"

"About that. And I know where to find him."

Without waiting for permission, Duval and Hendrix headed for the door. Behind them Hodges called, "Who the hell is Brent Thomas?"

Chapter Three

KANSAS STATE UNIVERSITY proved to be larger than Hendrix or Duval had expected. Its twenty thousand students matriculated amid ancient vine-covered buildings that sprawled across a mile-wide campus. Towering willow trees and thick-trunked pines and firs lent friendly support to the old, brick buildings as though without their symbiotic friendship the structures would tumble into a rubble of legends.

The University dean had been most helpful when Hendrix and Duval explained they were two old army buddies passing through town and wanted to say hello to Brent Thomas. After consulting a curriculum, the dean told them that Professor Thomas was coaching in the field house. Before they left his office, the dean gave them explicit directions about how to find the field house—all of which proved to be wrong.

The agents questioned their way through a maze of shady, cement paths and through echoing hallways until they approached a large building that had the appearance of being a gymnasium.

"Maybe we should have called ahead," Marc Duval said.

"Nah. He'd start asking questions. And I don't want him thinking until we get in our pitch."

"We? You're the one with the load of bullshit."

"You can back me up. I've got a feeling he might be hard to pry away from this place."

Duval looked at the green lawns, the shady, tree lined walks and the many young students. "I sure as hell would be."

"Me, too."

They walked in silence for a moment, each wondering what his life would've been like if he'd elected the academic life as had Brent Thomas, instead of opting to associate with drug dealers, snitches and a general breed of killers and other bad dudes.

"Professor," Marc Duval said. "He called him a professor."

"Yeah. He went to college after he got out. I guess he took up teaching."

"Jesus. He isn't gonna want to leave some cushy job to chase junk dealers."

"Maybe. He liked soldiering. Damn good at it, too, if I remember."

"Yeah."

They walked a few steps in silence.

"Coaching?" Marc Duval said. "You think he's into basketball?"

"Nah What is he? Six-one? Six-two? You've gotta be six-six minimum today before they'll let you touch a basketball."

"It's been five years. Maybe he grew."

"Not that much." Duval held up a finger. "Coaching. That coach at DePaul is about five-six. Hell, John Wooden was only about five-ten."

"They were coaching before kids started turning into fuckin' giants. My guess is swimming. The kid always looked like a swimmer to me."

"Swimming? In Kansas? They don't even know what water looks like unless it's in an irrigation ditch. I figure karate. He was damn good if I remember."

Hendrix shook his head. "That stuff we learned in the army wasn't karate. It was killer stuff. They wouldn't let anybody teach that in college."

"Okay. So maybe..." Duval snapped his fingers. "Gymnastics. He was a hell of an athlete."

"I hope he still is. He'll fit right in at Frankie's gym."

Remembering why they were here sobered them until Duval said, "Funny kid. A real straight arrow. Eagle scout. He might not like the idea of putting Frankie away. They were pretty good buddies."

"You're right. We'll have to ease him into it."

They walked in silence, each feeling a shade of guilt for what they were about to do. Or try to do.

Hendrix tightened his lips. It never got any easier. Here he was getting ready to screw somebody else. Why did this job have to deal so much with lying? Normal people didn't live like they did. Playing roles. Lying. Living from one crisis to another day after day after day. Or did they? Hell, maybe everybody lied and played games the same as agents did. The big difference was that other people's stakes weren't lives. Anyway, it was all part of the deal.

Hendrix broke the silence. "If he goes for the deal, we'll have to run him through the Institute. Some kind of an accelerated course."

"Yeah." Duval took a few more steps before he said, "Maybe we'd better not tell him it's about Frankie."

"Good idea," Hendrix agreed. "We can tell him when he gets to L.A."

Duval shook his head. "I hate to lie to the kid."

"We won't be lying. We just hold back a little."

"A little? If Fat Frankie is the man, he'll blow away anybody he thinks is a threat—friend or not."

Hendrix was silent. *What the hell. It ain't our asses.* The thought was depressing. You really had to be some kind of an asshole to talk a buddy into suicide.

They entered the large building through glass doors that opened into a wide corridor. They stopped the first student they saw and asked where they could find Brent Thomas' office.

"Coach Thomas? He's in the gym. Through those big doors there."

"Coach Thomas?" Duval shook his head as they walked toward the indicated double doors. "Sounds weird."

"Not as weird as Professor Thomas. Now that worries me."

At the doors, they paused to listen to sounds that filtered through the door panels. There were grunts and what sounded like a body being slapped and a voice giving unintelligible directions.

The two agents looked at each other. "Sure as hell isn't swimming," Duval said.

Hendrix cocked his head. "Shit! Boxing."

Duval nodded. "He could handle that."

He pulled one side of the double-doors open and they walked into a huge gymnasium. They stopped, staring. At the far end of the gymnasium, beyond a basketball court, was a boxing ring. Near the ring were boxing paraphernalia, punching bags and weight equipment.

A group of male students, some wearing warm-up suits and punching bag gloves, were watching two boxers inside the ring. The fighters wore large training gloves and protective headgear as well as codpieces over their shorts.

Brent Thomas, wearing a gray, stained sweat suit, was acting as referee, circling the fighters and giving directions in a firm, hard voice.

"I was right," Hendrix said.

"Yeah," Duval acknowledged. "They're big on boxing in the farm belt."

Duval started to walk across the basketball court toward the boxing ring, but Hendrix grabbed his arm. "Let's watch a minute."

Both men studied Brent Thomas carefully, not so much watching the way he moved as trying to get a feeling for his leadership capability.

Brent circled the fighters calling instructions. "Footwork, Joe. Footwork. That's it. Curt, watch your right. Keep it up! Out of the corner. Don't get trapped. Footwork! Joe, combinations. Use your left to set up. Good. Good."

Hendrix liked what he saw. He remembered Brent as a shy kid with a belly fully of guts and a head full of under-utilized brain power.

He still looked as though he wouldn't be at a loss talking to a rocket scientist, even though he'd retained the scrubbed, fresh-faced look of someone who'd be more at ease around cows and horses. His ash blonde hair was no longer worn in a military cut and perspiration had turned it into a mass of curls. But he'd filled out and his voice had deepened, acquiring a sure tone of command.

"He looks bigger," Duval whispered.

"Yeah," Hendrix said with a tight smile of satisfaction. "And tougher."

Someone rang a bell and Brent slapped each of the sweating boxers on the back. "Coming along, guys. Looking good."

The two boxers were starting to duck out of the ring when Brent said, "Curt. Hold on a minute. Mind if I use you to demonstrate something?"

"Okay, coach," Curt said. He moved back into the center of the ring.

Brent picked up a pair of boxing gloves from the ring's apron and slipped them on. While one of the students tightened the gloves' laces, Brent said, "You heard me telling Joe and Curt to work in combinations, setting up your opponent for a telling punch. Always think combination whether you're on the offense or the defense."

He straightened and moved to the center of the ring. "First, let me give you an idea of an offensive combination, setting up with the left and ending the combination with either the right or—if you've got a killer left—with the left." He slipped a mouthpiece into his mouth and turned. "Ready, Curt?"

Curt nodded and began circling, his gloves ready. Hendrix watched, fascinated. Brent looked decidedly over matched. Curt was bigger than Brent and heavily muscled. Brent had good shoulders, but was leaner. A panther against a lion.

"Don't hold back, Curt. This is your chance to get the coach," Brent said.

Accepting the invitation, Curt moved in quickly and began shooting lefts at Brent's head. Brent blocked and slipped the punches, making it look easy.

"Footwork, Curt," he said. "Footwork."

Curt nodded and renewed his attack, moving well. But this time, when he closed in, Brent met him with two left jabs like lightning bolts that snapped Curt's head back. Brent followed with a straight right to Curt's jaw. It was obvious that Brent pulled the punch, but still Curt was driven back a step, his eyes wide in surprise.

Brent stepped back. "You can also use combinations when you're in a defense mode. Curt, put me on the defense."

Curt's pride had been stung by the ease of Brent's blow to his chin. Now he dropped his chin against his left shoulder and came at Brent, throwing a series of hard, fast blows in rapid combinations that forced Brent to backtrack and circle.

"Brent's gonna get creamed," Duval whispered to Hendrix.

"Nah," Hendrix said. "Look at his feet. You can't hurt somebody who moves like that."

Curt was in the process of launching a right hook when Brent stepped inside the punch and snapped a short left to Curt's midsection, followed by a right hook around Curt's protecting left hand that slammed against the headpiece protecting Curt's jaw with the sound of a meat cleaver hitting a side of beef. Curt staggered back, his gloves down, his eyes glazed. Brent leaped to catch him.

"Sorry, Curt," he said. "You okay?"

Curt's legs steadied and he shook his head like a duck coming up from a deep dive before he rubbed his jaw with his glove. "Yeah," he said. "What the hell did you hit me with?"

"Combination," Brent answered. He turned to the students. "As you can see, a good combination generates speed with power by forcing your shoulders and legs into the punch. Like a golfer uses his back swing to put power in his front swing. Speed with power. That's the key."

"Jesus!" Hendrix said. "Did you see that?"

"Hell no," Duval answered. "It happened too damn fast."

Hendrix began a slow applause as he walked across the basketball court toward the ring. Brent looked toward the sound, shading his eyes against the glare of the overhead lights with his gloved hand. The students also turned to look at the two men in business suits walking toward them, their heels loud on the wooden floor of the basketball court.

"Go around," Brent said. "No walking on the court with street sho—" He stopped, staring hard. "Marc? Jim?"

Hendrix stopped applauding. "You got it."

Brent lowered his hand and grinned. "I'll be damned. I don't believe it. What're you guys doing here?"

"Looking for you."

Brent turned to the students. "Okay, guys. Enough for today. Wait a minute. You've got fifteen minutes. Give me fifty pushups and a hundred sit-ups."

Amid loud groaning from the students, Brent ducked under the ropes and dropped to the floor. The smooth grace of the move was not lost on the two agents.

Brent used his teeth to unfasten the laces on his right glove. He pulled off the glove and held out his hand. "You guys. Damn. It's good to see you."

When he shook Duval's hand, the agent winced. "What the hell have you been eating? You're going to hurt somebody."

Brent's face reddened, and Hendrix smiled. The kid might have matured, but he still blushed when he was embarrassed.

"Sorry," Brent said. "I guess I got excited seeing you guys."

"I know," Duval said. "You're Spiderman."

"No, no. I work out with weights." Brent nodded toward the students straining through their exercises. "It's part of the program."

"I know. Speed with power."

Brent laughed. "Yeah. Right." He stared at Hendrix and Duval with a wide grin. "What are you guys doing in Kansas?" His smile abruptly faded. "Not bad news, is it? We're not called back?"

"No," Hendrix reassured him. "No bad news. In fact, it just might be good news."

"Depending on how you look at it," Duval added.

"Yeah?" Brent said. He attacked the strings on the other glove with his teeth. "I could use some good news."

"You'll love this," Hendrix said. "When can we talk?"

Brent glanced at a huge clock high on the wall of the gym. "I've got a class in World History. Then I'll be free."

"You're studying history?" Duval said. "I thought only eggheads went in for that stuff."

"I don't study it," Brent said with a smile. "I teach it."

Duval's face reddened and Hendrix laughed. "Put your foot in cow dung that time, didn't you, partner?"

Duval grinned. "Not the first time."

"Or the last, I'll bet." Hendrix grinned at Brent. "You're looking good, kid. Where can we meet?"

Brent though a moment. "You guys still like beer?"

"Somewhat," Hendrix said and Duval nodded.

"Okay. There's a tavern a couple of blocks east of the main campus entrance. You got wheels?"

"Yeah. Rental car."

"Fine. It's called the Lode Stone. I'll meet you there in, say, an hour and a half."

"*Bueno*," Hendrix said. "The Lode Stone in an hour and a half."

"You married?" Duval asked abruptly.

Brent's happy expression changed. He shook his head. "I was. Not any more."

Duval glanced at Hendrix. "Oh. Sorry to hear that," he said, but his voice said he wasn't sorry at all.

"So am I," Brent said. His grin returned and he poked Hendrix's shoulder. "Hey, it sure is good to see you guys. You're going to have to tell me everything that's happened to everybody. Big Frankie. You ever see Big Frankie? He lives in L.A."

"Yeah," Duval said. "All the time. We see him all the time."

"Gee, I sure would like to see him again."

"Who knows," Hendrix said dryly. "Maybe you will."

"Okay," Brent said. "See you guys in an hour and a half."

Watching Brent walk away, Duval noted the width of his shoulders and remembered how easily he'd almost knocked out the fighter in the ring. And he had acquired a set to his jaw and a look in his dark blue eyes that made Hendrix think he was probably not a man to provoke.

"Jesus," he murmured. "World History?"

Chapter Four

BY THE WEEKEND, Brent was still unable to make up his mind about Hendrix's surprising offer. The idea of becoming a DEA agent was as foreign to his thinking as going to Mars. Despite the two agents' salesmanship, he knew the job would be as fraught with as much danger as intrigue.

Did he really want to give up his secure little niche for something so threatening? He needed to talk to someone whose judgment he respected. Brent called his dad and said he was coming home for a visit.

He was still undecided late Friday night when, after the two hour drive from Manhattan to Mankato, he pulled his Camaro up in front of his parents' old frame farmhouse. He turned the engine off and sat quietly for a moment, savoring the memory of evenings on the big screened porch that stretched the full width of the house, and of hours spent lying on the grass reading in the shade of the big cottonwood trees until it got so dark his eyes would almost fall out from the strain.

The screen door opened and Dad, Mom and his brother, Mike, came out. There was still light enough so he could see his parents hadn't changed much since he'd seen them a few months ago. Funny how you looked for signs of aging in your parents, as though you expected them overnight to look like the ads that showed an old couple about 90 helping each other walk. But his dad was only fifty-two.

Alvin Thomas had been a Navy lieutenant during the Viet Nam War, and he was still big and strong. His shock of rich, brown hair only had a few hints of gray. When he and Brent put their arms around each other, Brent could feel the corded muscles in his dad's back. They came from a lifetime of using a pitchfork or a shovel. When the day he could no longer feel steel in his dad's muscles, was the day he'd start to worry. Or maybe a greater cause for worry would be the day the perpetual sparkle of curiosity left his dad's eyes.

But that would never happen—not to Alvin Thomas. The day he stopped having a zest for living would be the day he died.

It was the same with his mother who was only fifty. When he hugged her, he noticed she'd put on a little weight. But that was good. Susan Thomas had always kept herself work-thin. Now she deserved a few pounds. There were a few new lines around her eyes, too. They made her look more like the grandma she was always telling him she could hardly wait to be. He thought she'd been more disappointed than he when his brief marriage to Connie had come apart. It meant another long wait for a grandchild.

But maybe not so long. Shaking Mike's hand and giving him a hug he could tell his brother was no longer an adolescent. Like Brent himself, Mike had been slow maturing, but now at twenty-three, he showed the family trait—an air of quiet confidence. Thank God Mike also had their dad's love for farming.

Over supper they talked about farmers' problems, and the country's, while Brent watched in awe as Mike stowed away enough food to feed a starving mountain lion. Then he noticed he was pretty well keeping pace with his brother, so it didn't seem like so much after all.

Brent waited until they were almost finished with pieces of his mother's apple pie before he casually said, "I've had an offer for a new job."

They looked at him quizzically, waiting for him to give them the details.

"Working for the government."

"Not the Department of Agriculture, I hope," Mike said with a smile. "The farmers have got enough problems."

"You're not going back in the service?" his mom asked, and he sensed her flash of fear.

It suddenly occurred to him that this decision was going to be tough on her. He'd never told her the particulars about his two-year hitch in the army, but she'd suspected he was doing dangerous work. She'd shown obvious relief when he had decided not to reenlist, electing instead to work on a bachelor's degree. Now, if he took the DEA job, she would again have to go through each day and night wondering about his safety.

He tried to find words that would assuage the shock. "Nope. Not the military," he said, and relief flooded his mother's face. He hesitated before he added, "Justice Department."

"Justice Department?" his mother said. "Like the Supreme Court?"

"Well, not exactly."

The concern that had left his mother's eyes returned when his dad asked, "FBI?"

"Something like that."

"I thought you had to have a law degree for that."

Brent shook his head. "Not for the DEA"

"DEA?" Surprised, his dad sat back in his chair. "Drug Enforcement Administration?"

"Yeah."

There was silence as though Brent had told them he was going to the moon. He hadn't realized his dad also harbored a fear for his safety until he saw his dad's jaw tighten and a curtain come down in front of his eyes. *Damn.* He'd thought that after his divorce, his life would be his own. Now he realized it would never be entirely his.

Mike finally said, "Drugs? Dope? You're getting into that mess?"

"It's that university," Susan Thomas said bitterly. "You should've left after you graduated. It's all changed. It's a bad atmosphere."

"It isn't like that, Mom," Brent said, forcing a chuckle. "The DEA is a lot like the FBI. You're kind of policemen."

"Don't try to fool me. You'll be dealing with killers."

Brent squirmed uncomfortably. It might have been a mistake to tell them anything. But if he left the university, they'd find out. There could be no hiding that. "Well, I guess that would depend on the case."

"Sounds exciting," Mike said, his eyes glowing.

"Sounds dangerous," Alvin Thomas interjected. "Where would you be stationed?"

"I wouldn't know that until after I graduated from the National Training Institute in Washington."

His dad couldn't keep the anxiety from his voice, "But it would be in the United States?"

"That's what I understand."

Brent could've slugged his brother when Mike said, "Drug enforcement agents go all over the world. Columbia. Mexico. The Middle East. And what about those drug czars in Asia? Some of them have their own armies. Did you run into them when you were in Pakistan?"

"No. Not really," Brent said. "They stay pretty much to themselves."

"You'll get a good pension working for the government." Mike said as he helped himself to a second piece of pie. "Only twenty years?"

"Your military time might count," Alvin said. "You should look into that."

"Yeah," Mike said. "Eighteen years. You could go back to the university. With a government pension, you'd be in great shape."

"You'll never get tenured that way," Alvin said.

"You'd get just as good a pension if you stayed at the university," Susan Thomas replied. Brent could tell by the tone of her voice that she'd decided against the move.

"Not as much, I'll bet," Mike persisted. "Isn't that right, Brent?"

Brent shrugged. "I couldn't say for sure."

His mother stared at him, and Brent had the same disquieting feeling he'd had as a kid that she could read his mind. "You've already decided, have you?"

"I'm not sure, but..." Brent moved the remains of his pie around on his plate with his fork so he wouldn't have to look at his mother's face. "Maybe I need a change. When I think of spending the rest of my life at the university..." He shook his head. "It seems like I'm missing a lot. Manhattan is kind of—closing in."

Nobody mentioned Connie and his divorce. They'd all lived through that and had put it behind them. But they knew what he meant. The university-dominated city held memories that were constantly being thrust upon him.

"You think it'll be like in the movies?" Mike asked. "You get shot at every time you turn around?"

Brent saw the shadow of pain on his mother's face, and he gave his brother a warning glance. "No," he said quickly. "It's nothing like that. Mostly paper work. They use computers now."

"It seems to me," Alvin Thomas said softly, "that you're going straight into a war nobody wants to win. But the whole country is going down the tube because of drugs. We gave up on one war. But we damn well better not give up on this one. This is home. There's no place we can run."

Brent looks at his father with surprise. It was unusual for him to use expletives, even one as mild as 'damn'. He had to have a deep hatred about what drugs were doing to the country he loved. *Or was it fear?*

"It is a war," Susan Thomas said. "And people get killed in wars. He's had his. Let somebody else fight this one."

"They've asked him," Alvin Thomas said flatly.

"And what kind of people will he be associating with? Addicts. Killers. You lie down with dogs, you get up with fleas."

"He's going to run into dogs and fleas everywhere. If by this time he can't handle 'em, he's going to get them anyway."

Susan Thomas glanced at Brent and slowly nodded. "I guess if you can't handle it," she said, "we've done a miserable job of bringing you up."

Brent grinned. "Not too many dogs with fleas in Kansas."

His mother bristled. "You know very well what I mean, Brent Thomas." Then she sighed. "I guess you can't win wars without fighters."

"Don't worry," Brent told her. "I promise I won't get shot–if I take the job."

She came to stand behind him and put her hands on his shoulders.

"Take it. I know you want to. Just promise you won't do anything foolish."

Brent had to fight back a smile. That was one promise he could definitely make. "I promise," he said. "I definitely promise."

"If things get too tough, you can always come back here," Mike said. "We'll have a shovel waiting."

Chapter Five

TWO MONTHS LATER, Brent was still trying to convince himself that becoming a DEA agent hadn't been a mistake. Throughout the long flight from Washington D.C. to Los Angeles, he'd pondered why he'd been accelerated through hectic weeks at the DEA's National Training Institute. It all seemed like a dream running at an accelerated pace, like a movie out of control.

Even so, when the taxi dropped him off in front of a three-story white-stucco apartment building in Santa Monica and sped away into the summer dusk, Brent felt as though he'd just cut off his last connection with anything familiar. Time may have settled into normal speed, but now the surroundings were unreal.

He looked at the towering palms lining the quiet street. Through space between adjacent apartment buildings, he could see a small patch of blue that was the Pacific Ocean. Occasionally, he could just make out the sound of surf. The air was balmy, spiced with salt from the sea and scented with the perfume of exotic flowers. There was none of the oppressive humidity he'd found in Washington D.C.

"Well, Toto," he muttered to himself. "This sure as hell isn't Kansas any more."

The entrance to the apartment complex's lobby was blocked by glass security doors. On the wall near the doors was a call box and a list of apartment residents. Brent rang the manager's number.

When a voice came on the intercom, he gave his name. Instead of releasing the door's lock remotely, the manager told him to wait. After a moment, he came to the lobby, probably so he could see whether his new tenant was acceptable. Apparently Brent passed the inspection because the manager let him in and led the way to an elevator. He explained that Brent's company had taken care of everything. Brent could sign the necessary rental agreement in the morning or at his convenience.

Apartment three-eighty-eight proved to be a one-bedroom bachelor on the building's top floor. The furniture was new, functional, and what Brent thought of as 'early apartment.' The bedroom was small with a smaller bathroom that smelled of stale air and Clorox. Brent forced open the small bathroom window before he went to inspect a tiny kitchenette separated from the living room by a counter which doubled as a bar. Brent pulled polyester drapes aside from a large sliding glass door. The door opened onto a small balcony that overlooked the quiet, cement-paved street.

That night, lying in the strange bed listening to unfamiliar night sounds, Brent was unable to sleep. He couldn't stop wondering why Hendrix and Duval had sought him out. They said he had 'special qualifications,' but he certainly didn't feel special. At the academy, his questions had gone unanswered.

Well, tomorrow he was scheduled to meet at DEA headquarters with a supervisor named Cleveland Zylo. Then he'd get some answers.

Still he couldn't sleep. What's it going to be like being an agent? Had he enlisted in a losing battle? Could people really be saved from destroying their bodies with drugs if they didn't want to be saved?

At six a.m., after drifting in and out of sleep, his mind was still threshing a harvest of doubts. To cut off the painful introspection, he got up, shaved and showered. Afterward, he felt better. His mind was clear and his body had begun to shake off the effects of jet lag.

He wasn't certain what DEA agents wore at headquarters so he played it safe by putting on a dark gray suit with a conservative necktie. Since this was California, he left off the vest.

At nine o'clock, following breakfast at a nearby Denny's Coffee Shop, he used a pay phone to call the DEA.

A woman's voice answered. "DEA. May I help you?"

"Good morning," Brent said. "I'd like to speak to Mr. Cleveland Zylo, please." He hoped he'd pronounced the man's name correctly.

"One moment, please. May I tell him who's calling?"

"Brent Thomas." Brent wondered if he should've identified himself as an agent. He didn't feel like an agent. He felt more like a university professor who'd somehow found himself in a strange room, in a strange place, trying to contact a stranger and wondering why he was doing so. He'd never realized what a sheltered life he had been living.

Except for his hitch in the army—two exciting years that now seemed like two months—he'd spent his entire life in Kansas. There'd been brief vacations, but always with his parents and always to one of the nearby national or state parks. Although once they'd ventured as far away as Chicago.

"Agent Thomas?" A man's voice interrupted his ruminations.

"Yes, sir."

"You get in okay? Get settled in the apartment?"

"Yes, sir. I got in last night."

"Fine, fine," Zylo said. "I'll be out to see you later this morning."

"Shouldn't I could come in there, sir?"

"No." There was a pause. "We'll come there. Hang loose. 'bye."

The line clicked dead and Brent slowly hung up. They were coming out to see him. How did he rate such VIP treatment? He wondered if the 'we' included Hendrix and Duval. He hoped so. But why didn't they want him to come to headquarters? One more mystery that needed answers.

After he walked home, Brent turned on the TV and tried to watch the news. But he had trouble concentrating, and after a moment, turned it off. He walked out on the small balcony and stood looking down at the unfamiliar street. He didn't like uncertainty. He was used to having total, or almost total, control over his situations.

Is this what it meant to be an agent? Waiting? Always waiting for something to happen?

An hour dragged by before the intercom buzzed. Brent pushed the black button on the intercom, hoping it was the correct one. "Yes?"

"Brent?" a familiar voice asked.

"Jim? Jim Hendrix?"

There was a chuckle and Hendrix said, "Welcome to the land of fruit and nuts."

Some of the tension went out of Brent. With Hendrix in attendance, he wouldn't be talking to a bunch of strangers.

"Hey," he said. "Come on up." He pressed the red button that he assumed unlocked the apartment building's front security door. Now he'd get those answers.

He opened his apartment door and stood waiting in the doorway. After a moment, Marc Duval and Jim Hendrix left the elevator and strode down the hall. Duval was wearing western style boots, jeans, and a plaid shirt with the tail out. Jim Hendrix was similarly dressed. Except for a brown attaché case that Hendrix carried, they could have passed for freight handlers.

"Hey, man, it's good to see you." The two agents pumped Brent's hand and slapped him on the shoulder. "Understand you got your gold badge. You're all set to get in the game."

"Yeah," Brent said. "If I could only figure out what the game is."

Duval and Hendrix glanced at one another and lost a little of their cheer.

"Yeah, well..." Jim Hendrix said. "We'll get into that."

"Hey, got something for you." Marc Duval tossed Brent a set of car keys secured by a twisted paper clip. "These are for the dark blue Chevy Caprice parked outside."

"It's a coupl'a years old and maybe a little...uh...beat up, but it's the best we could do," Hendrix added.

Brent stared at the keys. "Gee, thanks, you guys. But...how much are the payments?"

Duval laughed. "Payments are on Uncle Sam."

Jim Hendrix opened the *attaché* case and took out an envelope that he handed to Brent. "This is the registration. Inside are gas credit cards for four different oil companies. Sign here." He handed Brent a DEA-12 receipt that listed the credit cards by serial number. Brent signed, keeping a copy.

Hendrix took a shiny new pair of handcuffs and Colt Agent .38 Special with a two-inch barrel out of the case and handed them to Brent, along with another form to sign. "You won't be needing these for a while," he said. "But you've got to be issued them anyway. SOP...standard operating procedure."

"I won't be needing them?" Brent asked as he signed the receipt. "Don't all agents carry them?"

"Uh...not when you work undercover."

So that's it. It had been in the back of Brent's mind since he'd been hustled through his NTI classes in Washington. He'd dismissed the idea as preposterous. Only experienced agents went undercover. That's what they'd said at NTI. So why me?

"Isn't that kind of...uh...unusual?"

"Yeah," Hendrix said. "Kind of."

Brent waited for additional information. When it wasn't volunteered, he asked, "Will I be working with you guys?"

"Yeah. We'll be your main contact. Zylo'll explain the whole thing when he gets here." Hendrix glanced at his watch. "Which should be pretty soon."

"Okay," Brent said, realizing Duval and Jim weren't going to tell him anything. "I'm sorry I don't have any coffee or beer or anything to offer you guys."

"That's okay. I hope this place is okay for a while. We had to dig up something on short notice."

"Yeah," Jim Hendrix said. "We figured they'd let you finish up at NTI. But Zylo and Hodges think this thing is too hot to wait."

"What thing?"

"You'll get that. I just wish we'd had time to get you some experience on the street."

"You don't really need street time," Duval said. "You won't be involved in raids and shit like that." His voice trailed off as he added, "But then...uh...U.C. is kind of like—more dangerous."

"Thanks a lot," Brent said. He meant it to be humorous, but it didn't come out that way.

"Yeah," Hendrix said. "Undercover work is something that can't really be taught. It's like screwing. You've either got it or you haven't—a natural aptitude."

"Suppose you haven't got it," Brent said. "How do you find out?"

Duval and Hendrix glanced at each other.

"The hard way," Hendrix said softly.

The buzzer sounded and Hendrix said, "That'll be Zylo."

He used the intercom to make a check, then unlatched the downstairs door.

"Zylo is a little officious," Duval said, "but he's okay. He's the SAIC." He pronounced it 'sack.'

"SAIC?" Brent said, trying to recall the designation.

"Special Agent In Charge. He coordinates our undercover work."

Marc Duval opened the apartment door and stood where he could watch the elevator at the end of the hall.

"Look, Brent," Hendrix said. "Before Zylo gets here, I'm kind of sorry—we're kind of sorry, in a way, we got you into this. But you were the only guy we could think of. After you hear the deal... Well, I guess you could refuse."

Brent felt a quick chill of apprehension. He knew, just as they did, that he couldn't refuse a U.C. assignment without looking like a coward. He was committed from the instant he'd accepted the gold badge.

Before he could form an answer, Duval said, "He's here."

They waited while Zylo came along the hall and into the room. He was a slim man in his mid-thirties; younger than Brent had expected. He was carrying an attaché case. To Brent's relief, he was wearing a dark gray suit, no vest. As he entered, Zylo said, "'Morning, Hendrix, Duval."

"'Morning, sir," the two agents answered.

The SAIC crossed to Brent and held out his hand. "I'm Cleveland Zylo. Welcome to L.A."

Brent shook his hand. "Thank you, sir."

Zylo seated himself on the sofa, balancing the attaché case on his knees. He motioned Brent to the chair facing him, the only one in the room. Duval closed the door, and he and Hendrix brought chairs from the kitchenette and sat down.

"I'm sorry you had to miss the graduation ceremony at NTI," Zylo began. "I know you worked hard for it."

"I don't mind, sir," Brent lied. He'd hoped to bring his folks to Washington for his graduation, but the abrupt assignment had ended that. And he still didn't know what the hell was going on.

"Well, anyway you got your badge." Zylo glanced around the room as though to give it his stamp of approval. "It isn't often we do something like this, so we're sort of playing it by ear. I hope you understand that."

"Not really, sir."

"Yes, well... Please keep in mind, Thomas, that this is a rather unusual set of circumstances."

For Christ's sake, Brent felt like screaming, cut the bullshit and get to the point.

Zylo looked at Hendrix and Duval as though he'd read Brent's mind. "Have you showed him the file?"

Hendrix shook his head. "No, sir. I thought it better if you were here."

"Very good." Zylo held out his hand.

Hendrix took a thin file from his attaché and handed it to Zylo. "Do you mind, sir, if I tell him who the suspect is?"

Zylo waved his hand. "Go ahead. You know him better than anyone."

Hendrix and Duval didn't miss the implication. They were the ones closest to Fat Frankie, and consequently, the ones the stink was rubbing off on.

Hendrix turned his kitchen chair around and straddled it so he faced Brent who simply stared at him wondering if he was going to get more bullshit. Hendrix lit a cigarette as he talked.

"The guy we're talking about is Fat Frankie."

"Fat Frankie? You mean Big Frankie?"

"Yeah. Only now he's Fat Frankie."

"What about him?"

"It has come to our attention that Fat Frankie is the *numero uno* drug dealer in this area."

Brent should have felt stunned at the news. But, strangely, he wasn't. Frankie had always had the air of a man who'd do anything if the price was right. Brent had always liked him—everybody did—but he couldn't say he'd have trusted him.

"I don't understand," he said. "If he's involved, why haven't you busted him?"

"It's...uh...kind of delicate." Hendrix went on to explain Fat Frankie's rather unique role with the DEA and how he'd been fingered by a snitch. The only way they were going to get the evidence they needed to make a conviction stick was through an undercover agent. The problem was that Fat Frankie would never let a stranger in his organization.

"That's why we thought of you. You and Frankie were pretty close. He knows you're not a narc."

Mentioning Frankie's name had brought back vivid images of the most exciting period in Brent's life—images of exotic Middle Eastern cities and villages, of deserts, jungles and peculiar people. The SOG had spent a lot of time tooling around the Middle East. Big Frankie and Brent were the only ones who'd really enjoyed it, especially Frankie. He'd told Brent more than once that Pakistan and Turkey were the keys to getting rich.

"Yeah," Brent said. "We got to be pretty good buddies."

"That's why we think that if you went to Frankie and asked for a job in his gym, he'd give it to you," Hendrix said.

"Just because we were army buddies? If he's really a dealer, he won't want anybody straight around."

"It's not likely everybody who works for him is part of his trafficking," Zylo explained. "In fact, we believe that one reason Frankie's been able to stay in business so long is because only a few of his people know what he's doing. He keeps his legitimate operations entirely separate."

"We think," Hendrix interjected. "We can't be sure."

"We've got another card," Marc Duval said. "If you remember, Frankie was into boxing before he enlisted. Tell him you're the best trainer in the world. He'll jump at the bait."

"He won't buy that. Karate, maybe. He used to tell me I had potential."

"Nope. Frankie's not into karate. How about bodybuilding?"

"He's got a bodybuilder," Hendrix said. "Jaime Ortega. Frankie says he's going to be a champion."

"Yeah," Duval said. "But Frankie's first love is boxing. He's been trying for years to get a contender from his gym. He's had a few good fighters, but no cigar."

"Frankie's hungry," Hendrix said. "When you tell him you were a pro trainer, he'll roll out the red carpet."

"I wasn't a pro trainer."

Hendrix shrugged. "So lie a little."

Brent shook his head. "I'm no pro. It's not the same thing."

"Doesn't matter. It's what Frankie thinks that counts. When you see him, spread it on."

Brent's brain seemed to be spinning, making it almost impossible to fit the new pieces in place. He'd taken the job to fight drug dealers, not to spy on a friend. But undercover work was part of the job. He'd known that going in. And he certainly owed no loyalties to Frankie Rodriguez. If Frankie really was a dealer, he was the enemy. But professional trainer? It didn't make sense.

"I don't know," he said. "How much time do I have?"

Hendrix and Duval looked at Zylo. The SAIC pursed his lips. "None really. Frankie's organization is giving us fits."

"If it is Frankie," Duval reminded.

Zylo ignored him. "How soon can you be ready?"

Brent hesitated. A year from now, he'd be no more ready than he was now. "Any time," he said.

Zylo looked pleased. "Good. Make it tomorrow."

"Tomorrow?" Brent sucked in his breath. He looked at Hendrix and Duval, but they wouldn't meet his eye. "What the hell. Okay."

"There are a few details to work out," Zylo said. "First thing is communications. Number one. Unless it's an emergency, you'll deal exclusively with Assistant Supervisor Hendrix or Agent Duval.

"Number two. Never come to the office. Never. Your contacts with Jim or Marc will normally be by telephone."

"I don't have a phone."

"You'll have one. But when you do, don't use it for contacts. Use a pay phone somewhere."

"Not the same one all the time," Hendrix interjected.

"Right. Third. If you do have to meet with Jim or Marc, it'll be in a restaurant or in a car or some other place where you're not likely to be recognized."

Zylo stood up. "I know it's a bitch, but you're all we've got. This is really sensitive. Frankie carries a lot of weight in the Latino community—local and state. We've got to get hard evidence or we can't do a damn thing. Find out if he's got any books. Keep track of his contacts. See if you can find out how he's getting his junk into the country. If he's got anything incriminating on the premises, we can make a bust. It's up to you." He held out his hand. "Good luck."

Brent didn't want it to be up to him. Not on his first case, for God's sake. What did he know about anything? Still, he tried to keep the uncertainty out of his voice as he said, "How much time do I have?"

Zylo's thin lips parted in a tight smile. "All you need. But we want results."

"I'll keep that in mind, sir."

"Fine." Zylo nodded to Hendrix and Duval. "Good work. If you need anything, and I mean anything, let me know."

"Yes, sir," the agents said and Zylo went out, leaving the door open.

Brent watched Zylo walk away, trying to sort questions through his numbed mind. "Big Frankie," he said. "Are you sure? I mean, that snitch could be wrong."

"We know," Hendrix said. "That's why we need more information. If it's Frankie, we don't want him to suspect anything until we're ready. If it isn't, we don't want to get him on somebody's shit list."

"Okay," Brent said flatly. "But if you don't mind, I'm going to consider him innocent until proven guilty."

"Very noble," Marc Duval said. "But you might live longer if you considered him guilty."

"He means don't get careless," Hendrix added. "If Frankie is our man and finds out you're DEA, he'll have to kill you."

"But he knows I know you guys. He might put two and two together."

Duval and Hendrix glanced at each other as though to exchange thoughts. They reminded Brent of identical twins who often seemed to know what each other was thinking.

"We considered that," Hendrix said. "But it's been almost six years. And he knows we haven't been in touch."

"You didn't even know we were in L.A., did you?" Duval asked.

"No. And I sure as hell didn't know you were DEA."

"So there you go."

"Look at it this way," Hendrix said. "When you meet Frankie, see if he talks about all of us getting together. Kind of a reunion. If he doesn't, that could be significant."

"Or maybe not," Brent said. "Which is a great deal of ignorance founded upon a very little knowledge."

"Huh?" Duval said.

"A quotation. '*Bernard le Blovier de Fontenelle.*'"

"Oh."

"I know it's thin," Hendrix said. "But as long as Frankie doesn't know you're DEA, you'll be okay. If he's clean, he doesn't ever have to know."

Brent sighed, his mouth dry. He wanted to believe in Frankie. Assuming a person guilty without proof went against everything he'd been taught. But in this business everything seemed distorted, twisted. Suspicion was a way of life. It was the suspicious ones who survived.

Hendrix shook Brent's hand and moved to the door. "Sorry to get you mixed up in this, Brent, but they've got our asses in a sling."

"Don't worry about it," Brent murmured, thinking that the sling had now been transferred to his own ass.

"Keep in touch," Duval said. "Numbers where we can be reached and Frankie's address are in the envelope."

"Better memorize them," Hendrix said. "Destroy the paper."

"We'd like a report every day at first."

"Okay," Brent said. The two agents gave him tight smiles, and said, "See ya," and went out, closing the door softly.

Brent sank onto a chair. Depression deadened his senses. He felt as though he'd been battered by a gorilla. What the hell was he doing here? He stared at the ugly shape of the pistol that had been left on the counter. Its muzzle was pointing directly at his heart. Was it an omen? He shivered.

"Well, idiot," he muttered. "You wanted a change."

Chapter Six

FRANKIE'S GYM WAS located on Eastern Avenue just north of the Pomona Freeway, heart of the East Los Angeles Latino district. After parking in the building's tarmac-paved lot, Brent Thomas studied the building. It certainly didn't match his image of a drug dealer's headquarters. He'd expected a run-down warehouse in a littered alley.

Instead he found a modern, three-storied building constructed of beige-colored bricks. A verdant lawn between the building and the parking lot had just been mowed and the air was sweet with the scent of cut grass. Yellow and gold marigolds lined the walkway. Next to the building, tall ferns gently waved lacy boughs over brightly colored beds of flowers.

As he walked toward the building, Brent reminded himself not to be impressed. This was no ordinary gym and this would be no ordinary meeting. If Frankie were a drug dealer, behind all the beauty lurked the grinning skull of death. But here in the bright sunshine, it was hard to believe he was in any real danger. In truth, he was more afraid of being found out a liar than of being shot.

What was it he'd been taught at NTI? The lies must be presented properly, at the right time. No quaver of the voice or wariness in the eyes to betray the liar. All the very tiny signs—the nervousness, the dampness of the palms, heavier than normal perspiration—these had to be guarded against, and when possible, controlled. Maybe he could bring it off if he just forgot he was an agent and pretended he really was just an old army buddy looking for a job. It was his only hope.

He took a deep breath and pushed through the chrome-and-glass front doors. He was committed.

The building's foyer was spacious with a high ceiling and a polished terrazzo floor. Two glass display cases were placed to provide the best view of trophies inside. On the wall were pictures of bodybuilders and boxers. A pretty Latina receptionist was seated at a desk behind a gleaming white plastic counter. She was typing slowly and painfully on a computer's keyboard.

She didn't look up as Brent said, "Good morning."

"'Morning," she replied curtly.

Brent had taken Hendrix's advice and wore a tight-fitting T-shirt and old blue jeans. When the receptionist finally glanced at him, her look of annoyance changed to a bright smile.

"May I help you?" She sounded as though she meant it.

"I'd like to see Big Frankie," Brent answered. "Ah...Mr. Rodriguez."

"Regarding?"

"Just tell him it's an old buddy, Brent Thomas."

The girl looked happy as though she'd feared Brent might be a salesman of some sort she'd have had to send on his way.

She picked up a white phone and punched an intercom button. She spoke softly into the phone, then set it back in the cradle and informed Brent in a surprised tone that Mr. Rodriguez would come down to meet him.

Brent thanked her and she said, "My name's Carla."

"Carla? Nice to meet you."

"Thank you. You must be a good friend of Mr. Rodriguez."

"Used to be. We were in the army together."

Her beautiful lips formed a round O. "Oh, yes. Were you a general, too?"

"A general?" If Frankie wanted her to believe he'd been a general, it was fine with Brent. "No. Frankie was the only general. I was a corporal."

"Well, you must've been good. Mr. Rodriguez doesn't usually come down to meet anybody."

"Really? Well, thanks."

Brent noticed a small security camera set high in the wall. Just in case Frankie was watching, he walked over to look at the trophies in the cases with his face toward the camera. Most were for bodybuilding. A few were for boxing. Brent checked the names. He'd never heard of any of them. But that wasn't surprising. He'd never bothered to keep up with the professionals.

He examined the pictures of bodybuilders. Their degree of physical development always filled him with astonishment. How was it possible to dedicate oneself to such narcissism? It took hundreds of painful hours to create such incredible muscular development. But in a way, except for the pain, it was no different that the tremendous number of hours other people spent in developing skill at basketball, baseball or even chess and bridge. He was reminded of a Latin phrase: "*de gustibus non est disputandum*" meaning "there is no disputing about tastes."

He was about to turn aside when a name on one of the pictures caught his eye. Jaime Ortega. That was the name Hendrix had mentioned. Frankie's potential bodybuilding champion. The picture showed a darkly handsome man facing the camera, crunching to show off his lats. He had wavy black hair and a scowling face with piercing dark eyes under thick eyebrows that almost met at the bridge of his long, thin nose. He had the widest shoulders and superbly developed lats Brent had ever seen. But his legs didn't quite match his upper body development. Still, he looked as though he was in the championship ballpark.

A set of double doors to the right of the receptionist opened and Frankie's voice boomed, "Brent! How the hell are you?"

Brent turned—and stared. Frankie had always been overweight, but his heavy body was now swathed in layers of fat. His thighs were so huge he had to move in a wide-legged waddle. He was wearing an expensive single-breasted suit with the pants pulled up over his bulging stomach. The shirt was open at the throat while its remaining buttons strained to retain their grip. His hair was still thick and dark, and he'd grown a stubble of beard shot with gray.

His eyes, however, had not changed. Although almost buried in his round face and overhung by heavy black brows, their gleam was as shrewd and piercing as ever.

Brent held out his hand, but Frankie brushed it aside and clasped him in a bear hug while he pounded Brent on the back. "Damn, it's good to see you." He released the hug, but continued holding Brent by the shoulders. "How the hell have you been?"

"Great, Frankie." Brent grinned. "You're looking—healthy."

"Damn right." Frankie laughed. He stepped back and slapped his huge stomach. "Living right." He lowered his voice and winked at Brent. "Carmen made me do it. She says this way I can look at the girls, but I can't do nothing." He laughed. "Which goes to show what she knows." He took a good look at Brent and whistled softly. "*Aye Dios mio!* You grew up, kid."

"Yeah. Looks like we both did."

Frankie laughed again. Then he stared at Brent thoughtfully. "You into bodybuilding?"

"No, not really. I work out, but nothing serious."

"You should be. God damn. You looking for a place to work out? What're you doing in L.A.? I thought you lived in Kansas or someplace."

"I did. I...uh...I just moved out here. As a matter of fact, I am looking for a place to work out."

"Yeah? You came to the right place, *amigo*. I've got the best gym in town. Let me show you around." He moved to the double doors. There was no knobs on the doors, only large brass push plates. "Come on. I'll give you a cook's tour."

The receptionist pressed a buzzer under her desk and Frankie shoved the doors open, leading the way into a wide hallway carpeted with indoor-outdoor synthetic fiber. On the walls were more pictures of boxers, and male and female bodybuilders. Most of the pictures were autographed to Frankie. But what interested Brent more than the pictures was a another security camera in the ceiling, aimed to monitor the door and the hallway. Frankie wasn't taking any chances on being surprised by unannounced visitors.

"This place used to be a candy factory," Frankie said as he moved down the hall. "When I got it, there was nothing here but broken down machines." He chuckled. "Now we got broken down bodies."

At the end of the hall were two doors marked *mujares* and *caballeros*. Frankie opened the *caballeros* door and led Brent into a spacious room that had the familiar locker room odor of sour sweat and antiseptics. The immaculately clean room was carpeted with hard-weave nylon. Rows of large steel lockers were separated by wooden benches. Individual showers were in the back. Brent had the impression that Frankie wasn't running a gym for a bunch of bums.

"I got steam rooms for both sides," Frankie said with a note of pride. "Women don't have to worry about getting groped by some horny pervert. That's class. Right, *amigo?*"

They were walking back down the hall when Brent became aware of music coming from the floor above and the thump of people exercising in rhythm.

Frankie noticed his upward glance and grinned. "Dance class. You know. That jumping around kind of exercise."
"Aerobics?"

"Yeah, that's it. We got everything here."

Brent wondered whether Frankie ever used any of the equipment. He had to suppress a laugh at the mental picture of Frankie doing aerobics.

Partway along the hall, Frankie pushed open double doors and led Brent into a huge gym that occupied the entire length of the building. Brent stopped in amazement.

"How you like that, *amigo?*" Frankie said. "I got the best damn stuff money could buy."

Brent could well believe it. The place was a Hollywood version of a gymnasium. The ceiling of the long room reached to the building's roof where colorful banners dangled from freshly painted steel trusses and beams. The floor was roughly divided into three areas: a men's bodybuilder area, a women's bodybuilder area, and at the far end, a boxing area with two rings.

In the boxing area, a couple of men were skipping rope and another was filling the gym with the machine-gun sound of a light bag being expertly battered.

In the carpeted bodybuilding areas were stationary bicycles, treadmills, Universal Weight machines and Nautilus machines plus workout benches, reclines, wall racks, and racks of barbells and dumbbells with their associated assortment of chromed and knurled bars and heavily embossed Olympic weights. Mirrors lined one wall so bodybuilders could watch their progress. All the equipment gleamed with polished brilliance.

There was also a posing room, completely mirrored, where the bodybuilders could perfect their posing routines.

"It's got a Bose hi-fi system," Frankie said, "so they can practice with their music."

Near large freight doors was an equipment storage room. The freight doors looked as though they were made of riveted steel. It would probably take a tank to break through them.

Still, so much security might be standard for L.A. With its expensive equipment, the place would be a great haul for a gang of thieves with trucks.

"Looks great, Frankie," Brent said. "Must've cost a fortune".

"Money is to spend, amigo. You got to spend it to get it."

Brent's attention was drawn to the women's bodybuilding area where a man was giving instructions to a blonde girl in a lycra leotard who was working out with dumbbells. The man was the one in the lobby picture, Jaime Ortega. In person, his back and shoulders appeared to be even more developed than they had in the picture.

Frankie noticed the direction of Brent's gaze. "Them's our instructors. Hey, Ortega. Jennifer."

Frankie preceded   Brent across the room, and the two bodybuilders came to meet them. Ortega was bigger than he had looked in the picture, probably six-two and on the other side of two hundred pounds. But he moved with the lithe grace of a dancer. He was very handsome with piercing eyes. His wavy black hair was tied back in a pony tail.

"Ortega, Jennifer," Frankie said. "Meet an old army buddy. Brent Thomas. Brent, Ortega and *mi amor*, Jennifer Pierce."

"*Amor* nothing." Jennifer smiled. "He's a dreamer." She held out her hand to Brent.

"I don't blame him," Brent said.

Jennifer shattered Brent's conception of female bodybuilders. Her grip told Brent that she was very strong, but she didn't bulge with muscles. Her perfectly proportioned body was slender with soft contours. Unlike many female bodybuilders who dieted to the extreme to strip away every ounce of fat, and as a consequence, lost much of their bust, Jennifer had somehow managed to retain an intriguing cleavage. Her long, ash-blonde hair was plaited into two thick braids she wore coiled around her head and caught with combs. Her Nordic features were more chiseled than delicate. Her eyes under level brows were the gray-blue of water in an icy fjord. Her naturally pale skin was tanned to a light gold.

Brent released her hand and turned to Jaime Ortega. The pupils of Ortega's eyes seemed to dilate until his eyes were orbs of darkness that bored into Brent's as though to intimidate him with the intensity of his stare while he squeezed Brent's hand in a grip designed to be equally intimidating.

Brent grinned at him and tightened his own grip to match Ortega's. "Nice to meet you," he said.

Ortega's scowl deepened as he respond with a reluctant, "Hi."

Brent had the impression Ortega did very little smiling. He reminded Brent of an oversized flamenco dancer who worked hard at projecting machismo—an image that any display of *bonhomie* would shatter.

"Ortega's Western Region champ," Frankie said. "Some day he'll be world champion."

"Congratulations."

Ortega's scowl didn't change as he said, "Yeah," and Brent wondered how he managed to establish any sort of rapport with his audience and the judges when he posed. Unless he developed a better attitude, he'd never make it above the regionals. Maybe he practiced smiling in front of the mirror.

Jennifer took a step back and studied Brent's body. "Nice," she said. "You gonna work out here?"

"I'm not sure yet," Brent answered. "Depends."

"It's the best gym in L.A.," Jennifer said. "If you're going to work out at all, you won't find a better place."

"Damn right," Frankie agreed. "And the best damn instructors. You saw those trophies out front? About a dozen of 'em belong to Jennifer."

Brent took Frankie's words as an excuse to stare at Jennifer's body. "I can well believe it."

The color in her face heightened and Ortega's scowl deepened. "I think you'll like it here," she said with an amused twist to her lips.

"You're right. It's terrific. But..." Brent paused before beginning his first big lie. "I'm not sure I'll be staying in Los Angeles."

"Why not?" Jennifer said. "You'll like L.A. It's where things happen."

"Well," Brent said, followed by what he hoped was a convincing hesitation. "I've got to find a job first."

Jennifer smiled at Frankie. "Hey, Frankie. We need another instructor."

Frankie looked uncomfortable. "Yeah? Well, we can talk about it. Come on. I'll show you the rest of the place."

As they moved away, Brent said, "Nice to meet you."

"You, too. If Frankie says no," she said loud enough for Frankie to hear, "tell him I'll quit."

"Bull shit," Frankie said without turning. "You love me too much to quit."

Brent heard Jennifer laugh as she went to help a woman struggling with a treadmill. He noticed that Ortega, however, didn't move. He stood staring toward Brent and Frankie, his eyes hard. Brent wondered why the man had taken such an instant dislike to him. Maybe he considered Brent a competitor. Or maybe he just didn't like anybody. The latter seemed the most likely.

In the hallway, Frankie led the way to an elevator. The elevator was small and Brent had to squeeze in beside Frankie. "Frankie, you've got to go on a diet or get a bigger elevator."

Frankie chuckled and pushed a button marked 'P' which Brent assumed meant Penthouse and the car began a shuddering ascent. "I am on a diet. I been on a diet for ten years. Enchiladas and broads. Put it in one end and take it off the other." He laughed and the car shook.

"Jesus," Brent said. "Don't laugh, Frankie. I don't think this machine can take it."

"Who cares? If we fall, I'll just bounce."

"Yeah, but you might bounce on me."

Despite Frankie's laugh, the car creaked past a second floor and stopped. The door slid open to reveal a large foyer reception room. Frankie had gone all out designing his suite of offices. A thick pale-gold carpet covered the floor and the walls were paneled in blonde mahogany. Frankie explained that the hand-carved, leather-upholstered furniture was from Mexico. Mariachi music, a shade above subliminal, oozed from concealed speakers.

There was a secretary's desk opposite the elevator, but no secretary. A computer and its monitor were on a computer-stand beside the desk. Neither the desk nor the computer looked as though they got a lot of use.

Frankie crossed the room and used a key to open a thick, heavily paneled door with a small, built-in mirror. He stood back and motioned Brent into his office.

When Frankie closed the door, Brent noticed that the mirror in the door was actually a one way window so Frankie could see into the reception room. Two large steel deadbolts could be shot into reinforced steel on the thick door frame. It would take dynamite to force that door.

Brent carefully surveyed Frankie's office. Frankie hadn't spared money on his office. The wall-to-wall carpet was a dark gold, its pile even thicker than the one in the reception area. The paneling was also darker and richer, the furniture more massive and intricately carved and upholstered in leather so thick it might have come from a rhinoceros. A massive oak desk squatted in front of large windows overlooking Eastern Avenue. Traffic sounds were a mere whisper filtered through the thick glass.

A massive teak coffee table dominated the center of the room. Video monitors wired to security cameras were set into the wall near the door opposite Frankie's desk. On the right side of the room, shelves of books that looked as though they'd never been touched were on either side of a large, stylized image of a haloed Christ made of ceramic tile.

The other wall was covered with autographed pictures of boxers, bodybuilders, ball players and celebrities. The focal point, however, was a life-sized oil painting of a handsome woman with black hair drawn back severely from an imperious forehead. Dark eyebrows arched over luminous eyes. She was wearing a flamenco dress with a tight bodice and flounced, flaring skirt that swirled at her feet. Her poise was also flamenco with her hands curved above her head, glancing over one shoulder.

The pose displayed her slender figure and her expressive face to their fullest advantage. Brent knew it was a picture of Frankie's wife, Carmen, and he wondered how Frankie had been able to hold onto such a woman. Of course, the painting might be years old. By now, she could be as fat as Frankie.

"What do you drink?" Frankie asked as he crossed to a corner bar. "I got everything. Just name it."

"Oh, make it a beer."

"Beer, shit. Man, this is the land of plenty. Okay, what kind?"

"Kind? Have you got any Coors Lite?"

"Lite? Shit! I got Mexican beer. Corona. You'll like it."

"It's done all right by you."

Frankie opened a bottle of Corona and handed it to Brent. "I don't drink beer. That's for you peasants." He picked up a bottle of Cuervo. "*Tequila*. Puts hair on your *cajones*."

He poured a glass of the golden liquor and fired up a black cigar. "I hope you're not one a them jerks who don't like cigar smoke." Frankie's smile was jovial, but his inflection said that if anybody did mind it was just too damn bad.

Brent shook his head. "You want to kill yourself, go ahead."

Frankie was a good example of everything physically bad for a person: grossly overweight, heavy on booze, strong cigars. If he was a drug dealer, it'd be a wonder if he didn't die from a heart attack before they could get around to busting him.

Frankie carried his drink behind the desk and sank into the huge leather executive chair with a sigh. "All that exercise," he grunted. "Bad for the heart."

Brent nodded. "Everything is bad for something."

"Ain't that the truth? You pick up the paper today and they tell you something you've been eating or doing for years has killed every monkey in India. Shit. They'll tell us next that fucking is bad."

"It would be for you, Frankie. I think that'd push you right over the edge."

"Yeah, yeah. Is *verdad*. It sure as hell would kill the girl." His chuckle trailed off and he motioned Brent to a seat. "Sit down, *amigo*. What've you been doing since that horse shit army?"

Brent sat in one of the leather armchairs. He sank so far into the leather he wondered if he was going to be able to get up. It was like sitting in quicksand. Nobody could get out of that chair in a hurry. Frankie had probably planned it that way. He was not the kind who left much to chance.

"Went back to the university. Been teaching since then."

"In Kansas?"

"Yeah."

"So how come you left?"

"Got bored. Thought I'd come out here where it's 'happening.'"

"You got that right. You married?"

Brent thought for an instant before answering. How much should he tell Frankie? The easiest thing to do would be to just say no, which was mostly the truth, and wouldn't open old wounds. But what difference did it make now? He'd be doing enough lying in the next few weeks. Better to stick to the truth as much as possible. That way he wouldn't have to keep track of so many lies.

"I was," he admitted. "For two years. We met when she came from Arizona for post-graduate work at the university. It didn't work out."

There was no reason to tell Frankie that Connie hadn't been able to cut the umbilical cord. She couldn't stand living so far from her parents and had gone back to Phoenix. There was no reason to tell Frankie about the hurt caused by the breakup; no reason to tell him about the pain and bitterness that now, almost three years later, he still felt. After Connie left, he found that living in Manhattan with all its memories of her was increasingly painful. It had taken time to realized that, subconsciously, it had been one of the principle reasons he'd decided to take Hendrix's offer to join the DEA

He almost smiled when the thought struck him that he'd succeeded beyond his wildest dreams.

"How about you?" he asked. He nodded toward the portrait. "You still married to Carmen?"

"Sure. Who else is gonna have me? Besides, now I got the big restaurant and this place, she thinks I'm too rich to get rid of. Where else she gonna find somebody like me?"

"That's sure as hell true, Frankie," Brent agreed. Brent wondered how much Carmen knew about Frankie's real source of money.

Frankie had been studying Brent through a haze of cigar smoke. "You gonna keep on teaching?"

Here it comes, Brent thought. Watch yourself. "I don't think so. I'm looking to change my whole life."

"So you're looking for a job."

Brent had the idiotic feeling that ever since Hendrix and Duval had reentered his life he'd been trapped in a whirlpool. He'd started at the edge and each day had been whirling faster and faster, being sucked closer and closer to the vortex. Now he was on the verge of hurtling down the black tunnel to—where? But there was no way he could get back.

"Yeah," he said. He closed his eyes, plunging over the edge. "You got anything here?"

"A job?" Frankie rubbed his chin. "I don't know. You done any instructing in bodybuilding?"

"Not exactly," Brent admitted. "I have a degree in Physical Education. I was more into coaching."

"Coaching? What kind? Football? Basketball?"

"No. Boxing. Wrestling.

"Wrestling?"

"Yeah. Wrestling's big in Kansas. We were regional champs last year."

"What about boxing? You any good?"

"Damn good—for Kansas."

Frankie shook his head. "Kansas. Shit." He swallowed the last of his *tequila* and grunted with effort has he hauled himself to his feet. He went to the bar and refilled his glass. "Okay. Jennifer's right. She needs more help in the bodybuilding."

"But," Brent started to protest. "I'm not a—"

Frankie interrupted with a wave of his cigar. "Not you. Ortega's been handling most of the boxing. But his background was more in that damn karate shit. You take over the boxing. That'll free Ortega up so he can work full time with the bodybuilders. Okay?"

Brent had been holding his breath. Now he let it out with a sigh. "Yeah. Sounds good."

"How much money you want?"

Money? Brent hadn't thought about that. Hell, he'd have to give it all to the DEA anyway. He lifted his hand. "I'll leave that up to you. Whatever's fair."

"Okay. I'll work that out. I'll try to leave enough after Uncle Sam gets his so you can have a few *frijoles*." Frankie paused and his voice hardened. For the first time Brent caught a glimpse of the steel under Frankie's fat as he said, "Just one thing, *amigo*. I've got some pretty good fighters. I don't want them screwed up by no amateur."

Brent felt tension drain away. He'd been afraid Frankie had caught him in a lie. He had to hide his emotions better or Frankie really would get suspicious. "You're the boss," he said. "If you think I can't hack it, don't be shy."

Frankie's belly shook as he chuckled. "Shy? That'll be the fuckin' day."

Frankie walked to the door and pulled it open. "Get your gear and come back in the morning. That'll give me time to set this up with Ortega."

Brent took the last swallow of his beer and set the bottle on the floor so he could use both hands to heave himself out of the chair. "Okay." At the door he said, "Thanks, Frankie. I really appreciate this."

"*Por nada, amigo*. We'll work your butt off."

Brent grinned. "Just leave me enough for fooling around."

"How much you need?" Frankie said with a wink.

"Well, you can't drive a spike with a tack hammer."

"You got that right, *amigo*. Look at me."

Frankie was still laughing when he closed the door. But he wasn't laughing when he crossed back to his desk and put down his glass of *tequila*. He picked up the phone and punched in an intercom number. "Ortega. Come to my office. I think I've fixed it so you can make more trips."

He hung up the phone, went behind his desk and sank into his chair. He picked up his glass of tequila and stared at the amber liquid. His lips smiled, but there was no humor in his eyes as he muttered, "This is gonna be good. This is gonna be very good." He drained his glass.

In the parking lot, Brent started the Caprice and drove out of the lot. He picked up the Santa Monica Freeway and headed west toward the ocean. He should have felt elated. He'd succeeded in penetrating Frankie's organization. Instead, he felt miserable. He wasn't used to lying. It didn't come naturally to him the way it seemed to for some people—like his ex-wife. But the thing that really bothered him was what Frankie would think of him when he learned the truth. And, eventually, he'd find out.

Brent gripped the wheel hard. He'd almost rather be dead than be labeled a cheat and a liar—almost.

Chapter Seven

THE NEXT MORNING, Brent pulled into the parking lot at Frankie's Gym shortly before eight. He'd forgotten to ask Frankie what time he was supposed to report for work, but he figured eight should be about right. Then he noticed with chagrin that the lot was full. He probably should've come in earlier. Most athletes were early risers. He was himself.

But he had no way of knowing how they trained in East L.A. If they came in before going to regular jobs, he'd have to get here a lot sooner. And what about the afternoon? Some would probably come in on their lunch break or after work. He hoped he wouldn't have to work too late. But then—he smiled ruefully—why not? What else did he have to do?

Spotting an open place between cars, he was maneuvering the big Caprice to pull into the space when a red Porche convertible with the top up roared in front of him and Brent slammed on the brakes. The driver of the Porche executed a skidding stop that whipped the rear of the Porche around, and without a pause, shot into the space like an arrow shot into a bull's-eye.

Brent cursed softly. Instead of seeking another parking spot, he waited, seething with rage. It was important to him that the Porche driver knew what his opinion of him was.

When the Porche's door opened, Brent reached for the handle of his car door. He froze. A girl. A heart-stopping girl. She was wearing a sweater over leotards that clung to her petite, slender figure. Latina. Her curly black hair was pulled into a long pony tail.

She reached into the back seat of the car and lifted out a sports bag that she swung across her shoulder with the smooth grace of a dancer. She walked past Brent's car, her face as placid as a Madonna gazing at her baby.

The fact that she didn't even glance in his direction brought back Brent's anger, and he rolled down his window so he could say, "Thanks a lot. Didn't your mother teach you any manners."

She stopped and turned her head to look at him, totally unconcerned. "What's your problem?"

Up close her beauty made it difficult for Brent to speak. She had thick, dark brows that curved sardonically over level brown eyes. Her slightly concave cheeks highlighted pouting lips and even white teeth.

Her skin was a delicate bronze like the newly formed petals of a dusky rose. She stood with the bag thrown over her shoulder, her free hand on her hip. It was the insolence in her eyes and her pose that brought him back to reality.

"That was my place," he said. "I was here first."

"You were driving with your finger up your nose. You got what you deserve."

"I didn't think I'd run into somebody with the manners of a redneck."

She'd started to move away. At his words she stopped and turned back. Now there was more color in her cheeks and her lips were tight. "At least I know how to drive."

"Yeah, sure. There's a place over there small enough for your Porche. Why didn't you take that?"

"So what's your problem? Take it yourself."

"Oh, yeah. You couldn't get his heap in there with a shoehorn."

Her lips curled. "Want me to do it for you?"

Heat that had been creeping up Brent's neck flushed his cheeks. He opened his door. "Be my guest."

He slid across the bench seat to the passenger side. She dropped her bag to the tarmac and climbed behind the steering wheel. She slammed the door shut and at the same time yanked the shift lever into gear and hit the gas. The tires squealed and Brent's neck snapped as the car shot forward past the narrow parking slot. The girl hit the brake pedal and Brent saved himself a bloody nose by quickly bracing himself on the dash. Before he could recover his balance, the girl shoved the gear shift into reverse and hit the gas pedal again.

The tires yelped in protest as they yanked the car back. She spun the wheel, whipping the front end of the car around, then spun the wheel back the other way, backing the car into the slot like a cartridge being levered into the breach of a rifle. She jammed the brake hard, bringing the car to a shuddering stop, its rear bumper only fractions of an inch from the car behind it.

She turned off the engine and took out the keys. "You need any more help," she said as Brent was pulling himself upright, "let me know."

Brent's throat tightened. He was torn between disgust and admiration. It had been a magnificent bit of driving, except for one minor detail. "Great," he managed to say. "Now how the hell are we going to get out?"

"No problem."

There were only inches between cars on either side, but it was enough so she could open her door and edge her slender body through.

She closed the door and winked at him through the open window.

"Have fun," she said and walked away, her hips and ponytail swinging impishly.

If he could have reached her, Brent would've gladly throttled her. But she had already picked up her bag and was trotting toward the gym.

Brent slid across the seat and tried the door. He could never squeeze his one-eighty-five pound frame through the narrow opening. Damn. Damn. He'd have to pull out so he could open the door. He reached for the ignition key. Gone! Oh, shit. She'd taken the keys with her.

His fist lifted to pound on the steering wheel in rage. Then he paused as his rage turned to amusement. He'd been screwed expertly. In about twenty seconds, the girl had made him look like an inept fool. He put his head on his arms and laughed. "You idiot. The next time you think you're so damned smart, remember this."

It was impossible to get out of the car through either door, but by straining and wriggling, he was able to pull himself out through the open window leaving, he was certain, a few patches of skin from his back. He'd have to locate her to get his car keys, and when he did... Well, he hoped she wouldn't goad him into carrying out his original desire to throttle her. But remembering the mischief in her eyes, he knew she would.

She probably saved her life when he discovered she'd left his car keys on the trunk of the car so he was able to get his equipment bag from the car's trunk.

In the reception area, Carla returned his smiling good morning. "Welcome aboard," she said and handed him an envelop. "Your locker number and combination."

Brent took the envelop. "Thanks."

"There are a couple of papers in there you'll have to fill out. You know—address, taxes, social security...phone number."

"Okay."

"No rush. When you finish, just drop them off."

"Okay."

"...at my house."

Brent grinned. "I might do that."

In the men's locker room, he changed into his shorts, tank-top and sweat suit, and hung his street clothes in his locker. It was already busy in the gym, especially the boxing area where several men were working out. Most were Latinos of the lower weights. Brent hoped they all understood English.

In the bodybuilding area, Jaime Ortega and Jennifer were working with clients. Jennifer was wearing an electric-blue skin-tight lycra leotard that looked as though it had been painted on. Her legs were bare except for leg warmers which she wore pushed down below her knees. She looked over at Brent and waved a greeting.

When Ortega saw Brent, he jerked his head for Brent to follow him and he strode to a nearby water cooler. "You're supposed to be here at six," he snapped. "Where the hell've you been? You might be Frankie's boy, but down here you work like the rest of us peons. *Comprende?*"

Brent suppressed a quick burst of anger. Getting mad now wouldn't do him a bit of good. "Sorry," he said crisply. "Six it is."

"And get rid of those slimy looking clothes. You're supposed to be an example. If people want to throw up, they can go to Main Street."

Brent's muscles tensed. What the hell did this guy have against him? Maybe he did look a little unkempt, especially compared with Ortega who was wearing immaculate white warm-up pants and a tight-fitting tank top shirt that accentuated his powerful shoulders. Brent realized his old gray sweat suit had seen better days, but at the university, old sweats were almost a badge of honor. If he'd dressed like Ortega, his students would've laughed him out of the gym. But this was a long way from Kansas.

"Sure," he said. "I'll do that."

"Okay," Ortega said curtly. Apparently he was a little disappointed Brent hadn't lost his temper. He jerked his head toward the boxing area. "Go help those *estupedos*. There's not much to do right now, but there'll be a big bunch coming in about noon."

"Yes, sir." Brent smiled inwardly at the way Ortega shot a look at him to see if Brent was being sarcastic. But he managed to keep the smile off his face, and Ortega grunted and went back to the bodybuilding area.

Working with the boxers, Brent quickly discovered that virtually all were experienced fighters who knew their workout routines so he had little to do except supervise some of the sparring in the ring. From time to time during the morning, Ortega came to watch Brent work with a client. The only time he said a word was after he'd watched Brent in the ring working on a young fighter's footwork.

"Don't waste too much time on the dancing," he said. "Our boys like to hit."

"You're the boss," Brent said, and satisfied, Ortega moved away and Brent continued working on the young man's footwork.

Just before noon, the lunch crowd began arriving. But almost all were bodybuilding clients. Another girl had come in to help Jennifer and Ortega. Occasionally, Ortega came to help Brent with the fighters who spoke little or no English. Observing him, Brent realized Ortega knew what he was doing. He must've been a fighter at one time. The young fighters knew him and listened when Ortega told them something.

By one-thirty, the activity had begun to die down as clients went back to their jobs. Ortega said to Brent, "I'm gonna get some lunch. You can go when I get back."

Brent looked at the group of fighters using the equipment. He'd been working steadily all morning and he was beginning to drag. But it looked as though he had another hour to go before he got a break.

"Right," he said, but Ortega was already moving away.

For the next hour and a half Brent moved from fighter to fighter. It seemed that as one finished working out and left, two would take his place. Brent began to believe that every Latino male in East L.A. wanted to make it in the ring.

Jennifer came over once and asked how he was doing. Brent wiped sweat off his forehead and told her it was a piece of cake, but he knew that by the end of the day he was going to be walking on his heels. She laughed and told him to check with her when he went to lunch.

"If I go to lunch," Brent muttered. "I think it's going to be more like dinner."

"Even better," she said and went back to her sweating and grunting mastodons.

It was almost three when Ortega returned and the gym was virtually deserted. Even the flood of fighters had subsided. Brent was so hungry he felt sick and he wondered what he'd do if Ortega told him to forget lunch and work right through to quitting time—whenever that was.

"You've got forty-five minutes," Ortega growled. "You'd better get moving."

Brent didn't point out that Ortega had taken almost two hours. He'd learned a long time ago that rank had its privileges. He noticed Jennifer was still there helping a middle-aged man use a Nordic treadmill. When Brent asked if she wanted lunch, she nodded.

"Be right with you." She called to the other girl. "Chris, would you keep an eye on Mr. Brennen?"

Chris, a muscular girl in a bright red spandex leotard over a black T-shirt, waved that she understood and Jennifer pulled on a jacket as she came to join Brent.

"I don't know about you," she said, "but I'm starving."

"Me, too. I thought for a while that Ortega was the only one allowed lunch around here."

"Sometimes he runs errands for Frankie. That means the rest of us have to wait."

Brent wondered what kind of errands Jaime Ortega ran for Fat Frankie. Hendrix had thought Ortega was part of Frankie's dope dealing. That made sense. Frankie could hardly run a major operation by himself. He'd have to watch what he said around Ortega.

As Jennifer and he walked outside, she said, "There's a coffee shop over on Soto where I usually go. Want me to drive?"

Brent remembered how his car was parked. "Good idea. I don't know these streets."

Jennifer drove a white Corvette which she wheeled through busy traffic like a broken field runner. Brent was rapidly getting the impression that any California driver could easily handle an Indianapolis 500 race without additional training.

Slumped in a booth of the coffee shop, Brent ordered steak and eggs while Jennifer asked for chicken salad.

"Is that all you're having?" Brent asked. "You're going to die of malnutrition."

Jennifer made a small shrug. "Got to watch my weight."

Brent eyed as much of her slender body as he could see above the table top. "You need a diet like I need another head."

"You're thinking like a sane person. Not a bodybuilder."

"The operative word is 'builder.' Not 'anorexic.'"

"You've got to build muscle, not fat."

"What fat? You don't have an ounce."

"You just can't see it. But there's a small layer of fat between skin and muscle. It's hard to get rid of. But if you're a bodybuilder, you've got to do it or you can't get any definition."

"Definition?"

"Muscle striation. That kind of ropy cut-up look that the really great bodybuilders have when they pump up."

"Pump up? You mean loosened up?"

Jennifer shook her head. "I mean... Well, when a bodybuilder is relaxed he doesn't look much different than anybody else. He might look bigger in the chest and arms, but you don't see much in the way of real muscles. In other words, he's smooth. And smooth doesn't win contests. So before they go on stage, builders do a little warm-up pumping and some flexing exercises. That pumps up the muscles, gives them that exaggerated ropy look. Provided, of course, they've worked hard to bulk up in the first place."

"So they don't walk around looking like they're having a bad bowel movement."

"God, no. Do I look like that?"

Brent took advantage of the opportunity to stare at her. She was one of the silkiest looking females he'd ever seen. Her muscles were lean, her skin smooth, no bunchiness at all. "You can do that? Pump yourself up?"

"I can do a pretty fair job. But that's what turns a lot of women off from bodybuilding. They think they're going to turn into King Kong or some monster. They don't understand that that isn't what bodybuilding's all about."

Brent recognized an opportunity to obtain some information. "What about drugs?"

Jennifer's face hardened. "Drugs?"

"You know. Steroids. To bulk up."

Some of the hardness went out of her expression. "Steroids. God, no. They're illegal. All the major contests make you test for steroids."

"I'm not interested in contests. You think they might help me?"

"Stay away from them," she said sharply. "They'll screw up your brain. Besides, if Frankie catches you fooling around with any of that junk, you'll be out on your keester."

"That's good to know," Brent said. "Believe me, that is really good to know."

"Just take it easy," she said. "It'll get easier." She leaned forward and looked directly into his eyes. Her own blue-gray eyes were warm, but flecked with steely glints. "I think you're going to like working at the gym. I know I will."

Brent's smile seemed transparently false and his stomach felt as though he had swallowed ice. What would she think of him when she knew the truth? He wanted her to like him. Who wouldn't? But at the same time he warned himself to go easy. She might also be part of Frankie's dealing.

"I already do," he said.

He tried to keep his smile looking genuine, but inside he writhed in despair as he realized he couldn't trust a single person he'd meet at the gym. Any of them might be part of Frankie's dope operation. He had to keep close tab on his lies. One misstep, one minor change in a story from one person to another, and he could be dead. It was going to be a lonely—and nerve wracking—job.

Chapter Eight

THE NEXT MORNING, Brent was at the gym before six. Getting out of bed in four a.m. darkness had been a painful chore. He'd thought he was in reasonably good shape, but every muscle in his body told him he'd been fooling himself. Only one day on the job and he was falling apart. If he was going to survive, he was going to have to start a training program for himself.

During one of the morning's slack periods he was skipping rope when Jaime Ortega came up to him carrying a pair of beat up, sixteen-ounce boxing gloves. "Here." He tossed the gloves at Brent who was just able to stop the whipping rope and catch them with one hand. "Get your butt in gear. There's a guy wants some sparring. Ring one."

Brent had just begun to feel the euphoria that extended exercise always produced, but Ortega's insolent voice instantly depressed his mood. "Okay."

Ortega stalked away and Brent looked toward the ring. A young Latino heavyweight, wearing headgear and a protective cup, was standing in the center of the ring impatiently smashing his gloves together. His powerful shoulders, arms and legs were covered with enough black hair to qualify him as an animal. He was staring at nothing, but his eyes were hard under his heavy brows as though he was thinking about killing somebody. When he saw Brent walking toward him and putting on his gloves, his eyes focused like those of a lion on an approaching gazelle.

Brent ducked under the ropes and held out his gloved hand. "Hi. Brent Thomas."

The guy reluctantly touched Brent's glove with his own. "Hernandez."

"Okay. What do you want to work on?"

"Footwork."

"Okay." Brent stepped back. "Come at me. We'll take a look."

Brent, his hands down, began circling away, keeping his eyes on Hernandez's feet. Hernandez shuffled forward expertly, moving fast, his left hand out, his right fist cocked. Brent moved away, saying, "Good. Good. I might suggest—"

Bam! The unexpected blow slammed into the side of Brent's head, sending him reeling against the ropes. He almost fell. His vision was blurred; his legs didn't want to respond. He shook his head, turning.

Bam! Bam! He was hit again with two hard left hooks that straightened him against the ropes.

Surprisingly, because they were so rusty, Brent's instincts took over. Somehow he knew the next blow would be the man's right, and even thought his eyes were so glazed he couldn't see, he ducked down and away and felt a thrill of satisfaction when Hernandez' right fist whistled past his head in a blow that, had it landed, would've put him on the canvas.

Before Hernandez could recover his balance, Brent wrapped his arms around him, clinging desperately. Hernandez jerked away, but Brent had hung on long enough for his head to clear and he backpedaled across the ring. Hernandez followed quickly, his right fist poised.

Brent's legs still had all the strength of butter in a hot skillet, but his eyes were now clear. When Hernandez shot out a left jab immediately followed by a hard right, Brent easily let the blows slide past his head.

Brent tied up Hernandez again, but this time, he was the one who broke the clinch. The brief respite had brought life back to his legs, and when Hernandez began his next charge, Brent danced away. He caught a glimpse of Ortega standing near the ring, his lips twisted in a sneering smile. A set up! Hernandez wasn't interested in learning anything. His job was to teach Brent a painful lesson.

But Ortega had sent in the wrong man. Hernandez was strong as a bull, but his post-like legs didn't move him very fast. All right. Hernandez said he wanted to learn footwork. That's what he'd get.

Dropping his arms to his sides, Brent danced around the ring, circling just out of Hernandez' reach. "Feet!" Brent said, pointing. "Move your feet. Come on. Get off your heels. Balance. Balance. On your toes."

Stung, Hernandez lunged at Brent, his fists punching with the speed and skill of a professional. But Brent, his arms dangling, slipped the blows with a quick duck, a twist of his head, a skip of his feet. Brent was surprise at how easily he slipped into old habits, old routines. It seemed his body had been so honed and conditioned that even weeks of inactivity couldn't wipe away the ingrained responses. And to his dismay, the old thrill came back just as easily.

He was like an alcoholic taking a drink after a long absence. His body responded as though there'd been no interruption. One reason he'd stopped competitive boxing was because he'd begun to stop thinking of his opponent as another human being. The man was prey; something he wanted to batter senseless—not because he wanted to win a fight, but because he wanted to destroy an enemy. It was the thrill of mortal combat. One on one. Body against body.

During some matches, the sensation of combat had become so intense that, like a Viking berserker, he scarcely felt the blows of his opponent. They were merely annoyances that had to be endured so he could achieve the ultimate thrill of feeling his own blows inflict damage.

Perhaps if he'd been savagely beaten, he would've changed. But it had never happened. It was when the thrill had bordered on obsession that he had hung up his gloves and become a coach.

Now, dancing the dance with Hernandez, the old thrill began to return with alarming force.

But something had changed. Some part of his mind had acquired a new set of values that told him he could enjoy the combat without having to brutalize his adversary. Like now. There was tremendous pleasure in being able to elude the efforts of his opponent, to tantalize him, to make him miss with his best shots. It was even more of a thrill to watch his opponent unravel, to sense his mounting anger as he began to realize his ineffectiveness.

Brent almost smiled as he saw Hernandez' face turn a muddy red and his lips pull back to bare tightly-gritted teeth. Sweat began dripping from Hernandez' nose and chin and his breath came in ragged gasps. And as his anger mounted, his blows lost their crisp snap. Brent began offering him inviting targets like a bullfighter offering his cape to the bull, only to pull it aside when the bull charged. And, like a bull, Hernandez responded. He tried to take Brent's head off with wild charges and looping swings.

"Easy! Easy," he told Hernandez, knowing his advice was only goading the man. "Balance! Balance! You're swinging too hard. Keep your arms up. You're leaving yourself open."

Hernandez responded as Brent knew he would with increasingly wild charges. Brent continued his unwanted instruction even though the taunting he heard in his voice sickened him as much as its success imbued him with pleasure.

He had to bring this macabre dance to an end before it really took possession of him.

He could've simply ducked out of the ring. But, somehow, he couldn't bring himself to do that. Not with Ortega watching. Not with his instincts pouring gasoline on fires already blazing in his brain. His response was made inevitable when Hernandez paused for an instant, and some of the madness in his eyes was replaced by a look of shrewd calculation. He feinted left, then with the sudden speed of a striking snake, his right hand arched in a hook like a swinging sledge hammer.

Anticipating the blow, Brent stepped inside and hit Hernandez on the side of the jaw with a hard left hook. The jar of the blow traveled up Brent's arm into his brain with malicious joy. Hernandez' head snapped back, sweat flying, and his eyes opened wide in stunned surprise before they glazed over. His legs collapsed and he fell to his hands and knees where he swayed with his head down, gasping for breath.

Brent stared down at Hernandez in dismayed surprise—dismayed because his instincts had taken over again, and surprise because it had been so easy. He went to help Hernandez to his feet.

"Sorry about that," Brent said.

Hernandez snarled and yanked away. He used the ropes to haul himself to his feet. He was still staggering when he climbed out of the ring.

As Brent slowly stripped off his gloves, he heard a slow applause behind him, coming from the place where Ortega had been standing. It surprised him. He'd thought Ortega would only have applauded if he had been spread-eagled on the canvas.

When he turned, he saw he'd been right. Ortega was gone. The applause was coming from Frankie.

Frankie said, "*Aye, aye, Chihuahua.* Not bad, *amigo.*"

Brent touched his cheek where Hernandez' first blow had landed. "Not good either. I almost got my head knocked off."

"You weren't looking. You got a good chin. That's good. That's damn good."

Brent climbed out of the ring. He was considerably pleased at his own quick recovery from Hernandez' blow. It had been a long time since he'd been hit that hard. And an even longer time since he'd been angry enough to deliberately hit someone the way he'd decked Hernandez. He wasn't too proud of that, although he realized his anger had really been directed at Ortega. Hernandez had just been available.

"And that left!" Frankie mimicked the blow, his big body moving with surprising speed, and Brent remembered Frankie had once been a fighter himself. "Hernandez is a good boy. Like iron. One punch! *Bomba!*"

"Luck," Brent told Frankie. "A lucky punch."

Frankie stared at Brent like an eagle measuring the size of a rabbit. "Luck. Sure. That's my kind of luck." He rubbed his hand across his heavy cheek. "You been keeping in shape?"

"Not really." He looked toward the ring. "I guess I'd better start."

"Yeah. You doing any road work?"

"Not lately. I was thinking about starting in the morning. I could get a little in before I come to work."

"Good, good. Tomorrow I want you to check in with Maria."

"Your daughter? What for?"

"Aerobics. She's got a class in the morning."

"Aerobics? What good will that do?"

"Stamina. Footwork. You looked a little slow."

"If I'd been slow, I'd be dead."

Frankie smiled. "You could do better. Eight a.m. Be there."

Frankie walked away, punching at the air. Brent watched him go.

"Aerobics!" he muttered. "What I need is sleep."

Chapter Nine

FOR BRENT, GETTING out of bed was even more painful than it had been the previous morning. Every muscle in his body shot forth a protesting jolt of pain, and the side of his face felt as though it had been struck by a anvil. It took every bit of his will power to pull on his old sweats, go out into the predawn darkness and begin jogging the empty street.

At first, his jogging steps were slow and plodding. He felt logy—out of shape. At the university, he'd rationalized that he didn't really have to be in great shape to coach. It wasn't as though he was the one having to go five or ten rounds in the ring. He just had to prepare the other guys to do it. And at the DEA's National Training Center, he'd concentrated more on the academics than the physical preparation. Now he was paying the price.

Still, after five minutes, he was feeling better. The pain had subsided and he was able to pick up his pace to an easy run. And he wasn't breathing hard. Maybe he was in better shape than he thought.

"Aerobics," he said aloud, his voicing echoing from the palm trees along with the slap of his footsteps. "Ciminetly."

At five to eight Ortega came to take over the boxers. He said nothing, but Brent could tell he was seething. Ortega probably thought Frankie was grooming Brent to take his place as *numero uno*. If Frankie and Ortega were working together on drug dealing, Ortega's resentment could be dangerous for Brent. And for Frankie. A resentful man could do foolish things.

Brent took the elevator to the second floor. There was no one in the aerobic dance area except a girl going through a series of stretching exercises. She was the same girl who had humiliated him in the parking lot. Now she was wearing brilliant blue spandex tights with candy-striped leg warmers. Instead of wearing her hair in a pony tail, her mass of loose curls was caught with a blue headband that matched the color of her tights.

She didn't see Brent standing just inside the door and he paused, fascinated by her display of harmony and strength. She'd obviously studied gymnastics because her warm-up included a series of floor exercises all performed with an easy grace.

Then she noticed Brent and turned to face him, her hands on her hips. "I don't like spying," she said.

"Spying? I just got here. I'm looking for Maria Rodriguez."

The girl's voice reflected her irritation. "Oh? Why?"

An awful suspicion was beginning to worry Brent and he studied the girl more carefully. She could be Frankie's daughter. She had the ivory skin and the lustrous hair. But she weighed a hell of a lot less than Frankie. However, judging by the picture in Frankie's office, Carmen Rodriguez was a very beautiful woman. That would have to explain it.

"Frankie told me to see her," he said. "I'm supposed to take a class."

Maria favored him with a wintery smile. "So you're the great Brent Thomas."

"And you're Maria, the perfect."

She cocked her head, staring at him. Brent was fascinated by how clear were the whites of her eyes and how their dark pupils and golden irises made him feel so strangely uncomfortable. Maybe it was because he really had been spying, if only for a moment. But then, he'd do it again if he got the chance.

"I don't appreciate people watching when I'm warming up." She walked to the ballet exercise bar in front of the mirrored wall and retrieved a towel which she wrapped around her neck. Despite the displeasure in her voice, its timbre reflected a humor that the rancor couldn't hide. And, judging by her syntax and diction, she was well-educated. Frankie probably had spared no expense on his only child.

Maybe he'd been grooming her to help with his dope operations. If so, and the DEA was able to bust Frankie, Maria might well end up in a federal prison. That gorgeous body and all that education would go to waste for a lot more years than Brent cared to think about.

He pushed such disturbing thoughts aside. "Sorry," he said. "I didn't know you were working out."

Maria wiped a film of perspiration from her forehead with the end of the towel. "All right. Forget it. Daddy did tell me to get you started." She tilted her head slightly to one side and studied him. "What kind of endurance do you have?"

Brent suppressed a smile. He wanted to tell her it was a stupid question. It took a hell of a lot more endurance to go even one round in the ring than she could put him through in any aerobic class. Instead, he said, "Enough."

"Fine," she said. "I'll put you in with the advanced class. If I see you can't keep up, I'll drop you down to the intermediate."

Brent felt insulted. What did she mean 'keep up?' It was going to be a pleasure to run her—and her class—into the ground. He smiled at her through his teeth. "Fine. When do I start?"

"Right now. We'd better go through some of the routines so you won't be totally lost when you get in class."

For fifteen minutes she demonstrated the various aerobic exercises she used during her class routines. Brent picked them up rapidly, much to her surprise. She couldn't know, of course, that he'd spent years memorizing routines for wrestling, boxing and other sports. As the first members of the class began drifting in, Maria finished the last demonstration, and for the first time since they'd begun, she smiled.

"Not bad," she said. "Are you sure you haven't done this before?"

"Nope. But I've done a lot of calisthenics. Most of it is kind of familiar."

"Calisthenics, huh?" She took off the towel and draped it over the exercise bar. "When we start, pick a spot near the back where you can watch what the others are doing. And try to keep up," she added as she walked toward the front of the room.

Brent's growing sense of camaraderie vanished in a burst of pique. They'd been bouncing around for ten minutes and she could see he wasn't breathing hard. So why the snide remark? Maybe he was reading her wrong and she really did have an irascible disposition.

He was still fuming when Maria called the class to order. As they took up positions in a loose formation, Brent noticed with a sense of relief that there were a few other men in the class. Maria told them to do a little stretching and she went to a big hi-fi console. Sorting through the stack of tapes, she looked over at Brent and smiled. But it was the same kind of smile a headsman gives his victim before bringing the axe down.

The thought that flashed through his mind was, "Another Ortega. She's going to set me up." His jaw tightened. Forewarned was forearmed. He was ready for anything she could throw at him.

Maria clapped her hands sharply and the students snapped to attention like well-trained troops. "Today," she said with a wicked smile, "we're going to start right out with disco." There were several groans and her smile broadened. "Don't worry," she said. "We'll start slow with a few stretch patterns. Ready?"

She turned to the tape console and pushed the start button and the rollicking strains of a medium-speed rock song boomed from the strategically placed speakers.

"Ready and stretch. Around Sways," she shouted as she swung into a routine that appeared to be familiar to the group members because they all faithfully copied her bends and sways in perfect sync with the music. Brent, after an awkward start, was just settling into the routine when Maria shouted, "Lunge Present!" and launched into a series of forward and back lunges with her arms working like pistons.

After a minute, the music segued to a faster tempo and Maria shouted "Side Lunge!" and the group began a synchronous lunge and arm swing, first to the right, then to the left. Brent watched Maria and tried to copy her movements, but it was difficult to respond with the same easy rhythm. He always seemed to be a beat behind.

As he moved, Brent studied Maria, feeling something building inside him like water behind a crumbling dam. She was so damn beautiful; so full of life. She was crystal and light, radiating a kaleidoscope of brilliant colors. Was he to be responsible for extinguishing that joie de vivre? More than ever, he fervently hoped Frankie was clean. If not, taking Frankie down would be like a falling tree crushing all the smaller trees in its path.

His only salvation, and the one thing that kept Brent going, was the knowledge that if Frankie did fall, it was due to Frankie's own activities, not his. As the old saying went, 'You can't con an honest man.'

Ten minutes later, Brent didn't have enough energy left to think of anything except survival. His arms and legs ached and his lungs were beginning to burn as he gasped for breath. The only thing that kept him going was the sight of some students who'd given up and were standing with their heads down and their sides heaving. That and the amused glances Maria was directing at him as she effortlessly bounced, clapped, twisted and turned.

When the music climaxed in a thundering crescendo and stopped, most of the students dropped to the floor without waiting for Maria's voice telling them to take a break. She walked around to Brent who forced himself to breath without wheezing.

"How do you like it?" she asked, her hands on her hips.

Damn. She wasn't even breathing hard, but there was a telltale heaving of her lovely bust line, and Brent realized she was putting on as much of an act as he was.

"Fine," he said in a clear, strong voice that belied the fire in his lungs.

"Our next one is a 'Hustle,'" she said. "You'll love it."

She turned away and Brent said, "Wait."

She looked back over her shoulder and he said, "Can we...talk about this? Lunch?"

She stared at him, her eyes speculative. "I'm supposed to have lunch with Jaime. But—" She made a small shrug. "—business before pleasure. Okay."

By pacing himself, taking it easy when he could and fudging on some of the hops and jumps, but clapping his hands vigorously so it'd look like he was really on top of it, Brent managed to last through the remaining twenty minutes of exercise.

When he walked into the gym, Ortega was in a bad mood. "It's about time," he growled. "Get your ass in gear."

At noon, Ortega left without saying a word. Brent wondered if Ortega was on his way to see Maria. He'd like to see Ortega's face when she told him she was going to lunch with Brent. More likely she'd either forget their luncheon date, or simply ignore it and go with Ortega. The only way he'd know was to wait and see. At least it would put off unpleasant questioning about her father. It would also allow him more time to keep his illusions about her innocence.

Surprisingly, Ortega came back in a little more than half an hour. If anything, he was even more surly, which meant that he'd probably talked to Maria.

"I'm going to lunch," Brent said and when Ortega glared at him without answering, Brent knew for sure that Maria had told him. Brent wondered whether his surge of joy was because he was going to be with Maria or because it made Ortega so angry.

On his way out of the room, Jennifer fell in beside him. "Lunch?" she asked. "I can get away."

"Okay if I take a rain check?"

She stopped, disappointment in her eyes. "Sure," she said. "Another time."

She was turning away when Brent reached out and took her arm. "Wait. I... It's for Frankie."

"You're going to lunch with Frankie?"

"Well, no. His daughter." He saw the sparkle go out of her eyes, and he hastily added, "Frankie wants me to go over some things with her."

He hated himself for the lie. Frankie had nothing to do with it. The truth was that he wanted to see Maria. In fact, Frankie might not be at all happy about it. And Ortega probably already wanted to kill him. He could very well have his eye on Frankie's daughter for himself, most likely with Frankie's blessing.

The smart thing to do would be to deliberately 'forget' the lunch date. But, as Maria had said, business before pleasure. Now that he thought about it, he wished she'd phrased that statement a little differently. Well, in his case, it would be a mix of business and pleasure.

He heard Jennifer say, "Well, you've got to do what the boss man says. What about dinner?"

"Okay. I'll check with you around five."

As he walked to his locker for a jacket, Brent wondered whether he'd have enough strength left by five o'clock to go anywhere except home. But then, he had to eat, didn't he?

Maria was waiting in the deserted studio checking through her tape collection. She'd put on a red warm-up suit and fastened large loop earrings in her ears. They gave her the exotic look of a gypsy. When she saw Brent, she said, "I have another class in fifty minutes. Can we make it?"

"We can if you like hamburgers."

She laughed and to his delight, took his arm in both of her hands, swinging into step beside him. "I love hamburgers. But nobody ever buys me one. They think I'm supposed to eat health food."

"Stick with me. You'll get your fill of hamburgers. And if you're good, maybe a hotdog."

Brent drove to the coffee shop where he and Jennifer had gone. They found a booth in the back and ordered barbecue burgers.

Sitting across from Maria, Brent found it hard to keep from staring at her even though the beauty in her face and the laughter in her eyes were knives twisting in his stomach. But the job had to be done, and right now his job was to get her talking about her father.

"I take it you were born here in Los Angeles."

"Why? You think I'm an *espalda mujado?*"

"A what?"

"Wet back."

"Oh, you mean illegal. No, no. I know Frankie was in the army, so I guess he's a citizen."

"Our family has been in Los Angeles for more than a hundred years. I'm fourth generation."

"Did your family own one of the big *rancheros?* What were they called? *Hidalgos?*"

"Nobles? No. We were peons. Poor dumb Mexicans the missions made into slaves."

"That would make you a good Catholic."

She shrugged. "It goes with the territory." She didn't seem overjoyed with the declaration and Brent made no comment. "Nobody in our family had any money," she said after a moment. "My dad had to quit school and go to work when he was in the eighth grade. He never finished high school."

"He's some kind of guy," Brent said. "It takes brains to be a first sergeant."

"It takes brains just to survive in L.A. if you're Mexican. But Daddy made it. He's got a restaurant—one of the best in L.A.—and the best gym. That's a long way from the gutter."

"The gutter? I thought you were fourth generation."

"Practically. When he was nineteen, Daddy was a collector for a bunch of loan sharks. That's as close to the gutter as you can get."

"Loan sharks, huh?" Hendrix and Duval had told Brent that, in those days, part of Frankie's job had been collecting from dealers and junkies who were slow in paying. Frankie had a reputation of being a very rough customer with a real hatred for people who he felt were trying to rip him off—or his employers, which was the same thing to him.

"How did he get out of it?" he asked. "Not many do that."

"Hard work and brains. He joined the army."

"A lot of people wouldn't give him an 'A' for that."

"He knew what he was doing. It broke the cycle. When he got out, he took the money he'd saved and bought the restaurant. Made it pay off, too. He's done the same with the gym."

The words she uttered so casually couldn't conceal her admiration for her father. Frankie had fought his way 'out of the gutter' and was now a force in the city and even in the state. People in Sacramento knew Frankie Rodriguez and his power in the Latino community. That was one reason why he was so hard to touch. If he was a dealer—and so far Brent had no reason to believe he was—they'd have to build a very solid case or Frankie's political friends would have their heads.

And Maria? How could anyone with that much affection for her father not be aware that he could have blood on his hands up to his elbows? But then—maybe her hands were also dripping.

"Dad told me you're from Kansas."

Her voice jerked Brent out of his introspection. "Yes."

The name of his home town was on the tip of his tongue when he caught himself. If she was part of Frankie's dealing, he sure as hell didn't want her or her father questioning his parents.

"I spent most of my life in Kansas. All of it really, except for the time I was in the army and when I went to—" Brent stopped. He'd almost said 'when I went to Washington.' Then she'd want to know what he was doing there and he'd have to make up another lie. He covered by saying, "Except for a short time I spent in Phoenix."

"Phoenix? Is that were you went to college?"

"Post-graduate studies." He paused, wondering how much more to tell her. Then he decided it'd be best not to hold back anything he didn't have to. "That's where I got married."

Her hands that had been toying with a spoon went still. The waitress had brought coffee, and Maria began stirring it thoughtfully even though she drank it black. Brent considered changing the subject, which would leave the impression he was still married. It'd be an easy way to keep her at arm's length. She'd refuse to see him any more, and he wouldn't have to make her more of a pawn in this game than she already was.

But he couldn't accept that. It was even more important—not to the DEA, but to him—that she knew he was no longer married.

"We got divorced about two years ago."

He was rewarded by a lift of her head. Her eyes briefly lifted to his face, and he felt a tingle of joy when he thought he saw renewed interest in their dark depths. "That's one reason I left Kansas. Out here I'm starting a—to use a cliché—a whole new life."

She stopped stirring her coffee and sat watching him, her full lips puffed into a thoughtful pout that was so enchanting he had to look away. "So, how do you like it so far?"

"Love it," he replied with a smile.

"That's L.A. Love it or write about it."

She'd regained her humor and her smile made Brent's breath quicken. Had she really been upset when he'd said that he was married? More likely he'd seen what he wanted to see. She was Frankie's daughter and probably Ortega's girl. He'd be a fool if he didn't remember that. Or maybe there was nothing between her and Ortega. Suddenly, he was desperate to know.

"My stay might be kind of short," he said carefully. "When Ortega finds out I had lunch with his girl, he'll kill me."

He watched her face and was rewarded with a slight grimace of irritation before she replied, "Jaime and I are just... Well, friends."

Brent suppress a visible sigh of relief. "Yeah?" He picked up his coffee cup and drained it. "Well, if we don't get back, your 'friend' is going to have my hide."

She arched a darkly beautiful eyebrow at him and her eyes sparkled. "You think he could?"

"Could?"

"Have your hide?"

Brent shook his head. "Let's hope I never have to find out."

Chapter Ten

"FOOTWORK. FOOTWORK. Pivot. Snap! Hit through your target."

Brent turned his head, taking Julio's punch on the top left side of his head protector where it could do the least damage. He could've evaded or blocked the blow, but it was important for a young fighter to make contact some of the time.

Julio, his eyes narrowed with intensity, shuffled in and tried to take Brent by surprise with a hooking right lead. Instead of ducking or moving away, Brent moved inside, lifting his shoulder and turning so the hard blow harmlessly glanced off his upper arm. Caught off balance with his arm fully extended, Julio was wide open for Brent's left and his eyes snapped wide in alarm.

But Brent slipped away, dancing out of reach.

"If you're going to switch, you've got to switch your defense, too," he said, demonstrating. "Get your left up to block a counter. Let me show you."

With a swift step, he snapped his right toward Julio's face, deliberately missing so his gloved fist slid past Julio's ear. Julio, with the speed of a striking rattler, launched a short, hard left to Brent's exposed jaw. Except it wasn't exposed any longer. It was protected by Brent's left hand that he used it to brush the blow aside like a fencer brushing aside a *riposte*.

Brent stepped back. "See how it works? Keep thinking defense. Even when you're on offense. You can bet your *cullo* he's gonna counter. You've got to anticipate that counter."

For the next two minutes, Brent sparred with Julio. The young light heavyweight was fast and strong, and Brent took a few blows that jarred him. But, strangely, they brought more pleasure than pain, like diving into a pool of cold water. After the initial shock, the water brought life to his body. It was as though the blows intensified his concentration. When he'd begun sparring with Julio, his vision took in more than the man in front of him. He was aware of his surroundings, of men watching, of others going about their training. His ears, too, were unfocused. They registered the rhythm of fists pounding a light bag, and the grunts and thudding blows of someone working on a heavy bag.

But as the sparring continued, his body began a familiar response that always amazed and, in a way, alarmed him. It was as though some primordial instinct for survival was locked in his brain and the jarring blows of his opponent awakened the instinct. Gradually, all sounds, all sights, all senses began to compress until there was no other light, no darkness, no sound. He was locked inside a bubble that gradually encompassed him and his opponent like a zone of energy—a bubble that shut out all outside elements, narrowing and refining his concentration until his total focus was on the other man.

When he entered this zone, he wasn't even conscious of his own body, his own actions and reactions. Time seemed to slow as his entire being—all his senses—became centered on the man in front of him, a man who was trying to harm him, to kill him. They were partners in a savage dance that could only end with the death of one of them. Only he could save himself, and a heat of something akin to rage, but not rage, began to build inside him. He wanted to hit! To batter! To harm!

Brent shook his head, bursting the bubble, and sight and sound came back in a flood. He danced away fighting the desire to explode in savage combat. Stop it, he reminded himself sharply. This was sparring. This was not a battle for survival.

He relaxed his set jaw and the muscles in his shoulders. Now he had it under control.

Teach. Talk. That's what you were here for. "Don't turn so much. Face me. Snap your punches. Good. Good."

Julio was sweating heavily and breathing hard. Brent was pleasantly surprised to find he was breathing easily and his legs still felt nimble. Just a week of daily workouts on top of his normal energy-draining work had increased his endurance remarkably.

Clang. The sound of the bell startled Brent. They weren't working to a bell and he wondered why it had been rung. Then he saw Frankie was standing with his hand on the bell cord.

Brent dropped his arms and began stripping off his gloves. "Okay, Julio. *Basta por hoy.* You're coming along good. Go do a little shadow boxing. Practice what I told you."

Brent climbed out of the ring beside Frankie. "Kid's coming along," he said. "Did you see him?"

"Yeah. Great. He's a good boy." Frankie plopped down on one of the folding steel chairs near the ring. "But he isn't the one I came to see."

Brent took off his headgear. He was sweating, but it was a good sweat. Workout sweat. Not nervous sweat. There was a big difference. He was sure that even the odor was different.

"Yeah?" he said. "Who've you got in mind? Johnny Ponce? He doesn't fight until Tuesday. He'll be ready."

"Not Ponce. I've been watching you. You're damn good, you

know that?"

Brent grinned. "Thanks, Frankie. Does that mean my probation is over?"

"Probation. Shit. You ever considered fighting?"

Brent stared at Frankie to see if he was serious. "Me? You kidding?"

"You fought before. I can tell."

"Well, yeah. Eight bouts. Amateurs. But that was years ago."

"How'd you do?"

Brent shrugged. "I won."

"All eight?"

"Yeah."

"How?"

"Points. Six knockouts. One technical."

Frankie grunted with satisfaction. "I knew it. So why'd you quit?"

"I got smart."

"You get smart when you lose."

Brent picked up a towel and wiped his face. "Maybe I didn't like getting hit."

Frankie shook his head. "Yeah, some guys can't take that. But I've been watching you. It wasn't that. You can take a punch."

Brent grinned. "To tell the truth, Frankie, I only did it to get some experience. For coaching. I never really took it seriously."

"Maybe you should've."

"There are thousands of fighters. Only a handful ever make it to the money. There's more future in teaching."

"I think you could've made it."

Brent slowly wiped at the sweat on his neck. What was Frankie getting at? It was nice that he was flattering him, but he couldn't see where this conversation was heading, unless Frankie was trying to trip him up in a lie.

"I doubt it," he said carefully. "Anyway, those days are long gone."

"No, *amigo*. I've been watching you all week. You got the moves. You got the punch."

Brent nodded toward the ring. "For here, yeah. But a real match? There's a hell of a lot of difference."

"You should give it a shot. You could do it."

Brent shook his head. "I'm too old for amateurs."

"Not amateurs. Professional."

Brent stared at Frankie, thinking he might be joking. When he saw the intensity in Frankie's gaze, he said, "No thanks."

"Why not?"

"I know my limitations."

"How could you? You never had to find out."

Brent looped the towel over the lower ring rope. "I hope I never have to."

"Why?" Frankie raised his voice. "Not many men ever get the chance. Wouldn't you like to know?"

His words sent a chill through Brent's sweaty body. He was afraid his limitations might be far too great for the battle he was already fighting. And yet, like every man, he'd often wondered how he'd behave if he was ever pushed to the limit. There had been times when he'd been in the army that his endurance had been tested. But never his courage. The tests had always been during training or in non-life threatening situations.

He had never been in combat where his courage was threatened by death. And his courage in the ring had never really been tested in any of his eight fights. In fact, he'd won them rather easily. But it had never entered his mind to turn pro. Did he really have what it takes?

Brent shook his head as reality drove away the pink haze of euphoria. "Only a fool would turn pro at my age."

"Hey," Frankie said. "A lot of guys were in their prime when they were your age."

"Yeah? Like who?"

"Marvelous Marvin Hagler, Sugar Ray Robinson, Muhammad Ali, George Foreman. Archie Moore was fighting 'til he was almost fifty."

Brent waved them aside. "I'm not in their league."

"How do you know? Let me set you up with one or two bouts."

"You've already got contenders here. You don't need me."

"Yeah, but they're all lightweights and middleweights. I want the big one." Frankie heaved himself up from the chair. "Brent, let me tell you something. I was a fighter once. I was damn good, but not good enough."

"Let me guess," Brent said with a grin. "You were a super heavy."

Frankie's laugh rumbled through layers of fat. "You got that right, *amigo*. Two hundred- thirty pounds. And not an ounce of muscle." He laughed again, then his face hardened and his eyes gleamed. "Brent, I think you might have a shot. How much you weigh?"

"One eighty-five. That's not enough."

"You can put on another five."

"Still not enough. Every heavyweight today is over two hundred."

"Shit. Dempsey was only one-eighty-seven. Joe Lewis was less than two hundred. Rocky Marcinano was only one-eighty-two."

The eagerness in Frankie's voice surprised Brent. It bordered on desperation. Actually, he shouldn't have been surprised. He had seen the same obsession in many people. The popularity of boxing around the world was testimony to *homo sapien* fighting instincts. He didn't believe the non-aficionado's mantra that fans only went to fights to see somebody get hurt, ideally killed.

The true fan wanted to see a display of raw courage in the only sport capable of such a display. And how could one display courage unless he was matched with someone of equal or superior skill? It was often said that boxers who were too good were never given a chance to prove if they had real courage. Sometimes, if they fought long enough, it was only when they'd lost the speed and power of youth, and had to fight only on 'heart' that their courage could be proven.

But Frankie might have another agenda. Having a heavyweight contender in his gym would bring in a lot of money. But if the DEA was right, the gym wasn't the source of Frankie's wealth. Money alone couldn't be the reason for his desperation. If Brent read him correctly, Frankie was obsessed with boxing, and the possibility of developing a real contender probably gave him spasms of ecstasy.

But while Frankie might be willing to do most anything for a championship, it'd be Brent's brains being scrambled.

"I don't know, Frankie," he said. "What if I get the crap beat out of me? Do I get fired?"

"Hey, no, *amigo*. If it don't work out, that's it. What do you say? One fight."

Brent's rejection froze on his lips. Like most instructors, he'd often wondered how he would fare against real fighters. Could I have made it as a pro? This was his chance to find out. What the hell! How bad could he get hurt in one fight?

He was just about to tell Frankie he'd give it a shot when he was struck by a chilling thought. He wasn't free to make such a decision. He was an agent of the DEA. How the hell could he justify being in the ring getting his brains beat out? On the other hand, this might be a way to gain Frankie's confidence. What would Hendrix say about it? He'd have to check.

"Let me think about it," he said.

Frankie smiled as though Brent had already said yes. "Sure, *amigo*. Think about it. I'll start looking at contenders."

As Frankie moved away, Brent said, "Look for one so far over the hill I'll need a telescope to see him."

Frankie waved his hand without turning around. "Leave it to me, *amigo*."

Brent stared at Frankie's retreating back. What the hell had he done? Now if Hendrix told him not to do it, Frankie would think he was a coward and would probably fire him. The best thing to do was not even ask permission. As the saying went, 'It's easier to obtain forgiveness than to obtain permission.' He should take the fight.

If he lost, which was likely, he wouldn't even have to mention it to the DEA. If they found out after the fact, he could tell them it was part of his cover. And it would put him in more solidly with Frankie. They'd like that.

Brent was turning away when he saw Jaime Ortega watching him, his eyes hooded, their pupils black with malice. Ortega was standing in the men's workout area and Brent assumed he was far enough away he couldn't have overheard his discussion with Frankie. But Ortega couldn't have missed the look on Frankie's face, and the body builder's malevolent expression caused the hair on Brent's neck to prickle. He hoped Ortega wouldn't have a hand in picking his first opponent. It would probably be a *tyrannosaurus rex*.

That same afternoon Brent was working hard on the heavy bag, his body drenched with an unaccustomed degree of sweat, when he looked up to see Jennifer standing beside him. Her blonde hair was bound in a French braid as tight as her spandex leotards. She was standing with her feet slightly apart, leaning toward him, her fists clenched. Her mouth was partially open in a little smile, and her eyes flashed each time Brent's gloved fists smacked into the heavy bag.

Brent caught the bag to stop its movement and stepped back. He was breathing hard, harder than he should be even after a vigorous workout. If he was going to be any good in a real bout, he'd have to work harder on his endurance. Unless, of course, he got knocked out in the first round.

"Don't stop," Jennifer said.

Brent exaggerated his heavy breathing. "Why? You want to see me die?"

She reached out and touched his arm, trailing her fingers along his glistening skin. "Frankie said you were going to fight."

Brent didn't know whether to be angry or simply chagrined. He'd told Frankie he would think about it. To someone as eager as Frankie, he must have taken it to mean yes. "Frankie's a little premature," he said. "I told him I'd think about it."

"I hope you do." Jennifer's eyes lifted, promise in their depths. "I like fighters."

"Wait'll you see me," he said. "You'll change your mind."

"I doubt it."

Brent turned back to the bag. "I don't know why I'm doing this. I should practice running. It'll be my only chance."

"If there's anything I can do to help, let me know."

"Okay, you can pick up the pieces."

He went back to work on the heavy bag, hitting it harder than he would've if Jennifer hadn't been watching. After a moment she said, "Oh, Frankie wants to see you."

The bag made a satisfactory 'whap' as Brent slammed it with a left hook. "When?"

"Now."

Brent backed away from the bag. Apparently, Frankie didn't want to wait long for a definitive answer, even though he must have assumed the answer would be in the affirmative since he'd told Jennifer about it. "Okay."

He pulled off his gloves and handed them to Jennifer. "Here. Take over for me."

She took the sweaty gloves. "Great," she said. "I'll pretend its Jaime."

"Pity poor Jaime," Brent said, moving away. "I hope you never get mad at me."

"Keep that in mind," she said. "I hit hard."

Brent took a quick shower, ending with icy cold, but he was still damp with perspiration when he pulled on his warm-up suit and took the elevator to Frankie's office.

The door to the outer office was open and Brent walked in. He was startled to see Maria sitting behind the secretary's desk typing expertly on the computer's keyboard. She was wearing a white blouse with a thin red necktie. Her hair was unbound and rampaged around her face in a tumbling mass of curls as exotic as an houri dancer.

Instead of pleasure, however, Brent felt a wave of dismay so intense it almost made him dizzy. He'd assumed that Maria's only connection with her father's business was as an aerobics instructor. But if she also worked as his secretary, perhaps she had knowledge of his real business. Very likely she was part of it.

She looked up at Brent as her fingers automatically completed the line she was typing. When she recognized him and said, "Hi," the sparkle in her eyes, and her smile gave Brent the sensation of having been punched in the gut. How was it possible for anyone to be that beautiful? It was difficult for him to keep from blurting out some stupid remark such as 'Wowee.'

As it was, he had to clear his throat before he said "Hi."

Her smile broadened, driving through him like a steel spike. "Go right in. Daddy's waiting for you."

He paused, his hand on the knob of the inner door, reluctant to leave. "Uh...I didn't know you worked up here."

"Sometimes. Somebody's got to see that the bills get paid."

"Don't you have bookkeepers?"

"Yes, but I mean his personal things. He's such a baby about business."

Brent nodded. "Yeah. That sounds like Frankie."

Actually, that didn't seem like Frankie at all. While Frankie evinced a slap-on-the-back *bonhomie*, Brent had always had the impression that Frankie was as shrewd as a pawnbroker. He undoubtedly gave a different impression to his family.

It occurred to Brent that since the subject was open, he might be able to get a line on Frankie's bookkeeper without arousing suspicion. "How do you keep from getting your accounts mixed up? With your bookkeepers', I mean?"

"No problem. Separate banks; separate accounts. They do their thing. I do mine."

Brent pasted on a grin. "Glad to hear it. Let them get the gray hair."

"You got that right. See you in class."

When Brent opened the door and entered Frankie's office, he was wondering which of the two accounts handled Frankie's drug dealing. He desperately hoped it wasn't the one being administered by Maria. More likely, Frankie had three accounts. He probably kept his own books on his dealing—if he was a dealer.

Frankie, seated at his desk, looked up as Brent entered. "*Hola, amigo.*"

"Hello, Frankie. You wanted to see me?"

"Yeah." Frankie used both hands flat on the desk to push to his feet. He went to the bar and opened a bottle of Corona beer that he handed to Brent. "Here, *amigo*. It'll be the last one for a long time."

"You're assuming I'm going to say yes, huh?"

Frankie poured himself a glass of Jose Cuervo Special. "Not an assumption, my friend. You can't say no."

Brent felt a momentary surge of alarm. Does Frankie know? "Why do you say that?"

"Because I know fighters. They're a different breed. Some people think they only fight for money. I admit that money has got a lot to do with it, especially when you've got nothing. But how many of them really make any money? A handful. But they keep on fighting even when they know they're going nowhere. Why is that, my friend?" Frankie slapped his chest. "Something in here."

"You've got to know. Not can 'I beat that bum?' No. You've got to know what you've got inside yourself. I've seen fighters so scared they couldn't talk before they went in the ring. But I never saw one of them—not one—refuse to climb through the ropes. I've seen a couple of them quit in the middle of a fight, but they're the exception.

"Usually it's the other way. You see guys trying to keep fighting when they're out on their feet and getting the crap beat out of them. They won't stay down when they're knocked down. They could be dead, and they'd still be trying to get up. Why? Because they've got to know. You, my friend, this is your chance to know. You've got to say yes."

Brent stared at Frankie. He was right, of course. He might be able to rationalize that he was going along with Frankie's plan just to stay on the inside. The truth was he couldn't pass up this opportunity to find out if he could've made it in the ring. He wondered if all his intentions were so transparent.

Brent studied his beer as though it could prove a shield to his anxiety. Frankie couldn't possible know about his DEA role. If he did, he surely wouldn't be making this offer. Unless the whole scheme was merely a setup to get him out of the way without arousing suspicion.

There was only one way to find out. He had to take the fight. "You're right, Frankie. I've got to know."

Frankie walked over and slapped Brent on the back. "Good! I've got you set up for ten rounds a week from Saturday."

"A week from Saturday? That's too soon. I can't go ten rounds."

"No *problema*. Knock him out in two."

"Yeah, sure. Or get myself murdered in two."

"Naah. This guy's a bum. You can take him with one hand tied."

"What's his name? I'll see what I can find out about him."

"You don't have to find out nothing. Take my word. I set it up myself."

"Yeah, well, I'd still like to know if he's right- or left-handed, fast or slow, a boxer or puncher, like that."

"Yeah, yeah. Okay. Chester Walker. Club fighter. Been around longer than my wife. Fatter than me."

"Yeah, I'll bet."

Still, when he left Frankie's office Brent felt less apprehensive. Frankie didn't seem to have a clue about Brent's DEA connection. And if this guy Walker was a club fighter he was probably a puncher. Hopefully, without a hell of a lot of punch left. If Frankie was true to his word, Walker shouldn't be too much of a problem. Even so, ten rounds was a long time.

He'd really have to concentrate on his workouts. It was important he make a good showing. If he was ever going to move into Frankie's organization, he was going to have to get the big man's complete confidence. Bringing a couple of trophies to the gym would help. Provided he didn't get himself killed in the process.

Of course, there was still the possibility Hendrix wouldn't allow him to fight. But Frankie's speed in setting up the fight practically ruled out the possibility of backing out without seeming like a coward. The solution was to keep his mouth shut. After the fight, there wouldn't be anything Hendrix could do about it.

Provided—Brent almost chuckled—provided he didn't talk while he was unconscious.

Chapter Eleven

BRENT PACED THE stained cement floor, working his arms and shoulders to keep loosened up. His nostrils wrinkled as he tried to breathe without drawing in the odor of stale sweat and liniment.

He'd warmed up by shadow boxing in front of a large cracked mirror with moisture-blackened edges that was cemented against one wall of the small dressing room. Now he had nothing to do but wait for the first preliminary fight to end. Waiting to fight was always depressing. The room itself was dolorous enough. The walls of rough cement had at some time in the distant past been painted a dark green that was now faded to a bilious verdigris.

A row of six steel lockers with broken locks lined the wall opposite the single door which wouldn't close all the way so Brent could hear the shouts of the fight spectators. One of the fighters now engaged in the preliminary bout shared the dressing room with Brent. He was a Latino welterweight and this was his first fight. When he'd gone out, he was trying to look tough, but to Brent, he'd just looked scared.

"Probably the same way I'm going to look," Brent muttered.

In truth, he wasn't overly concerned. He'd obtained a videotape of one of Walker's fights, and while the black man looked tough, and like all club fighters, could take a punch, he wasn't especially fast. He looked as though he'd been around a long time and would welcome an excuse to retire. Studying the tape, Brent thought Frankie was right— he should be able to handle Walker.

Brent was getting restless. He wanted to sit down for a minute to rest his legs, but there was no place to sit except for the massage table and its worn naugahyde was tacky with ancient perspiration and, probably, blood.

Brent stared around the room and shook his head. Nobody could accuse him of not starting at the bottom.

The sound from the crowd swelled to a roar, and as though the sound had a physical force, the door abruptly opened and Frankie entered closely followed by Jaime Ortega. Frankie's face glistened with sweat generated by excitement and unusual activity.

"Okay, *amigo*," he said. "*Vamanos*."

Ortega, holding the door open, was the opposite of Frankie. His face was a study in a blank canvas. Only his eyes glowed as Brent walked past, and for an instant, Brent thought that in Ortega's stare there was a trace of disdain and—something else. Anticipation? Pleasure?

In the narrow cement corridor leading to the arena, they passed the young fighter who was sharing the dressing room. His face was bloody, his nose crooked and welling blood. But he was grinning and talking excitedly in Spanish to his trainer and a pretty girl who looked as though she'd been crying.

"Hey," he said as he passed Brent. "*Bueno suerte.*"

"Yeah," Brent answered. "*Gracias, amigo.*"

As they left the tunnel and walked down the narrow aisle leading through the crowd to the ring, Brent could see that every seat in the arena was taken. And not a blonde in sight.

"You got a good crowd," Frankie said. "All my friends. And the ref's practically family."

"Good," Brent said. "I hate to fight in broken glass."

A shout went up and everyone leaped to his feet as though one of their idols had just entered. At first, Brent thought it was for him, and he grinned and started to raise his arms in greeting. Then he saw that nobody was looking at him. They were concentrating on his opponent who was approaching down the opposite aisle.

Brent stopped and stared at the man who crawled through the ropes into the ring and raised his arms. The man's face twisted into a menacing scowl, and the cheering increased to a roar. Who was this? Although the fighter was wearing a robe, Brent could see he was big— at least two hundred-twenty pounds—with bulging muscles. And he sure as hell wasn't black.

Brent turned to Frankie. "What the hell is this? That isn't Walker."

"Walker scratched," Frankie said. "This guy was available."

"But holy shit, Frankie. I thought we were going to start with somebody small."

Frankie shrugged. "He's smaller than me."

"Dad!" someone called, and Brent was surprised to see Maria leave a ringside seat and push her way through the crowd closely followed by Jennifer.

Brent moved to meet them, clearing a path. "Maria. Jennifer. What are you doing here?"

Almost surrounded by heavy, sweating men, all standing and yelling, Maria looked slender and vulnerable. She was wearing a coffee-colored blouse and black slacks that could have been molded to her hips. High-heeled shoes brought her eyes almost level with Brent's. Her mass of dark hair was worn loose and flowing so it formed a lion's mane framing her strong but delicate features.

Jennifer, wearing heels, was as tall, in fact taller, than most of the men. Her eye-popping figure was accentuated by a low-cut mini-dress. Her hair, usually worn in a tight braid, was loose, tumbling across her shoulders. It wouldn't have surprised Brent if she couldn't have given a heart attack to any man in the room if she smiled at him.

"We came to watch," Jennifer said.

"But not this," Maria added. She turned to her father. "Dad, what's going on? That's Hector Molino."

Frankie attempted a small shrug. "Walker scratched. Molino was all I could get on short notice."

"Brent's not ready for him."

"Sure, he is," Frankie said, but he had the grace to look uncomfortable. "Anyway, this'll be a better fight than that bum Walker."

Maria turned to Brent. "Brent, you shouldn't do this. He's a killer."

"Bull," Frankie said. "He's a puncher, a *toro*. Stay away from him. He can't touch you. When he's wore out..." He smacked his fist into his palm with a flat 'whap' that made Brent wince. He suspected he was going to be on the receiving end of a lot of those 'whaps.'

"Yeah, sure," he said. "Sounds easy."

"It will be, *amigo*. Piece of cake."

Brent looked at Maria. "Have you ever known him to lie?"

Maria tried to smile. "It's called being a con man."

"Brent, you can't do this," Jennifer said. "You could really get hurt."

"She's right." Jaime Ortega spoke for the first time. "You wanna quit?"

Brent studied Molino who was leaning over the ring ropes shaking hands with some of the spectators. Molino didn't look particularly worried.

"No," Brent said. "I've come this far."

He started to climb into the ring and Maria took hold of his arm. "Brent, don't be a fool."

"He won't get hurt," Frankie hastily said. "We'll watch him. You got that, Jaime?"

"Sure," Ortega answered, and this time Brent knew he was smiling. "I'll have the towel ready."

"You'd better," Jennifer said. "Brent, when he knocks you down, stay down."

"That's right," Maria added. "Don't get up."

She turned back to her seat as Brent muttered, "When? What

happened to 'if'?"

Brent climbed into the ring followed by Ortega. The ring announcer nodded to the bell man, and he clanged it a couple of time. The announcer used a hand-held microphone to begin the introductions in Spanish.

"*Mujares* and *caballeros*. The fourth fight of the evening." He turned to Hector Molino's corner. "In the blue corner, wearing black trunks, weighing two hundred-twenty pounds, from East Los Angeles, Hector Molino!"

Molino made a slow pirouette waving to the crowd who responded with a thunderous cheer. The man at the bell clanged it again and the announcer moved to Brent. "And in the red corner, wearing white trunks, weighing one hundred eight-five pounds, from—" He lowered the mic and said to Brent in English, "Where you from, kid?"

Kid? Brent would've smiled if he'd been anywhere else. "Kansas City," he said.

"Where's that?"

"Kansas."

The announcer raised the mic. "From Kansas City, Kansas. Brent Thompkins."

"Thomas," Brent told him.

"Thomas," the announcer corrected.

The announcer walked away and the referee waved the two fighters to the center of the ring. Molino was three inches taller than Brent and he glowered down at him from brows that looked as though they belonged to a gorilla. Slick scar tissue surrounding Molino's eyes made them appear as piercing as chipped obsidian. But Brent wasn't interested in the man's eyes.

He looked at Molino's legs. He had a broad chest and heavily muscled arms covered with tattoos. His legs were equally powerful with heavy thighs, and thick calves and ankles. Not the legs of a boxer. They were made for power, not speed. Better yet, it looked as though at least ten pounds of Molino's weight was carried in a tire around his waist. There was a suspicious softness in his solar plexus region. The largest ganglia in the body, the semi-lunar, was located in the solar plexus.

Maybe Frankie was right. Molino couldn't be in really good condition. If Molino had slow hands, he just might be able to keep away from him until the guy ran out of gas, making him vulnerable. Punches to Molino's head would be like hitting a brick. But if he could get at his middle....

"You guys know the rules," the referee said in English. He looked directly at Molino. "Hector, when you knock him down, don't forget the neutral corner."

"Yeah, yeah," Molino snarled without taking his eyes from Brent.

"I mean it, Hector," the referee snapped. "I'm not starting a count 'til you're in a neutral corner."

"Take your time," Molino said. He pounded the faces of his gloves together with a hard 'whap.' "You're gonna have all night."

Brent was aware Molino's display was designed to intimidate him, and it made him wonder why intimidation was such a part of all sports. The answer, naturally, was because it often worked. The history of sports was rife with stories of people and teams whose superior talent had been blunted or even eliminated through intimidation. Which was nothing more than the demoralizing effect of fear.

Some day he'd have to write a dissertation on the art and efficacy of intimidation.

Molino, of course, had no way of knowing his act was totally unnecessary. Brent was already resigned to getting his lumps. But he was also determined to find out whether he was qualified to be in the same ring with a real pro. He was as anxious to prove himself as he was apprehensive about the fight's outcome.

They touched gloves and Brent went to his corner where Ortega helped him out of his robe. "I think it's going to be a long night," Brent said before he inserted his mouthpiece.

"I don't," Ortega answered.

Ortega climbed out of the ring and Brent pulled on the corner ropes in the time-honored fashion of fighters. Brent hated this part of a fight. The crowd had grown quiet in anticipation like a pack of hungry cubs waiting for their mother's kill. In a sense, they were more than spectators. A real fight aficionado participated vicariously in every punch, every move. It was as though they were proving their own courage by imagining themselves to be one of the fighters. Brent wondered whether anyone in the entire stadium imagined himself to be him. If they did, they were as stupid as he was.

The bell rang and he turned. Jesus! Molino charged across the ring like a rampaging bull, his huge right hand already launched at Brent's head!

Brent ducked and twisted away. Molino's fist grazed the top of Brent's head and pain ripped through his skull. Feeling as though he had been scalped, Brent quickly moved to the center of the ring and waited for Molino's next charge. The big Latino bounced off the ropes like a rubber ball, but instead of launching another charge, he slowed and shuffled toward Brent with his left fist out, his right cocked behind his chin, his eyes burning.

Brent danced away, circling right, away from Molino's right hand. Molino shuffled after him, moving faster than Brent had thought he could.

Bam! Molino's left snapped out like a striking mongoose, powering through Brent's blocking right, and pounding into his temple.

Rocked back on his heels, Brent knew what was coming and he lifted his left arm and shoulder. *Bam!!* Molino's right cross exploded against Brent's protective shoulder instead of his jaw. Brent quickly danced away, feeling as though his left arm was paralyzed. For a moment he was unable to lift it and Molino, sensing a quick kill, attacked with a series of hard rights and lefts.

But Brent hadn't been dazed by the blow and he danced, twisted and ducked away. The few punches Molino managed to land were taken on his arms or shoulders, or were blunted by Brent's slipping, sliding movement.

Brent was startled by the sound of the bell. Three minutes already? His face felt numb from the blows Molino had landed. But he hadn't thrown a single punch!

In his corner, Ortega was slow in placing the stool so Brent had to wait before he could sit and a shred of anger began to form in his gut. Ortega wanted him to lose, just like everybody else in the place!

Brent waved away the water Ortega offered and glanced toward Frankie and Maria. Frankie was smiling and giving Brent a closed fist of encouragement. Maria shouted something Brent couldn't hear because of the crowd's noise, and he put his gloved hand to his ear. Maria cupped her hands around her mouth and he made out the words, "Try hitting him!"

Brent grinned at her around his mouthpiece and made a fist. It seemed like a good idea.

When the bell sounded, he moved quickly to meet Molino. He wasn't going to be taken by surprise a second time. He was sure Molino would expect a resumption of his evasive maneuvers so, instead, he feinted as though he was going to move right, stepped in and hit Molino with two quick left jabs to the nose, followed by a hard right to his jaw.

Molino grunted and his eyes glazed. He grabbed Brent, wrapping him in a bear hug that felt like it was breaking his ribs. The referee made no move to pull them apart and the two men lurched around the ring like drunken dancers before Brent could force his way out of Molino's grip.

Brent had wanted to follow his attack with an other combination, but he saw that the delay had given Molino time to clear his head, and he was watching Brent warily, his fists ready, his injured nose dripping blood.

Brent danced away. The fight had entered a new phase. Molino had stopped fighting with his machismo and was starting to fight with his head. The position of Molino's hands and feet, his head sunk between his shoulders, his eyes wary with the coldness of a coiled rattlesnake, told Brent his punches had taught Molino that this man could hurt him. He wasn't going to leave himself open again.

Now, Brent thought, I'll find out if I'm a fighter or not. Until now, it had been the rapier against the broadsword. Now it was saber to saber.

Molino, relying on his longer reach, began snapping left jabs at Brent's head, sometimes following with hard rights.

Brent kept up his dance, shuffling, slipping or blocking the punches, taking the sting out of those that got through by going away. Molino's guard made it difficult to get at his head and Brent went to work on his body. He developed a pattern of blocking or slipping Molino's left jab or hook, and countering with a right to Molino's stomach and ribs. To his surprise, the blows seemed to have little effect. There had to be a network of tough muscles beneath that layer of fat.

Sitting on his stool at the end of the round, he carefully watched Molino who was drinking a large amount of water while his trainer talked to him. Molino was also beginning to breath heavily and Brent reminded himself to stick to his plan. Go for the body. Slow the man down.

The bell rang and Brent moved forward. When Molino snapped the expected left, Brent slipped it and hammered a right to Molino's heart.

Bam! Brent's head exploded in a blackness shot with geyser of white and red sparks.

What the hell? Canvas, bloody canvas, was under his head. Dimly he heard a voice saying, "*tres, quatro, cinco—*" He was down!

Something, something he couldn't fathom, got him to one knee. But it was the sound of the voice close above him saying "*siete*" that generated the raw anger that brought him to his feet. Son of a bitch! The bastard was counting in Spanish, probably hoping he wouldn't understand the count.

Surprisingly, his legs were strong and he was able to get to his feet, although his eyes seemed to be peering through a red curtain. Instincts, honed by years of physical and mental training, allowed Brent to keep away from Molino's pounding fists. Molino tried to force him into a corner where there'd be no escape, but a cold place in the center of the pain and anger told Brent not to let that happen.

Move! Keep in the center of the ring! Grab and hold! Protect the head! Take the body blows! Keep the gloves up! Move! Move!

But he couldn't escape! Molino bored in, battering Brent's

protective arms and shoulders with both hands, trying to force his guard down. And that was his mistake!

It was there... Molino's jaw! Inches from Brent's gloves. Exposed by his mad flurry of roundhouse swings.

As though it had a life of its own, Brent's right fist slammed upward into the inviting target. *Bam!*

Molino's attack stopped as though he'd hit a stone wall, and Brent retreated, grateful for the momentary respite.

God! What's happening? Why doesn't Molino attack? The red curtain was rapidly lifting from Brent's vision, and it dawned upon him that Molino was sagging against the ropes. The sight was like a sniff of ammonia and Brent's reflexes sprang to life.

Molino came off the ropes, his hands lifting, his eyes clearing. Attack! Before he recovers! Not the head! Head too damn hard! The body! Like hitting the heavy bag. Forget defense!

Bam! Bam! Bam! He was in the zone. And there it is was! The solar plexus! Now! Hard!

The blow exploded in Molino's gut like a mortar shell. He made a gagging sound and fell face down, bile pouring from his mouth. The hands pushed futilely at the canvas, trying to force the body back into battle. But the body was finished, devoid of energy, its stomach heaving, its spirit pouring out of the mouth.

In the stunned silence, the referee stared stupidly. Brent gave him a shove. "Start counting, damnit!"

The referee slowly moved to Molino and began the count. He could have taken all night. Molino was too sick to get up. His eyes rolled, his hands pushed, his lungs sucked for air, but there was no strength, and his body sighed and gave up. He was inert when the referee's slow count reached *diez*. Reluctantly, he straightened and raised Brent's hand. The only sound was a yell from Frankie, who was already standing and applauding. Maria and Jennifer jumped and yelped with joy.

Brent walked to his corner and climbed through the ropes. Ortega was staring at Molino, his eyes wide, his jaw slack. Brent removed his mouthpiece and grinned. "Frankie was right. He's a bum."

Frankie slammed into Brent with a force like one of Molino's blows and wrapped him in a powerful hug. "*Lo hizo! Lo hizo,*" he shouted. "What a punch!" He released Brent and spun toward Maria with astonishing alacrity. "You see that, Maria? One punch! Right in the gut. Look at that! They got to carry him out!"

"You were terrific," Jennifer said. She touched Brent's face with tender fingers. "My God, does it hurt much?"

Brent put his gloved hand to his face, surprised that there really was no real pain, only a dull ache. Then he saw blood on his glove. "I don't think it's mine," he said. "I'm okay."

"Yeah, yeah," Frankie chortled. "You're okay. We got to celebrate. My *restaurante!* Anything you want, my friend. You know who that was you beat? Hector Molino! You beat him. Three rounds! I can't believe it."

"Yeah, I'll bet," Brent said. "You set me up."

"Yeah, yeah. But you did it."

Brent looked at Maria. She was studying him with an expression between pleasure and concern, like a mother who'd just found out her child had a talent for lying. "Did you know about this?" he asked.

"No," she said. "But you did okay anyway."

"Okay? Is that all?"

"Okay, great. Well, maybe not great. Adequate."

Brent was trying to analyze the look of mischief in her eyes when Frankie pulled on his arm. "Come on, come on. We don't want you to catch cold."

He started pulling Brent toward the aisle, but Brent held back to speak to Maria and Jennifer. "The celebration. You'll be there."

"Are you kidding?" Jennifer said.

"Wouldn't miss it," Maria grinned. "I want to watch your face turn purple."

"Sadist," Brent said. But when he turned to follow Frankie's broad back up the aisle, he was smiling.

AT FRANKIE'S PLUSH Mexican *restaurante*, Frankie was lost somewhere in the crowd, basking in the hot sunshine of congratulations while a *marimba* band tried to be heard above the shouts and laughter. Jaime Ortega had not shown up for the party.

Seated on soft leather upholstery in a horseshoe-shaped booth with Maria and Jennifer, drinking a beer that was a gift from some fan, listening to the happy music and cheery voices, Brent was struck by the contrast between his life tonight and what it had been only a few months ago. Back in Kansas it was possible he'd also spend the evening in a club. But he'd most likely be nursing a solitary beer and feeling miserable about losing Connie. This was considerably better.

But as with everything good, there was a price. Maria had been right about his face. It was starting to hurt. There were lumps on his cheeks and both his eyes were blackened. Fortunately, and surprisingly, there were no cuts. Even so, he was going to look like a bad loser for a few days.

But here, everyone seemed to look upon his messed up features as a badge of honor. He could hardly find time to drink his beer. He was constantly interrupted by men and women stopping by to shake his hand. The women, some of them gorgeous, were more fascinated by his battered face than the men. He knew boxing was popular among Latinos, but he'd had no idea boxers were held in such esteem. He could see how the adulation could become addictive, on the edge of megalomania.

But it was a false adulation with no heart behind it. No heart. Sycophancy could be withdrawn as quickly as it was bequeathed. Somewhere Hector Molino was probably wondering what had become of all his friends.

It occurred to Brent that the attention he was getting from Maria and Jennifer could be part of the same hypocritical unctuousness. Perhaps not. They'd been friendly enough before the fight. Jennifer had made it starkly clear that if he accepted her invitation, their relationship could spiral to heady heights.

And Maria? It was difficult to read her. She'd been friendly, but cool, as though he was just one more male client with more on his mind than aerobics. As near as he could tell, the fight hadn't changed her attitude. When they had sat down in the booth, she'd practically insisted Jennifer sit next to Brent.

At first, she'd been reserved, joining in the laughter and banter more with her mind than her heart. Gradually, however, she'd thawed, opening up, laughing and talking. But it could have been because of the party and not because of him. It seemed everyone knew her and liked her. And she enjoyed them, occasionally speaking fluent Spanish, her eyes sparkling and her smile indelible. During the brief moments they had to themselves, her warm animation carried over into effervescent conversation with Brent and Jennifer.

But the real test, Brent knew, would come tomorrow when the party was over.

What the hell. Enjoy it, he reminded himself. Today, it might be 'roses, roses all the way, and after that, the dark.' And the dark might be only as far away as his next fight. Next fight?

The thought that Frankie might want him to fight again gave Brent a chill, and he took a long drink, emptying his glass of beer. Instantly, another bottle mysteriously appeared on the table and he laughed. It seemed that gods, even those with clay feet, didn't have to order their own drinks.

Frankie plunked his glass of *tequila* on the table and shoved into the booth forcing Jennifer to press her warm body close against Brent, closer he was sure than necessary, her thigh tight against his, her shoulder against his arm, her hair brushing his cheek. Maria smiled knowingly, but to Brent's chagrin, without a trace of jealousy.

"*Aye, Chihuahua*," Frankie breathed. "A good day. A very good day, no?"

Jennifer raised her glass of Chivas Regal. "I'll drink to that."

"Me, too." Frankie took a swallow of *tequila*. "*Amigo*, this is just the beginning."

Brent lifted his hand. "Hey, Frankie, we've proved our point. It's over."

"We proved you can win."

"Who did I beat? Some nobody."

"Hector Molino. He's a good boy. Tell him, Maria."

"Nineteen fights. Eighteen wins. Fifteen by knockouts."

"So why was a guy that good fighting a greenhorn like me?" Brent stared suspiciously at Frankie. "That wasn't a fix, was it?"

Frankie spread his hands. "Hey! Molino wouldn't take no dive. He figured that if he got by you, he was a contender."

"What gave him that idea?"

Frankie's grin was lopsided. "Well, I kind of lied a little."

"About me? What did you tell him?"

Frankie shifted uncomfortably and Maria said, "He told him you were the Kansas champ. He didn't know Kansas from Russia."

"Jesus, Frankie," Brent muttered. "You almost got me killed. I've never been hit so hard in my life."

"Yeah, but you took the shot. That's the important thing. You took Molino's best shot and you came back. Nobody else ever did that."

"God!" Jennifer said. "I thought I was going to die."

"So did I," Brent said.

"You got it, *amigo*. You got the will! You go down. You get up. That's what makes a champ."

"Spelled c.h.u.m.p. I'm glad we got that out of the way."

"Brent." Jennifer put her hand over his. "You can't stop now."

"Yes, I can. I'm retiring undefeated."

Frankie leaned forward as much as his bulk would allow. "Uh, *amigo*, we said a couple of fights. Remember?"

"You also said the first one would be with some over-the-hill bum. I figure this one equals two."

"Well...uh...I've already got something set up. I can't back out now."

Brent leaned back, staring at Frankie accusingly. He should give Frankie a flat 'no.' But to his surprise, he hesitated. He'd barely escaped taking a bad beating. He had no desire to climb into the ring with someone who might be even better than Molino. And yet, there was a niggling thought in the back of his mind. Just how good am I?

After all, he'd beaten Molino. He'd survived a crushing blow. Frankie believed he could make it. He kind of owed Frankie one more fight. If he won, he won. If not, what difference would it make? It would make Frankie happy, and that's what counted.

"Okay," he said, and Jennifer squealed. "But just one more. And this time no lying. I want to know who I'm fighting?"

"You got it, *amigo*. I'll get somebody who can give you some practice."

"Practice! One more 'practice' like tonight and I'll be in permanent retirement."

"Who do you have in mind?" Maria asked.

"Depends who I can line up." Frankie rolled his eyes up in thought. "Maybe Pablo Cruz."

"I know him," Jennifer said. "They call him 'the snake'."

Maria said, "Twenty-six fights. Twenty-four wins. One knockout."

Twenty-four wins? What had he gotten himself into this time? Brent felt an increasingly familiar sense of helplessness. Lately it seemed that every aspect of his life was being manipulated.

"I don't know, Frankie," he said. "That's a lot of fights."

"He's a boxer. You can handle a boxer."

Brent felt a slight easing of tension. A boxer? That shouldn't be too bad. In a sense, he was a boxer himself. That's what a trainer did—get a boxer in shape and teach him to box. The ability to take a punch or to knock out an opponent couldn't be taught any more than a baseball pitcher would be taught to throw a ninety-five mile-per-hour fast ball. They were God-given talents. What he taught was primarily how to keep from getting knocked unconscious while piling up points against an opponent. That was the Olympic way—the amateur way.

But the pros? They were always looking for the knock out. That's where the money was. This Pablo Cruz might be an accomplished boxer, but he wouldn't be a pro if he didn't have a knockout punch.

"Okay," he said without enthusiasm. "When?"

As though he knew the answer, Frankie quickly said, "Three weeks. In Acapulco."

"Three weeks! Jesus, Frankie. I won't hardly be healed up in three weeks."

"Sure you will. When I was your age, I used to fight every couple of days."

"You were crazy."

"No, *amigo*. I was hungry."

Brent looked at Frankie and had to laugh. "Well, you sure took care of that."

Frankie guffawed, and Maria and Jennifer laughed. Brent really enjoyed seeing Maria laugh. The way she tossed her head so her dark hair became wild like smoke in the wind, and the way her eyes sparkled like moonlight on deep ocean water, gave him a sense of joy that had been out of his life for a long time. He could hardly keep from staring at her.

To keep from making a complete fool of himself, he concentrated on Frankie who was saying, "*Amigo*, tomorrow we celebrate at my *casa*. Be there at eight. Okay?"

Brent glanced at Maria and nodded. They'd have to shoot him to keep him away. "Sure," he said. "I guess I can break training for one night."

"Right," Frankie agreed. "One night. Then we're gonna break your butt. Right, Maria?"

Maria looked at Brent and her smile was malicious. "Right. You're gonna wish you'd stayed in Arkansas."

"Kansas."

"Wherever."

Chapter Twelve

DURING THE DRIVE home, Brent was scarcely conscious he was driving. His mind was lost in the wonder of Maria. He enjoyed visualizing every nuance of her smile, the way her eyes sparkled when she was happy, and the way they smoldered when she was angry. The glow of her skin seared his memory leaving warm embers of pleasure. And he'd be seeing her tomorrow night, assuming of course that she'd be at the dinner. If she wasn't, the entire evening would be a big disappointment. In truth, there'd be no real point in going if Maria wasn't there. He had no interest in meeting Carmen. And he could talk to Frankie at the gym.

A dark thought snapped him out of his reverie. The DEA. The reason he should be going to dinner at Frankie's home was to insinuate himself farther into Frankie's life, not to stare at his daughter. It'd be a major mistake to allow her hypnotic eyes to pull him into an impossible fantasy. Nothing could possibly come of it except pain.

Damn! It had been so easy to forget his real job—probably because he wanted to forget it. But it wasn't going to go away. The best course of action was to end the job as soon as possible. The dinner at Frankie's house should help move it along faster. That should make Hendrix and Duval happy.

Thinking about the DEA made him realize he hadn't checked in for two days. He checked his watch. Almost midnight. Should he call Hendrix at his home? Or wait until tomorrow? Better make it tonight. He might not get a chance tomorrow.

Brent drove slowly, searching for a pay phone. When he saw a large supermarket that was still open, he pulled into the nearly deserted lot at the market's rear entrance. As he expected, there were pay phones against the wall of the market.

He called Hendrix, using the agent's home number he'd committed to memory. Hendrix answered with a sleepy sounding, "Yeah?"

"It's me. Brent."

Hendrix's voice sharpened. "Yeah. Where you calling from?"

"It's okay. A pay phone."

"Yeah, good. Where the hell have you been? I've been trying to get in touch with you."

A blade of dread pierced Brent. He was sure Hendrix wouldn't try to get in touch with him to rely good news. So whatever he had to say would be bad.

"What for?" he asked.

"To see if you're still alive. How does it look?"

"Well, I'm in pretty solid with Frankie. He's invited me to dinner at his place tomorrow night."

"Hey, good. Maybe you can hit on his daughter."

For an instant, Brent debated whether to tell Hendrix that he'd already met Maria. He decided there was no point in implicating her any more than necessary. "Yeah, maybe."

"See if you can get close to her. She might be easier to crack than Frankie."

Hendrix had no way of knowing the illness his words were generating in Brent's stomach. If Maria were involved in Frankie's dealing, he didn't want to know anything about it. He shifted the subject away from Maria. "I'm going to Mexico with Frankie next month."

"Mexico! Jesus! Great! We think that's Frankie's major source. I thought you said you hadn't found out anything."

"I haven't. Not yet."

"So why is Frankie taking you to Mexico?"

Brent tried to chuckle, but his throat was dry with apprehension. He had to tell Hendrix about his fighting. There was no way he could keep it from them for long. Even DEA agents read the papers. "You're going to get a kick out of this. I'm supposed to fight some guy down there."

"Fight? What the shit do you mean fight?"

"Fight. Like boxing."

Again there was a pause, this time longer. "Oh, Christ. What the hell is going on?"

"Well, Frankie wanted me to try a couple of fights. I figured it'd be a good way to get in with him."

Brent heard Hendrix take a deep breath before he said, "Yeah, okay. Maybe it'll help. Just don't get hurt. I'm not sure your insurance would cover it."

"I thought about that, too," Brent said dryly.

"Actually, this might be good. If Frankie is using his trips as some sort of cover, it could get you on the inside. You any good? I mean, for real."

A movement caught Brent's eye and he turned. A black Chevy Camero had pulled into the lot and was slowly driving past. There were two men in the front seats and one in the back. Latinos, he thought. All three stared at him as they drove by and Brent suddenly realized how dark it was behind the market.

He kept his eye on the car as he said to Hendrix, "I hope so. I'd like to get this thing wrapped up before I get my brains beat out."

Hendrix chuckled. "Yeah, okay. Maybe we can think of something to speed it up."

The Camero pulled to a stop and the man in the passenger's seat got out and began walking past Brent toward the market entrance. He had lean hips and the shoulders of someone who'd spent a lot of time lifting weights. His straight, black hair was pulled back and caught in a ponytail. There was a fresh scar on his jaw that looked like a knife cut.

Brent watched the man out of the corner of his eye as he sauntered past, saying to Hendrix, "I hope so."

"But have you got any leads on his dealing?"

"Well, no. So far, I haven't seen a sign of it."

The Latino passed Brent, then suddenly, whirled. There was the snick of a switch-blade knife popping its blade, and Brent felt its point dig into his back just below his shoulder blade. The Latino put his head close to Brent's and gritted, "Hey, man, hang up the fuckin' phone."

The man's breath reeked of beer and Brent turned his head slightly. "Okay, okay," he said. "Take it easy." To Hendrix he said, "Hold on, Jim."

The smart thing to do was to give up his money, and if the man hadn't been so stupid as to stand so close, Brent would have surrendered the money. But years of martial arts, wrestling and boxing had taught him that there's a lag in human reflexes, and if one moved fast enough, it was possible to attack faster than a person could react, especially if the other person was not expecting it.

"Easy," he said softly. "Easy."

Brent sensed the man relaxing and he exploded around, away from the knife point, and smashed the telephone against the man's temple. The man's eyes went dead and the knife dropped from his hand. His knees buckled, and without a sound, he slid to the ground.

Moving fast, Brent strode toward the car. The driver was getting out on Brent's side with a gun clutched in his hand while the smaller man in the back seat was struggling to get out the passenger's door from the rear seat.

Brent was upon the driver before he could get both feet on the ground. He grabbed the man's gun arm and yanked him so he fell head first, half out the door. Then Brent slammed the door hard. The man screamed as the heavy door crashed into him. The gun fell from his hand and bounced on the asphalt.

The small guy was out of the opposite door and coming around the front of the car, holding a knife, and Brent went for him. Like a fool, the man slashed at Brent's eyes and Brent ducked under the swing and grabbed him under the armpit with his left hand and seized his balls with his right. The man gasped in pain as Brent lifted him and threw him at the driver who had staggered out of the car and trying to pick up his gun with his good hand. They collided with a sickening thud and fell to the asphalt, the small guy with both hands between his legs, retching. The driver lay motionless, blood running from his smashed nose.

Brent picked up the gun and put it under his belt. Then he picked up the fallen knife and walked around and stabbed each of the car's tires.

As air hissed from the tires, he used his foot to break the knife blade off at the handle, and after wiping off his fingerprints, tossed the handle to the ground. He did the same to the knife of the man by the telephone.

Brent picked up the dangling telephone, "Hello, Jim," he said. "You still there?"

"What the hell happened?" Hendrix snapped.

"Slight interruption. I'll call you after the party at Frankie's house. Okay?"

"Yeah. Watch yourself."

"Don't worry."

Brent hung up and wiped his prints off the phone. He didn't believe the Latinos would call the police, but maybe someone in the market had witnessed the incident and called 911. He kept his lights off when he drove away until he was out of the lot so his license plate number couldn't be seen.

Strangely, instead of being elated that his training had worked to perfection, he was weary with disgust because it had been necessary to use it. Why the shit did the world have to be filled with such human scum? If he'd been an ordinary citizen, he'd now be without his money and more than likely on his way to a hospital.

The trouble was that there were plenty more under the rock that had spewed forth those three. Would there always be? Probably.

During the remainder of the drive home, the streets looked darker than usual.

Chapter Thirteen

THE FOLLOWING EVENING, Brent drove carefully through heavy rush hour traffic, heading west on Sunset Boulevard toward Pacific Palisades, an affluent area of West Los Angeles located on a plateau above the blue-gray Pacific. The boulevard undulated through cool canyons past expensive homes with spacious lawns and perfectly manicured shrubs and beds of flowers. Brilliant waterfalls of crimson and pink Bougainvillea spilled over high walls and spiked ornamental fences as though to hide the ominous purpose of the barriers.

On a bluff where all the homes overlooked the ocean, Brent located the address Frankie had given him and drove through open wrought iron gates and down a long driveway to a circular, brick-paved parking area in front of a two-story California Spanish-style home painted a delicate pink. Colorful impatiens, peonies, dianthus and marigolds were artfully displayed in beds and path borders. Tall royal, Madagascar and coconut palms, rising from green lawns, waved their fronds gracefully above the house's red tile roof.

Frankie's Cadillac was parked in front of the house, and through open doors of a nearby four-car garage, Brent could see Maria's red Porche and a white Bentley. Brent stopped behind Frankie's Caddy and sat looking at the house. At California prices, the estate had to be worth millions. Frankie had certainly come a long way from the *barrios* of East L.A., not only in distance, but in affluence.

Then Brent remembered where the money had come from and the house lost much of its beauty. If what they suspected about Frankie was true hundreds, perhaps thousands, of people had paid for this grandeur with their careers, their health, and many, with their lives.

But for the time being, Brent choose to give Frankie the benefit of the doubt. It would make him feel less like a scumbag when he ate Frankie's food and drank his wine.

Almost as soon as he'd rung the bell, the paneled front door was opened by Frankie. He was wearing white pants, white shoes and a pale blue Guayabera shirt with brocade panels. He had a large cigar in his hand and a broad smile on his face.

"Hello, my friend," he chortled. "Come in. *Me casa es su casa.* Have any trouble finding the place?"

"Nope. Couldn't miss it. It's the only place on the block."

Frankie laughed. "Yeah. You're right. Come on in. I want you to meet my folks."

His steps echoing off Spanish tile, Frankie led the way through a circular foyer to a sunken living room with wall-to-wall white carpeting so thick Brent felt the nap turning beneath his feet. To his right was a grand piano on a slightly raised dais. To the left, a curved stairway with ornate, polished oak balusters led to the house's second floor.

The walls were hung with large oil paintings that looked as though they had been carefully selected and positioned for the effect of their brilliant colors. On the far side of the room, huge picture windows looked out on a slope of verdant lawn flanked by beds of flowers and incredibly tall eucalyptus trees. Beyond could be seen the blue of the ocean, spangled gold by the setting sun.

An older man and woman, and a slender, younger woman were standing with their backs to the door looking out at the view. There was no sign of Maria, and Brent felt a pang of disappointment. Perhaps Maria wasn't going to be in attendance which meant it was likely to be a very boring evening.

The slender woman turned and came toward them, and Brent realized she was Frankie's wife, Carmen. Although the painting of her in Frankie's office had to be years old, Carmen Rodriguez had lost little of her beauty. She was hardly more than five feet five inches tall, but her imperious posture made her seen taller. She had the same long, almost-black hair as Maria. Her tawny skin was smooth without a wrinkle or blemish. She could easily have passed for being in her thirties instead of her fifties. She wore a long-sleeved, white evening gown that sparkled with thousands of tiny beads. Walking across the room, she moved with the grace of a dancer despite the thick carpet and her high-heeled shoes.

"Brent," Frankie boomed as he put his arm around her shoulders. "This is my beautiful Carmen."

She held out her hand to Brent in a gesture that had the grace of a ballerina. "I'm so glad you could come." Her voice was low and throaty with the faintest trace of an accent. "You're all I've been hearing about lately."

Brent tried not to show his embarrassment as he took her hand. "Thank you. I hope that none of it was the truth."

She laughed and Brent saw where Maria got her brilliant smile and flashing eyes. "No one could make up such accomplishments," she said. "And now I've seen you, I know they must be true."

Brent thought of the bruises on his face and knew she was being the perfect hostess. Most of the swelling had gone down and he'd used a little Max Factor protection makeup to hide the worst of the bruises, but he knew his face still looked as though he'd been in a fight.

However, he could take refuge in the thought that if clothes made the man, he should be okay. He thought he looked pretty good in his tailored white dinner jacket with black pants and a white-on-white shirt with a black and red silk necktie. They had to count for something.

He smiled at Carmen Rodriguez while a dozen clever replies raced through his mind, but they might be misconstrued as being flip or condescending, so Brent answered with what he considered a stupidly lame, "Thank you."

"We been married twenty-five years," Frankie said. "Can you believe that?"

"Sure, Frankie," Brent said. "You grow on people."

Frankie chuckled. "You better believe it." He stepped away from his wife and smiled at her. "A very beautiful woman, eh, Brent?"

Brent nodded. "Very beautiful. It's easy to see where Maria gets her looks." Then he realized the implication of his remark, and he felt his face grow warm as he quickly said, "I mean, you're good-looking, too, Frankie—"

Frankie waved the faux pas aside with his cigar, "Hey, *amigo*. I agree. Thank goodness you're right."

"Anyway, thanks for the compliment," Carmen said.

Frankie turned to the couple by the window. "Brent, *mi padre* and *mi madre*."

Brent said hello as Frankie's father, followed by his wife, crossed the room. Frankie's father was a small man, perhaps five feet six inches tall and so slender he was almost skinny. He had thick, white hair and a white, precisely-clipped, military moustache. His skin was webbed with fine lines. He wore a dark gray, sharkskin suit that could've been made in Italy. When he shook Brent's hand, Brent felt calluses that came from hard physical labor—the kind that never went away.

His wife was about the same height, but she was as heavy as her husband was skinny. She had a body like a barrel with a huge bosom that almost spilled over the top of her sequined gown. Her hair, fastened in a low bun, had the jet black color of dye and was pulled back so severely that it looked painful. Like her husband, she spoke with the faint accent that, while she might have been USA-born, gave Brent the impression she'd spent her formative years speaking Spanish as her primary language. They both gave the impression of being warm and friendly with none of the animosity toward Anglos harbored by some Latinos. Brent liked them immediately.

Frankie had poured glasses of white wine and he passed them around. "You'll like this. French," he said. "I don't buy American no more. Nothing but the best. Right, Carmen?"

She raised her glass. "That's right, *Franquito*."

Brent smiled at Frankie. *"Franquito?* Little Frankie?"

Frankie laughed, spilling wine on the white carpet. His mother and father winced, and Brent guessed that all their possessions had been hard-earned. Carmen, however, didn't deign to notice. If she'd come out of poverty, she'd left it far behind.

"She gave me that name before I put on a couple of pounds," Frankie said.

Carmen looked toward the stairway and her face took on a new warmth. "Maria. You look lovely."

Brent turned and sucked in his breath. Maria was descending the stairway, one hand resting lightly on the banister, her chin up, her back straight, moving with the easy assurance of a fashion model. A totally black evening gown of some filmy material clung to her lithe body like a lover until at the swell of her hips it flared into a multi-layered long skirt that swayed exotically with each step. The gown had long sleeves and a wide décolletage that began at the tips of her shoulders and exposed the tops of her ivory breasts.

Her high-heeled sandals were fashioned of thin strips of cleverly woven silver-colored leather. Her dark hair was pulled back and fastened in a loose, cascading ponytail, highlighting her face and neck. Around her neck she wore a small emerald heart on a gold chain so thin it was virtually invisible. Her earrings were long, and the light sparkled from diamonds and emeralds. Light from the setting sun, striking through the window, caught the green in her eyes which seemed to perfectly match the green of the emeralds.

As she stepped into the room, she saw the stunned look on Brent's face, and came to him with both hands outstretched. "Brent," she said, and her smile tore at his eyes. "Is it really you? I've never seen you with your clothes on."

Brent blinked and again he felt his face begin to heat. He ripped his eyes from her to see the effect of her joking words on Frankie's mother and father.

Thank God, they're smiling.

Maria laughed as she held both Brent's suddenly nerveless hands and came up on her toes to kiss him on the cheek. "I've only seen him wearing gym clothes," she explained to her grandparents. She touched one of his bruises delicately. "Or in the ring." She stepped back, still holding his hands and looked at him. "I must say I like this better."

Brent studied her making no attempt to hide his admiration. "So do I," he said. "Wow!"

She smiled before she turned to hug her grandparents. Frankie poured another glass of wine and handed it to Maria. "Here, *querida.* French. 1965. A good year."

"Really?" she said taking the glass of wine.

"*Franquito* is becoming a real dilettante," Carmen said.

Frankie's chest rumbled out a snort. "No way. I'm as much a man as I ever was." He patted Carmen on the derriere. "Tonight, I prove it."

"*Aye, carumba,*" she replied with a wry smile. "Me and my big mouth."

A few minutes later, Frankie led the way into a huge dining room. Brent stopped just inside the door, impressed. The room's walls were covered with a patterned silk cloth. A ten-foot-long table flanked with wooden, Mexican-style chairs was set for dinner. The table cloth was made of Spanish lace; the place settings were Aztec-patterned with matching linen napkins. The flatware was solid silver, heavy, deeply patterned. Matching candlestick holders were also silver.

The meal was *pollo mole*, chocolate chicken, prepared in the Mexican style and served by an obsequious group of Mexican servants wearing black suits and bow ties. Frankie was in his element, laughing and telling stories to Brent and Maria about the old days in the *barrio* while his mother and father nodded in agreement and added bits of information. Maria was almost as animated as Frankie, laughing at his jokes and asking questions that made Brent realize she hadn't heard many of the stories.

Carmen was generally silent unless Frankie asked her a question. She looked so supremely elegant that Brent wondered what she'd seen in a rough character like Frankie who must've been broke when she married him. Perhaps, like many Latin women who grew up in a male-dominated environment, she'd allowed Frankie to overwhelm her.

Studying her, Brent gradually altered his impression. In small, almost imperceptible ways, she revealed she was a very, very tough and determined woman. He wondered how much of Frankie's career and his success was due to her guidance. He had to assume she knew about Frankie's drug dealing, if in fact, he was dealing. It was difficult to believe that Frankie could keep anything from her for very long.

And Maria? Brent didn't want to believe she knew. It would be so totally out of character for her, unless she was the greatest actress in the world. She had her mother's looks, but not her mother's flinty coolness. Carmen was an orchid, a waxen epiphyte—beauty without warmth or fragrance. Maria was a dusky rose—warmly beautiful, emitting allure like a perfume.

After dinner and an aperitif of fine *Amaretto de Saronno*, Carmen turned to Brent. "*Franquito* tells me you have another fight."

Brent nodded. "That's what he says. Someone named Pablo Cruz."

"Ah, yes. The champion of Mexico. A wonderful boxer."

Brent sat up straight and looked at Frankie. "Mexican champion? You didn't tell me that."

Frankie blew smoke from his cigar. "*No problema.* You can take him."

Carmen voice was casual as she asked, "And where is this fight to take place?"

For the first time, Frankie looked uncomfortable. "Acapulco."

Carmen's expression didn't change, but her voice became as cold as a glacier-fed stream. "Are you taking Jennifer with you?"

"Yeah," Frankie said.

Carmen's eyes flicked toward Brent. "Do you think that's wise?"

Her words produced an expression on Frankie's face that instantly made Brent realize that Carmen might be an advisor, but she'd never be the boss. Frankie's voice was hard as he said, "That's for me to say."

Carmen features froze as though Frankie had struck her. Then her lips lifted in a small smile. "Of course. Give Jennifer my regards."

"I'd like to go," Maria said. "I can work out something for my group."

A glance passed between Carmen and Frankie before he said, "Not this time, *querida.*"

"This time? You never take me."

"Next time. I promise."

"But you're taking Jennifer."

Frankie's voice lashed out in rapid Spanish. Maria sat for an instant, holding her breath, her face pale. Then she pushed back her chair and stood up. "Would you excuse me? I have some things to do."

Before Brent could stand, she stalked out of the room.

Carmen turned to Brent. "Please excuse my daughter's manners. I'm afraid she's still suffering from a very bad experience."

Brent wondered if her 'bad' experience had anything to do with discovering the truth about her father. The thought was like a sword of Damocles over his head as he said, "I hope it isn't because of me."

"Perhaps in a way, it is," Carmen said. She hesitated, then continued, choosing her words carefully. "Two years ago, Maria was engaged to be married. Her fiancée was a fine young man, a flier with the Navy. From a very good family. He was killed in a crash."

Brent sat motionless, hardly breathing, torn between sadness and joy. He felt a vast sense of relief that the outburst hadn't been about drug dealing. At the same time, he wanted to make some sound of regret, of condolence. But even his pleasure was sundered between an awful sadness that Maria had already given her love to someone else, and a joy that it was over. So he said nothing, feeling foolish and intrusive.

"She is young," Frankie's mother said softly. "She will get over it. She needs time."

There was a painful pause that Frankie broke by pushing back from the table and heading for the living room. "Hey, Maria," he called. "How about showing Brent around the place? Tell him what a great guy your dad is."

As Brent walked beside Carmen into the living room she said, keeping her voice low, "Frankie is sometimes a little impatient. If Acapulco is too soon for you, you must make him understand."

Three weeks was, indeed, too soon. But, as Hendrix had said, he couldn't miss the chance to accompany Frankie to Mexico. He'd just have to take his beating as one more occupational hazard.

"Frankie's been around for years," he said. "If he thinks I've got a chance, then maybe I have."

Even as he mouthed the words, Brent was telling himself it was a lie. He had no chance against the Mexican champ. But maybe in three weeks, if he repeated the lie often enough, he might actually begin to believe it.

A short time later, obeying her father's wishes, Maria led Brent on a tour of the estate. The sun had vanished below the ocean's horizon and the air of dusk was spiced with the delicate scent of flowers. But the beauty was lost on Maria. Instead of describing their surroundings as they strolled past a swimming pool and through winding paths beneath a variety of trees and flowering bushes, she was silent, walking far enough away from Brent so their hands wouldn't accidentally touch.

Her chilling aloofness mystified Brent, and he searched for words that would break through her reserve. She had to be hurting. Or, perhaps, she was burning with anger. If he made a wrong analysis, he might just make her attitude worse. It was best to start with something neutral and listen for a clue.

As dusk turned into velvet darkness, a slight onshore breeze brought a salt-tanged chill and he used that as his opening. "Are you cold? I'll lend you my jacket."

"No," she said. "I'm okay."

They walked a few more steps in silence. In the distance, Brent heard the faint sound of surf breaking on rocks. "How's the swimming down there. Is there any beach?"

"Not really. The water comes right up to the bluffs."

"Oh."

They turned onto a cemented path leading toward horse stables and exercise areas surrounded by high wood fences painted a gleaming white. "I'm not going to like this trip to Acapulco," Brent hazarded.

"Why not? You might win."

Unbidden words seemed to leap from his mouth. "Can't you talk Frankie into letting you come with us?"

He was immediately aghast at what he'd said. If Hendrix was right and Frankie was, somehow, using the trips to Mexico to set up drug dealing, he didn't want Maria there. And yet, once again, his desire had overcome his intellect.

She didn't answer immediately and Brent wondered if he should try to take back the admonition. Then she said, "Daddy doesn't want me along on business trips." Her voice dripped with bitterness as she added, "He always takes Jennifer."

Brent's steps developed a new spring. Obviously, Frankie was protecting his daughter from the real reason for his 'business' trips. And she thought it was only because her father favored Jennifer. She might even believe there was something between Frankie and Jennifer. But he could be wrong about that. He could've sworn Maria and Jennifer were friends.

"I'm sure it's got something to do with business," he said. And his words brought a quick pang to his heart. If, as she said, Frankie always took Jennifer, could she be part of his real business? The thought was almost as difficult to accept as the idea that Maria might be involved.

On the other hand, the fact that Frankie took Jennifer on his business trips and not Maria made it definite that Maria was out of the loop.

Suddenly, the night was crystal with joy.

"Besides—" Maria said, and some of the mischief had returned to her voice. "—you won't be lonely. There are lots of pretty girls in Mexico."

"You wouldn't mind if I went out?" Brent kept lightness in his voice, but he waited anxiously for her answer, hoping she'd say she wanted him for herself.

Instead, she said, "No. Why should I?"

They had reached the corral and a horse came to Maria, offering its soft nuzzle for her to caress.

"No reason, I guess," Brent said.

She didn't answer. Her fingers gently stroked the horse's muzzle with a caress Brent would've killed for. He had to swallow hard before he said, "When you were out of the room, your mother told me about your engagement and what happened."

Her back stiffened. "She had no right to do that."

"I'm glad she did. Now I can tell you about my divorce."

Maria was silent, not looking at him, but her fingers stroking the horse's soft muzzle now moved absently as Brent continued. "I was in love. But it went sour for her. She didn't like my job or where we lived.

I guess that when respect for someone goes, love doesn't stay around long. Anyway, she gave up on me. She thought I'd never be anything except a small-time hick. She left—went back to Phoenix. I guess they've got more lights there. At least, they're a lot brighter than they are in Kansas."

Despite his desire to be objective, bitterness had crept into his voice and Maria turned her head to look at him. "Do you still love her?"

Brent shook his head. "No." He didn't tell her that if she'd asked him the same question a month ago she might have received a different answer.

"When was the last time you saw her?"

"Almost two years ago." The significance of the time didn't escape Maria and he saw pain flare in her eyes before she turned her head away. "I still had a lot of...affection for her then. But things change. Memories fade. Emotions die."

He was speaking as much for her as to her and she responded by saying, "I know." Her voice was a whisper as though for the first time she was consciously betraying her memory.

"And then..." Brent put his hands on her shoulders and turned her to face him. She came around without resistance, but didn't look up. "And then you meet someone else and your world comes back together."

For answer she swayed toward him and lifted her head and he saw tears in her eyes. Something turned inside him, wrenching deep inside his chest. He gazed at her a moment, trying to determine her reason for the provocative move. Her lips were close to his, parted and moist, and his heart hammering, he took a chance that he'd read the move correctly and kissed her lightly, half-expecting her to push him away. His emotions exploded with joy when he felt her warm lips return his kiss, and he put his arms around her, pulling her close as he deepened his kiss.

Then she turned her head and pushed him away. "No, Brent," she whispered. "I'm not ready for this. Not yet."

But before she turned to walk back toward the house, she rested her head on his shoulder for a brief instant and he brushed her hair with his cheek, almost overcome by a desire to hold her so fiercely that she'd never go.

HE REMEMBERED LITTLE of the drive back to his apartment. His mind was a turmoil, filled with despair for what he'd allowed to happen and a wonderful elation because of the possibility Maria might be falling in love with him. One of the blessings he missed about being married was the sharing—the feeling of belonging to someone and of them belonging to him. And now it was happening again.

But he couldn't allow that! His love for Maria was star-crossed from the beginning. When she found out he was a spy, it wouldn't matter whether her father was guilty or innocent, she'd hate him. An emotional attachment now could only end in hurt for both of them. She had already been through one wrenching loss, and once was enough—for her and for him.

He'd driven as far as Santa Monica before he remembered he'd promised to check in with Hendrix after dining with Frankie. He checked his watch. Eleven-thirty. Not too late.

This time, when he stopped at a pay phone, he was careful to pick one in a well-lighted area.

Hendrix answered on the first ring and Brent filled him in on the conversation, omitting his involvement with Maria.

"About your trip to Acapulco," Hendrix said. "We were thinking it might help get a line on his operation if you were on the inside before you went down there."

Brent paused, puzzled by Hendrix's words. "I don't understand. I am on the inside."

"Yeah. But we mean on the inside of his drug dealing."

Brent's skin prickled with a sudden chill. "How can we do that? We don't even know if he is dealing. That's why I'm there, for Christ's sake."

There was a pause. "We thought of a way we might be able to speed it up."

Brent tensed. Was it all going to be over? Did he want that? "Yeah?" he said. "How?"

"We make Frankie think you're a dealer."

Brent felt his jaw sag. "Huh? A dealer? Me?"

"Look at it this way. If Frankie finds out you're dealing small time, he either invites you in or he fires you. If he fires you, he's probably clean. But if he invites you in..." Hendrix left the sentence dangling, but the implication was clear.

"There's one more option," Brent said. "He could just tell me to give it up and we're right where we were."

"That's a possibility. Right. But it's low percentage. The odds are that if he's dealing, and he likes you, he'll open up."

"One more option. He could kill me."

Hendrix's pause was an indrawn breath. "Yeah, I guess there's that. If this goes down, you'd better be ready to split."

"If what goes down? What have you got?"

"Well, we'll think of a way to make Frankie think you're dealing.

Maybe catch you with a few ounces of coke. Then the ball's in his court."

Brent found his breathing was fast and shallow; his heart thudding. It was happening too fast. "Where do I get this coke?" he asked.

"From me. We got a bust going down in a couple of days. We'll use the junk from the bust."

Brent lowered the phone and rubbed at his face with his palm. What had seemed so very simple when he'd agreed to go undercover had taken on ramifications that threatened the destruction of every life he touched, including his own. He'd thought it took a lot of courage for a fighter to keep fighting when he was getting his brains punched out. But that kind of courage was nothing compared to this. A fighter had only himself to think about. But his battle could not only destroy Frankie and his entire family, it might also bring down Jennifer.

But that was his job. He had to keep reminding himself that if it happened, it would all be Frankie's fault, not his. "Okay," he said.

Another thought struck him and he started to reject it, then changed his mind. His first allegiance was to his conscience, and his conscience told him it was his duty to do the best he could. And what the hell. In for a penny, in for a pound. "I've got an idea. Let me go along on the bust."

"No way. It might get back to Frankie."

"Not as DEA. What if Frankie heard that some blonde guy, a fighter, almost got busted? Then I turn up with the junk. He'll go ape."

There was a brief pause while Hendrix thought about it. "You were there, but got away. Yeah. That might do it."

"Okay. When? I've got to set up an excuse to get away from work."

"Call me at the office late tomorrow afternoon. Don't use your name."

"Yeah, I know. I'll lie about that, too."

He hung up without waiting for Hendrix's reply. He didn't feel like talking any more—to anyone.

Chapter Fourteen

THE SIXTY MILE drive to the little town of Pearblossom in LA County's Antelope Valley took an hour. Marc Duval drove one of the DEA's unmarked 2002 Cadillacs along Highway 14 through the San Gabriel Mountains that separated LA from the Mojave desert. The car was a beauty, highly polished—the kind that might be driven by a dope dealer, which it had been before being sized by the DEA from a dealer now vacationing in a federal penitentiary.

Hendrix was sitting in the passenger's seat with a briefcase balanced on his lap and a brown-paper bag on the floor between his feet. Brent sat in the back seat. All wore worn jeans and shirts with the tails out to hide guns holstered in the small of their backs. Brent's gun felt hot against his back, but for the first time, he felt as though he was really DEA.

"You sure Fat Frankie'll get wind of this?" Duval said. "It's out of his territory."

"Count on it," Hendrix answered. "If Frankie's as big as we think, he's got his fingers in just about everything."

"But he might not buy me being a dealer," Brent said.

"He will after today."

"Yeah, I guess you're right."

Brent's voice was listless, and Duval turned to look at him. "How're you holding up?"

"Okay, so far."

"Yeah, well, if this goes down right," Hendrix muttered, "it should help bring this thing to a head."

"I hope so," Brent answered.

"Yeah," Hendrix echoed. "We can't keep all these balls in the air forever."

At the parking lot of the L.A. County Sheriff's Office in Pearblossom, they met Tony Ramos, a DEA agent working undercover who was their contact with the three dealers they planned to bust. When Hendrix explained Brent's role, Ramos wasn't happy about keeping the sheriff out of the loop or about putting Brent into it.

"Too damn many cooks," he muttered. "No dealer is gonna deal with three strangers."

Hendrix realized that Ramos might be right. It was always a good idea to get as many agents as close to the bust site as possible, but most crooks were so suspicious that, if possible, they wouldn't deal with more than one or two strangers. That was the reason for a U.C. like Ramos. He was someone they trusted.

Still, if the crooks were hard up for money, they might deal with three strangers.

"They got three. We got three," Hendrix said. "They might go for it."

"We'll have four," Ramos pointed out.

"Yeah, but they think you're on their side."

Reluctantly, Ramos said he'd go along with the deal as long as his own nose was kept clean.

Hendrix glanced at his watch. "Okay. Let's go over this again. Here's the deal. Ramos has got three dealers set up to sell him half a kilo. Brent, you're going to be his money man." He handed Brent the paper sack. "There's thirty-five grand in there. Checked and logged. You want to count it?"

Brent opened the sack and stared at the bundles of hundred-dollar bills. He knew from his training that each bill was entered by serial number on a serialization sheet as required. The purpose of the serialization sheet was to allow the agents to know exactly which bills were missing in the event an agent was robbed or ripped-off by the traffickers.

Brent closed the sack, feeling as though he was holding a bomb. "Okay," he said. "What do I do?"

"The way it works is that one of them will come to the car to see the money," Hendrix said. "You flash it. But don't give it to him. We go with him to the house. You wait in the car. When we see the dope, we'll come back and get the money. We bust the guys and you take off in their car like you're escaping."

"What if they don't have a car?"

"Then take off in ours. Just make sure they get a look at you first. We might even take a couple of shots in your direction."

"Okay. I hope you guys are good shots."

Hendrix grinned. "Don't worry. We won't hit the car. It'll be DEA property when we pick it up."

"Leave it where we can find it," Duval added. "Somewhere over by your pad."

"Okay." Brent's heart was already thudding and they hadn't even left Pearblossom. He wondered how he'd react if there was any shooting? Judging by the way his heart was pounding already, he might just drop dead of a heart attack. Wouldn't that be a kick in the ass? "If I take your car, how will you guys get back?"

Hendrix opened the briefcase and took out a cell phone. "We've got guys standing by. They'll pick us up."

Brent rubbed sweat off his forehead. "I hope to hell this works."

"What've we got to lose?" Hendrix said. "When Frankie finds out you're dealing, he'll probably bring you into his organization."

"If he's got an organization."

"Right. If he isn't dealing himself, he'll just want to know what the hell you're doing. Either way, we'll get this thing off the dime."

Brent had no enthusiasm for the plan. It seemed to him that even if everything went right, he was going to look stupid. If it went wrong, he could get shot. Or Frankie might have him killed. Not a great choice. But Hendrix was right about one thing—it would precipitate some move by Frankie.

Hendrix took two small glassine envelopes containing white powder from his open briefcase. "Here. When you get back, put these in your locker. Make sure Frankie finds out. He'll put two and two together, and voila, you're in."

"Don't lose them," Duval cautioned. "That's real junk. It's checked out to you."

"Thanks a lot," Brent muttered. He put the envelopes inside the money compartment of his wallet and was putting his wallet back in his rear pocket, when Duval asked, "You bring your gun?"

The question sent a shock through Brent. This was it. This was the situation he'd dreaded all through training—when he might be forced to actually shoot someone. He'd been deadly against targets. But shooting at a person? In the army, it had been different. He could've shot an enemy soldier. But could he shoot a civilian? Even a drug crook? He wasn't sure. His gun pressed against the small of his back like a festering boil.

"Yeah," he said. "I brought it."

"Good. Keep it out of sight unless you need it."

His words echoed in Brent's mind as Hendrix drove out of the parking lot and turned east on Highway 138. On their left was the purple haze of the Mojave Desert. On their right, foothills lifted to the towering mountains of the San Gabriel Range. The desert heat was beginning to build toward its usual hundred plus degrees and Hendrix turned on the car's air conditioner.

Riding in the back seat next to Ramos, Brent had the eerie feeling this was all part of a training exercise and there was no real danger. Except that in his wildest dreams he'd never visualized anything as bizarre as riding through the California desert with thirty-five thousand dollars sitting on his lap and his loaded gun poking him in the back.

He tried to keep his mind focused on reality by reviewing what he had been taught at the training academy. Concentrate on the deal. Don't let the nagging little worry that you might get killed take over your ability to reason. Stick to the plan. Be alert, ready for anything and you'll be okay.

He hoped to hell they were right.

After driving for ten minutes, Ramos directed Duval to turn off the highway onto a narrow, black-topped road leading toward higher country. Two miles up the road, they turned off onto a meandering dirt road that cut between brush of mesquite and sage, and dipped in and out of shallow arroyos. Their passage was announced by a plume of reddish-tan dust that billowed from beneath the tires.

"About half a mile now. There's a shack with a couple of sheds," Ramos said. "The road ends there." He looked at Brent. "You'll have to come back out this way."

"Okay," Brent acknowledged. "Got it."

They topped a last low rise with a superb vista of the Mojave desert, and pulled into the dusty yard of a small, frame house with a sagging porch. The house, more shack than house, had once been painted white, but the paint was mostly a memory, sandblasted by wind-driven dust and blistered by desert sun. Its wooden structure looked so dry and dilapidated that one small spark would turn it into an inferno. Two peeling, electric power wires led to the house from a distant pole. The front door sagged half open.

There was a new 4X4 Jeep Cherokee being sun baked in the yard, but no other sign that the building was occupied. When Duval shut off the Cadillac's engine, they heard the whir of an air conditioning sump.

Nobody moved.

Duval nodded toward the 4X4. "If they're smart they left the keys."

"Yeah," Hendrix agreed. He looked over his shoulder at Ramos. "As soon as you're inside, I'll look."

Ramos licked his lips and said, "Okay. I'm going in."

He got out of the car and slammed the door, the sound like an explosion in the dead air. He wasn't taking any chances on walking in unannounced.

He walked carefully toward the house, his hands swinging loosely, his shoes making little puffs of dust. A lizard scurried out of his path. His footsteps thudded on the wooden porch. When he knocked on the door frame, Brent wouldn't have been surprised to see the shack collapse. They heard no reply to Ramos' knock before he went inside.

Hendrix quietly got out of the car and crossed the few steps to the Cherokee. He peered in through the open window, then quickly returned to the car and got in. "Keys are in the ignition."

Hendrix checked to make sure his revolver was securely in place in his waistband holster. Duval took his 9 mm pistol from its holster and slid it into his western boot. Taking his cue from the two agents, Brent took his shiny new revolver from its holster. It felt cold in his hand despite the heat. Cold and heavy. A metallic machine, designed for killing. He placed it between his thigh and the seat where he could grab it quickly.

Ramos came out of the house followed by a big man wearing old chinos and a torn T-shirt hanging outside his pants. Brent estimated that he was at least six-three and weighed close to two-hundred-fifty pounds. His unkempt beard and hair were red-brown. His eyes were mean. A skinny woman came out of the house and stood with them on the porch staring at the car. She could've been pretty, but had let herself go. Her blonde hair was stringy, and there were dark circles under her dull eyes. She had to be in her twenties, but she stood like an arthritic, old woman with her neck bowed, her skinny arms folded.

"You figure she's the third one?" Hendrix said.

"Could be," Duval answered. "Where's the second guy?"

"Probably inside the house with the dope."

Ramos and Red Beard stepped off the porch and walked toward the car.

"Put down your window," Duval said to Brent. "He'll wanna see the money."

Brent kept his eyes on Red Beard as he rolled down the window. Desert heat poured into the air-conditioned car like a blast from hell. Brent's heart was racing. If the guy had a gun, it was out of sight under the T-shirt.

Ramos and Red Beard stopped beside the car. Up close, Red Beard looked even meaner. Brent was fascinated by the man's eyes. They looked flat, lifeless, like the eyes of zombies in horror movies. His voice was as lifeless as his eyes when he said to Ramos, "You said two guys."

"Guy in the back's my score," Ramos said. "He's got the money."

Red Beard's reptilian eyes swiveled to focus on Brent, and Ramos said, "Show him."

Brent opened the mouth of the sack and held it to the car's open window, fighting to keep his hands from trembling. Red Beard bent down and looked inside the sack. His eyes took on life, a stare of menace as they lifted to look at Brent. Brent stared back. Every red vein in the man's eyes, every unshaven hair on his ugly face, every scabrous pimple, every bead of sweat stood out in sharp relief, giving him the look of a grotesque Beliel.

The eyes went dead, and Red Beard straightened with a grunt and walked back toward the shack. Ramos jerked his head at Hendrix and

Duval, then hurried to catch up with the man.

Hendrix took a set of scales from his briefcase. As he and Duval got out of the car, Hendrix said to Brent. "Don't give 'em the money 'til we give you a signal."

"Okay," Brent said. "Watch yourself."

The two agents followed Ramos and Red Beard, and Hendrix surreptitiously held up three fingers so Duval, walking behind him, could see them. They meant that if the woman on the porch was not the third trafficker, there should be two more inside the house. Duval acknowledged with a grunt.

Their steps thumped as they crossed the porch and followed Ramos and Red Beard inside the house.

IT WAS EVEN hotter inside the house than it was outside, and with their eyes accustomed to blinding sunlight, a hell of a lot darker. Both agents were sweating. They were tense...ready to go for their weapons. Inside the door, Duval and Hendrix separated, keeping their hands in plain sight at their sides. If anything was going to happen, it would be now before their eyes adjusted to the gloom.

Nothing happened.

Hendrix made out that the room was small, furnished with a battered couch and a pair of crippled wooden chairs. Dim light from grimy windows was pierced by brilliant shafts of light that streamed from holes in the roof. Dust motes played tag in the beams of hot sunlight. An open doorway led to a second room where there was no light at all.

A man who looked like a cadaver with wisps of gray hair sprouting from his wrinkled pate was seated behind an old card table in the center of the room. One of his thin, bony hands rested on a bag of clear plastic on the table. The bag contained white powder and looked as though it could weigh the required half-kilo.

Cadaver's sunken eyes swiveled toward Red Beard. "They got the money?"

Red Beard grunted, "Yeah."

Cadaver shoved the package across the table. "Here it is." His voice was as gaunt and bony as his hand.

Hendrix hoped Duval and Ramos noted that the man kept one hand out of sight under the table. It made him feel a little more secure when Ramos put his back against a wall where he could watch the black hole that was the other room.

Hendrix put the scales on the table and Cadaver lifted his chin toward Red Beard. "Get the money."

Red Beard went out and Hendrix jerked his head toward Duval to follow him.

Outside, Duval swung in beside Red Beard. He had no intention of allowing the trafficker to get his hands on the money before Hendrix checked the weight and content of the package so they could make the bust. According to the rules, traffickers were supposed to wait until verification before getting their money. But maybe these guys were amateurs who didn't know the rules.

Then again, maybe they weren't and this was the beginning of a rip. He hoped to hell that Hendrix read it the same way.

FROM HIS PLACE in the back seat of the car, Brent watched Red Beard and Duval approach. He bunched up the top of the bag, getting it ready to hand to the man. He froze when he saw Duval fall slightly behind the man, and flash one of his hands palm out in the ancient sign for 'stop'. What the hell was Duval trying to tell him? He slid his right hand under his thigh and closed it around the grip of his pistol.

He got his answer when, as the two men came even with the front of the car, Red Beard suddenly pulled a large revolver from under his shirt, and with a backhand swing, hit Duval on the side of the head. Duval crumpled without a sound and Red Beard put the barrel of the gun through the open window, aiming it between Brent's eyes.

"Gimme the money," he snarled.

Brent handed him the money bag with his left hand. Red Beard took the sack. Instead of backing away, he used his thumb to pull back the hammer of his pistol, and his eyes widened into a baleful glare. Brent knew he was going to fire! He feinted with his head to the left and twisted right. Red Beard went for the feint and the gun boomed like a Howitzer. The muzzle flash blinded Brent, but his gun was out and he fired three times.

Bam! Bam! Bam!

Through a red haze, he saw Red Beard stagger back. His big pistol boomed again, but it was pointed at the sky, its recoil spinning it from Red Beard's nerveless hand.

INSIDE THE SHACK, Hendrix had just put the package on the scales when Red Beard's first shot reverberated through the dry desert air. Cadaver, moving faster than Hendrix thought possible, yanked his concealed hand from beneath the table holding an army .45 cal. pistol. Duval upended the table, knocking Cadaver back against the wall, and went over it in a headlong dive, landing on top of Cadaver with the full weight of his hundred and seventy-five pounds. Cadaver gasped as the air was driven from his lungs and Hendrix ripped the gun from his hand.

Bam! Bam!

Two shots sounded so close together they were almost one, and Hendrix heard the ugly sound of a bullet hitting flesh.

Oh, God, the third man.

He rolled, clawing beneath his shirt for his own gun, expecting any second to feel the shock of a hit.

He came to a stop, his gun swinging toward the black hole of the door.

There he was! In the doorway!

Hendrix leveled his gun. But his finger refused to pull the trigger. Why? Then he saw why. The man was already falling! A rifle fell to the floor with a clatter an instant before the thud of the man's body.

Hendrix jerked his head around to look at Ramos. The agent stood with his gun clutched in both hands, his eyes wide.

Hendrix picked up Cadaver's .45 and got to his feet. "You okay?" he said to Ramos.

Ramos' big eyes swung to Hendrix, but his hands kept his gun pointed at the fallen man as though they didn't believe his eyes.

"I saw the gun," Ramos said. "I couldn't see him, but I saw the gun. The idiot stuck it out through the door before he fired."

Hendrix, clutching a gun in each hand, leaped toward the door. "Keep an eye on 'im," he gritted.

The woman was off the porch running toward the car. Her hands were empty so Hendrix ran after her. Beside the car, Red Beard was lying on his back in the dirt, and Brent was kneeling over Duval.

Hendrix groaned in anguish. Oh, Jesus. Let him be okay!

To his vast relief, Duval sat up with Brent's help. At the same time, the girl gave a scream and tried to snatch up Red Beard's gun. Hendrix leaped past Duval and Brent, and smacked her on the wrist with the butt of his gun. She yelped and dropped the pistol. Hendrix pushed her away and shoved Cadaver's .45 in his pocket so he could pick up Red Beard's pistol.

He turned to Duval. "You okay?"

Duval nodded, grimacing. "Yeah, I guess so. Ramos?"

"He's okay."

Hendrix looked at Brent who was leaning against the side of the car staring at the girl kneeling beside Red Beard, her face in her hands. Red Beard's eyes were staring into the sun. He had three closely spaced bullet holes in his shirt over his heart.

"Nice shooting," he told Brent.

Without looking at Hendrix, Brent said, "He tried to kill me."

"Yeah. It was a rip all the way." He jerked his thumb toward the Cherokee. "Get the hell out."

Brent, riding an adrenaline high that made him feel as though he was flying, sprinted past the girl, yanked open the door of the Cherokee and threw himself behind the wheel. He started the engine and spun rooster tails of dirt as he charged away. Behind him he heard the sound of two shots, fired for the girl's benefit.

Tony Ramos came out of the house carrying the bag of white powder in one hand and the rifle in the other. "A good bust," he said.

Hendrix stared out across the dozing desert where the sun still shimmered as though nothing had happened. "Yeah," he said. "A good bust. Ten seconds of fun and ten hours of making reports."

Duval snorted. "Ain't that the truth."

Driving the Cherokee as fast as he dared on the rutted dirt road, Brent tried to generate some degree of satisfaction. The bust had produced the desired effect. The girl had seen him run. He was branded now as a dealer.

One thing puzzled him. Where was the remorse that was supposed to make him sick to his stomach for having just killed a man. The feeling failed to come. This was probably how a soldier felt after having killed an enemy in battle. He felt no connection to the lump of flesh that was now lying in the hot sun. It had been a non-entity then, and it was a non-entity now. That's all it would ever be.

Maybe sickening reproach would come later when he had time to think. But, somehow, remembering the sound of the gun booming beside his head, he didn't think it would.

Chapter Fifteen

"SIT DOWN, JAIME," Frankie said, and Ortega perched on the front edge of a leather armchair. "You want a drink?"

"Yeah. I could use one."

At the bar in the corner of his office, Frankie poured himself a glass of Cuervo Special and one for Ortega. The floor quivered as he crossed to Ortega and handed him the drink, and it shuddered when he flopped into his desk chair. He lit one of his black Cuban cigars, and cigar in one hand and glass of tequila in the other, he smiled at Ortega.

"What is it, *amigo?* You said *muy importante.*"

"Yeah." Ortega cleared his throat. He didn't want to rush this. It wasn't often he had such good cards to play. And these cards should put him back solidly in Frankie's corner. "It's about Thomas. Brent Thomas."

Frankie's eyes chilled and his hand holding the cigar stopped half way to his mouth. "Yeah?" he said softly. "What about Brent?"

Ortega licked his lips as he tried to read Frankie's thoughts. Frankie was no fool. He was well aware there was no love lost between him and Brent. "You told me yesterday to keep an eye on him."

Frankie didn't move and Ortega edged forward a little more. You never knew how Frankie was going to take bad news. He might look soft with all that flab, but underneath he was as bad an *hombre* as Ortega had ever seen, and anybody raised on the Chicano/Black border around southeast L.A. had seen all the really bad guys. "Remember?" he added.

Frankie remembered all right. Yesterday when he'd stopped by the DEA office, he'd been badly shaken when Hendrix told him about a bust they'd made in Antelope Valley. Frankie had been only mildly interested until Hendrix had told him about one of the traffickers who'd gotten away—a young, blonde guy, who for some reason, reminded Hendrix of their army buddy Brent Thomas.

While Frankie was certain it couldn't have been Brent, he'd asked Ortega if Brent had been at the gym all morning. When Ortega had said no—that Brent had been gone a couple of hours—Frankie had told Ortega to keep an eye on him.

"Yeah," he said to Ortega. "I remember. So what?"

"So okay. I saw him standing by his locker this morning. He looked funny. You know, like he was trying to hid something. So when he went to lunch, I checked it out. He was trying to ditch something all right."

From his pocket, Ortega took two small glassine envelopes full of white powder and tossed them on Frankie's desk. "These," he said with a hard smile.

Frankie's eyes flicked to the envelopes, then back to Ortega. He had to use all his iron control to keep his dismay from showing. What the shit was the stupid kid doing?

He took a sip of tequila, a large sip. During an almost sleepless night, he'd almost convinced himself that the guy Hendrix had seen couldn't have been Brent. Now this. It was a bomb because if Brent was a dope head, there went any hope of a championship.

Ortega mistook Frankie's silence for disbelief. "It's coke, man," he said. "Two one-ounce baggies."

Frankie knew full well what it was. The thought churning through his mind was that he wished it was grass. A hit of marihuana wouldn't be too bad. But coke? Shit. He took a long drag on his cigar as though the aromatic smoke could sooth his pain. "Did you say anything to him?"

"Hell, no. I came straight up here."

A possible solution to the problem spun free of the churning thoughts and Frankie smiled. "Does he look like a user to you?"

Ortega blinked, unable to comprehend the reason for Frankie's smile. "Shit, I don't know. He'd have to be an idiot."

"That's what I figure. And I don't think he's an idiot."

"So what the fuck was he doing with it? You think he found it?"

"I think he's dealing it."

An expression of incredulity crossed Ortega's face. "Dealing? In L.A.? We'd know about it if he was."

Frankie waved his cigar, suddenly very happy. "*Amigo*, you might've solved a problem for me. Yes, I think this is going to work out all right."

Ortega sank back in the chair and Frankie could practically read his mind. If Brent was dealing, he'd been lying to Frankie. And Frankie didn't like liars. He didn't like them so much they usually ended up dead. So why was he so happy?

Frankie opened his desk drawer and swept the two baggies into the drawer. "Don't say anything about this. I'll talk to him."

Ortega slowly got up and went to the door. He turned before going out. "If you kill him, can I do it?"

Frankie laughed. "Who said anything about killing? He's going to bring me a championship."

Ortega stared at him a moment as though he'd lost his mind. Then he went out, closing the door softly. Frankie continued to chuckle. Poor Jaime. He had to think he'd scored brownie points by catching Brent with the baggies. But he didn't have to worry about Brent taking over his job. Not yet.

THAT NIGHT AFTER he was off work, Brent was in the middle of his weight work when Frankie came in to watch him. Brent had been wondering how long it would take Frankie to show up. Brent had made certain Ortega had seen him put the baggies in his locker. When he'd checked later, they were gone. And Ortega would've gone straight to Frankie, hoping to get Brent's ass thrown out. Or even get a bullet in his head.

He continued his rep of bench presses while trying to read Frankie's expression. Which was it going to be—a chewing out or a bullet? If it was the latter, it probably wouldn't happen here. Frankie must have come to talk. Good. That's what he wanted, too.

Brent had worked his way up to pressing three hundred pounds and he was pushing through the burning pain in his deltoids.

"Burn it," Frankie said. "You can do it. Smooth, smooth. Don't bounce it."

Brent finished the set and relaxed, breathing hard, feeling the pain replaced by a pleasant warmth as blood surged through his strained muscles.

When Frankie still didn't say anything, Brent moved to a Nautilus machine and began working on his legs.

Frankie watched for a moment before he said, "You left your locker open today."

Brent interrupted his routine for a moment as though fright had suddenly hit him, which wasn't too far from the truth. "Yeah?" he said. "Did I break a rule?"

Frankie took the two baggies out of his pocket and held them in front of Brent. "Somebody could've taken these."

Brent stopped his workout. He stared at the baggies as though wanting to deny their existence. Then he clamped his mouth shut and started another set, working slow and smooth.

"You using it?" Frankie asked.

Brent waited an appropriate beat of time before he gritted, "No."

Frankie sighed as though a weight had been taken off his shoulders. "I believe you, my friend. I believe you. So, if you don't use the junk and you've got this much, it means one thing. Correct?"

Again, Brent stopped. His legs felt weak. It still wasn't too late. Even if he admitted the dope belonged to him, he could still walk away.

Frankie might be disappointed, but he wouldn't know the truth. The hollow place in his stomach seemed to swallow him and he heard his voice say, "Yeah, Frankie. I'm dealing. So what?"

Frankie shook his head, his eyes sad. "Why, *amigo?* Why?"

Brent drew a deep breath. There's no backing out now. "Why else? Money." He started another rep as though the subject was unimportant.

"You've got money. Your share of the Molino purse was a hell of a lot more than you made in Kansas."

"A drop in the bucket. I got bills you wouldn't believe." Brent finished the rep and picked up a towel and began drying off. "In a way, Frankie, I did it for you."

This time Frankie couldn't hide his surprise. "Me?"

"Yeah. I know how much you've got your heart set on me fighting. But you know I don't make a hell of a lot. It was either take a second job and cut down the training or find a way to make some easy money."

"Easy!" Frankie snorted. "How much business do you do?"

Brent felt a thin chill of victory. Frankie was taking the bait. Brent bit his lip so he wouldn't smile. "Not much. You know, this and that."

Frankie's control snapped and his breath exploded. "You dumb son-of-a-bitch. If you get busted, it could ruin everything, you know that? You've done a good job here. Everybody likes you. They respect you."

"Shit," Brent interjected. "It's a damn dream, Frankie. I'll never be a champ."

"Forget the fucking champion." Frankie grabbed the towel out of Brent's hand and slammed it on the floor. "Damn it, Brent. You could screw things up in a way you don't even know about."

Brent fought an impulse to shout that he did know. He knew every fucking thing. All of it.

Through gritted teeth he managed to say, "I won't get busted. It's easy."

Crash!

In raging fury, Frankie pushed over a rack of weights, the heavy barbells smashing to the floor. "Like shit!" he shouted. "It ain't easy. It's hard! Damn fuckin' hard! You *stupido!* You've got to be smart. You got to take your time. Most of all, you got to be lucky!"

Catching the opening, Brent said, "How the hell would you know? You've got it made."

Frankie's face contorted and his shoulders shook. Brent couldn't tell if he was laughing or crying—or building to a killing rage. "How do I know? How do I know?"

Brent realized that Frankie was laughing, but there was no humor in it.

"How much do you deal?"

Strength drained out of Brent as he realized Frankie wasn't going to attack and he sat down on a bench, his head bent, his hands clinched between his legs. "An ounce a week. Sometimes two."

"So you take in about two, three grand a month. Shit! You risk your career, your whole fuckin' life for that? Stupid." Frankie turned away, then quickly turned back. "Where do you get it?"

Brent shrugged. "I get it. People I know." He was intentionally evasive. What was he going to say? The DEA?

"Trustworthy? Reliable? Competent?" Frankie's voice was hard and flat.

"Sure. I trust them."

"Like those idiots yesterday?"

Brent looked up at Frankie, blinking as though he were surprised. "You know about that?"

Frankie's face worked, and for a minute, Brent though he was going to spit on the floor.

"Idiot!" he snapped. He put his thumb and finger close together. "You came this close to getting busted. Or killed, like that other *stupido.*"

"Yeah, but I wasn't! I guess I was lucky like you said."

"Lucky! Shit!" Frankie shook his fist in front of Brent's nose. "Don't trust nobody. You deal in shit, you don't trust nobody. *Comprende?*"

Brent nodded. He'd expected anger and disappointment from Frankie, but the depth of his rage astonished Brent. The man was on the edge of a stroke. "Yeah, sure, Frankie," he said. "What do you want me to do?"

"Do? What the shit do you think I want you to do? I want you to stop fooling around with that God damned junk."

"Yeah, but—what do I do for money?"

Frankie moved away, his hands working. This was it, Brent thought. He was either dirty and was going to invite Brent in, or he was clean and would have to come up with something else. Brent held his breath hoping Frankie would prove the guys in the DEA were a bunch of idiots.

When Frankie turned back, Brent's face was calm but his stomach was a Gordian knot. "I've been thinking." Frankie paused and the knot tightened while Frankie made up his mind. "How would you like to move up a little in my organization?"

Brent suppressed a sigh as all the hope he'd been holding in check drained away. He fought to keep despair from his voice. "You mean like working in your restaurant? No thanks, Frankie."

"Not the restaurant. I have...other interests."

Brent clinched his fists. How did actors manage to keep the believability in their voice and manner when they were dying inside? He was being pulled apart by relief because he was succeeding, and by sorrow because it also meant he could no longer hope it was all a mistake and that Frankie was Snow White.

Still, he cautioned himself, clinging to a faint thread of hope, Frankie's 'other interests' could be anything. "Depends," he said. "If you want me to keep on fighting, I can't be working in an office some place."

Frankie laughed, a short, hard bark. "No office." Frankie sat down on the bench-press bench. "My friend, have you ever wondered where I got the money for this place, the restaurant?"

"I never gave it much thought."

"Not from the *barrio*, I can tell you that. I got it in Pakistan."

Brent squinted at Frankie. "Pakistan? You mean when we were in the army?"

Frankie nodded. "People were making fortunes over there, *amigo*. I got in on it. It's still working for me."

The knot was gone from Brent's stomach replaced by a hollow emptiness as though he'd lost something irreplaceable. "How? The only guys making money were the big contractors. And you sure as hell weren't one of them."

"There were others. Bigger."

"Yeah, but they were drug dealers and..." Brent let his voice trail off. He put shock into his voice as he said, "Jesus! You're not into that?"

Frankie was watching him, unblinking, his eyes hard, flat. "Would such a thing bother you?"

Brent shook his head, although it did bother him more than Frankie would ever know. He began working the Nautilus again, but his muscles felt as though they'd been drained of more than energy. "Why should it?" he said. "These days it seems like everybody is picking up a little extra dough."

"That's right," Frankie chuckled. "A little extra."

"So how would I fit in?"

"One of the problems in this business, my friend, is supply. That's where the big money is. I'm sure you know that. The street dealer like you who sells five-dollar bags don't make shit. The guy who handles the pure stuff, who can do the big cut, he's the one making the big money. Right?"

"Yeah. Right."

"So that's the end you get into."

Brent stopped working so he could concentrate on what Frankie was saying. He noticed Frankie wasn't committing himself. He was weasel wording, not trusting Brent all the way. So okay. If Frankie wanted to ease him in gradually, that was fine with him.

"So where would I fit in?"

"Simple. You'll be a courier."

"A courier? How can I do that?"

"They don't check fighters. You can handle a lot of pure stuff."

Brent forced a smile and resumed his workout. What was the old expression? The show must go on even if you did feel like you were dying. From some unknown source inside, he dredged up a fake enthusiasm. "Pretty damn good, Frankie. A perfect alibi."

Frankie nodded. "You got it."

Although the truth about Frankie now sat on Brent's shoulders like vultures, in a way he had to admire the man. Frankie had taken a bad situation and turned it into an asset. He still had Brent fighting and he also had a new courier, one who could travel anywhere in the world without suspicion. He'd probably been doing the same thing with Ortega, using his bodybuilding contests as cover. And Jennifer? Was she also a courier?

"All right," he said as though making up his mind, although his road had been carved in rock the moment Hendrix and Duval had walked into the gym in Kansas. "I'll do it."

"Good." Frankie heaved himself to his feet. "Lay off the dope. Concentrate on your work. You'll soon have more money than you ever dreamed of."

Brent laughed. "That'll be the day."

"Believe me, my man. You stick with me, you'll have it all. Carmen likes you. I think Maria likes you." He stared at Brent a moment. "And that presents a problem."

Maria! Is she involved? The thought turned his muscles to stone. Whatever Frankie was going to say now wouldn't be good. "A problem? How?"

The pupils of Frankie's eyes were like chips of black granite as he stared at Brent. "She knows nothing of this. It must stay that way."

Brent's shoulders sagged as tension drained from his body like water from a ruptured dam. He hadn't realized it, but fear about Maria's involvement had been building to an impossible pressure. He wondered if he could've continued with the assignment if Frankie had said she was part of his operation. The thought of Maria in prison was an image he couldn't endure. Now, thank God, he could continue knowing that she was out of it.

"I'm glad to know that," he said, relieved that for once he didn't have to put on an act.

"So you don't see her no more. You don't even talk to her. That way she stays out."

Brent felt his body sag. It was a odd feeling, and he thought that this must be what it felt like to be shot, to feel your life drain away and not be able to stop it. "That..." He had to stop and draw a breath. "That's going to be tough, Frankie."

"I understand. But it must be done."

Brent licked his lips, his mind roiling, searching for a way out. "What if I say no?"

Frankie stiffened as though he hadn't heard Brent correctly. His hard eyes seemed to sink deeper into his round face. When he spoke, his voice was soft and dark like the body of a black widow spider. "You work for me, *amigo*, you don't say no. Ever."

"Suppose I say no to that, too?"

The look that crossed Frankie's face made Brent feel as though someone had walked across his grave. "That's up to you." Frankie's voice was almost a whisper. "But you still don't see Maria. You don't talk to her. Nothing!"

Brent knew if he did say no, he might not talk to anybody again. Desperately, he tried to sort through his options. He could, of course, turn and run back to the safety of the DEA. Or even back to the safety of Kansas. But even that might not be far enough to stop Frankie from closing his mouth.

And every one of his options meant losing Maria.

If he ran, it also meant his loss would be for nothing.

So he laughed and said, "Okay, boss. I just wanted to see what you'd say."

Frankie's return smile had all the sincerity of a hyena grinning at a lamb. "Okay, *amigo*. But you don't see Maria. *Comprende?*"

"*Comprendo.*" Despite his effort at control, bitterness crept into Brent's voice. Searching for a way to defuse the charged atmosphere, he added, "There are plenty of other fish in the ocean."

Frankie's cold stare continued a second before his face broke into a smile. "Damn right. I wish I was your age. And size. You'll have all you can handle."

"It'll be a great way to die."

Frankie laughed and took a cigar from his jacket pocket. "Later, *amigo*. You're in training. The main thing right now for you is to concentrate on the fight. You got to cut out the women." He bit off the end of the cigar and spit it out before he started to light it with a lighter. "We'll talk more about this later."

"Okay, Frankie."

Frankie's eyes hardened. "Just remember what I said." He walked away, trailing a cloud of pungent smoke.

Brent resumed his workout, but his heart wasn't in it. Could he give up Maria? In a way, a forced separation might be for the best. It was only a matter of time before Frankie was busted and his dope dealing was revealed. Maria might be shocked and disappointed in her father, but she wouldn't hate her father the way she would hate him.

He had nothing to offer her but heartbreak. And, truthfully, her heartbreak could never be as deep as his own. It was best he end their relationship while it was still possible. Frankie didn't know it, but he'd done Brent a favor.

So why did he feel so miserable? He knew the answer. The raft was getting close to the falls. When it went over, it could very likely take him with it.

Chapter Sixteen

THE NEXT NIGHT, it was six-thirty by the time Brent had made the drive from East L.A. to Fairfax Boulevard where he was to meet Hendrix and Duval. The trip seemed like a waste of his dinner hour. He'd called the two agents to tell them their plan was working, but they didn't want to discuss it on the telephone and had set up the meet.

The slow drive in the L.A. traffic had given Brent time to think—time he didn't want. His thoughts were full of black holes that he fought to keep from overwhelming him.

One of the black holes was a growing guilt about having killed a man. Never mind that the man had been trying to kill him. Never mind that if he'd murdered Brent, it wouldn't have bothered the son-of-a-bitch one iota. This was another bitter memory that would take a long time to disappear.

Another growing black hole was Frankie and his organization. But he was diving into this one with his eyes wide open, knowing it could rip him to shreds. It had already stripped him of Maria and was slowly stripping away his moral ethics. It was becoming easier to lie. He was actually getting good at it. And he was already conditioning his conscience to trafficking in drugs.

The saving grace was that none of it was his fault. It was all designed to trap Frankie.

But how many lives would he have to ruin in order to do it? Every delay ran up the score. The sooner Frankie was brought down, the better.

Brent's black thoughts were still swirling when he pulled into the parking lot beside the designated liquor store. There was no sign of Hendrix's bronze Camaro, so Brent pulled up close to the building, shut the engine off and waited.

He wasn't surprised the agents were late. It seemed to be de rigueur in California for everyone to be late. And even more typical for government employees. Back in Kansas they might be considered hicks, but it was considered bad manners to keep someone waiting.

Ten minutes later, just when Brent was beginning to think he'd made a mistake in the location or that the agents weren't going to show, he saw the bronze Camaro pull out of a parking space half-way up the block on the opposite side of the street and nose out into the traffic. Across from the liquor store, it made a left turn into the lot. Brent had to smile. Suspicious bastards. They'd been waiting for him, watching to make sure he hadn't been followed.

Hendrix and Duval got out of the Camaro and walked to Brent's car. Each was dressed in worn jeans and long-sleeved T-shirts with the shirt tails hanging out. Hendrix was wearing black basketball shoes and Duval had on scuffed western boots. Brent reminded himself that if he ever needed help to look for a guy wearing jeans and cowboy boots with his shirt hanging out because he was probably a cop.

"Hi, sport," Duval said as he got in the back seat.

Hendrix slid into the front passenger seat. "Hi, buddy. How's it going?"

Brent said hi and added, "Okay, I guess. Like I told you on the phone."

"So Frankie took the bait."

"Looks that way. He gave me hell about dealing. Said it was stupid."

"He should know," Duval agreed.

"Yeah, but it still didn't mean anything 'til he said I could ruin everything."

"What everything?"

"That was my thought. He could've been talking about the boxing– By the way, he's got me set up for a bout in Acapulco."

Duval shook a limp hand. "Acapulco. Hey, hey."

"But that wasn't it, huh?" Hendrix said.

"No. He was talking about his organization. The upshot was he invited me in."

Hendrix and Duval both leaned forward. "He admitted he was dealing?"

Brent took a deep breath. His next words could turn the key on Frankie's cell. "Yeah."

Hendrix and Duval glanced at one another. There was no satisfaction in their expressions. They probably were as disappointed as he. But now the game had changed from trying to learn if Frankie was dealing to trying to get evidence to convict.

"So where do you fit in?" Hendrix asked.

"I'm supposed to be some kind of courier."

"Good."

"You said you've got a bout coming up in Acapulco," Duval said. "I'll bet it ties in."

"Right," Hendrix added. "Mexican cartels have turned into major players. They've taken over most of the drug distribution business from the Columbian cartels. They've got pipelines that traffic in all the biggies—cocaine, heroin, marijuana, amphetamines."

"What about the Mexican *Federales?*" Brent said. "Are they cooperating?"

"Yeah. But they're having their problems, too. There's a lot of corruption."

Duval said, "And damn near every member of a cartel is related, either by blood or by marriage. It's possible—in fact, it's damn likely—that Frankie or his wife, Carmen, are related to his supplier."

"Yeah," Hendrix said. "You should be very flattered Frankie invited you to be part of his organization without the blood connection."

Brent's rueful smile was filled with pain. Frankie had cut off any possibility of that happening when he insisted he stay away from Maria. "Yeah," he said. "I guess I'm just lucky."

"See if you can find out how he brings the dope in," Duval added. "It's got to come in bulk. Probably goes to a factory where the cuts are made. See if you can get a line on that."

Brent nodded. "I'll try. But I don't think he trusts me that far. Not yet." His voice sounded weary even to his own ears.

Duval and Hendrix glanced at each other again. Hendrix's voice was softer when he asked, "How are you making out with his daughter? Maybe she can give you a lead."

"She doesn't know a damn thing," Brent snapped. "Leave her out of it."

Hendrix took out a pack of cigarettes and lit one, blowing the smoke out the open window.

Duval rubbed his face. "You sure about that?"

"Yeah. Frankie ordered me to stay away from her. He doesn't want her involved."

"Oh. Well, I'm glad to hear that."

"Did you bring the baggies?" Hendrix asked.

Brent dug the two glassine bags out of his pocket and handed them to Hendrix. The agent took a pen and a folded sheet of paper from his shirt pocket. He unfolded the paper. It was the DEA 12 form Brent had signed for the dope. Hendrix signed that he'd received the two baggies and handed the paper to Brent. "Keep this somewhere it can't be found."

Brent took the paper and refolded it. "Yeah, sure. I'll hide it with my gun and badge."

Hendrix blew a cloud of smoke out the window before he said, "Look, kid. We know how you're feeling—"

Brent turned his head to stare at Hendrix. "You don't know a damn thing about how I'm feeling."

"Yeah, well, that's true. We're all different. But none of us are robots with no feelings. When you're working U.C. you're bound to get involved. They've even got a name for it. What the hell is it, Marc?"

"Stockholm syndrome. It happens when people are held hostage for a long time. After a while, they begin identifying with their captors. They might even get to liking them if they aren't too brutal."

"That's what's happening to you, Brent," Hendrix said. "You met the family. You find out they're nice people, just like the neighbors back home so to speak. Then you start to wonder what the hell you're doing to them and maybe if it's right or not. Well, let me tell you, kid, I've been there. So has Marc and most agents. It's a shitty thing."

"A fuckin' bitch," Duval interjected.

"Shit," Hendrix said. "Hitler was a monster, but his father and mother could've been the nicest people in the world. But does that mean we let Hitler go on killing millions of people because we don't want to hurt his parents?"

Brent sighed. "Okay. You can skip the lecture. I get the point."

"I know, but let me finish. To get back to Frankie... What he's doing is wrong, legally and morally. Look at what happens to people who use the junk he sells."

"Not to mention the people whose lives are ruined even if they don't take it," Duval said. "Like the addict's family and friends."

"Why didn't they say anything about this at the academy?" Brent asked bitterly. "I never would've gotten involved."

"Yeah, I know," Duval said. "I really get pissed at the academy. They spend hundreds of hours teaching you how to catch the bad guys, but they completely ignore how the job affects an agent psychologically and emotionally. They teach you that dope dealers are such bad asses and how they're ruining thousands of lives and costing the country billions of dollars. Then you go U.C. and you find out they aren't so damned bad. They're a lot like you are. The only difference is that they sell dope." He shook his head. "It can be a shock."

"Yeah," Brent said. "It sure as hell can."

"But let me remind you. Just who is causing their families the pain and suffering when we bust them, huh? You? Shit, no! It's them. They screwed up their own lives and the lives of everybody around them. Not you. Not me. They did."

"I don't know," Brent said. "What's it all for? It's like the Gorgon's heads. You cut off one head and two take its place. Maybe they're right. Maybe we should legalize drugs."

Hendrix spit out the window. "Shit. The only people who want to legalize are users or ghouls after the money. They don't give a shit about addicted babies or overdosed kids or people trying to do their jobs while they're high as a kite."

"People get high on alcohol and that's legal."

"Most people who drink don't do it to get high," Duval said. "Some do, yeah. And we've got to control them. But everybody who takes dope does it for one thing—to get stoned. You want to make it easier for them? I sure as hell don't."

"Yeah," Brent said. "I know. It's just that...what a shitty way to make a living."

"Yeah," Duval said. "We're the thin, brown line."

"Hang in there, kid," Hendrix said. "It won't be long now. All we need is some hard evidence."

Duval looked hard at Brent's set expression. "You're gonna be all right, aren't you, buddy?"

Brent's head snapped up and his disgust with himself and his job spilled out, "I said I'd do it. So get off my back. Okay?"

"Okay, okay," Hendrix said. He opened the car door and got out. Duval did the same from the back seat. Before he closed the door, Hendrix bent down and said, "Don't call us from Mexico. Wait 'til you get back."

"Jesus," Brent said. "You can't even phone now. What's the world coming to?"

"It's coming to what shitheels like Frankie make it," Duval said with a harshness that made Brent look at him sharply.

"Yeah," Hendrix agreed. "A fuckin' cesspool."

The two agents went back to their car and drove away. Brent sat thinking about what the agents had said. He was truly surprised at the depth of their anger. Like most people, he'd given little or no thought to the feelings of the agents. What was it that made them stick with a job where they had to suppress so many of their finer instincts, and instead, deal with the assholes of the world...assholes who'd kill them if they could?

They might say they took the job for the excitement, the desire to get away from a 9-to-5 desk job. But that kind of shallow motivation would soon wear off, especially if you got shot at a couple of times, or a buddy got his brains all over your clothes. There had to be something else—something inside that made you care if the world became a cesspool or not.

Brent started his car and headed back to the gym. He had at least two more hours of working out to do before he could go home. As he drove, he wondered about the depth of his own commitment. He felt like the little Dutch boy with his finger in a hole in a dike trying to hold back the rising tide of the sea. Only in his case it was the rising swill of a cesspool.

He wondered if he had the fortitude, the commitment to keep his finger in the dike. He had been shot at and not folded. But worse than being shot at was the loss of Maria. Was the job worth that? At the moment, he wasn't so sure.

Chapter Seventeen

THE THREE-HOUR flight from Los Angeles to Acapulco, Mexico should've been among the happiest hours of Brent's life. He'd accomplished some of his major goals. First, he was solidly entrenched in Frankie's organization. Second, tomorrow night he'd be in a fight that would put him even more solidly in Frankie's corner. In addition, he was traveling—something he had always wanted to do—flying first class, sitting next to Jennifer, a beautiful girl with an exciting body and a fascinating personality. To some people's way of thinking, he had it all.

Except that images of Maria kept intruding. He couldn't help but wonder if there was some way he could resign from the DEA, break away from Frankie, and get some kind of a job in L.A. that would allow him to see her. They'd have to meet in secret. Frankie would go ballistic if he found out. If Frankie really was obsessive about keeping Maria innocent of his drug trafficking, he could never allow a renegade from his organization to have dates with his daughter. He would do whatever was necessary to remove the threat.

So he was stymied. He couldn't quit the DEA and he couldn't quit Frankie. His only hope—and it was a futile hope—was that after Frankie was busted, Maria would allow him to see her. He had to cling to that. It was all he had.

Brent sat back in his seat with a sigh. Stupid! Stupid! She would hate him. Whatever happened, he was finished.

"You sound like you're carrying the weight of the world."

Brent turned his head to look at Jennifer who was sitting in the window seat. "I guess I am. I was thinking about the fight. In about forty-eight hours, I'll probably be a basket case in a Mexican hospital."

Jennifer reached over and ran her fingers gently across his jaw. "Don't let anything happen to your face. I like it the way it is."

Brent noticed Ortega staring at them from his seat next to Frankie directly across the aisle. Ortega hadn't been happy with the seating arrangement. But it had been Frankie's idea, not Brent's. Throughout most of the flight Frankie and Ortega had been conversing in low tones. Brent wished that he knew what they were discussing. From time to time, Ortega's voice had risen in an angry retort, but Frankie had quickly brought the level of their conversation down so Brent had been unable to hear a thing.

"So do I," he now told Jennifer. "But I think our friend Jaime might enjoy seeing it rearranged."

Jennifer's glanced flicked to Ortega. "Oh, forget him. He hates everybody."

"Everybody but you, I think."

"That's his idea, not mine."

Brent's smile at her was sincere "I'm glad to hear that."

The engines changed their tone and the plane gently nosed downward in a slow descent. Jennifer looked out the window, "Are we there?"

"I guess so. Have you been here before?"

"Sure. Lots of times. Want a guide?"

Lots of times? With Frankie? He was almost certain she was one of Frankie's couriers. But why come to Acapulco so many times? Unless it was a major buying point for Frankie. Maybe Jennifer could supply some of the answers.

"Yeah," he said. "I don't know a *tostado* from a *taco*."

Jennifer laughed and linked her hands around his arm. "Acapulco is really a fun place. The fight isn't until tomorrow night so that gives us the rest of today and tomorrow." She looked into Brent's eyes and touched her lips with the tip of her tongue. "I'll show you the sights."

Brent grinned at her. There was something very exciting about a beautiful woman making it clear she was attracted to you even if you had no intention of taking advantage of the implied offer. "Wonderful," he said. "Sort of eat, drink, and make merry."

"Oh, no," she said. "No eating and drinking."

"And no making merry?"

She grinned at him. "You're in training. Remember?" Then her eyes grew hot. "Until after the fight."

Brent was still trying to shake off the feeling he was teetering on the edge of an even deeper pit of trouble when the plane landed at Acapulco's AeroMexico Terminal. The smart thing to do was steer well clear of Jennifer. All he needed now was to have Ortega stick a knife in his ribs.

When Brent stepped out of the plane, he walked into humid heat laden with the scent of the nearby sea.

Leaving Ortega to make arrangements for their luggage and equipment that had been shipped, they boarded a waiting limousine that took them along a winding boulevard called *Carretera Escénica.* During the six mile drive from the airport, Brent gazed out the taxi window at the palm trees, the structures and the Spanish language signs. If it hadn't been for the humidity and the nearness of the ocean and the hills, he could've been in California. Everything looked the same, yet somehow, different.

Frankie saw Brent's interest. "This isn't Mexico, my friend. Too many hotels. Too many tourists. If we had more time, I'd show you some of the real Mexico."

"Maybe we could take a couple of days after the fight," Brent said. "If I can still move."

Frankie laughed as though Brent had made a real joke. "Maybe next time, *amigo.* This time we've got business."

Brent turned back to the window thinking about what Frankie had said. The 'business' would have to be about dope. If he could get a line on who Frankie was meeting, it would be a big step in bringing him down.

When he saw the *Las Brisas* Hotel, Brent knew why it was considered by many to be the most elegant and certainly the most expensive hotel in Mexico. Multi-tiered, it was situated on the side of a hill overlooking the beautiful Acapulco Bay. Everything was in shades of pink—the building, the uniforms of the staff, even the lines in the road leading to the hotel. Masses of pink bougainvillea grew on the sides of the pink stuccoed walls.

Although the hotel had three large swimming pools, Brent's air-conditioned suite had its own small pool on a private terrace. The bathroom was tiled in imported pink marble. The bedspread and pillows were also pink. *Mariachi* music, that somehow seemed pink, oozed from speakers in the walls.

Standing on the terrace, Brent had a perfect view of the city across the vivid blue waters of the bay where he could see people water skiing and parasailing. The wide beaches that encompassed the bay were dotted with people soaking up the sun or relaxing under colorful umbrellas or small umbrella-like structures thatched with palm fronds. Barefoot venders tramped through the sand offering T-shirts, ice cream, and cold drinks.

It looked like a fairy-tale existence if one could afford it. As Frankie had said, all Brent had to do was stick with him and it could all be his.

Or almost all. His daughter was not part of the dream.

Brent's telephone buzzed and he went back inside. It was Jennifer asking if he was ready for a swim. He laughed and said sure. He was in the land of fun. Why not enjoy it while he was capable of doing so.

"Good," she said. "Fifteen minutes. My pool."

"Your pool?"

"Sure. Didn't you get one?"

Brent glanced out the sliding glass door at his terrace pool. "Well, yes. But—"

"Okay, then. I'm in six-twenty-three. Right next door if you get lost."

She hung up, leaving Brent staring at the phone in his hand. He'd been wanting a chance to speak to Jennifer alone. He'd have to be careful about his questions, but he'd like to find out how much she knew about Frankie's operations. If she was working as a courier, she might know how he got his dope across the border.

He found Jennifer stretched out in a lounge chair beside her pool, a glass in her hand. A large plastic bottle of Diet Pepsi was in an ice bucket on a table by her side. She was wearing a thong bikini; her sun glasses covered a larger area than the wispy bra over her marvelous breasts. Apparently she hadn't been lying about having been to Acapulco many times because her body was warmed by a golden tan.

With her long hair flowing down her back, she stunned Brent with her beauty. But instead of being attracted, he was struck with a quick, burning anger that anyone with so much beauty and so much intelligence could throw it away dealing in drugs. It was a dead end street that, sooner or later, had to lead to prison or personal destruction.

When she saw him, she pushed her sun glasses up. "Hi. You got here in a hurry."

"Who wouldn't?"

She laughed and poured him a glass of Pepsi. "Sorry about the drink. If you want something stronger..."

Brent shook his head. "This is fine."

Brent wore a plain white T-shirt in addition to his bathing trunks and Jennifer studied him for a second. "We've got to do something about your tan. You look like an albino."

Brent looked down at his white legs. "I don't get out in the sun much. Frankie keeps my nose to the grindstone."

Jennifer put down her drink, and in one fluid move, got to her feet. She took the beach towel from her lounge chair and spread it on the pool deck. "Stretch out," she said.

Brent didn't move. "All I need is to climb in the ring tomorrow with a sun burn."

"We can fix that." Jennifer reached into a bag and took out a plastic bottle of sunscreen. "Come on," she ordered.

Brent looked at her wide smile for an instant before he stripped off his T-shirt, then stretched out on his stomach on the towel. Jennifer knelt astride him and poured lotion on his back and began spreading it with slow strokes of her palms.

Brent closed his eyes and gave himself to the intense pleasure. Her fingers moved gently across his back like warm lips, making it impossible for him to think of anything except the touch of her hands and the pressure of her thighs against his hips. The warmth of her hands laved his body with sensuous heat, and he could feel an erection begin to form. He considered ending the encounter. He had to stop this before it got out of hand. But somehow the part of him that wanted to resist was overwhelmed by the power of her touch.

Still, he felt a brief sense of disappointed relief when she slid back and began applying lotion to his legs. But when her probing fingers moved up the inside of his thighs, he groaned and lifted his hips to relieve the painful pressure.

"Am I hurting you?" Her voice was a husky whisper with a hint of laughter.

"No, no," he said. "I just had to...uh...get comfortable."

She gave his bottom a gentle whack. "Okay. Turn over."

"Turn over?" Brent didn't think that was a good idea. Not a good idea at all.

But Jennifer whacked him again. "Turn over," she ordered. "I won't look."

So. She knew.

As though his body had a will of its own far removed from any connection to his brain, Brent rolled over and Jennifer began working on his legs. Brent put an arm across his eyes to shield them from the sun and peeked at her. She'd lied. Her eyes were open and her lips were set in a smile.

He shouldn't have looked. The way she was leaning forward caused her breasts to strain at the tiny strip of cloth covering them and he felt his erection harden. Oh, Jesus. He had to end this!

He was tensing to get up when Jennifer moved up to straddle his hips. "Now for the chest," she said. "I hope you're not ticklish."

"I wish to hell I was," he groaned.

She snickered and began rubbing lotion into his chest, drawing her fingers delicately across his nipples and he gasped. "Don't—do—that."

"Okay. This better?"

Her hands left his chest and moved down to caress his stomach and he shuddered, his jaws rigid, unable to answer. When she untied the drawstring of his bathing suit and pulled it from his hips, he was gripped with a delicious expectation that flooded his mind like hot lava. Only for an instant did a vision of Maria intrude and a small part of his mind told him to forget her. For him, she was dead.

Live for today.

Then Jennifer impaled herself with a soft cry and leaned forward and kissed him, her tongue seeking his while her hips began a slow dance and there was no tomorrow.

Chapter Eighteen

THEY SLEPT LATE the next day, luxuriating in warm caresses, exploring the wonder of each other's bodies.

"I heard this is bad for a fighter before a fight," Jennifer murmured at one time.

"I won't be fighting for hours," Brent vaguely remembered answering.

For lunch, they went into the hotel's dining room, but they spotted Frankie sitting in a booth talking to several men who looked like reporters so they found a small coffee shop where they ordered hamburgers and tacos.

Jennifer had grown pensive and suddenly she looked up at Brent, her eyes clouded with concern. "You're part of Frankie's organization, aren't you?"

The question dismayed Brent. Until now he'd been able to put the unpleasant task of interrogating Jennifer out of his mind. Her question was also desponding because it took away any doubt he had about her ties to Frankie's dope trafficking.

"I am now," he said wearily. "As of last week."

"Then you know what he does."

"Some of it. I'm not sure what I'm supposed to do."

"Well, in a way you're already doing it."

"Oh? How?"

"You're helping him bring the stuff in from Mexico."

"He mentioned something about a courier. Is that what you do? Courier?"

She looked away, her face drawn with pain. "Yes. But that's it. I'd never do anything else?" She paused before adding softly, "What about you?"

"You mean dealing?"

"Well, yes."

Brent shrugged. "What's the difference?"

She stared at him as though he'd said something she didn't want to hear. "There's a big difference."

"Is there? You think it's less a crime to steal a quarter than it is to steal a dollar?"

Her voice dripped with bitterness when she said, "Oh, I see. You think a courier is as much a crook as a dealer."

Brent nodded, hoping he was leading the conversation in a direction that would give him more answers. "You got it. In for a penny, in for a pound. So what difference does it make if I try to move up to the really big bucks?"

Jennifer put her hamburger down and stared at it as though it was more interesting to look at than Brent. "You've just ruined my little illusions. All I had to do was leave the country once in a while for a fight or a body-building competition and bring back a little junk. I was only doing what everybody else was doing. No big deal."

"That's right," Brent said, his voice hard. "No big deal."

Jennifer looked up at him. Light from the window made her eyes bright and incredibly blue. "I've thought about quitting but... I like my job at the gym. I like competing. I like the money. I owe all of it to Frankie." She smiled, her lips twisting ruefully. "Now I guess I owe him even more."

"Oh? For what?"

She turned her head to look out the window and her voice was so low he almost missed her saying, "For meeting you."

Brent's dark depression deepened. Another relationship built on lies. He didn't love Jennifer. She was wonderful—a fantastic lover. But he wasn't in love. What had happened between them had been spontaneous, an accident. He didn't intend to let it happen again. She would have reason enough to hate him when she learned the truth without adding the betrayal of love.

When he didn't answer, Jennifer leaned forward and put her hand over his. "I'm sorry, Brent. I didn't mean to make you feel guilty."

Brent bit back a bitter laugh. Guilty? What was one more grain of guilt on top of the mountain already tearing at his gut. "There's nothing to feel guilty about," he said. "Never between you and me."

She smiled at him and her eyes became smoky and heavy-lidded. "Frankie's going to have a party after the fight. Maybe we can have our own."

Brent chuckled. "It might have to be in a hospital room."

"You can fix that," Jennifer said without smiling. "When he hits you, fall down and stay down."

"Good advice." The conversation had taken a turn away from the direction Brent wanted it to go, and he steered it back. "Speaking of Frankie, I'm curious. How does he do it? Get the stuff back? What do these trips have to do with it?"

Jennifer straightened and picked up her hamburger. "I have no idea. I do what Frankie tells me." She was going to take a bite of the hamburger, then paused and her voice became low and bitter as she added, "We all do."

"Did I hear my name?"

Brent looked up to see Frankie approaching. It seemed incredible that a man of Frankie's bulk could have come close enough to overhear Jennifer without Brent seeing him. Brent reminded himself that he couldn't afford to lose himself in a conversation. Not in his occupation.

"Sure, Frankie," Brent said lightly. "We were hoping you'd show up so we could stick you with the check."

Frankie laughed. "Just sign for it. It goes with the room." His eyes flicked between Brent and Jennifer like the shutter of a camera, taking in the picture and filing it in his mind before he pulled up a chair and sat down gingerly, testing the chair for his weight. "I'm glad I found you. I've made arrangements for you to use the hotel fitness center to work out this afternoon."

"Okay," Brent said. "What time is the fight?"

"The main card is at ten."

"Ten? That late?"

"They start late down here. Lots of prelims. It'll give you time for a light workout." His glance turned to Jennifer. "And a nap, if you need one."

Jennifer's face flushed and Frankie grinned.

Brent quickly said, "Tell me about the rules here. Anything I should know?"

"No. Everything's the same. The ref will probably hate your guts." Frankie looked toward the window. "Thank God we've got good weather. You can't always tell down here."

"Good weather? What's that got to do with it?"

"We'll be outside. The only place big enough for a fight this big is the bullring. Good thing it's out of season."

"The bullring," Jennifer murmured. "How appropriate."

Frankie chuckled. "Yeah." He looked at Brent. "You'll have the hotel's exercise room to yourself. If the reporters find you, don't talk to them. I'll take care of that." He pushed to his feet. "I'll pick you up at seven. Okay?"

Brent nodded. "Okay."

Frankie started to move away, then turned back. "I'm having a victory party after the fight."

"What if I lose?"

Frankie shrugged. "Don't come."

Chapter Nineteen

THE NIGHT WAS clear; the weather balmy. A huge moon rode a thin band of clouds. It was a beautiful tropical night—a night for lovers. But for Brent, walking in a blaze of lights toward the ring, romance was the last thing on his mind. Derisive yells, scream, catcalls and whistles came from fanatics jamming the bullring stands and from hundreds of people in chairs that had been set up on the arena sand. Brent wouldn't have been surprised if bottles had come flying out of the crowd toward him.

In contrast to the old robe he'd worn in his first fight, Brent wore a new satin robe with the name and logo of Frankie's gym emblazoned on the back. A towel was draped over his head, its ends tucked inside the collar of his robe.

He stayed close to Frankie's broad back as Frankie led the way, pushing aside people standing in the aisle like the prow of a supertanker pushing through heavy seas. Jennifer was directly behind him while Ortega guarded the rear. Ortega was not happy about his vulnerable position and he kept glancing over his shoulder at the crowd as though expecting an attack.

At the ring, Brent received a quick good luck kiss on the cheek from Jennifer. As he and Ortega climbed through the ropes, the screams from the crowd escalated. There was no sign of his opponent. Traditionally, the challenger entered the ring first. Occasionally, someone would try to psyche out his opponent by upsetting the order, but it seldom worked and was generally considered amateurish.

However, keeping your opponent waiting was acceptable and most champions delayed their entrance, giving the challenger plenty of time to think about the punishment he was going to receive. But Brent was prepared for the tactic, so it failed to bother him. He could use the extra time to acquaint himself with the ring and the atmosphere.

He went to his corner and began a series of exercises designed to keep him loose and to test the ring surface. He noticed that the ring was large, probably twenty feet square, undoubtedly designed to give Cruz maximum room to maneuver. It confirmed what he knew about Cruz. The man was primarily a boxer, but with a knockout punch in his right hand. The size of the ring would make catching Cruz difficult, but not impossible.

The sound from the crowd had diminished, and now it rose to a thundering roar interspersed with shrill blasts from trumpets. Brent knew without looking that Pablo Cruz was making his entrance. He ignored the sounds, refusing to turn until the bell was rung and the announcer had introduced him in Spanish.

When he turned and acknowledged the introduction, the waves of sound were so vehemently pejorative that Brent had to smile. He couldn't detect a single friendly sound. If the fight came to a decision, it wouldn't go his way. Any judge who voted for him would be signing his own death warrant.

Brent glanced toward Jennifer who was sitting with Frankie in the first row near his corner. She had left her seat and was jumping up and down cheering, but he could not hear her above the roar of the crowd.

Then Cruz was introduced and the sound crescendoed. Brent wondered if this was the same kind of sound a bull in the arena heard just before the matador's sword gave him the *coupe de grâce*. He noticed that Cruz also was aware of the irony of having the fight in the bull ring since he'd pulled his hair back into a matador's traditional small pony tail and was wearing a matador's *montera* which he swept off his head and saluted the crowd just as a matador would before the kill. Brent wouldn't have been surprised to see a matador's sword in Cruz's other hand.

The referee motioned the two fighters to the center of the ring and spit out the rules in rapid in Spanish. Brent assumed they were the usual. He used the moment to study Cruz. The man was taller than Brent so he was able to carry his two hundred and ten pounds without looking fat. He was even more handsome than he appeared in the videos. His features were unmarked, giving Brent the impression Cruz was careful to avoid being hit in the face. Or he had a damn good plastic surgeon.

Through the open robe, Brent noted that Cruz wasn't quite as lean and hard as he had looked on the video tapes. Because of Brent's miniscule record, he probably wasn't taking the fight seriously.

Cruz hardly looked at Brent as they touched gloves and went to their corners and the sound of the crowd gradually died. When the bell sounded, Brent and Cruz advanced toward each other in almost total silence. Cruz danced forward and his left snaked out.

Splat!

It came in over Brent's guard so fast he scarcely had time to duck his head and the blow hit him hard on the right temple. Its power surprised him, snapping his head back. Before he could recover, Cruz followed with a slashing right cross.

Bam!

Brent was on the canvas, his head ringing. The roar that erupted from the crowd was so loud he couldn't hear the count and he watched the referee's fingers. They appeared to be moving unusually slowly and he suddenly realized why. The referee didn't want the fight to end so quickly. If Brent was knocked out in the first ten seconds, the crowd wouldn't be happy.

The referee almost looked relieved when Brent got up at the count of six. Surprisingly, Brent's head was clear and he wondered if he'd taken Cruz's best punch. If so, he didn't have to be terribly concerned about being knocked out. In truth, Cruz's surprisingly fast left had knocked him off balance so the right cross had been able to knock him down.

Apparently, Cruz also didn't want the fight to end quickly because he didn't follow up his advantage. He danced around Brent, lancing out with his lightning left.

But forewarned, Brent was able to block or slip most of the punches. When Cruz tried the same rapid one-two that had decked Brent the first time, Brent moved his head aside and countered with a hard left to the ribs under Cruz's right cross. Cruz grunted and skipped away with a new look in his eyes.

It was almost the only punch Brent was able to get in throughout the round, and when the bell rang, Cruz walked back to his corner with a wave to the appreciative crowd as though to say that he'd give them a good show before going in for the kill.

While Ortega applied grease to Brent's face, Frankie came to the ring apron. "You okay?" he asked.

Brent nodded. "Lucky punch," he said.

Frankie stared at him. "Yeah, I hope so."

Frankie went back to his seat. Ortega didn't say a word, and Brent asked facetiously, "Any advice?"

"Yeah. Try hitting him."

Brent nodded. Ortega didn't realize it, but he'd echoed Brent's own thoughts. He was never going to inflict any damage on Cruz unless he could slow him down. There were two ways he could do that. The first was to let Cruz use him as a punching bag until he tired himself out. That method did not seem too inviting. The second method was to hit Cruz in the stomach and ribs until he wouldn't feel much like moving.

Sure. Easy. All he had to do was catch Cruz without getting the shit beat out of him in the meantime.

At the bell, he came out in a lower crouch, forcing the taller Cruz to hit down at him so his straight left jabs that did get through Brent's guard glanced off his forehead. After a minute, they didn't even hurt any more and Brent was able to handle them automatically while concentrating on Cruz's right. That's where the killer blow would come from.

Forced into being the pursuer, Brent shuffled after Cruz feeling like a bull futilely pursuing a nimble matador's cape. But, unlike a bull, he didn't waste energy swinging at his elusive target. He followed, his fists and feet ready, slipping and blocking the jabs, waiting for Cruz to make a mistake.

His chance came! Cruz wearied of the cat and mouse game and stopped, flat-footed, to launch a series of quick lefts and rights. Brent slipped one of Cruz's left hooks and came over the top with a right lead that hit Cruz square on the nose and blood spurted. Cruz's eyes glazed with pain and his head snapped back, bringing his chin up for Brent's hard left hook.

Cruz staggered and Brent leaped forward, and the referee grabbed him from behind. He swung Brent around and yelled something at him in Spanish, motioning him to a corner. Cruz was standing near the ropes, both hands to his face. Brent tried to push the referee away, but the referee clung to him while he shouted in Spanish.

Before Brent could twist free, the bell rang. The referee let him go and Brent stalked back to his corner. "What the hell was that all about?" he asked Ortega.

Ortega nodded toward the center of the ring. "He wanted to clean up the blood."

The referee had a towel and was mopping up blood from Cruz's nose.

"In the middle of a round?" Brent said. "Nobody does that."

"Yeah. You tell him."

Brent looked across the ring at Cruz's corner. They were working on his nose. But Cruz was paying little attention. He was staring across the ring at Brent, his eyes full of hate.

When the bell rang, Cruz almost leaped into the ring. He came at Brent, whipping his long arms out in vicious jabs that Brent had to work hard to avoid. Cruz had abandoned his skillful boxing and had become the aggressor, pounding Brent with hard blows all aimed at Brent's head.

Brent danced away, analyzing Cruz's change of tactics. The man's eyes blazed with anger. His handlers had effectively stopped the bleeding in his nose, but it was obviously broken. And, suddenly, Brent realized why Cruz had changed. He wanted to break Brent's nose in return. He really didn't care if he knocked Brent out. Not now. He wanted revenge.

Brent smiled to himself. All right. He'd give Cruz what he wanted.

Deliberately, he lowered his guard giving Cruz a clear shot at his face. Cruz's eyes widened and he surged forward his right fist aimed in a vicious blow at Brent's exposed nose.

Except it wasn't there.

Knowing what was coming, Brent ducked under the blow and hit Cruz in the solar plexus with a hooking right. Cruz stopped as though he'd been shot, and Brent hit him on the broken nose with an overhand left.

Cruz staggered across the ring, hands clasped over his stomach, his nose dripping blood. The crowd was screaming in anger as Brent charged after him. And he was again grabbed by the referee who whirled him away, shouting in Brent's face. From his gestures Brent realized the referee was warning him for a low blow and he shook his head angrily.

"No way!" he yelled around his mouthpiece.

He shoved the referee aside and surged forward, but to his surprise, the ring was suddenly filled with people yelling and screaming while the bell was being rung furiously. Someone hit him in the back of the head. Another blow landed on his cheek. He ducked and bulled his way to his corner. Ortega was standing on the ring apron watching the melee with a thin smile. Brent wouldn't have been surprised if he'd found Ortega inside the ring trying to get in a few punches himself.

What was surprising was the image of Frankie trying to climb into the ring. But he was having no luck, and he cursed and yelled in Spanish as he struggled to get his legs up on the ring apron.

It appeared that the safest place was outside the ring so Brent ducked through the ropes and dropped down beside Frankie. Frankie dragged him close where his bulk provided a small island of protection in a dangerous sea of screaming, yelling fanatics.

"You okay?" Frankie shouted.

"Yeah." Brent warily looked around, ready to duck. But the most outraged of the fans were trying to climb into the ring and were ignoring anybody outside. "Where's Jennifer?"

Frankie pointed to the ring. "Up there."

Then Brent saw her. She was just above them, inside the ropes, shoving and punching anyone within reach, ignoring blows, her hair flying, the only blonde in a melee of brunettes.

Brent reached up and grabbed her ankle with his gloved hand. "Jennifer!"

She tried to shake free, but he clung desperately. When she was forced to look down, she saw the glove and looked toward Brent, her eyes wild.

"Jennifer," Brent yelled again. "Get down."

Her eyes cleared and she ducked through the ropes, dropping down beside him. "Wow!" she exclaimed. "These guys are crazy. I thought they were going to kill you."

"I'm okay." She had the beginnings of bruises on her face and her blouse was torn from one shoulder. Her hair was a tangled mane. "You look worse than I do."

She grinned and he was happy to see she had all her teeth. "That was kind of fun," she said. "I think I'll go back."

"Hey, you're hurt." He used the side of his glove to wipe at a smear of blood near her mouth.

She probed at the spot with her fingers. "Nope. Not mine. I got in a couple of good shots."

"Let's see if we can get the hell out of here," Frankie said.

Brent shook his head. "Wait. I think they're getting it under control."

In the ring, a battery of police, using batons with abandon, had succeeded in forcing most of the combatants from the ring. The few remaining received the police's full fury, and with blows raining down on their heads and shoulders, they scrambled from the ring.

Cruz was standing in his corner surrounded by a phalanx of handlers. One of them was repairing the new damage to his nose.

With the ring cleared, the policemen climbed through the ropes and began forcing the crowd back to their places. Those who had remained in their seats or hadn't been able to reach the ring continued to shout and shake their fists in helpless anger.

But now the ring announcer, who'd found shelter inside the circle of Cruz's handlers, had the microphone and his voice urged the people to take their seats so the fight could continue. Given the choice of rioting or continuing the fight, the commotion began to subside.

The referee pushed into the center of the ring. He looked for Brent, and when he saw him beside Frankie, he motioned him to get back in the ring.

"Well," Brent said. "Here we go again."

He started to climb back upon the ring apron, but Frankie grabbed his arm. "Work on that nose," he said. "He don't like that. Try to make him mad."

"Frankie, I think he's already mad."

"Don't let him do it to you," Jennifer said. "I like your nose the way it is."

Brent grinned, climbed back into the ring and went to his corner. When they saw him, the crowd broke out in cat calls and whistles, but they stayed in their seats. Ortega put out his stool and Brent sat down. He picked up a towel and mopped his face and Ortega applied a fresh coat of Vaseline.

In the other corner, Cruz had also sat down. He seemed to be fully recovered from Brent's blow to his solar plexus and his nose was replugged. But his eyes were as hard and mean as ever as he glared across the ring at Brent.

The announcer ducked out of the ring and the girl with the round-card strutted around displaying the figure three

Brent breathed deeply. Only the third round. He wasn't tired, but it seemed as though he'd been fighting all night. The long delay might have given Cruz time to recover, but it had also given Brent time. It was as though they were just starting. But this time, Brent knew what to expect.

When the bell sounded, both Brent and Cruz shuffled forward in almost dead silence. As Brent expected, Cruz was still after his nose, but now he was not swinging in a blind fury. He had listened to his trainer and he returned to his boxing, ignoring Brent's body, lancing out at his face with long lefts, looking for an opening for his right.

But Brent was intimately acquainted with that left jab and he handled it with no more damage than a few glancing blows that got through his guard to his forehead and cheeks.

Brent wasn't sure it would work a second time, but again he lowered his guard, exposing his nose as an inviting target. To his surprise, Cruz went for it again.

But this time, Cruz switched tactics and led with his right.

Bam!

Caught partially off guard, Brent was able to block some of the blow, but it slammed against his left cheekbone with stunning power.

Brent staggered back. Cruz leaped forward. He slammed another right that Brent was able to take on his shoulder. Off balance, he fell against the ropes.

Cruz pinned him there, slashing him with lefts and rights. Brent knew he had to get away. The ropes could kill him.

But Cruz would not let him escape. He had Brent pinned like a fly against the wall. Thus far, Brent had been able to duck or block the most damaging of Cruz's blows, but he knew he couldn't do that for long. He had to get away. And there was only one way to do that.

Abruptly, he abandoned his guard!

Bam! Bam! Bam!

He smashed as hard as he could at Cruz, not caring where the blows landed. His objective was to force Cruz to relinquish his attack. He had to put up a guard, and he couldn't do that and punch at the same time.

Bam! Bam! Bam!

Brent's fists were like pistons, driving Cruz back to the center of the ring.

Bam!

Brent's right powered through Cruz's guard and hit him on the cheek. Cruz's legs buckled and he grabbed Brent, wrapping him in his long arms.

Brent struggled to break free. He looked toward the referee for help, but the referee continued to circle them, making no move to break Cruz's grip.

Whack! Whack!

Twice Cruz's butted Brent, trying for his nose.

But Brent's shorter stature saved him. Cruz's butts hit him above the eye and Brent felt blood spurt.

His sudden fury gave him strength, and he ripped away from Cruz. Coming free, he hit Cruz on the point of the jaw with a hard left hook and Cruz went down.

Brent stood over Cruz, blood running down his cheek, and dripping on the canvas. Where the hell was the ref? Why didn't he begin the count? Cruz was struggling to get up.

Suddenly the referee was there. But not counting! He stopped in front of Brent, and stared at the cut above Brent's eye.

"Count, God damn it!" Brent shouted. "Count."

The bell rang.

Brent knew it was too early for the bell, but there was nothing he could do. He went back to his corner and sat down breathing heavily, not with fatigue, but with seething anger.

Ortega went to work on the cut in his forehead, sealing it with collagen. The referee came over with a doctor. They looked at the cut and said something to Ortega in Spanish and Ortega nodded. Brent had the impression that they meant to stop the fight. He'd lose on a technical knockout.

Furious, he surged to his feet. "What the hell is this? He butted me. You can't stop it!"

The doctor shook his head. But suddenly Frankie was there. Beside the apron. He didn't yell, but he said something to the doctor and the referee, and the edge on his voice would've cut steel. The referee and doctor stared at him a second, then the doctor shrugged and climbed out of the ring. The referee went back to Cruz's corner.

Frankie said something to Ortega in the same cutting tone, and Ortega scowled, but said nothing.

Frankie looked at Brent. "Calm down, my friend. You can win this. Don't try to box him. Fight him. Like you did coming off the ropes. Punch the son-of-a-bitch's lights out."

The bell sounded and Brent moved forward. Frankie was right. If he boxed Cruz he could probably survive without being knocked out. But he could never win. Not on points. Not with these judges. And he wanted to win. For the first time, he wanted to win!

Cruz came out, his left flicking. He was going for the cut above Brent's eye. To hell with the nose. If Cruz could start that eye bleeding again, he could win on a technical.

But Brent wasn't about to give him the technical. The first time Cruz's left snaked out toward his eye, Brent ducked under it and slammed his right into Cruz's heart.

Cruz backpedaled, using his speed and a long right to hold Brent off. Brent didn't rush. There was plenty of time.

Again Cruz circled. The left lashed out.

Bam!

Brent hit him again above the heart.

Cruz backed away, his face contorted, his left elbow pressed against his side.

Brent's smile was thin. That hurt, didn't it? Okay. Give me that left again.

But Cruz was no fool. He came dancing in again and the left lanced out. A fake!

When Brent went under it his head exploded in a burst of light.

He couldn't see! Black and red explosions rocked through his head. He felt Cruz's fists searching for his head, and he fought back desperately, blocking, throwing weak punches, running, held up by instinct and the bestial roar of the crowd.

Strangely, his legs were strong, and he knew what had happened. Cruz's uppercut had jammed his jaw bone upward and it had disrupted the nerves controlling his eyesight.

But he'd survived. He was still on his feet, and now, his eyes were clearing. If only he could evade a killing blow for another ten seconds!

Desperately, he ducked, weaved, danced away and held until he could see. But something was wrong! His sight was blurred like he was looking through a red haze. Blood! Damn! Cruz had opened the cut. This time the ref would surely stop the fight.

He'd lost!

Like hell!

Cruz had dropped all pretense of boxing and was charging after Brent with both fists swinging. He didn't expect a counterattack. Clearly Brent was surviving purely by instinct and guts. Trained fighters sometimes continued to fight when they were out on their feet, all senses shut down except the primitive urge to fight. But they were done—out of it. Like Brent, they just didn't know when to fall.

So Cruz was totally unprepared when Brent suddenly came alive. He was totally unprepared when Brent stepped inside and hit him with a left hook that snapped his head to the left, bringing his jaw in perfect position for Brent's short, thunderous right cross.

Bam!

Cruz's eyes rolled back and he fell face down, his arms at his sides. He hit the canvas so hard he bounced, the sound like a clap of thunder in the dead silence of the arena.

Brent walked to a neutral corner and stood watching. The referee stared at Cruz, stunned, unable or unwilling to move. From the crowd came the sound of a deep sigh.

Desperately, the referee looked toward the bellman, but the man was staring with the others, frozen in disbelief. With no choice, the referee slowly dropped to his knees and began counting.

It was a waste of time. Everyone in the entire arena knew Cruz wouldn't be getting up for minutes, perhaps hours; maybe never. Long before the referee had reluctantly counted to ten and stood up, the crowd was filing out, their voices stunned mutters.

Brent walked to the center of the ring, and the referee shrugged and raised Brent's right hand. Frankie and Jennifer yelled and applauded.

Chapter Twenty

A PARTY WAS already underway in the bar when they got back to the hotel. Several revelers saw them and came to shower congratulations on Brent and Frankie. Brent tried to make his way to the elevators, but Frankie, basking in the glory, allowed them to be escorted to the bar that was jammed with Latin *aficionados* and North American fans. A Mexican band was banging out a disco rhythm with a *mariachi* flavor, and the small parquet dance floor was awash with writhing bodies. Jennifer was immediately surrounded by hopeful Latinos. Several girls tried to pull Brent onto the dance floor, but he easily convinced them he was in no shape to dance. His face was discolored, swollen. The cut over his eye was closed by a taped strip of gauze. He was tired, but not dead tired. Victory produced a lot of adrenaline.

Frankie glowed with the high of elation, telling everybody about the virtues of Frankie's Gym. He'd been waiting for this moment for years, so Brent was surprised but grateful when he suggested they leave.

"Let's get out of here," Frankie said. "I've got a real party set up."

"Okay," Brent said. "I'll get Jennifer."

"Forget her. This is for us."

Brent was uneasy about leaving Jennifer, but she looked as though she was having a great time. If he stayed, he might be here for hours. Better to go with Frankie, then slip away at the first opportunity.

He'd thought that Frankie's idea of a party would be a few beers and a crowd of friends. He was wrong.

Frankie's suite was deserted except for Ortega and half a dozen waiters setting up a table loaded with cuts of exotic fruit, shrimp and cracked Alaska King crab on ice, cold cuts, and Mexican hors d'oeuvres surrounded by small dishes of hot *salsa*. Several bottles of champagne were chilling in silver chalices filled with crushed ice. A trio of musicians on the terrace filled the night with *mariachi* music.

Frankie gave the waiters a generous tip and they left. Frankie poured three glasses of champagne. He was in the middle of a toast when the door opened and three breathtakingly beautiful Mexican girls walked in. None could have been more than twenty. Their brilliant red lips and scarlet fingernails were a bit too gaudy for Brent's tastes, but their low-cut mini-dresses displayed figures that more than made up for their lack of class.

Brent expected other guests to be following, but to his dismay, the door was shut behind them.

One of the girls, whose name turned out to be Chio and who was slightly more buxom than the others, knew Frankie and Ortega and she introduced the other two as Juliana and Rosario.

The girls took the glasses of champagne that Frankie poured and made directly for the table of goodies. Brent watched in fascination as they proceeded to devour the food as though it was going to be their last meal in this world. Champagne apparently did not appeal to them because they quickly switched to heavy red port wine. Frankie and Ortega had already switched to *tequila.*

It was easy for Brent to look as though he was drinking by walking around with a champagne glass filled with soda water. Since there were three girls, he assumed one of them was meant for him, which would make slipping away pretty obvious.

Chio was sitting on Frankie's lap when the musicians switched to a *salsa* beat and she leaped up and began writhing in an imitation of a go-go dancer while stripping off her clothing. Frankie, Ortega and the two girls cheered and clapped their hands in time with the music. She stopped when she was down to red-laced panties and an equally red bra, and crawled back into Frankie's lap.

The *tequila* was getting to Ortega and he moved unsteadily as he grabbed Juliana and wrapped his arms around her like an amorous octopus, fumbling for the zipper on the back of her dress. Brent wondered how much of her laughter was real.

Brent stood by the table attempting to engage in conversation with the other girl, Rosario. Unfortunately, she didn't speak a word of English. Her body language, however, easily bridged the language barrier. She took Brent's drink from his hand and set it on the table and wrapped both arms around his neck, pressing her soft lips to his neck below his ear.

Brent was attempting to explain he wasn't in the mood. "*No amor, por favor.*"

She laughed as though it was a good joke. Across the room, Frankie heaved to his feet, clutching the hand of Chio who now was wearing only her panties.

"Time for bed," he said, his voice slurred. Supported in part by the girl, Frankie moved unsteadily toward the bedroom. As he passed Brent, he winked and said, "This is 'nother part'a the business we don' talk 'bout." He almost bumped into the door frame as he turned back. "See ya a' bre'fst." The girl steered him into the bedroom and shut the door.

Brent stood with his arms around Rosario who had started to work on him with professional expertise. She wrapped her warm body around Brent, one leg locked behind his, her hands gripping his hair while her lips explored his neck, all designed to lift him quickly to a fever pitch of passion.

And yet, the soft, perfumed flesh of Rosario's back felt unreal under Brent's hands. It was as though he was caressing a body without life. The soft lips on his neck, lips searching for his own, had all the warmth of dead leaves. And the nubile hips, undulating expertly against his, possessed the programmed passion of a robotic machine.

Brent stared at the wall trying to make his body respond. But it was useless. His mind was more concerned about how he could escape without hurting the girl's feelings than it was about making love. Ortega was having no such problems. Over Rosario's bare shoulder Brent could see Ortega lying on the couch with Juliana. He already had her clothes off and she was helping him tear at his own.

Brent's excuse for escape came when Rosario moved her hands from his hair and locked them around his waist so she could pull him harder against her insistent hips. Brent winced, grunting in simulated pain, and pulled away.

Rosario's huge, mascaraed eyes glanced up at him, compassion replacing death. "*Que pasa, querido?*"

"Sorry about that." Brent traced a path across down his rib cage. "I think Cruz broke a couple of ribs. I think I'd better get to a hospital."

Rosario's look of concern deepened. "'ospital? *Tiene dolor?*"

Brent recognized the word for pain. "Yeah. *Mucho dolor.* I'm sorry. *Yo siento.* But I'd better go to a hospital." He walked quickly toward the door, pausing only to indicate the table of food. "Help yourself. If you get lonesome, maybe Chio or Juliana can use some help."

Rosario shrugged. When Brent went out, she was lifting the bottle of *tequila.*

Walking back to his room, Brent couldn't believe what he'd just done. The girl was young, beautiful. And very willing. But he'd felt nothing.

A year ago he probably would've romped with her all night. So why not now? Maria was out of his life; Jennifer was only a friend. She was certainly having no compunctions about coming on to those Latinos in the bar. Perhaps his lack of interest was the culmination of all his guilts. Was it going to be like this from now on?

The price he was paying suddenly seemed bigger. A lot bigger.

Chapter Twenty-One

THE SUPPLIER'S HOUSE was not the sumptuous mansion Brent had expected. The Spanish-style *casa* was relatively modest, set behind an eight-foot wall topped with broken glass facing a small side street on the back edge of Acapulco away from the cool bay. Behind huge ornate oaken doors in the wall was a wide private patio paved with flagstone and tastefully landscaped with dozens of hanging potted plants and stands of semi-tropical ferns, rubber plants and towering banana trees. The house was old, maybe more than a hundred years, and much of the outside stucco had fallen away, revealing adobe bricks.

An old man, as weathered as the house, led Frankie, Ortega and Brent across the courtyard and through a carved oak door. A tiled vestibule opened to a living room with a high, beamed ceiling. The hardwood floors gleamed with a luster of wax. A patio could be seen through opposite windows. Brent could see the house was built in the form of a hollow square with the patio in the center. It reminded him of pictures he'd seen depicting old houses in Spain and Italy.

The living room was furnished with heavy, hand-carved furniture made of some dark wood that had achieved a hand-rubbed luster. All the upholstery appeared to be of thick, tooled leather, also rubbed to a high luster through years of use. A large rectangular table dominated the center of the room. A fireplace, blackened through much use, occupied most of the left wall. Hugh, massively-framed oil portraits and scenes of bullfights, dark with age, looked down from the ancient walls.

Brent was admiring a pair of crossed sabers, heavily embossed with gold and silver, crossed on one wall when he heard footsteps and a man's voice said, "*Bienvenidas, amigos.*"

The man who had spoken was in his middle fifties, quite slender, so that he looked tall. He had black hair, graying at the temples and a closely-cropped gray beard and moustache. He wore a white tropical suit with a narrow, black tie. His shoes were white with the leather woven into intricate patterns. He might have been a wealthy retired gentleman except his eyes were hooded, hostile. When he smiled, they darted with quick glances from face to face.

"*Hola, amigo. Como esta?*" Frankie said, and shook the man's hand.

In answer, the man nodded a fraction of an inch.

"You know Ortega, of course," Frankie continued. "And this is my friend I told you about—Brent Thomas. Brent, *Señor* Hector Corillo."

Hector Corillo, Brent thought as he shook the man's hand. So this was Frankie's Mexican connection. Corillo probably wasn't his real name. This probably wasn't his house either.

However, if what Brent had learned about drug law enforcement in Mexico was true, Corillo might own key members of the *policia* and the necessary judges to operate pretty much in the open.

"Welcome," Corillo said. He looked at the bruises marking Brent's face and the bandage on his brow, and his thin lips parted in the barest smile. "Congratulations. You were—most impressive."

"Thanks," Brent said. "I hope you enjoyed it."

"I would not have missed it." His gaze flicked past Frankie. "*Señorita* Pierce is not with you?" The disappointment in his voice made Brent wonder if Jennifer had lied to him. Perhaps her job in Frankie's organization went beyond being a courier.

"No," Frankie said. "We had a little party last night. I think she's going to be passed out until time to catch the plane."

Corillo spread his hands, palms up. "Ah, yes. The celebration. I heard about it." He looked at Brent and Brent was not sure whether his eyes were clouded with hate or with regret. "I had a small celebration of my own planned. But you cancelled that rather effectively."

"I hope you didn't lose any money on Cruz," Brent said. Actually, he hoped Corillo had lost a bundle.

He got his wish. "A small sum," Corillo said. He looked at Ortega, and this time, there was no hiding the displeasure in his eyes. "I had some very bad advice."

Ortega's lips twisted, but he said nothing.

"Next time, *amigo,*" Frankie said. "You can make it all back. And more. *Mañana.*"

"*Mañana,* of course," Corillo murmured. His flat eyes turned toward Brent. "You will want something to drink."

As though his words were a command, the old man appeared with a tray holding four glasses of amber-colored liquid and a bottle of Gold Patron *tequila.* When he passed them around ,Brent said, "Excuse me, *señor.* If you don't mind, I'd prefer beer or a Coke."

"Ah, yes, the training," Corillo said with a deprecating smile that made Brent want to twist him a little. "But of course." He nodded to the old man. "*Dos Equis.*"

The old man went to a sideboard and opened it. Inside were shelves containing varieties of expensive liquor and a small refrigerator. He opened the refrigerator and took out a bottle of the Mexican beer and a beer glass.

When Brent had his beer, Corillo lifted his glass of *tequila*. "I'm sorry you do not appreciate our native liquor," he said to Brent. "Good *tequila* is ninety-six proof."

"That'd knock me on my ass quicker than Cruz did," Brent said, and Corillo responded with a genuine smile.

"I remember," he said. "I thought for an instant that I had won a great deal of money."

"Sorry about that."

Corillo waved the thought aside. "I can afford it." He raised his glass. "Now *amor y dinero y tiempo a gustarlos*."

"I'll drink to that," Ortega said and took a long swallow of the *tequila*. He coughed and gave a strangled gasp, and Frankie and Corillo laughed.

"Easy, my friend," Corillo said. "You are used to that cheap eighty-proof *caca*. This must be savored."

"Yeah, Jaime," Fat Frankie laughed. "Stop hoarding your money like a *brujo*. Buy some good liquor."

Ortega glared at him and sat down in one of the big leather chairs. Frankie lit one of his big cigars and Corillo fired up a slender cigarillo.

"Okay," Frankie said. "Let's do some business."
He reached under his jacket and unfastened the ornate silver buckle of his belt. After sliding the belt out of the loops in his pants, he turned it over and opened a hidden zipper on the inside. Then he removed stack after stack of thousand dollar bills, all folded lengthwise. This was one situation, thought Brent, where Frankie's girth was definitely an advantage. He could carry a hell of a lot more money in his belt than the average man.

As Frankie stacked the money on the table, Corillo counted each stack. "*Bueno*," he said after counting the last stack.

"We check the quality as usual," Frankie said.

Corillo made a sneering smile. "As you wish, *señor*."

He left the room, returning a few minutes later followed by the old man who carried a plastic-wrapped package of brownish-white powder that he placed on the table. Mexican brown heroin. Brent wondered how much a hundred thousand dollars would buy.

Frankie nodded to Ortega. "Go with him."

Ortega set his empty glass on the arm of the chair and went out with the old man by the front door. Brent wondered where they could be going.

Then Corillo went to a cabinet and took out a heating coil, a small test tube and a hypodermic needle. Brent had seen a demonstration at the DEA Training Institute of how heroin could be tested for purity, but there was no sign of the necessary chemicals. Maybe Ortega and the old man had gone after the testing equipment. Unless the crooks had perfected some method that was ahead of what they were doing at NTI.

"The usual method of delivery?" Corillo asked as he put the equipment on the table and plugged the heating coil into a wall socket.

Brent increased his attention. This was the rope that could hang Frankie. If he could find out how the stuff got from Mexico into Frankie's hands, the DEA would know when to make their raid.

"Yeah," Frankie said. "It's worked good so far."

"Very well," Corillo answered. "I'll take care of it."

Brent relaxed, disappointed. Whatever the method was they either didn't want to discuss it in front of him or it was so familiar they had no reason to discuss it at all. Either way, he had nothing to report. Not yet.

The front door opened and Ortega and the old man came back in. Ortega was carrying a bundle wrapped in an old blanket. He placed the bundle on the table where Corillo had already melted some of the heroin into a liquid in the test tube. After suctioning it into the hypodermic needle, he bent over the bundle.

So that's it.

Ortega and the old man had picked up some small animal and they were going to test the heroin on it. Brent had read that such tests were common when modern technology was not available. If the animal died almost instantly, it would mean that the junk was between ninety and one hundred percent pure. If it died slowly, going into convulsions and choking to death on its own vomit and mucus, it would mean the purity was less than ninety percent. It was a sickening process and Brent walked over to the patio window and stared out, not wanting to watch.

There was a whisper of sound—a whimper—and Brent felt a chill as though he'd been touched by the finger of death. The whimper swelled into a choking gasp. My God, that's no animal!

He whirled and took two swift strides to the table. He yanked the blanket aside and stared at a baby. It couldn't have been more than three or four months old. Already it was fighting for breath, its tiny face contorted, its tiny hands tearing at the air while a white mucus spilled from the side of its rosebud mouth.

Brent whirled on Corillo who was standing with the needle in his hand watching the child with the intense stare of a vulture. "What the Christ have you done?"

Brent smashed Corillo aside, sending him reeling across the room, and snatched up the baby. Using a corner of the blanket he wiped at the baby's mouth. Then he closed its nose with his fingers and tried to breathe life into the tiny lungs.

"Hey, *amigo, amigo*," Frankie said and pulled at Brent's shoulder. "It's dead. Forget it."

Brent shrugged off Frankie's pudgy hand and continued to force air into the baby's tiny body.

Behind him he heard Ortega laugh. "Who you think you are, man? God? You gonna bring it back to life?"

Brent paused and stared at the baby. Its eyes were closed; its tiny fists lax. Ortega was right. All the CPR in the world would never bring it back to life. Slowly, he lowered the baby to the table, his temples throbbing with disgust and anger.

"Hey, that's good stuff," Ortega said. "It went out like that." He snapped his fingers and it was as though he had awakened Brent from hypnosis. With a growl of rage, he hurled himself at Ortega.

Taken by surprise, Ortega was unable to move before Brent's fingers locked around his throat. Ortega sagged backward under the onslaught, clawing at Brent's hands. Then he caught his balance and powered his hands up between Brent's arms in the classic maneuver to break a throttling grip.

It didn't work. Brent's rage had given him an almost superhuman strength and Ortega's eyes began to bulge. He brought his knee up in a vicious jab at Brent's groin, but his own writhing caused him to miss and the knee hit Brent's thigh. Brent lifted Ortega from the floor and shook him, his face inches from Ortega, his eyes wild with blind rage. Ortega's tongue came out and he clawed at Brent's hands, but Brent's world was filled with the feel of Ortega's throat in his hands and the sight of Ortega's blackening face.

Then he felt a jarring blow on his head, and his world erupted in a red geyser that blossomed into blackness.

Chapter Twenty-Two

BRENT AWAKENED TO the sensation of movement and of cool hands on his throbbing forehead. He moved his head and pain lanced through his body. He felt on the edge of vomiting and he swallowed painfully.

"Take it easy." The voice was Jennifer's. "Just lie still."

He cracked open his eyelids. Bright sunlight stabbed his eyes like knives. But he kept them open, squinting against the painful glare.

He was in the back seat of a limousine, his head on Jennifer's lap. He groaned and fought pain as he put his hand to the back of his head. There was a good-sized lump, covered with a bandage held in place by adhesive tape.

The fight? No. Ortega.

Memory flooded back and he gingerly sat up, fighting back nausea.

Jennifer put her hand on his shoulder to steady him. "Are you all right?"

"Yeah," he gritted. "I guess so."

"I wanted to get a doctor, but Frankie said you'd be all right."

He closed his eyes, trying to adjust to the sway of the limo so it wouldn't make his head throb. "I'll be okay in a minute." He knew he was lying. In a minute, he almost hoped he'd be dead.

"Here," she said. "Lean against me."

"No. I'd rather sit up." He squinting out the window. "Where're we going?"

"The airport."

"Airport? How long was I out?"

"A couple of hours. I still don't know what happened. Frankie said you slipped and fell."

"That's a damned lie." He turned his head slowly so he could look at her, the pain of memory wiping out the pain of the moment. "They murdered a baby."

Jennifer's face had drained of color. "A baby? But... Why?"

"They used it to test the junk."

Jennifer's hand went to her mouth. "Oh, God! I didn't know that."

Brent put his hands to his face, trying to blot out the memory. "I went after Ortega. Somebody hit me. I guess it was Corillo."

"You went after Ortega? Not Frankie?"

"Ortega brought the baby in. Him and an old man."

"But where did they get it?"

"I guess they just went out and took it. When I realized...I was too late." He took a deep breath that roiled his stomach. "Where are they?"

"At the airport. I told them I'd bring you as soon as you woke up. But...it was getting late." She touched his face, forcing him to concentrate on her. "Brent, don't do anything. It's too late. Don't do anything."

Brent stared ahead at the road. It was hard to believe the reality of traffic and obscenely bright sunlight. It all had to be a nightmare. Nothing so monstrous could be real.

He put down the window and leaned his face into the hot draft of air. It was real. It was all real. The baby. Everything. Too late. Too late for the baby. Too late for him. The only thing that was not too late was stopping Frankie and Corillo so it could never happen again. And to do that, he had to play out his role. Now, more than ever, it was imperative he do his job and not get caught.

By the time they arrived at the airport, his blazing anger had turned to a smoldering rage. But the pain in his head had diminished to a throbbing ache and he had the nausea under control.

Inside the airport terminal, he walked beside Jennifer toward the terminal's bar, ready to grab her arm if his legs failed. A man who looked like an American tourist was taking pictures of the AeroMexico lobby. He stepped back and bumped into Brent, sending a stab of pain through Brent's skull that wrung a grunt of anguish from him.

"Oops," the man said. "Sorry." He peered at Brent's battered face. "You all right?"

Brent knew instantly that the man was a DEA agent. He must have taken pictures of Frankie and Ortega for the record. He probably thought they'd broken Brent's cover, and perhaps, tried to kill him.

Brent straightened and smiled. "Yeah," he said. "I'm okay. No sweat."

The man said, "Okay. Sorry," and went away.

In the airport bar, Frankie and Ortega were sitting across from each other in a booth next to a large picture window that overlooked the flight line. Frankie saw them and waved.

"Over here." He grinned at Brent as though nothing had happened and asked, "How you feeling, *amigo?*"

Brent touched the back of his head and painted on a smile. "Okay. I guess I got carried away."

"You!" Frankie laughed. "Jaime was the one almost carried away. Show him your throat, *amigo.*"

Ortega growled and turned his head to stare out the window, but

Brent could see that his throat was bruised and swollen.

"Sit down," Frankie said. "You look like you could use a drink."

"You got that right," Brent said. He started to sit next to Ortega so Jennifer, who took up half the room he did, could sit beside Frankie. But Ortega was already sliding out of the booth.

"I've got to go to the can," he said and walked away.

"I think you ruined Jaime's sense of humor," Frankie chuckled. He shoved his glass of *tequila* toward Brent. "Here, *amigo*. You look a little pale."

Brent lifted the glass and took a swallow. The oily, raw alcohol burned his throat, taking his breath away and he gasped for air, his stomach churning.

"See," Frankie laughed. "You look better already."

Jennifer had been sitting quietly, staring at Frankie. "Is it true, Frankie?" she asked.

Frankie's eyebrows lifted. "True? What?"

"What Brent said. About the baby."

Frankie shot Brent a look that admonished him for mentioning what had happened. He made a small shrug. "It was only a baby. No big deal down here. They spit them out like watermelon seeds. *Powee! Powee!*"

Under the table Brent clenched his hands as Jennifer's stare turned into a look of disbelief. "What about the mother? The father?"

"Quintana'll take care of them. When they get the money, they don't mind."

"I can't believe that."

"Well, believe it," Frankie snapped, his voice suddenly ugly as though he'd had enough of the subject.

Brent looked out the window, wondering how he was going to keep working for a monster like Frankie.

Suddenly, Brent's eye was caught by a reflection in the glass that made him snap his head around. A young Mexican stood in front of their booth, facing them. But what had caught Brent's eye was the pistol in his hand. Behind the man, he caught a glimpse of Ortega watching.

The man raised the pistol. Somebody in the bar screamed and Frankie's head jerked around. The man's teeth bared in a snarl of rage, and he pointed the gun at Frankie's head. Trapped in the booth Frankie was a sitting duck. Brent was also trapped! His reflexes took over, and without thinking, he grasped the edge of the table and wrenched upward with all his strength. The table top tore loose from its base, and in the same movement, Brent upended it at the man just as the gun exploded.

Brent surged out of the booth, diving at the man who'd been driven to his knees. Too late. The gun muzzle was centered on Brent's head.

Boom! Boom!

The quick shots thundered in Brent's ear. The young man stared down at two small holes in his shirt, then collapsed, clawing at his chest. His legs convulsed, then he seemed to shrink inside himself and was still, his cheek pressed against the floor, his eyes staring into the future.

Standing over him, Brent couldn't believe he was still alive. He was sure the shots had been directed at him. He glanced toward the booth in time to see Frankie shove a pistol down between the seat cushion and the back of the seat. A crowd was already gathering, staring at the dead man.

"Come on, Jennifer," Frankie said. "Move it. Let's get the fuck out of here." He pushed her and Jennifer fell sideways off the seat, hitting the floor with a jarring thud.

"Oh, Jesus!" Brent said, and knelt beside her, lifting her head. Her face was still and white except for a trickle of blood that oozed from a hole in her temple. He put his fingers to her throat, praying for a pulse. He looked up at Frankie, unable to believe it. "She's dead, Frankie. She's dead."

"Yeah, yeah. Let's get the shit out of here."

Brent stared at him. "We can't leave her. Call an ambulance."

"What the shit for? Let's get out of here! This place'll be swarming with cops in a minute."

Frankie reached down and grabbed the back of Brent's jacket, trying to pull him to his feet. Reluctantly, Brent stood up. Frankie was right. There wasn't a damn thing he could do for Jennifer. He stumbled after Frankie who pushed his way through the crowd. Ortega came to meet them and took Frankie's arm, steering him toward the exit. Brent saw the DEA man trying to push through the crowd, and he grabbed the man's arm, not caring if Frankie saw him or not.

"Take care of her," he whispered harshly. "Take care of her."

Then he hurried to catch up with Frankie and Ortega, hating himself even more than he hated Frankie.

Chapter Twenty-Three

BY THE TIME the airport shuttle-bus from LAX dropped Brent off at the long-term parking lot on 111th Street, it was almost midnight. Frankie and Ortega had picked up Frankie's car from the airport's main lot where the tab was considerably higher and had long since departed, so Brent wasn't worried about being followed.

Walking from the shuttle-bus to his car, he took his time. He was sick, almost too weary to move. It was easy to understand now why some people committed suicide. If he had his gun, he would have been sorely tempted. He felt responsible for Jennifer's death and the death of the baby, although he knew deep inside that he wasn't. Every one of the events could have happened if he'd remained in Kansas. Still, if he hadn't thrown the table, the man might not have missed. Frankie would be dead and it would all be over—for Frankie, for him, for everybody.

He'd almost reached his car, which he'd parked at the far north edge of the huge lot, when he saw the shadowy figure of a man leaning against the Caprice smoking a cigarette.

Brent stepped into the concealment of a parked van and studied the man. He was obviously waiting for him. One of Frankie's goons? Had Frankie found out who he was? Or was the man simply a mugger waiting for whoever chanced by. Well, he was in for a surprise.

Brent took off his shoes and left them with his bag against the lot's chain-link fence. He waited until a landing jet thundered low overhead, reaching for a LAX runway, then he quickly circled behind parked cars to come up behind the man. He was less then five feet away, crouching for his attack, when the man sucked on the cigarette, and in the dim glow, Brent saw that it was Jim Hendrix.

"Hey," Brent said softly. Hendrix snapped his head around so fast he dropped his cigarette on the front of his jacket, his hand reaching for the back of his belt.

Brent moved forward, "Aren't you up kind of late?"

"Christ!" Hendrix yelped, beating at the sparks on his jacket. "Don't sneak up like that."

Brent leaned his back against the side of his car. "I didn't know it was you. How did you know I was here?"

"Our guy in Acapulco told us what plane you were on. I figured you'd park in a cheap lot, so I looked 'til I spotted your car."

"But why? I was going to call in."

"I wanted to talk to you tonight. And I don't like to call you at your place."

"Okay. But first let me get my shoes. This gravel is killing my feet."

Hendrix walked with Brent as he retrieved his shoes and his bag.

"So?" Hendrix said. "How'd it go?"

"Great." The bitterness in his tone caused Hendrix to stare at him. "I won."

"We heard. I don't mean that shit. There was a shooting down there. What the hell happened?"

"Some guy tried to kill Frankie. Instead, he got Jennifer."

"Yeah. We heard. I'm sorry as hell about that. Was she involved in Frankie's organization?"

Brent considered lying to Hendrix. But Jennifer was beyond being hurt now. He nodded. "Yes. She was one of his couriers. But I don't know just how."

"Well, that makes it a little less bad. Getting shot in that business is an occupational hazard."

"What about ours?" Brent asked.

"Ours? Nobody gives a shit about us. They figure we're expendable. That's why we get the big salary. Anyway, I heard the guy got shot himself. Who did it? You?"

"No. Frankie. He was carrying a gun."

"Figures. Most dopers do. You sure that guy was after Frankie?"

Brent hesitated, taken by surprise. "You think he might have been after me?"

"Maybe your cover got busted."

Brent shook his head. "I thought of that." He thought back to the scene just before the man had raised his gun. An image of Ortega flashed through his mind. If Ortega had gone to the restroom as he said, it had been a very short trip. "It was something else. Just before the guy fired, I saw Ortega standing in the background watching. The guy was coming from his direction. They might have been talking."

"You think Ortega's on to you?"

"No. If it was me he fingered, it had to be for other reasons—I think. One of them is that I'm getting buddy-buddy with Frankie. Ortega might think I'm acing him out."

"Yeah. Could be. But if the guy was after Frankie, could be that Ortega's planning a takeover."

"That's possible."

"Yeah. Well... There's no way we can find out now."

Brent slowed his pace. "There's one way. If somebody doesn't try to kill me when I go in tomorrow, they were probably after Frankie."

They had reached Brent's car and Hendrix waited while Brent unlocked the door before he said, "You want out, Brent?"

Brent wanted to scream yes. He'd wanted out from the beginning. This whole affair was pulling him apart. He'd lost Maria. Jennifer was dead. He had killed a man. And he could be next.

He opened his mouth to tell Hendrix. Then he remembered the baby. "They murdered a baby. They do it all the time."

"A baby?"

"They use them to test the purity of the heroin."

"Oh, yeah. That started in Asia. They'd just go out and grab some woman's baby—any baby—and use it for the test. It's not common, but some traffickers still use it."

"My God," Brent breathed. "How do they get away with it?"

"Who's gonna stop them? They're the big guys with guns. There are a hell of a lot of places in the world where might makes right. And there'd be a hell of a lot more if the assholes of the world didn't have a bunch of stupid suckers like us to look after them."

Brent sagged against his car. "God, I've really lived in an ivory tower. When I took this job, I thought I'd run into some bad dudes, but nothing like this."

"Yeah, we all felt like that." Hendrix paused, then asked, "What about it, kid? You want out?"

"If I do, what happens to your case on Frankie?"

"Back to square one, I guess."

"I want that bastard hung up by the balls," Brent gritted.

Hendrix laughed. "Try and find them."

Brent had to smile. "Yeah, okay. I'll hang in. I think if I was the one Ortega was after, it was because he was jealous. I don't think he made me. I should be okay."

"If you're right."

"Yeah. If I'm right."

Then he told Hendrix he hadn't found out how the dope was being shipped. But he was working on it. It undoubtedly had something to do with the boxing and bodybuilding Frankie promoted.

"Good," Hendrix said. "Unless we can get Frankie and the dope together when we make the bust, we're going to have a hell of a time tying him in so it'll stick in court."

"There's another way. Frankie's got to keep books on his operations somewhere. They'd tie him in."

"Could be. But he'll have them damn well protected. If we knew the name of his supplier in Mexico, we might be able to make a connection."

"I met the guy. Tall, thin, wore a white suit. Graying hair and short beard. Called himself Hector Corillo."

"Probably a fake. He'll be long gone."

A thought had been nagging at Brent's memory and he finally pinned it down. "Quintana. Or something like that."

"Quintana?" Hendrix's head jerked up. "Are you sure?"

"I think so. Frankie used that name when I asked him about the baby. He was talking about Corillo. I'm sure of it."

"So that's where the son-of-a-bitch is. We've had a warrant out on him for a long time. If he's in Acapulco, I think we can get the *Federales* to pick him up. Man, that's a real break."

Yeah, Brent thought. And it only cost two lives.

Driving back to Santa Monica, Brent couldn't stop thinking about Jennifer. It was hard to believe he'd never see her again. She had been so full of life. How had she allowed herself to be sucked into dope dealing? How could she have ignored the lives of others she was helping to ruin?

But what was really depressing was the knowledge that her death had not changed anything. Even busting Frankie would cause no more than a ripple in the river of dope flowing into the country. Dopeheads would continue to ruin their lives and the lives of others whether Frankie lived or died.

Did Frankie ever think about the lives he was destroying? Unlikely. What was it that made some people into psychopaths with no regard for others? They'd destroy anyone or anything to gratify their own greed. The selfish were overwhelming the earth. Maybe it was foolish to even attempt to stop them. It all seemed so damn hopeless.

He had to take deep breaths to fight back tears. He knew he had to stop such thoughts or he'd never be able to go on. But he couldn't do it alone.

He stopped at a pay phone and made a collect call to his folks in Kansas. His dad answered with a sleepy, "Hello."

"It's me, Dad. Brent."

He pictured the alarm on his father's face as he sat up in bed and turned on the light as though he couldn't talk in the dark. "Brent, is everything okay? Are you all right.?"

"Yes, yes," he said hastily. "I just...wanted to talk."

He heard his father tell his mother, "It's okay. It's Brent. He just wants to talk."

"At this hour?" he heard his mother say. "Something's wrong."

"What is it, Brent?" his father asked, worry in his voice. "Is something wrong?"

"Not the way you think, Dad. Tell Mom I haven't broken anything or been hurt. It's just that... It's this whole damn business. I don't know if I can handle it any more."

There was a pause while his father read the pain in his voice. "You had a feeling it'd be like this, didn't you? That's why you came home before you went to Washington."

Brent hadn't realized it before, but his dad was right. He'd been preparing for the worst. But not this. "It's worse than I thought," he said. "I just...lost a friend."

Again there was a pause. Then his dad said, "It really is a war, isn't it?"

"Worse than any damn war I ever saw. This one kills babies and women. It rots everybody it touches."

"Including you, Brent?"

"Not yet. Not that way. It's just making me bitter. God, Dad, I used to be so damn naive."

Brent could almost see his father's face as he searched for words while his mother stared at him, her face drawn with worry as she tried to follow the conversation. Then his father said, "When you were here—when you told us what you were going to do—we had an idea of what kind of people you'd get involved with. The thing that worried us the most was just what's happening to you now."

Brent sighed, wishing he were back home in his old bed. "Not much I can do about it, I guess."

"There's one thing. You can quit. Go back to the university."

The statement surprised Brent. It sure didn't sound like the Alvin Thomas he knew. "Quit?" He paused, trying to determine in his own mind why he should dismiss the idea. "I can't," he said. "Not now. A month ago, I could've. Maybe even a day ago. But not now."

"Good," his dad said and Brent almost smiled. The old man had been putting him on. "Just remember, for every one of those scum you meet, there are hundreds of good people. We can't handle those killers. We're too old, too damn soft. We need somebody like you who can. We're part of you."

Brent tried to hold to that thought during the remainder of the drive home. His father was right. He was part of them and they were part of him. The trick was to defeat the enemy without becoming like them—to hold to your values; to lie down with the dogs without getting their damn fleas.

His resolve should have allowed him to sleep peacefully. But his dreams were filled with images of babies reaching toward him with tiny fingers that turned into bloody claws as their bodies slowly disintegrated until all that was left were their eyes staring at him accusingly.

Chapter Twenty-Four

THE NEXT MORNING, Brent felt miserable and the back of his head ached with a pulsing, nagging throb. Generally, he did fifty or sixty pushups and a couple of hundred sit-ups before his morning run. But this morning, he couldn't bring himself to do any of them.

He debated about going to the gym. Frankie certainly couldn't object if he took a day or two off. His face and body felt like he'd been run over by a tractor. The bruises had turned purple and the swelling made his face look like hell. Fortunately, the cut over his eye had proven to be smaller than he'd thought, and it was above his eyebrow where it wouldn't be a problem during workouts.

He decided to go to work. He didn't think he could bear sitting alone in the apartment. He needed hard physical activity, not just for his body, but for his mind.

Remembering Hendrix's warning, Brent was wary as he parked and walked toward the gym. But there was no sign of anybody with a gun.

Still, he was cautious when he entered the lobby, scarcely replying to Carla's congratulations for winning in Acapulco and her murmured regrets about Jennifer.

Ortega was working with a few men using the gym equipment while ignoring a couple of women who were standing around waiting for Jennifer. Brent told them Jennifer had been in an accident, and they'd have to work on their own until somebody else would take over for her.

In the boxing area, more than the usual number of fighters were working out. Apparently, being a winner brought in customers. Several congratulated Brent. Working with them, Brent noticed that there was a change in their attitude when he gave an instruction. They'd listened to him before, and had more or less complied with his suggestions. But now everyone could hardly wait to do whatever he said. Obviously, in the fight business, there was no substitute for winning.

At about ten o'clock, Carla came in and said that Mr. Rodriquez wanted to see him and Brent's heart began to beat faster. Was this it? Would Frankie be waiting for him with a gun?

Brent told his charges to carry on and he went upstairs. He wasn't surprised when he didn't see Maria at the desk in the outer office. Frankie would try to keep them separated as much as possible.

But there might be another reason why Maria wasn't there. Maybe Frankie wanted to keep her out of the line of fire. He walked toward the door to Frankie's office, ready to bolt at the first sign of trouble.

Everything looked normal. He knocked on the door and heard Frankie tell him to come in.

He was still wary when he walked in, but the room was deserted except for Frankie sitting behind his desk, his face obscured by a cloud of blue-white cigar smoke.

"Come in, my friend, come in." Frankie waved aside the cloud of smoke. "Glad to see you came in today. Good for you. Just don't push too hard for a couple of days."

"Don't worry. I don't feel much like it." If Frankie was angry, he certainly didn't show it.

"Understandable," Frankie said. "We're all very upset about Jennifer."

"Yeah," Brent said. But he was thinking, Not you, you bastard.

"The man who did it was the father of the baby," Frankie said. "I'm very glad of that. If it had been somebody hired to make a hit, they'd try again."

The baby's father? That would explain why he'd been so foolish as to try to kill Frankie in front of witnesses. He was probably so crazy with grief and anger that he didn't care who saw him. "What about the Mexican police? Won't they be after us?"

Frankie shook his head. "My friends in Mexico have managed to keep us out of the picture." With an effort, Frankie heaved himself to his feet and went to the sideboard, on the way, clapping Brent on the shoulders. "So, my friend, I think you are ready for the big one."

"The big one?"

"You beat Molino, then Cruz. People are taking you serious. I had a dozen calls this morning from managers and promoters wanting to set up matches."

Brent touched his sore face. "No, thank you. I think we've proven our point."

Frankie poured himself a glass of *tequila*. He lifted an eyebrow at Brent and Brent shook his head. Frankie carried the *tequila* back to his desk and sat down with a sigh.

"Why don't you just take the bottle?" Brent asked.

"Because, my friend, I know my temptations. If I had it here, I'd drink it. If I have to go after it, it's too damn much trouble. That's why I always get it myself."

"Put it down stairs. You'll never drink again."

Frankie shook his head. "One doesn't overcome a temptation that does not exist."

Brent wondered if Frankie's idea wasn't a lot like the DEA's reasoning about drugs—if dope could be made virtually impossible to obtain, a lot of people would simply give up. Getting the dope wouldn't be worth the trouble. The prohibition of alcohol back in the '30s was a case in point. Thousands of people had given up or never started drinking. When alcohol was again made legal, it was as though the government had put its stamp of approval on drinking, and consumption soared. It would surely be the same with dope.

Frankie motioned Brent to a chair. "I realize this is asking a lot of you, but you can't quit while you're winning."

Brent grinned, and the pain that shot through his jaw made him wish he hadn't. "That's the best time."

"Not in this case. You don't know how far you could go until you go as far as you can."

"What's that supposed to mean?"

"You don't know how good you really are. I was watching you, *amigo*. I've seen a lot of fighters. You're the best I've ever seen." Frankie leaned forward. All humor had drained from his expression. "My friend, I wouldn't be surprised if you couldn't go all the way."

"All the way where? An early grave?"

"Stop kidding around. You know what I mean."

In spite of himself, Brent felt a thrill of pleasure. Frankie was talking about being world champion. Was it possible? Frankie thought it was.

Then reality brought his dream crashing down. Two fights and he was thinking champion. Frankie might be living in a dream world, but it wasn't his body that'd be beaten to a pulp.

"Thanks for the vote of confidence, Frankie," he said. "But two fights don't make a champion."

"But suppose you beat a contender. A real contender."

"I thought that was Cruz."

"Cruz wasn't a top contender. I'm talking about Duncan."

Brent sat up straighter. "Duncan? Willy Duncan?"

Frankie nodded. "His manager was one of those who called."

Brent stared at Frankie. "You're out of your mind. Duncan would never fight me. He's second in line for a shot at the title."

"Two days ago, no. He would now. My friend, you're big news. And Duncan needs a good win and the publicity. He figures he can get both with you."

"Yeah, well, I pass."

Frankie paused and took another sip of his *tequila* before he said, "There's another consideration."

"Yeah. What's that?"

"The fight would be held in Vancouver, Canada."

"So?"

"The...incident...in Mexico has caused some problems. My supplier has suggested our next shipment be brought in from a different location." Frankie's eyes narrowed. "My friend, I need you in Canada."

Brent felt a jolt of satisfaction. Frankie was practically admitting that his promotions outside the country were somehow being used to bring in dope.

"I see," he said slowly. "But why me? Why not set up a bodybuilding competition for Ortega?"

"There's nothing in that direction. Not soon enough. I'm going to need another shipment in a month."

"A month? You want me to fight Duncan in a month?"

Frankie leaned back in his chair. "I know it's asking a lot. But it has to be done."

Brent stood up. He couldn't sit still. Not with the dismay building inside his chest. "But a month. Jesus, I won't hardly be healed up from Cruz."

"I didn't say you had to win. It would be nice, but not necessary."

Brent had moved away. Now he turned to face Frankie, leaning across his desk. "Oh, I see. You're willing to get me killed so you can get another shipment."

"Not killed. No. Just give it your best. If it's not enough..." He shrugged. "At least, you gave it a shot."

Brent straightened. "Well, that's nice. What was all that hogwash about having a shot at the championship?"

Frankie waved his hand. "I think you can beat him. But we've got to get our priorities straight."

Brent walked around his chair feeling like a caged rat. Priorities, for Christ sake. Frankie didn't know it, but Brent had only one priority—to bring Frankie down. He had to take the fight just to find out what the hell was going on. The DEA couldn't order him to fight Duncan, but they did expect him to do his number on Frankie and his organization.

"Okay, Frankie. But don't expect too much. I'm not going to get my brain scrambled for a little extra money."

"A little?" Frankie reached in his desk drawer and pulled out a thick sheath of bill. He tossed them to Brent. "Here's part of your purse. I'll get the rest in a few days." Brent glanced at the bundle. The top bill was a thousand dollars. He stared at it, stunned. He'd totally forgotten that fighters got big money when they started fighting in the upper echelons.

Frankie took another bundle of bills from his drawer and also tossed it to Brent. "And here's your cut from me."

The stack was slimmer than the first, but Brent saw that the top bill was also a thousand.

"Ordinarily," Frankie said, "I'd tell you to hide that money away somewhere. On your salary, it wouldn't do to be seen with so much. But fight money is a perfect cover. For both of us."

Brent felt as though the second bundle of money was burning his fingers. To him, it was covered with the blood of the baby and the baby's father—and of Jennifer. Well, he wouldn't have it for long. He'd have to turn it over to the DEA. He wondered about the fight money. Would he have to turn that over to the DEA also? Probably. He'd never known the government not to take anything they thought they could get.

Brent moved toward the door. "Okay, Frankie. You're the boss."

"Wait, *amigo*." Frankie motioned to the chair. "Sit down."

Mystified, Brent returned to the chair and slowly sat down, wondering what other surprises Frankie had in store for him. Whatever it was, he was sure he wouldn't like it.

"*Amigo*," Frankie said, "I think you've proved you can be trusted."

Brent stared at Frankie silently, trying not to appear as tense as he was.

"How would you like to go to work for me on a higher level?" Frankie continued.

"Are you talking about the fight? I thought we'd settled that."

"No. Not the fight." Frankie leaned back as though savoring what he was going to say. "I've been looking for someone to be my buyer. Traveling—" He patted his huge stomach. "—is getting harder all the time."

Brent turned to look out the window. The truth probably was that Frankie was worried about being caught in Canada. In the Latin countries he had contacts, so there were few worries. But Canada could be dangerous. Better to have some minion like Ortega or himself get caught if it came to that.

"What about Ortega?" he asked.

"Ortega is okay. Very loyal. But.." Frankie tapped his temple with a fat finger. "He doesn't have enough up here."

When Frankie used the word loyal, Brent remembered Ortega at the Acapulco airport. It had been very convenient for him to be gone when the baby's father had tried to kill Frankie. And how had the father known that Frankie was responsible? And how had he known they'd be at the airport? Perhaps Ortega wasn't as loyal as Frankie thought.

"No, my friend," Frankie continued. "Not Ortega. You saw how it worked in Mexico. You'll handle the money. I'll set up the contact. You'll make sure of the quality."

Brent went rigid. "No baby killing. I won't do that."

Frankie smiled. "I know that, my friend. It's against your nature, just like cheating is against your nature. That's why I trust you."

Brent got up and walked to the sideboard. He found a beer and opened it, tilting the bottle so he wouldn't have to look at Frankie.

"In Vancouver testing won't be necessary anyway," Frankie said. "They know better than to cheat Frankie Rodriguez."

"I guess I can handle it," Brent said. "I already know Corillo."

"Not Corillo. Not this time. There's a shipment coming in from Afghanistan. You remember Afghanistan? That's where I got my start, you know."

So the guys at the DEA were right. Frankie had set up his connections when he was with the army. "Is that right?" he said. "I never would've guessed."

Frankie's smile was filled with self-satisfaction. "I could tell you stories, my friend, you would not believe. But—" He lifted his hands. "—back to Vancouver. You'll make the payoff. Jaime Ortega will handle the delivery."

"Isn't his nose going to get a little out of joint about that?"

"I'll talk to him. He'll understand."

He'd better, Brent thought. "Okay," he said. He started to put his beer down, ready to leave, then stopped when it occurred to him that with Frankie in such a good mood, it might be a good time to pump him for information. "Damn, Frankie," he said. "I've got to hand it to you. You've got a hell of an organization."

Frankie nodded and reached for his cigar. "Brent, there's so much money in this business that sometimes I can't believe it myself."

"Don't you ever worry about getting caught?"

Frankie laughed. "In this country? No. They make a big thing out of stopping drug dealing, then they pass stupid laws that handcuff the police. Even if I'm caught, my lawyer can handle it. He plays golf with half the judges in the city." He chuckled again.

"Can you image a system where the defense lawyers are allowed to associate with the very judges who'll be trying their cases. Shit. They even buy drinks and dinners for each other." Frankie tapped his forehead. "I'm no fool, my friend. And only fools go to prison. Those who get careless. Those who use the junk themselves."

"I guess you're right, Frankie. It sure has worked for you."

"You are fortunate, my friend. You're coming into the organization at the top." Frankie got up and came around the desk. "You might as well get used to it, *amigo*. You're going to be a wealthy man."

"Even if I stop fighting?"

"There are other fighters. They don't have to know how they are helping us."

The admiration in Brent's voice was only partially feigned as he said, "Jesus, Frankie, you've really got this thing under control."

Frankie walked to the door and opened it. "*Tiene razon, amigo. Just remember what I told you.*"

"Sure, Frankie." At the door, he paused. "Oh, one thing. I've got an aerobics class with Maria. Should I cancel out?"

Frankie's eyes hardened. "Not necessary. I already told her you won't be seeing her any more. And, *amigo*, don't forget what I told you about her."

Brent felt a surge of anger. How could he forget? Images of Maria plagued his dreams and tortured his days. She was one more good thing that Frankie had taken from him. Holding his anger in check, he said, "Right, Frankie. You're the boss."

Frankie didn't have to tell him not to forget it. They both knew that.

Riding the elevator, Brent felt the weight of the two packs of money in his jacket pockets. He took out the heaviest package and leafed through it. The bills had to total at least two hundred thousand dollars! Holding that much money was so unreal it lost credibility. At the moment, the bills held no more excitement than when he'd won thousands of play-dollars playing Monopoly when he was a kid. Which was a good thing since he probably wouldn't be able to keep it anyway.

At his locker, he stacked the money inside. It should be safe until he found a better place. After all, who'd expect a beat-up locker of a beat-up fighter to contain almost a quarter-million dollars.

He was about to close the locker when he noticed a folded piece of paper on top of his clothing as though it had been shoved through the air slots in the locker door.

What the hell? A note? The DEA? Unlikely. They wouldn't jeopardize his cover.

He looked around to be sure he was alone before he opened it. It was from Maria. "Meet me tonight. 6:00. The restaurant on Olympic."

Slowly, he folded the note and put it in his pocket. The smart thing to do would be to tear it in small pieces and flush it down the john. Then forget Maria existed. But he knew he couldn't do that. The note might be an invitation to hell, but it was an offer he could never refuse.

Chapter Twenty-Five

BRENT WAITED IN the restaurant parking lot, impatiently watching each car that pulled in, searching for Maria's Porche. There was another reason he scanned each car carefully. The note might have been a ruse to get him to this isolated spot to kill him. Not by Frankie. He was sure that Frankie suspected nothing. But Ortega? He was a horse of a different color.

Brent was almost certain Ortega wanted him out of the way. And he knew Ortega wanted Frankie dead. Ortega could've written the note. Or had it written. Brent had no idea what Maria's handwriting looked like.

He glanced at his watch again. Maybe she wasn't coming. It would be a good thing if she failed to show. He had to be out of his mind to risk seeing her. She'd already taken over his mind more than he thought any woman could after his bitter divorce. Could it have been only a little more than two years since he swore he'd never again fall in love? And his feelings for Maria grew stronger every time he saw her. They could end up destroying the entire investigation. Destroying him.

He put his hand on the car's ignition key. Start the car, he told himself. Get the hell out of here while you still can.

But a vision of Maria's face clouded his mind and his hand dropped. He groaned in anguish. It was useless. He'd do anything, take any risk, to see her if she wanted to see him.

His deliberations broke off when Maria's Porche came wheeling in and spun to a stop beside him. When he saw her, Brent's heart soared. She had the top down on her car and the wind had whipped her hair until it framed her face in an exotic cloud. Her smile stabbed him with exquisite anguish.

"Hi," she said. She reached across and opened the passenger door and winked at him. "Come on, stranger. Want'a take a ride?"

Brent didn't argue. He quickly locked his car and slid into the passenger's seat, fastening his seat belt. "My mother told me never to do this," he said.

"Your mother missed a lot of fun." She flipped the car into reverse, made a pursuit turn and kamikazied out of the parking lot and onto Olympic Boulevard heading west toward the ocean. Brent leaned back in the seat, watching the way the wind played with her hair, happier than he'd been in days.

"Congratulations," Maria said. Then her expression changed as though she'd been caught laughing at a funeral. "Oh, I'm sorry. I'm so sorry about Jennifer."

"Yeah." Brent looked away. How much should he tell her? How much could he tell her? How had Frankie explained it? He had to be noncommittal. "It was pretty awful."

"Daddy said it was some kind of a maniac—with a gun."

"That's right. A total stranger. Jennifer just happened to be in the wrong place." At least that much wasn't a lie.

Maria drove in silence for a moment. At an entrance to the Santa Monica Freeway, she roared up the entrance ramp in the diamond lane and neatly sandwiched between cars in the rushing traffic.

"I've missed you," she said. Her glance was brief, but Brent caught a look in her eyes that made his heart race. "I thought I'd see you as soon as you got back."

"Well..." Here was the moment he'd dreaded. He had to find some way to tell her it was over between them before something stronger than friendship broke both their hearts. "Frankie thinks I should concentrate on my training."

"I know," she said. "That's what he told me."

Brent let out his breath. Maybe it was going to be easy after all. "He...ah...he told me to stay away from you."

"And you were going to do it?"

Brent ran his fingers through his flying hair. It wasn't going to be easy after all. "I don't know," he said truthfully. "It seems like lately I've been trying to please everybody and ending up pleasing nobody."

"So what do you want to do?"

He turned to face her. "I want to see you. I never want to stop seeing you."

She glanced at his face, but she didn't smile. He'd give anything to know what was going on in her mind. "Do you like Italian food?" she asked.

He shrugged. "What's not to like?"

"Good. I know a great little place near Malibu."

Whenever she talked, she gestured with one or both hands, turning to look at him as though the car was on autopilot. Brent noted that the car's odometer was hovering above seventy and decided to hold his questions. He clutched the seat and tried to remember how far it was to Malibu. The way they were flying it shouldn't take long to get there, if they made it at all.

The sun was making its final plunge into the distant rim of the sea when they turned onto the Pacific Coast Highway and zoomed north past the wide Santa Monica beaches and almost wall-to-wall beach houses. Maria was forced to slow to a sedate fifty so Brent's hair didn't feel as thought the wind was ripping it from his scalp. With amazing speed, the sun slipped out of sight leaving a luminous gloaming that settled over the brooding sea.

Where Temescal Canyon dead-ended into the PC Highway, Maria made a hard left into a huge parking lot that bordered the sand of a broad beach. The beach crowd had long since departed and there were only a few cars in the mile-long lot so Maria was able to park in a deserted section facing the beach and the breaking surf. She shut off the engine, and in the sudden quiet, the only sound was the regular boom of a small surf and the whisper of cars rushing past on the highway. Across the wide sandy beach an occasional bathing-suited jogger moved along the wet sand near the water like an image silhouetted on a travel poster.

They sat quietly for a moment. Despite the peaceful ambience, Brent sat tensely, his stomach knotting, wondering what he could possibly say or do that make it possible for him to hold onto Maria and still do his job.

It was Maria who broke the silence. "So what are we going to do?"

Brent pushed back his hair with both hands, avoiding answering as long as possible. Finally, he had to admit. "I don't know. I've been struggling with this for days and...I just don't have an answer."

"My father isn't the only reason, is he?"

Startled, Brent stiffened. Did she know? How was that possible? If she knew he was a DEA agent, she'd have told Frankie. "I don't understand. What do you mean?"

"It's this damn boxing thing. You had to make a choice and you made it."

Brent sucked in a deep breath. This had to be how a man facing the gallows felt when given a reprieve. Even a temporary respite was better than nothing. "It wasn't my idea. You're father sort of gave me an ultimatum."

"You could've said no."

"That's hard to do to Frankie."

She turned to face him, her wind-tangled hair framing her beautiful face and Brent noticed that her eyes were brimming with tears. "Brent, Daddy's obsessed with boxing. He'd give anything to have a champion. He'd sacrifice anything. Even us. But you don't have to buy into it. He's going to keep pushing you until you get hurt—really hurt."

"I don't think that's going to happen."

"That's your ego talking. I know you've done all right so far. But maybe you've just been lucky."

"Lucky?" Even as he uttered the protest, Brent realized that she was probably right. He had been lucky. But something in him refused to admit that. "Maybe. This next fight will tell if it's luck or not."

"What next fight? With whom?"

"Willy Duncan. In Vancouver."

"Duncan! Brent, you're not ready for him."

"Frankie thinks I am."

"He doesn't give a damn about you. He wants that title so bad he'd take a chance on getting you killed. You've got to be smarter than that!"

Brent grinned at her. She might be right. But then again, she could be wrong. "Hey," he said. "Give me a little credit. I'm not exactly a bum."

She stared at him a moment. The tears were gone, replaced by a frustrated anger. "I know that. But use your head. You're not in Duncan's league."

Brent knew she was right. He had convinced himself that he needed the fight in order to trap Frankie, but in truth, he also wanted to see if he could win. To beat Willy Duncan! It was a heady dream. "Maybe I can't win," he said, "but I'm not going in there to lose either."

"What's that supposed to mean?"

"Sometimes it comes down to who wants it the most."

"Oh, sure. I suppose if I really wanted to I could beat him myself."

He looked at her and grinned. "I wouldn't be surprised."

But she didn't return his smile. "I just want you to promise this'll be the last one."

Brent's smile faded. She didn't know that she'd prophesied his future. Because, win or lose, bringing Frankie down would spell the end of his ring career.

"All right," he said. "This will be my last fight. It's over."

She stared at him, hope replacing the anger in her eyes. "You promise?"

Brent crossed his heart. "Promise."

Her quick smile was so devastating Brent had to suck in his breath.

"Good," she said. "Then Daddy won't have any reason to keep us apart."

Brent's euphoria vanished. How wrong she was. She didn't know it, but she was as trapped in lies as he was. He needed time to think— time to find a way make it all seem right.

He opened the car door. "Come on. Let's go for a walk on the beach."

"You nut," she said, but her smile broadened. "We'll get all wet."

"Take off your shoes." He slipped off his own shoes and socks and rolled up his pants legs. Stuffing his socks in his shoes, he dropped them inside the car and walked out on the sand, which was still warm from the afternoon sun.

Maria shook her head resignedly, but she got out of the car. She was wearing slacks and a blouse with a light sweater so it was easy to follow Brent's example and slip off her own shoes and stockings and roll up the legs of her slacks. She quickly locked her purse in the car's trunk and wedged the car keys under the front tire before she ran to catch up with Brent.

When she reached him, Brent was slowly walking across the warm sand toward the ocean. She tried to slip her hand into his, but he scooped her up and cradled her against his chest.

"What are you doing?" she asked.

"The sand's hot." he explained as he continued walking. "I don't want you to burn your feet."

"Oh," she said as though his explanation was perfectly logical. "Thank you, kind sir."

She locked her fingers behind Brent's neck and half turned so her cheek pressed against his shoulder. Brent could feel her breath through his shirt and the soft pressure of her breasts. Under his palms, the muscles of her back and legs were firm and smooth, warm as the sand beneath his feet. In his arms, she felt as small and helpless as a kitten and he wished that somehow he could walk forever, holding her close, smelling the delicate perfume of her hair, the caress of her slender fingers against his neck and hair.

At the upper limit of the surf line, he stopped. He stood holding Maria, looking out across the phosphorescent glow of the breaking waves, out beyond the sullen ocean to the faint line of the darkening horizon. The thought struck him that this might be the last time in his life she'd ever be in his arms. He wished there was some way he could make it last forever. Then he wouldn't have to thread his way among the lies that waited like the teeth of sharks just below the placid surface, waiting to catch him in one little mistake so they could tear his life away.

But he wasn't living a dream. This was reality. Soon she'd be lost forever, and he had better start preparing for it.

Reluctantly, he lowered her feet to the sand. She gave a little moan of protest that turned into a squeal when the dying end of a wave washed cross her bare feet.

"Oh," she gasped. "That's cold."

Brent looked at her hopping from one foot to the other and laughed. "Impossible. This is California."

"Yes. But those waves are from Alaska."

She took Brent's hand and tugged him farther up the slope of the beach so the water wouldn't reach their feet, and they began walking slowly, watching the lights of distant Santa Monica wink on like night-flying insects.

After a moment Maria asked, "Is this the last time, Brent?"

Her words struck Brent's heart like the blow of a sledge hammer. She meant that it might be the last time they could be together until after the fight when she believed he'd be free to defy her father. But he knew it might well be the last time they would be together forever.

"No," he lied. "After the fight, we'll have the rest of our lives."

"When is the fight?"

"Next month."

She stopped walking. "Next month? You can't possibly be ready by then."

Brent lifted an eyebrow at her. "You want it to be longer."

"Well, no. Even a month is too long to wait. But you'll hardly be healed up from the fight in Mexico."

"Oh, I don't know. In the old traveling road show days, those guys used to fight every day. Sometimes several times a day."

"They weren't fighting Willy Duncan."

"How do we know? When you fight a thousand guys, some of them have got to be damn good. But they survived."

She was silent for a few steps before she said, "Maybe we can figure out some way to see each other anyway."

It was Brent's turn to stop. "You think that would be wise?"

"No. But who said I was wise?"

Brent began walking, sorting through her proposal. Was it possible? She didn't know he'd be risking more than Frankie's displeasure. He'd be risking death. And yet...he desperately wanted to continue seeing her. The last hour had made him realize just how much.

"Maybe we'll think of something," he said.

"I just don't understand what's gotten into Daddy. He never said anything when I dated Ortega."

Brent's breath stopped. "You dated Ortega? When?"

"A long time ago." She glanced at him and a faint smile tugged at her lips. "Don't worry. I haven't been out with him in ages."

"Why did you stop?"

"Oh, I don't know. I never was that interested. And he...just stopped asking me."

"Maybe Frankie told him to stop."

She thought about it, staring down at the sand. "I never thought of that. I was just glad. I never did care that much for him."

Brent slipped his hand into hers. "Funny," he said. "I feel the same way."

She chuckled before her face settled back into lines of worry. "I just don't understand why. A lot of our fighters have girl friends. Daddy never asks them to give them up."

"They weren't going with his daughter."

"I think it's more than that. It's got to be something else."

Brent didn't like the direction the conversation was heading so he tried to defuse the bomb with humor. "Religion, maybe. I'm not Catholic."

Maria shook her head. "Daddy's about as religious as Madeline O'Hara. I've got to ask him. He must think I'm a baby."

"No," Brent said sharply, and when she looked up at him, he added, "This way we've got a chance. If Frankie suspects something, we'll never get to see each other."

"Yes. You're right about that. He doesn't like people to double-cross him. I think it goes back to the time when he was a kid on the street."

Brent thought, You don't know the half of it.

They'd wandered away from the surf, across the warm, dry sand to a low dune that shielded them from the highway and she sat down, her chin on her fist. "It just doesn't make sense. He's been so proud of you."

"Maybe he doesn't want to mix business with family."

"So why did he invite you for dinner?"

"Maybe that's when he noticed that we were...uh...mixing."

"Well, maybe. But..."

Searching for an explanation she could accept, Brent sat down beside her and said, "He's just old-fashioned. When he saw the way I was staring at you... Well, he decided I was definitely dangerous."

"Are you?"

"What?"

"Dangerous?"

He laughed. "Sure. I'm big enough to take advantage of you. No wonder he's worried."

"I'll bet you can't."

"Can't what?"

"Take advantage of me."

There was a smile in her voice and he snickered. "Listen, little girl. You're on dangerous ground."

"I'll bet you can't even catch me." She leaped up and sprinted across the sand.

Brent jumped up and charged after her. He was fast, but he still had to run full out before he was able to overtake her flying form. He reached for her slender waist, but she made a quick stop and doubled back. His own stop was less graceful and he tumbled in the sand. He leaped to his feet and set out after her again.

It was like trying to catch a jackrabbit. He was faster, but she zigged and zagged sharply, doubling and turning, splashing through the surf and up into the slogging sand. She was inexhaustible and he was beginning to breath heavily when he guessed correctly on one of her quick turns and intercepted her, lifting her off her feet and whirling her to the sand.

But she wasn't subdued. She was lithe as a panther and she twisted free time and again, and he had to lunge to pull her down by an ankle or wrist. It wasn't until he had both legs around her waist in a scissors grip and her arms pinned behind her back with one hand that he was able to tilt her chin up with his other hand and kiss her. And still she struggled, making groaning sounds of protest and writhing her body against his chest and legs.

But he held her, his lips on hers, and gradually her struggles diminished and her lips began to respond.

Brent lifted his head and grinned at her. "See. I am dangerous."

"Yes," she said softly. "I guess you've got me."

"No." Brent's voice caught in his voice. "You've got me." He kissed her again.

This time her lips were warm against his, and he was able to be tender and soft until he could contain his desire no longer and he crushed her lips with his, searching for her tongue and thrilled when she came to meet his. He released his grip so he could put his arms around her, and abruptly, she hit him in the stomach.

She laughed. "Gotcha!"

She sprang to her feet and dashed away.

Brent started to get up, then flopped back on the sand with a groan, pressing both hands to his stomach. Maria stopped and looked back at him over her shoulder. When she saw he wasn't following, she came back warily like a puppy playing tag. She circled him, moving in closer. But he lay motionless, groaning.

"Give up?" she said.

He groaned.

She moved closer. "I knew you weren't dangerous."

He groaned louder.

She moved closer, peering down at him, concern in her eyes. "Are you all right?"

He struck like a cobra. His hand lashed out, grabbing her ankle and he pulled her down on top of him. "Gotcha!"

She bucked and writhed, but he wrapped both arms around her and squeezed until she gasped for breath.

"Give up?" he said.

"If you squeeze any harder," she gasped, "you'll be making love to a dead body."

Brent relaxed his grip and she lay panting, her body on top of his, her breasts pressed against his chest, her thighs molded to his, her soft breath on his neck. Her breathing slowed and she slid up and raised herself on her hands until her face was poised over his.

"Well?" she said.

Brent looked into her eyes. "Well, what?"

"Aren't you going to kiss me again?"

"What? And get my nose bitten off?"

"Coward," she said, and kissed him.

He lay passively, allowing her to explore his lips with her own, savoring her soft nips and gentle breath, but refusing to cooperate.

Finally, she lifted her head and grinned at him. "It won't work. You might play dead, but there's one part of you that's very much alive."

She laughed and wiggled her hips.

"Damn," he said, and lifted his lips to hers.

She rolled off him, lying on her back in the sand. He moved on top of her, and this time, there was no laughter when he gently moved his lips across her cheek. His lips nuzzled the hollow of her throat and she tilted her chin back with a sigh. His hand moved inside the neck of her blouse and caressed the upper slopes of her breasts.

She gasped. "Brent. No. Please."

But there was no conviction in her voice. He knew he could take her, and she'd allow it because it was right for both of them. Instead, he turned to lie on his back in the sand and put his arm beneath her head, snuggling her gently into the hollow of his shoulder.

They lay like that for a long time, her body warm against his, her breath soft on his cheek, listening to the sea and the whispering cars, watching the awakening stars, not wanting to think beyond the moment.

It was a long time later that Maria sat up and hugged her knees. "I guess we'd better go."

"Yeah." Brent got up and brushed sand from his clothes. "Besides, I'm hungry."

"You men." She chuckled. "All you ever think about is food."

"That's the second thing we always think about."

"And what's the first?" she asked coquettishly.

"Cars. Men are mad about machines."

Maria laughed and put her hand in his. They walked through the darkness and the warm sand, their hips brushing, each acutely conscious of the other, aware that it might be a long time before they saw each other again. Brent knew that sneaking around, meeting behind Frankie's back was only talk. Maria could never keep her father—or her mother—from suspecting something. And Brent couldn't take the chance. Maria might think their separation was temporary, but Brent knew it was forever.

At the car, Maria retrieved her keys. Before she walked around to the driver's side, she put her arms around Brent's neck and kissed him quickly and lightly. "Thanks," she said softly.

Brent climbed into the passenger seat. He was glad he'd retained control there on the beach. She was bound to hate him when she learned the truth. He couldn't live with himself if he'd made love to her before he betrayed her. The depth of such a betrayal would be more than he could stand.

Chapter Twenty-Six

THE NEXT DAY, Brent walked into a rented motel room carrying a brown paper sack. The air in the room already reeked with the odor of cigarettes and beer. Supervisor Zylo was seated on a couch leafing through a sheaf of papers from his open briefcase. Hendrix and Duval were standing near a small table in front of the window drinking Coors straight from the can and smoking cigarettes. What was left of the six-pack was on the table. The Venetian blinds were turned flat, shutting out the sunlight, so it was necessary to use the overhead light and two bedside lamps.

The agents said hello to Brent, but nobody moved to shake his hand. Brent wasn't offended. DEA meetings in some safe place like this motel room were not for social purposes. If anything, DEA agents tended to avoid ostentation. In their way of thinking, that was for FBI guys who wore suits and neckties.

Duval looked at Brent's face and grinned. "Have you ever considered ducking?"

Brent smiled. It had been less than a week since his fight with Cruz and his face still registered the results. "If I knew how to duck," he said, "I wouldn't be here."

Duval nodded. "That goes for all of us." He glanced at Zylo. "Almost all of us."

Zylo, if he heard, gave no indication. He looked up from the papers he was holding. "Quintana. What did you say he called himself? Corillo?"

"Right. Corillo."

"He's our man. We've got a warrant out on him. Killed a guy in a drug deal in Calexico."

"He's too smart to enter the *Ustados Unitos*," Hendrix said. "If he gets caught, it's up the river."

"Shit," Duval said. "I'll bet he's been in and out of the country a dozen times."

Hendrix took a can of beer from the six-pack and opened it before he offered it to Brent. "Beer?"

Brent hesitated. He shouldn't be consuming all the calories contained in beer. But he also wanted to be a good old boy, so he took it with a "thanks."

"I doubt it," Zylo said. He got up and went to the table where he popped a beer. Brent noticed that neither Hendrix nor Duval had offered a beer to the supervisor. "We've got the FBI in on it."

Hendrix and Duval glanced at each other. "That's great, Zylo," Hendrix said. "The FBI has been trying to take over our operation for years and you hand them one of our cases."

"Nonsense," Zylo countered. "We're all part of the same agency. We've got to work together."

"Together is one thing. Under is another."

The antagonism between the two federal agencies had seemed stupid to Brent when he'd encountered it at the NTI. It was no secret that J. Edgar Hoover, when he was running the FBI, had wanted to keep the agency out of narcotics. But since his death, the FBI had been edging more and more into areas the DEA considered their purview.

"That pisses me off," Duval said. "We've been busting our asses for year with too few agents and too damn little money. Now we're starting to make a real dent in dope, the FBI moves in and treats us like a bunch of idiots."

"And takes the credit for our big busts," Hendrix added. "Don't forget that."

"It sucks," Duval said. "Man, it really does."

"So what else is new?" Zylo said. He turned to Brent. "What's this about you going to Vancouver?"

"Frankie's got a fight set up there."

"For you?"

"Yeah."

"Who with?" Hendrix asked.

"Willy Duncan."

Hendrix's head lifted. His hand, raising his beer to his lips, stopped. "You're crazy," he said softly. "Get out of it."

Brent shook his head. "I can't. Frankie's made me his money man."

Hendrix and Duval both straightened. "Frankie's not going?" Hendrix asked.

"No. I'll be making the buy." When the DEA agents were silent, he added, "It might be the break we're looking for. I couldn't turn it down."

"Forget it," Duval said. "You can't do us any good if you're dead."

"Wait a minute," Zylo cut in. "He's got a point. If he's the money man, he can get a line on Frankie's Canada contacts. And he might find out something about his smuggling M.O."

"I don't know about that," Brent said. "Jaime Ortega is going along. He'll be handling the shipment."

"Good," Hendrix said. "That means you can get out of it. Let Ortega handle it."

"Forget that," Zylo snapped. "We might be able to get Frankie and the junk together on this end. This could be a real break."

"Not if he gets his head beat in," Duval said. "Kid, get sick. Break a leg. Don't go up there."

"Yeah," Hendrix echoed. "We'll get Frankie sooner or later."

"It had better be sooner," Zylo interjected. "With your picture plastered all over the sports pages, somebody's bound to make you."

"You've got a point," Hendrix agreed. "I think we should pull him out now."

Zylo put his beer on the counter. "Wait a minute. Let him decide for himself." He took a step toward Brent. "How about it? You want to go through with this?"

Brent had thought of little else for a week. He had the feeling his boat was in white water moving inexorably toward a deadly falls, and it was too late to make the shore. Frankie had already cost him everything that meant anything to him. His only reason for living now was to bring Frankie down.

"The fight doesn't matter," he said slowly. "It's only a means to an end. Nobody'll be surprised if I go down in the first couple of rounds. But Zylo's right. We've got to do it soon or it's all going to fall apart. I've got to do it."

Hendrix and Duval were silent.

"Good. Just don't screw up," Zylo said. "It's murder dealing with the Canadians." He picked up his beer and walked back to his seat on the couch. He picked up the papers he'd been holding. "You know how much we could confiscate if this goes down?" He consulted the papers. "If we can get a good paper trail all the way back to the time Frankie was in the army, we can confiscate his restaurant, his gym, about a dozen apartments, a twenty-seven-foot boat, his house, and God knows what else. We're talking millions here."

He was referring to the seizure law that allowed the government to seize property purchased with proven drug money. Its objective was to take the profit out of dope dealing so a trafficker couldn't sit out a prison term and reap the rewards of his loot when he got out.

"Frankie is no fool," Brent said. "I'll bet he's got everything in somebody else's name."

"We know he has—mostly his wife and father. Doesn't matter. If we can prove they were bought with drug money, we could hit it big."

Brent knew why Zylo was so excited. While the money realized from a bust belonged to the federal government, a portion of it was always given back to the local department making the bust.

"Zylo's right," Hendrix said. "Don't screw up. We can use the money to pay your hospital bills."

"This should help," Brent said. He picked up the sack he'd brought in and tossed it to Zylo.

The supervisor caught it gingerly as though Brent had tossed him a bomb. When he felt its weight, he put it on the table near the window and opened it. He looked inside and his eyes went round with surprise. He upended the sack and the sheaves of bills spilled out on the table.

"Jesus," he said. "How much is here?"

"Two hundred and ten thousand dollars," Brent said.

Hendrix and Duval walked over to examine the money.

"Is this the money you're supposed to use for the Vancouver buy?" Hendrix asked.

"No. The two hundred is my purse from the Cruz fight. The ten is from Frankie."

"God damn!" Duval said as he picked up the ten thousand dollar sheaf. "Dealing sure as hell pays more than busting."

"Temporarily," Zylo said. "Temporarily."

Hendrix picked up the larger sheaf of bills. "What about this? This isn't dope money. Shouldn't he get to keep it?"

Zylo almost grabbed the money from Hendrix's hand and thrust it back in the sack. "We'll have to get a ruling on that. Personally, I think the fight was part of his cover, so it should go to the agency."

"Shit, Zylo," Duval said. "You'd think it was going in your own pocket."

"Yeah," Hendrix added. "Maybe you can get your office renovated."

Zylo's face reddened. "I don't make the rules," he said. "If they rule it's his, you won't get any protest from me."

He put the money in his briefcase and took out a paper form. He began filling in spaces. "You'll have to sign this," he said to Brent. "It'll make sure you get it back if the ruling is favorable."

Hendrix and Duval finished their beers. "Keep in touch," Hendrix said to Brent. "Don't phone from Vancouver unless it's an emergency."

Zylo looked up from the paper. "You guys keep seeing what you can dig up on Frankie's assets."

The two agents looked at Brent and grimaced. They hated paper work. "Sure," Hendrix said. At the door, he said to Brent, "See if you can get a line on where Frankie does his cutting. If we're going to bust the place, I'd like to scope it first."

"I'll try. But Frankie's pretty closed-mouthed about that end of the business."

"What about Ortega? He must know. Why don't you buddy up

with him? He might spill something—if he doesn't kill you."

He laughed and went out.

Duval said, "Luck, kid," and followed his partner out the door.

Zylo got up and held the paper out to Brent along with a pen. "Sign at the bottom."

Brent signed the receipt for the money. Zylo had already signed.

Zylo tore off a carbon and gave it to Brent. "Put this somewhere safe," he said. He put his copy in his briefcase with the money and snapped it shut. He held out his hand. "Good luck." Brent shook his hand and Zylo said, "Look, Brent. I know those guys think I don't give a damn, but take care. If things get dicey, back off. Okay?"

"Yeah," Brent said. "Don't worry."

Zylo stared at Brent a moment as though to determine how Brent was holding up. Satisfied, he nodded and went out the door, leaving it open.

Brent sighed and looked around the room. The room fit the way he felt—sleazy.

Chapter Twenty-Seven

BRENT AND ORTEGA exchanged few words during the long flight to Seattle, then on to Vancouver. Brent didn't mind. He much preferred to dream about Maria. They'd had dinner the night before in a Japanese restaurant situated in the Hollywood Hills with a view of L.A.'s ocean of lights. Maria had been especially beautiful in a black silk dress. A double strand of pearls matched the luminescence of her skin. When they walked into the restaurant, Brent noticed people turned to look. He didn't blame them. Someone as lovely as Maria didn't pass very often.

And later, beside her car in the parking lot, she'd kissed him good night with a heavy sensuality that had left him aching for hours.

"Good luck in Vancouver," she said as she got in her car.

"Thanks," Brent answered. "I wish you could be there."

"Maybe I will be." She smiled mischievously at him and cocked her head. "Daddy isn't going. You should have some member of the family there."

"Don't even joke about it. If Frankie finds out we met even once, it'll be over for both of us."

"Okay," she said as she climbed into her car and fastened her seat belt. "Mother isn't doing anything. I'll send her."

She laughed, started the car and roared away.

Brent had stood staring after her, unwilling to move, trying to burn the image of her laughing face so deep in his memory he'd never forget. It would be the last time he'd see it.

The image was still clinging to his memory when the plane landed at Vancouver's international airport and they picked up their bags at the baggage claim area. Ortega had his usual two, large, battered Samsonites and a two-suiter carry-on. Brent had a two-suiter and a small carry-on bag.

The custom agent scarcely glanced at their passports. "Oh, yes," he said. "Mr. Thomas. Good luck in your fight."

Although it was after six, the sun was still high in the sky, painting a horizon of majestic mountain peaks with rosy splendor. The rented limousine was waiting, and as they headed for their hotel, Brent asked the driver, "Where's the B.C. Stadium?"

"On the west side. Only about a mile from the hotel. Want to go around that way?"

"No," Ortega answered. "Just get us to the hotel."

"Yes, sir."

Brent sat back in the seat. He didn't mind the way Ortega had taken over. He'd see the stadium soon enough. At the moment, the money he was carrying in a money belt provided by Frankie felt like a garrote around his waist. The sooner he got rid of it ,the better he'd feel.

A half hour later, the limousine pulled into the *porte cochére* of the Vancouver Hotel, which was located in the heart of downtown Vancouver. The hotel, with its French Gothic architecture, including a green roof and gargoyles, radiated old world elegance. Brent liked it immediately, although Ortega sniffed disdainful.

"Dead," he said. "There's more action out on Granville Island, but Frankie likes this place."

"I understand it's got an exercise room. We'll need that."

"You will. I've got other plans."

As soon as they had registered, Ortega said, "I'm going to the bar. Take care of the bags. Don't let anything happen to them."

"Don't drink too much," Brent warned. "We've got a big day tomorrow."

Ortega glared at Brent. "You just do your job. I'll do mine." He turned and strode away.

Brent shrugged and followed the bellman to the elevator. Ortega was right about one thing—he did have a job to do.

The size and furnishings of the suite surprised Brent. Frankie had spent some money. There was a living room with a grand piano in one corner, and picture windows that gave a magnificent view of the city and the waters of the sound. The bathroom had a shower big enough to hold a party inside. There was also a large Jacuzzi bathtub. Brent wondered what kind of a room Frankie would've reserved for him if he'd lost the fight in Mexico. Probably a broom closet in a flop house.

The bellman had gone and Brent was unpacking when the phone rang. He picked it up, expecting it to be Ortega. "Yeah."

It wasn't Ortega. A man's voice, harsh and raw, said, "Thomas?"

At first, Brent thought it might be a reporter. "That's right."

Instead of asking him questions, the man said, "Got a pencil?"

The supplier. It had to be him. Frankie had said he would be getting a telephone call from the supplier who would set up a meet. Brent had assumed it would take place after the fight the way it had in Acapulco.

"Wait a minute." Brent opened the top drawer of the small desk under the phone. Inside was a pen and stationary bearing the hotel logo. "Got it," he said.

"Call this number." The voice rattled off a number that Brent scribbled down. "Use a pay phone." There was a click as the man hung up.

The voice hadn't said when to call, but Brent assumed he meant right away. So he took the elevator down to the lobby and searched out the bank of public telephones.

Brent selected a phone as isolated from other callers as possible, deposited the necessary coins and dialed the number.

The same voice answered. "Yes?"

"It's Brent Thomas."

"Ah, Mr. Thomas." This time there was warmth in the voice. "You brought the gift from Frankie?"

Brent touched his new money belt. "The gift? Yes. I have it."

"Good. We'll meet the morning after your...ah...contest. That's the day after tomorrow. At the Empire. That's a motel on Beach Street at Howe. Room two-eight-six. Nine o'clock."

"No," Brent said. "Ten-thirty."

There was a pause and Brent had the impression that the man on the other end of the line wasn't used to being told what to do and wasn't happy about it.

His voice had lost its warmth. "Why not nine? There a problem?"

"No problem. I just don't carry the money with me. I'll have to pick it up."

This time the answer came quickly. "Very well. Ten-thirty."

Click. The line went dead. Brent quickly jotted down the name of the hotel, the room number and the time before he allowed himself to say, "Damn!"

He'd have preferred to wait a day or two after the fight. No telling what kind of shape he'd be in. It was possible he could be flat on his back in a hospital. Frankie should have thought of it before he set up the meeting. Or maybe he had, and the whole thing was nothing but a test.

Back in his room, Brent called Ortega, locating him in the bar, and asked him to meet him in the hotel restaurant. Ortega wasn't thrilled about it, but said he'd be there.

In the restaurant, Brent selected a table in a corner. When Ortega joined him, they ordered coffee. He told Ortega about the phone call and the meeting time, and Ortega's perpetual scowl deepened. "That's right after the fight. Suppose you can't make it?"

"I'll have to."

Ortega's scowl almost disappeared, and for a moment, Brent thought he was going to smile. "If you can't make it, I can handle it."

The thought that flashed through Brent's mind was wonder at why Ortega was so happy. Perhaps he was savoring the image of Brent so incapacitated that he couldn't make the meeting. But one thing was certain, he had no intention of allowing Ortega to get his hands on the money.

"We'll cross that bridge when we get to it," he said.

"Yeah." Ortega's scowl had returned. He stared at Brent, ice mirrored in his black eyes. "I don't know what the fuck Frankie was thinking about when he gave you the money. Where are you going to stash it when you're fighting?"

The question seemed innocuous, but Brent had a gut feeling there was something hidden in Ortega's desire to know, so he smiled thinly at Ortega. "That's none of your business."

Ortega's lips compressed and the ice in his eyes became more apparent, but all he said was, "Okay. Just don't screw up."

When he and Ortega separated, the money belt weighted as heavily on Brent's mind as it did on his waist. He hadn't trusted Ortega before, now he was even more apprehensive. He considered his original plan of putting the money in the hotel safe. That was the obvious thing to do. Perhaps too obvious.

In his room, Brent emptied his carry-on bag and put the money belt inside. Taking the bag, Brent left the hotel by a side entrance. Making sure he wasn't followed, he walked two blocks from the hotel before he hailed a taxi and had it take him to the Greyhound bus station. There, from a large bank of rental storage lockers, he picked out one on the bottom, deposited the coin, put the bag inside the locker and locked it.

Back in the hotel, he sewed the locker key into the waistband of his boxing trunks, using a needle and thread he found in a tourist's package in his room's writing desk. Then he folded all the hotel stationary he could find into a package. He wrote his name on an envelope, then placed the package inside and sealed the envelope.

He carried the envelope to the lobby's front desk and asked to have it deposited in the hotel safe. The clerk put the envelope in a large manila envelope. He wrote Brent's name and room number on it and gave him a receipt.

When Brent changed into his gym clothes and went to the hotel exercise room, he was conscious of the locker key snug against his back. He was probably being paranoid about the money, but what the hell. He had nothing to lose by being cautious. He wondered what the DEA would say if he lost Frankie's money. Would they take it out of his salary like they would if the money was the DEA's?

One thing was certain. Frankie sure as hell would take it out of his hide.

Chapter Twenty-Eight

THEIR LIMOUSINE dropped Ortega and Brent off at the side entrance of the stadium. Brent felt a shiver of dread when he saw an ambulance parked near the entrance. It was probably a normal procedure for any event at the stadium, but the feeling he might be its next passenger was disconcerting.

Later, walking behind Ortega down the isle from his dressing room toward the ring, Brent couldn't help but compare the situation to his fight in Mexico. That entire experience had been a circus—a nightmare. Here things had proceeded with cool efficiency. From the weigh-in the day before, the press conferences, and the pre-fight warm-up to preparations in the clean dressing room, everything had been conducted with typical Canadian efficiency. Even the crowd, although boisterous, didn't feel threatening. Some of them even seemed to be on his side.

During the weigh-in, as though caught up in the sober mood, Willy Duncan's usual flamboyant fight predictions had seemed more subdued than usual. One thing that hadn't seemed subdued, however, was Duncan's malevolent glare each time he looked at Brent. He was Jaime Ortega magnified, except this version weighed two hundred twenty-four pounds and would soon be given the opportunity to kill him.

Brent had studied videos of Duncan's fights, but he'd been unprepared for the sheer power the man exuded in person. He reminded Brent of a young Mike Tyson. The muscles in his arms and shoulders were so massive they made his arms seem shorter than they were.

"Brent! Brent!"

The voice cut through the sounds of the crowd like a wonderful memory cuts through despair.

Maria!

She was standing in front of a seat next to the aisle, and at first, Brent didn't recognize her. Her clothes were nondescript, her magnificent hair was tied back with a dark scarf, and her wonderful eyes were hidden behind dark glasses.

Brent stopped. "Maria! What are you doing here?" He glanced at Ortega who continued down the aisle, thinking Brent was following.

She grinned at him. "You don't want me here?"

"You know I do, but... Does Frankie know?"

She tossed her head defiantly. "I didn't tell him."

Brent felt an instant dismay. Since the weigh-in, he'd been telling himself what a fool he was to be in the same ring with Duncan. He'd been fighting a battle with himself about minimizing the damage by going down and staying down the first time Duncan got in a solid punch. Now, with Maria watching, he knew he could never do that. He'd have to hang in as long as he could no matter what the price.

"I've got to go," he told her. "I'll try to meet you after the fight. Don't let Ortega see you."

"Okay. I'm at the Vancouver, too. Room five-ten. Don't forget."

"Don't worry."

"This is for luck." She wrapped her arms around him and kissed him, and the people watching cheered and applauded. As he turned away, she said, "Don't let him hurt your lips. I like them like they are."

Brent was smiling when he hurried to catch up with Ortega and climb in the ring. His lips? Hell! His whole face would probably be like it was full of balloons for days after Duncan finished with him.

As Ortega was putting grease on his face, he said, "Don't get hurt too bad. We got work tomorrow."

"I'll keep that in mind."

"When he knocks you down, stay down." Ortega's eyes flicked toward Duncan's corner. "If you're still alive."

Brent was thinking much the same thing when the referee called them to the center of the ring for his instructions. Standing eye to eye with Duncan, he was again impressed by the man's strength. He radiated power. Brent felt a shiver of fear. What the devil was he doing here? This had to be how a soldier armed with nothing but a rifle felt going up against a tank. Unlike the soldier, however, he might get seriously wounded, but he probably wouldn't be killed.

Probably.

Waiting for the bell, Brent went over his strategy. With Cruz, who'd been a superb boxer, he'd been forced to be a puncher. Here the roles were reversed. Duncan was a brawler. It would be stupid to slug it out with him. He would have to be the boxer. If Duncan ever hit him cleanly with all the power in those massive arms and shoulder, it would be *sayonara.*

At the university and fighting as an amateur, He had met fighters who had muscles like Superman. But few of them had the necessary hand and foot speed to make it as a fighter. Duncan was the exception. You'd think that all those muscles would slow the man down. But, watching videos of his fights, Brent had been awed by Duncan's hand speed.

The man's foot speed was not great, but when he got close, those short, powerful arms lanced his fists like servo-driven pistons. Almost every one of Duncan's wins had taken place when he'd trapped his opponent in a corner where he'd been unable to escape those pile-driving fists. Ergo, he had to keep Duncan from pinning him in a corner.

The one unknown was Duncan's physical condition. Brent hoped that, like Cruz and Molino, Duncan took him so lightly that he hadn't trained hard. If Duncan had neglected his conditioning, then there was just a chance, if Duncan didn't tag him early, he could outlast him. Few people realized what a terrible physical drain it was for a fighter to keep his arms raised for round after round while being hit with blows like a wrecking ball.

If Duncan had neglected the long hours of light and heavy bag work, maybe, just maybe, arm fatigue would cause him to loose some steam from his punches. If that happened, and Duncan's arms began to sag, that's when Brent would go to work. He could help speed the process by not wasting his energy going for Duncan's head; instead pounding those heavy muscles on the man's arms and shoulders, tiring him like a *bandrillero* brings a bull's head down by plunging *bandrillas* into the muscles of the bull's neck and shoulders.

Of course, sometimes the bull killed the *bandrillero*.

Brent tried not to think about that as the bell sounded, and he moved to meet the man who wanted to dismember him.

Duncan came out slowly and the fight's pattern was quickly established with Duncan shuffling forward, his fists cocked, and Brent moving away, circling, with quick changes of direction, his left jab working hard to keep Duncan off balance. When he used his right, it was to hook Duncan's upper left arm.

Suddenly, Duncan struck.

Bam! Bam! Bam!

His speed astonished Brent. He was barely able to block Duncan's quick combination of left and two rights with his arms, but the blows sent him reeling, his arms feeling as though they'd been hit by a steel crowbar.

Frantically, he ducked, dodged and back-pedaled, fighting to stay clear of Duncan's follow-up attack.

Duncan's blow, however, had taught Brent something. Duncan's left did not have the devastating impact of his right. The left looked powerful and it could hurt like hell, but Brent doubted that Duncan's left could knock him out unless he got careless. His immediate task was to work on Duncan's right arm and ribs.

When Duncan realized he couldn't catch Brent, he slowed his charge and returned to stalking, his fists cocked.

But Brent was even more wary, and throughout the remainder of the round, he was able to stay clear of Duncan's quick combinations, using his own opportunities to hammer at Duncan's arms and ribs. Once he was able to hit the inside of Duncan's right bicep with a hard right hook and he noticed Duncan wince. His satisfaction was short-lived because Duncan countered with a quick left that Brent was able to deflect just enough to take the stunning blow high on his forehead, and again, he was forced into a fast retreat.

When Brent came out for the second round, instead of circling away, he took Duncan by surprise by a swift, aggressive attack. Before Duncan could get his guard set, Brent got in a stinging left jab to Duncan's cheek that showered sweat from his hair, and when Duncan's arms came up, he got in a hard right to Duncan's right bicep.

Quickly, before Duncan could counter, Brent went into his dance, moving fast, using his superior reach to keep Duncan away.

Then, like a fool, Brent began to develop a pattern: circle right, jab, jab, right hook to Duncan's right side. Even as he was doing it, Brent told himself to change. Duncan was no fool. He'd figure out the pattern if Brent did the same thing all the time.

The trouble was it wasn't working. He was getting in some good whacks on Duncan's arms and ribs. But the tactic seemed to be about as effective a hitting the side of a battleship with a tack hammer. Still, it was all he had going for him.

Then it happened. He'd made his two swift jabs and was throwing the right when Duncan stepped inside and hit him on the side of the jaw with a right hook that lifted Brent off his feet. He sensed that he hit the canvas on his side, but there was no feeling in his body. Somehow, he was able to keep his eyes open and he saw Duncan stalk to a corner. He saw the referee kneel over him. He saw the man's lips move. But he heard no sound.

Damn. Should've learned to read lips.

He had no idea what the count was. Then his eyes were attracted by movement and he noticed the referee's fingers. He was putting up four fingers. Or was it six? Six fingers on one hand? That didn't make sense. It had to be five. Then the referee was using both hands. That meant it was more than five. He had to get up!

To his total surprise, he was able to roll over and get to his hands and knees. The problem was that from that position, he couldn't see the referee's fingers.

Wait. There they were. The referee was considerately putting them where he could see then. But that was stupid. What made the idiot think he could count? It was all he could do to see them at all. He thought it was eight.

Was that right? Five on one hand and three on the other. Right. Eight. And damn close to ten!

Stay down! If you get up, he'll knock your stupid head off. Amazing how many thoughts could go through a brain in one second.

Nine! He definitely saw nine fingers, sharp and clear.

Then, for some reason, the referee stopped counting and Brent looked at him bewilderedly. Instead of counting, the referee was staring at him eye to eye. Eye to eye? Oh, yeah. Somehow he was standing up. Suddenly it struck him. Jesus! Duncan!

From the corner of his eye he saw Duncan coming toward him, his fists swinging. Instincts took over and he ducked away. He knew better than to try to tie Duncan up. Those powerful arms and shoulders would pound his ribs to a pulp.

Instead, he bicycled away, surprised at how quickly his head had cleared. Incongruously, the thought lightninged through his head that clean living paid off.

But he couldn't keep away from Duncan forever. He had to find some way to slow the man down. Attack! It had worked once. And Duncan was so overconfident he was coming at Brent with his guard down, his hands back, cocked for the put-away shot.

It was easy for Brent to stop abruptly, feint left, and hit Duncan on the point of the jaw with a hard right.

Duncan stopped as though he'd been hit by a cannon ball. His eyes glazed and his knees buckled. Brent followed up with a hard left and a harder right cross.

Duncan was falling when the bell sounded.

Brent stood staring as Duncan's handlers leaped into the ring and helped Duncan to his corner. Damn! Saved by the bell.

Brent walked back to his corner, cursing his luck. That would probably be the only chance he'd get.

Surprisingly, Ortega said, "Keep working on his right arm. I think you hurt him."

"Yeah," Brent agreed. "I think you're right."

Brent glanced down at Maria. She was bouncing in her seat, gesturing with both fists. It was too noisy to hear what she was shouting, but he thought it was something to the effect that he should "get the S.O.B." He gave her a fist to let her know he understood. There was no way to tell her he was amazed he'd lasted this long.

At the bell, Duncan appeared to be totally recovered. If anything, he was even more dangerous and, certainly, more angry because he said, "I'm gonna git you, boy. I'm gonna git you."

Brent had no answer. He rather thought that Duncan was right. It was simply a question of when.

But he could make Duncan pay a price.

He offered Duncan a right hand shot at his head. When Duncan took the opportunity, Brent slipped the punch and hit Duncan's right ribs as hard as he could.

A moment later, he tried the same trick again. And again it worked and he got in another hard shot to Duncan's ribs.

Better not try that again. Duncan was ready for him. But maybe he could make Duncan think he was going to try it again...

He faked the same pattern, offering his head. As he expected, Duncan ignored the invitation. Instead, he prepared to counter Brent's expected punch to his ribs. But Brent only faked the punch and when Duncan launched his counter, Brent countered with a hard left to Duncan's solar plexus.

Duncan grunted and his hands came down.

Brent shifted his attack to Duncan's head and was able to hit him three times. But he couldn't reach Duncan's jaw, and Duncan shook off the punches and resumed his relentless pursuit.

At the end of the round, Brent was able to get in a hard uppercut to Duncan's right elbow and he felt his fist jar against bone. When Duncan walked back to his corner, he carried his right arm pressed against his side.

"It's working," Ortega said. "Keep it up."

"Gotcha," Brent agreed. But he wasn't at all sure Duncan was going to give him the chance. By now he had to know Brent's strategy. He would protect that right arm like it was the mint.

Brent was right. When Duncan came out, he kept his right side turned away from Brent, his right arm held close against his side.

And, like a fool, Brent went after Duncan's exposed jaw. He set Duncan up with a left jab and launched his right. Big mistake! Duncan slipped the punch and countered with a battering right to Brent's jaw.

To Brent's surprise, he didn't go down. He was hurt, but not badly, and he was able to motor away from Duncan's follow up.

It was working. His pounding at Duncan's right arm and ribs had taken its toll. Duncan's pulverizing power was diminished.

But don't get stupid! Keep at the arm. Don't give him a chance to recuperate.

But he could take more chances now. Float like a butterfly; sting that right side like a sledge hammer. Move in with combinations, just like he'd told his class. Jab, jab, dance, jab, combination. Dance away. Bam! Smash that arm.

This time when the bell sounded, Duncan went to his corner, holding his arm across his chest, his eyes worried.

"He's getting tired," Ortega said. "He don't move like he was."

"Yeah, I noticed."

"Take him. You can do it. This round."

Was Ortega right? Could he actually knock Duncan out? It just might be possible.

At the bell, Duncan came out protecting his right arm and side, and Brent smiled. If Duncan kept his right hand low, he could be hit. This was it!

He feinted a right lead, crossed with a left hook that hit nothing but air!

Bam!

Sparks exploded inside his head and he reeled against the ropes.

Christ! Duncan had been faking. He still had plenty left in that right hand.

But not enough!

He'd taken Duncan's shot and was still on his feet!

Maybe that wasn't too smart. He was pinned against the ropes in a corner and Duncan was working him over with both hands.

But, amazingly, he was weathering the storm. Duncan had hit him twice on the chin and he was still up trading blows. Duncan's tired! His punches had lost power. Now! Inside! Move inside! Now!

Brent powered his right fist up in an uppercut that caught Duncan on the chin. Duncan staggered back and Brent followed, hitting Duncan again as hard as he could. Once! Twice! The jar from the blows on Duncan's jaw ran sweetly up Brent's arm.

Duncan fell backward to the canvas. This time the bell couldn't save him. He tried to get up at the six count but fell back, his eyes vacant. At the ten count, he wasn't moving.

Brent, standing in a corner, was suddenly aware of a bedlam of noise. He'd done it! He'd won!

Even when the referee walked over and raised his arm, he could hardly believe it and one thought kept driving through his mind. "What now? What the hell am I going to do now?"

Chapter Twenty-Nine

IT TOOK ALMOST two hours for Brent to work his way through the reporters, shower, dress, talk to more reporters and get in the waiting limo. It had been gratifying to see the ambulance parked at the stadium had left without him.

It was well after midnight when he arrived at the hotel. He was able to free himself from the few waiting reporters and from Ortega by saying—with absolute truth—that his swollen face was starting to ache and he was dead tired.

At the door to his room, Ortega told him, "I called Frankie. He saw the fight on TV. He wants you to call him."

"Okay. But I don't have his home number."

"Here." Ortega's smile, as he handed Brent a slip of paper, contained both a warning to Brent not to try to ace him out with Frankie, and a minor display of victory because he had Frankie's home number and Brent didn't.

"Okay. Can I use my room phone?"

"Yeah. Don't say anything stupid."

Inside his room, Brent put through the call to Frankie's home. Frankie answered on the first ring as though he'd been sitting with his hand on the phone.

"Frankie—"

Frankie cut loose with a flood of congratulations. "I knew it, *amigo.* I knew you could do it. How does it feel to be rich?"

"Rich?"

"Your end of the purse was a quarter million, my friend. The next one will be a hell of a lot more."

Two hundred and fifty thousand dollars? Brent had known the fight would make money, but he hadn't realized his purse would be that much. After all, he was almost totally unknown. Until now. A million? It wasn't out of the question now—win or lose.

"We're on our way," Frankie was saying. "I'll get you a shot at the champ."

Frankie's enthusiasm was so overpowering Brent wondered if he could be right. What if he really did have what it took to have a shot at the title? Maybe he could even take the title!

"Don't shit me, Frankie. Do you really think I could make it that far?"

"Yesterday, my friend, I'll admit I had doubts. You were good...damn good. The best I ever saw. But I didn't see you taking Duncan. But, God damn, *amigo*. You not only took him, you knocked him out. So today? Damn right. More and better training. I really think you could go all the way."

"You're not shitting me?"

"No, no. And to prove it, I'm going to get you a quality trainer—McCoy or Gil Clancy."

Frankie was serious. He might be able to go all the way. The idea raced through Brent's mind like wildfire, destroying every rational thought on its way.

World champion! The kid from Kansas. Champion of the world!

His folks would also be famous. His ex-wife would tear her hair out. And Maria? How could she resist him?

He was jarred back to reality when Frankie asked, "How'd the other thing go? You got everything else under control?"

Frankie's words drowned the fire in Brent's mind, leaving the bitter ashes of defeat. He could forget about any shot at the title. In a few days, this whole new world would come tumbling down. "Yeah," he answered. "We're set for tomorrow."

"Good. When're you coming back?"

Brent made a swift calculation. If Ortega was shepherding the dope, he wanted to arrive at the same time. "I'll come back with Ortega," he said. "When is he leaving here?"

"Tomorrow afternoon. You up to it? Why don't you take a few days? Rest. Enjoy the mountains."

"Naah. I like L.A. I'll come back with him."

"Okay, my friend. I'll see you at the gym."

Brent thought about the conversation as he cautiously walked down the deserted hall past Ortega's room to the stair well and started up the stairs. The buy had to be big. So how did they get the stuff over the border? The method had to tie in with the fight somehow. If he couldn't learn how, the DEA guys would have to follow Ortega from the airport. Eventually, he'd have to come together with the dope.

Fortunately, the fifth floor hallway was also deserted and he knocked softly on the door to five-ten, hoping he'd remembered the number correctly. He'd have a hell of a time explaining his presence to a stranger who might well scream at the top of his or her lungs at the sight of his beat-up face.

He let his breath out in a sigh of relief when the door was opened by Maria. "Hi," she said. "I was beginning to think you'd found someone better."

"Impossible," he said. He eased into the room and Maria closed the door.

The moment the door was shut, she threw her arms around his neck and kissed him, her warm lips moving gently on his swollen lips and cheeks. When she tilted her head back, she said, "That should make it well."

"It still hurts," he said. "Give me more."

She laughed. "You'll get more—and better—when it won't hurt." Her wide smile changed to one brimming with pride. "Oh, Brent, I knew you could do it."

"Then you knew more than I did. I still can't believe it."

She touched his face with delicate fingers. "I'll be glad when this is over. I can't stand to see you hurt."

"I'm getting used to it. Besides, it only hurts when I laugh."

She moved away from him, leaving his arms feeling empty and weary. "Would you like a drink? It might help."

"Okay. What have you got?"

She went to the kitchenette and opened a small refrigerator which the hotel kept stocked with various miniature bottles of liquor and liquors. "Most anything," she said. "How about some Amoretto? It's supposed to make you passionate."

"Better make it bourbon. I'm in no shape for passion."

She giggled and took a bottle of Jack Daniels from the refrigerator and placed it on the counter. "Then I'd better have bourbon, too, if I've got to stay an ice maiden."

She poured two water glasses a quarter full and added a similar amount of soda. She handed one of the glasses to Brent, then raised hers for a toast. "Here's to the next champion of the world."

"I don't think my luck can last that long," Brent said, but he drank the toast.

"Did you call Daddy?" Maria asked. "I'm sure he won't sleep a wink 'til you do."

Mention of Frankie's name chilled Brent's euphoria. "Yes. I called a few minutes ago. He was sitting by the phone."

"Did he ask about me?"

Brent stared at her as goose flesh prickled his skin. "He doesn't know you're here, does he?"

"No. I said I was flying to San Diego to visit a friend."

Brent's apprehension remained, but now it was different, hardened by jealousy. "Male or female."

She sucked in her cheeks and pursed her lips. "Why? Would it matter?"

"You know it would."

She smiled and sipped her drink. "It was a lie anyway. I flew straight up here." She looked at him and caught her lower lip with her teeth. "How long are we going to be here? I told daddy I'd be gone for days."

Brent could not look at her. The longing to take her in his arms was almost overwhelming. And the thought of spending hours—days—alone with her took over his brain, spinning it into a whirlpool of desire—a whirlpool with a vortex of despair.

"You can't stay," he said harshly. "If Frankie even suspects you're here, he'll... Well, you know him better than I do."

She put her drink down on the counter slowly, staring at him, her eyes luminous and inquiring. "I told you he doesn't know I'm here."

He turned to her. "Maria, believe me. You've got to go back as soon as possible."

"When are you going back?"

"Tomorrow. I've got to go back tomorrow."

"Then we only have tonight."

Invitation was naked in her eyes and in the way she moved toward him. Brent couldn't have resisted putting his arms around her if someone had held a gun to his head.

She molded her body against him, her firm muscles hot beneath his hands. "Brent," she whispered. "You can do anything you want."

Her words seared Brent's mind. Anything he wanted? Oh, God, he wanted her. He wanted to be champion. But the betrayal he'd soon have to make would end it all. He was about to lose everything he had ever dreamed of. Unless....

The impulse was so startling he went rigid and Maria looked at him, her eyes wide with alarm. "Are you all right?"

"Yes," he whispered and wrapped her in his arms again. "Oh, yes."

Because there was a way! A way he could have it all. It was so simple. All he had to do was call Hendrix and say that Frankie was clean! He could easily account for everything he'd told them so far—it had all been a monstrous mistake. Frankie was not the man they were looking for. He wouldn't have to betray Frankie, the man who'd been so good to him. He wouldn't have to betray Maria. He wouldn't have to make her hate him.

He could make love to her! Now. She wanted him. And it'd be all right. He could take her, knowing that soon they'd be married. Her ear was close to his lips. All he had to do was ask.

He opened his mouth, the wondrous words trembling on his lips. And he couldn't say them! Oh God, no. He couldn't sacrifice one betrayal for another!

Because if he turned his back on the truth, he'd be betraying everything in his life. Maybe for a time he could fool himself into believing he was happy and that he had it all. But he would know the lie. He'd be as evil as Frankie. Worse. Frankie had never betrayed his own principles.

If he married Maria, how long would it take before guilt turned his love to hate? If he won the championship, how long would it be before even that turned to ashes?

He stepped back, afraid to touch her for fear he'd never be able to let her go. "No, I can't."

She stared at him, stricken. Her tongue touched her lips, and the tears in her eyes tore at his heart. "You don't want me? Even for one night?"

"Want you? You know I do." He wanted to scream how much he wanted her. But could not. He had to find some way to avoid inflicting any more pain, on himself as well as her.

But, God, he wanted her. She was offering him her smooth, flawless skin, her soft breasts, her eager mouth. His hands were trembling and his voice was a harsh whisper as he lied, "But not like this. Not a one night stand in some damn hotel room."

She backed away from him, her face pale. "All right," she whispered. "I'll leave in the morning."

He went to her, drawn by the pain in her voice. "I'm sorry. I...I'll make up for it. I promise."

He tried to put his arms around her, but she shrugged him off and moved away. "Don't bother." She went to open the door.

Brent moved to the door, his gut twisting as he looked at her grim face, lifted proudly, the tears gone. "I'm sorry," he whispered.

"Sorry?" She stared at him, her eyes glistening with tears. "When you fight," she said, "I see something in you that scares me. You change. It's like you turn into some kind of killer. I didn't believe it was real. But now... Maybe inside you really are cruel."

Brent stood facing her, his hands at his sides, paralyzed, unable to make even a gesture of denial. He longed to pull her into his arms, to deny her cutting words. Because they were true. He was a killer. Fighting was only the proof. There his true nature came out. Outside the ring, he was filled with guilt and pain. But he was no less a killer.

When he was able to move, he put his hand over his face so she wouldn't see his pain. "I'll call you as soon as I get back," he said.

"Sure." Her voice was low, lifeless. "But you'd better ask Daddy if it's okay first."

As she turned her back and walked away, overwhelming despair wrenched a low moan from Brent's lips. Moving into the hall was the most difficult task he had ever forced from his body and his mind.

When he pulled the door closed behind him, the dull click of the lock sounded like the stroke of a headsman's axe.

Chapter Thirty

BRENT SLEPT LITTLE that night. His body shrieked for rest, but his mind was a pit bull with its teeth locked in the thought it still was not too late. All he had to do was tell one little lie and he could have everything. But it was a lie that could cost him every shred of self-respect.

And his brain responded with a thousand reasons why he should. What was self-respect compared to the rewards—Maria. Heavy weight champion of the world. Money. Fame. Everything.

Everything except his soul. Go on, his conscious said. Don't be a fool. Sell your soul to the devil.

But a terrible part of him knew he couldn't live with the self betrayal.

Betrayal? He'd have to betray someone no matter what he did. Why not betray himself? Either way, he'd lose! Which road to take?

By morning he knew. He'd always known. His road was set in stone. It was too late to change it now. Too late!

At nine a.m., Brent took the receipt for the package he'd left in the hotel safe and went to the lobby, certain that at this hour he wouldn't run into Ortega. His eyes burned from lack of sleep and his body hurt in so many places it was an effort to walk.

He was crossing the lobby when he saw something that brought him to a halt. Two uniformed policemen stood behind the registration desk talking to the hotel concierge. Two more policemen stood near the front door. Momentary panic gripped him. Could something have gone wrong? Were the police looking for him? Or Ortega?

He quickly dismissed the idea. If they wanted him, they wouldn't be standing around the hotel lobby. There had to be another explanation.

Brent walked boldly to the front desk. "Excuse me," he said to the desk clerk. The man turned and Brent shoved his receipt across the counter. "I'd like to pick up my package from the safe."

The clerk put his hands to his cheeks, looking so contrite Brent thought he was going to cry. "I'm sorry, Mr. Thomas," he said. "But the safe was robbed last night."

Brent felt a momentary pleasure. He'd guessed right. "Robbed? They got my package?"

The clerk's stricken look deepened. "I'm afraid so. He had a large gun. He forced the night clerk to open the safe. He took everything."

Brent tried to look bereaved. "That's terrible. Well, thanks anyway."

He turned to walk away and the clerk said, "But Mr. Thomas, the insurance..."

Brent said back over his shoulder. "It was of little value. Forget it."

In his room, Brent touched up the bruises on his face with Max Factor skin-colored makeup. When he put on dark glasses and pulled a cap low over his face, he was confident he couldn't be recognized as the fighter who'd been on TV the night before.

The walk to the Greyhound bus station loosened his sore muscles and gave him time to think about the robbery. Whoever had robbed the hotel safe had thought Frankie's drug money was inside. And the only one who could've known that was Jaime Ortega. Brent's suspicions that Ortega wanted to make him look bad had been right. If Ortega hadn't pulled off the robbery himself, he'd hired somebody. He would like to have seen Ortega's face when he opened Brent's package and found hotel stationary.

He walked past the Greyhound station, while he again made sure he was not followed. Then he doubled back and entered the station where he retrieved his bag from the locker.

He returned to the hotel and called Ortega from the lobby. Ortega sounded more surly than ever, and Brent had the feeling he hadn't slept well. He said he'd meet Brent in Brent's room, but Brent said no. He'd meet Ortega in the lobby. He didn't want to be isolated anywhere while carrying thousands of dollars, not when Ortega knew he'd have the money. Better to wait in the hotel lobby where two policemen remained.

A few minutes later, Ortega came out of the elevator carrying a briefcase. His face was drawn and pale, his eyes like those of a hungry weasel. They walked a block from the hotel before hailing a taxi. In the taxi, Brent casually asked Ortega if he'd heard about the hotel safe being robbed and Ortega, refusing to look at him, grunted an unintelligible answer.

At the Empire Motel, Brent waited in the taxi while Ortega went inside to check out the deal. Only a total idiot would walk into a strange place carrying thousands of dollars without first checking it out.

After a moment, Ortega opened the motel room's door and motioned to Brent that it was okay. Brent paid the taxi driver and told him to wait.

When he entered the motel room past Ortega, Brent thought about how easy it would be for Ortega to kill him and blame it on the trafficker.

But nothing happened. The trafficker sat at a small table near the curtained front window sipping a glass of dark red wine. He was squatty and dark, wearing a rumpled black suit. He had thinning dark hair which he combed forward and sideways to lessen the effect of a deeply receding hairline. His bushy mustache was salt-and-pepper. On the little finger of each hand he wore a ring with a huge diamond. His pierced ears displayed small loop earrings studded with diamonds. Apparently, dope trafficking paid well.

Another man—larger and wearing a loose-fitting dark gray suit that looked very expensive—sat on the edge of the motel bed watching Ortega and Brent with feral eyes. Near his feet were three cardboard cartons. The man's hands rested on his knees, but Brent was certain they could produce a gun as quickly as the hands of a magician. It made Brent wonder if Ortega was carrying a gun.

The deal was completed almost exactly as it had been in Acapulco. Ortega selected one of the cardboard boxes at random and took out a kilo of heroin wrapped in a thick layer of plastic. He put the kilo on the table, then used a pen knife to cut a small slit in the plastic. He raised the bag to his nose and sniffed. Brent could smell the odor of vinegar. He knew it was because the chemicals used in the manufacture of heroin created a sharp odor similar to that of vinegar.

Ortega grunted his satisfaction. "And the quality?"

"The usual. You know me."

"Okay. We take your word."

The trafficker nodded and smiled. "I have scales. Unless you would prefer to use your own."

"I'll use mine," Ortega said. He opened his briefcase and removed a roll of Scotch tape and a balance beam scale which he placed on the table. After sealing the cut in the bag with a strip of the tape, Ortega put the bag on the tray, then nudged the scale's weights over. It balanced out a slightly more than two thousand grams. One by one he took nineteen more bags from the boxes and weighed them. Each checked out within two or three grams of the same weight. Very professional. Very neat.

"Good," Ortega muttered. He nodded to Brent. "Okay."

Brent opened his bag and handed the trafficker Frankie's money.

The trafficker counted the money quickly, then said to Ortega, "Okay. How do you want to handle the delivery?" There was no mention of a receipt. People in the dope business operated on trust—or fear.

Ortega looked at Brent. "Your part is finished. I'll take it from here."

Brent's disappointment was edged with relief. He was glad his part of the deal was over. But it looked as though he'd have to find another way of learning how Frankie managed to get so much dope through Canadian and U.S. customs.

He nodded and went out the door. He got in the waiting taxi and had him leave. Ortega would have to find his own way back to the hotel.

The taxi dropped Brent a short distance from the hotel. From the lobby of a different hotel, he put through a collect call to Hendrix in Los Angeles using the name they had agreed on. Hendrix had no sooner got out his hello before he said, "What the shit is going on up there? I thought you were coming back with Ortega."

Brent wondered if he had heard Hendrix correctly. "Ortega? Yeah. We're leaving tomorrow."

"Like shit. Our guy said he checked out of the hotel over an hour ago."

"Checked out?" Brent's mind struggled to focus on the thought. Why would Ortega have checked out? Unless... "Damn! He's got the stuff. He never intended to come back with me."

Hendrix made a sound of disgust. "We still don't know how he's going to bring it in."

"It's twenty kilos. He can't very well carry..." He paused and gripped the phone harder. "The equipment. Ortega handles the equipment."

"What equipment?"

"Boxing stuff. We don't need much. I think it's shipped in a crate. Customs passes our stuff through without any inspection. I guess they figure that fighters aren't dopers."

"If the junk is in with the equipment, he'll watch it like a hawk."

"Find out what flight he's on. You can pick him up at the airport."

"We'll keep an eye on him, but shit, we don't want him. We've got to get Frankie and the dope together."

"I doubt Ortega would be stupid enough to take the junk back to the gym. He'll have to drop it off somewhere. It might give us the location of the lab."

"Yeah, well, that's something. Okay. I'll take care of it. What time does your plane get to LAX?"

"Six-thirty. Alaskan Air."

"Okay. Call me tomorrow. I'll fill you in on what happened."

"Okay. Talk to you tomorrow."

"One thing," Hendrix said.

"Yeah?"

"How much money you make on the fight?"

"Beats the hell out of me? Why? Can I keep it?"

Hendrix laughed and hung up.

Brent slowly hung up the phone. Tomorrow. If they could get Frankie and the dope together, tomorrow could mark a fateful Chapter in a lot of lives. Maybe even the final chapter for some.

Chapter Thirty-One

DESPITE HIS SLEEP being plagued by nightmares, sheer fatigue allowed Brent to sleep throughout the night.

The next morning, his body felt better, but depression had settled in his mind like a heavy weight. It was over. Everything he'd ever wanted was gone.

As soon as he was dressed, he went to a pay phone near his apartment and called Hendrix. "Hi," he said listlessly. "How'd it go?"

"Go? Shit," Hendrix exploded. "Ortega took a private jet. He didn't go through the usual baggage check. Our guys followed him from the airport, but he didn't stop anywhere. He went straight home, for Christ sake. We watched all night. Nothing!"

"What about the fight equipment? It could be in there."

"The crate's still in Canada. The Canadians checked it. Nothing. What the hell is going on?"

Stunned, Brent pulled the phone aside, trying to think. Where's the junk? When no answer came, he said to Hendrix, "Damned if I know. I'll try to find out. I'll call you back as soon as I know anything."

"You do that," Hendrix said tersely and hung up.

Brent stood holding the phone, his mind blazing with hope. A second chance. Call Hendrix back. Tell him that it was all a mistake. Tell him that Frankie was clean. Do it, you idiot!

He muttered an oath and hung up. When in the hell was he going to stop pretending he had a choice?

When Brent arrived at the gym he noticed that Frankie's big Cadillac was in its reserved parking spot. There was no sign of Maria's Porche. That was a relief. He wasn't sure his resolve could stand another attack. He was walking to the gym when he saw that his name had been stenciled on a parking spot next to Ortega's. His depression deepened. He wiped his hand across his aching face. The spot would never be used.

In the lobby he said hi to Carla who answered, "Hi, Champ." He grinned at her and she said, "Frankie wants to see you."

"Okay," he said. "Thanks."

Carla let him through the door, then called and told Frankie he was on his way up. Nobody ever walked into Frankie's office unannounced.

As he expected, the outer office was deserted. He knocked on the door to Frankie's office, and when the lock clicked, went inside, his nostrils flaring at the odor of cigar smoke. Brent again thought about how difficult it was going to be to catch Frankie in a raid. If he had anything to hide, he'd have plenty of time to destroy it by the time they got through all the barriers. You just didn't kick down a steel-reinforced door. Somehow, if they made a raid, he'd have to find a way to open the doors from the inside. Or Frankie would have to be caught out in the open.

Frankie heaved to his feet and ground out his cigar in an ashtray. Brent almost smiled. His name on the parking space and now this. It was the first time Brent had seen Frankie put out his cigar for anybody.

"Congratulations, *amigo.*" Frankie came around his desk and put his hands on Brent's shoulders. "But maybe I should start calling you 'champ'."

Brent exaggerated a wince. "Come on, Frankie. I'm not in that class."

"Yes, you are, my friend." Frankie waddled to the bar and took a bottle of champagne from the built-in refrigerator. "You just don't know it. You have no idea how good you are. How good you can be. But I do." He opened the chilled bottle and poured two whiskey glasses half full. He handed one to Brent and raised the other. "So, my friend. This is more than congratulations. This is to the future."

Frankie's words sent a shaft of pain through Brent. Frankie didn't know it, but his future was rapidly running out. He could not look Frankie in the eye as he said, "Thanks, Frankie."

Frankie moved back to his desk. "I've got plans for you. Big plans."

"You mean in your organization?"

Frankie shook his head. "No. That'll have to wait. We can't take foolish chances with your shot at a title match. From now on, I don't want you to even think about dope. I want you squeaky clean."

"What about you? Are you going to give it up?"

Frankie actually looked sad. "Impossible. I have too many...ah...responsibilities in that direction."

The way he said it made Brent believe Frankie would be taking his life in his hands if he tried to back away from his dealing. "What about Jaime?"

Frankie lifted his shoulders. "I'm going to have to go against my instincts there."

"How do you mean?"

"He'll have to remain your handler. At least, for a time."

"That's keeping it pretty close to me."

"I know. But Jaime is my primary courier. He understands what has to be done. But he doesn't understand money."

His primary courier? Could that mean Ortega was carrying the stuff personally? Those old Samsonite bags of his might be rigged with concealed compartments. Ortega was strong enough to carry twenty-two extra pounds in each one without effort. It seemed like a dangerous and stupid way to do it. On the other hand, Brent had seen the way customs officials waved Ortega and him through when they realized who he was. He would have to get the information to Hendrix as soon as possible.

"It doesn't seem to me," he said to Frankie, "there's much to understand. You've already made the arrangements. All the money guy has to do is hand it over."

Frankie nodded. "True. But sometimes we're talking real money here. A million or more. I'd prefer not to put that kind of temptation in Jaime's hands."

What Frankie didn't realize was that a million or more dollars was not enough for Jaime Ortega. Brent was quite sure Ortega wanted it all.

Brent considered putting another seed of doubt in Frankie's mind. If he could increase Frankie's distrust of Ortega, maybe Frankie would resume handling the money himself and it would enhance the chances of putting Frankie and the dope together.

"Speaking of money, did Jaime tell you what happened at the hotel?"

Frankie's eyes hooded and his body tensed. The change in him was so swift that Brent was startled. One moment he was warm and friendly. The next he looked as though he wouldn't hesitate if he had to kill you.

"What happened?"

"Somebody tried to rip off the money."

Frankie sat up straight. "Who? How?"

"Well, I had to make sure the money was safe. I didn't want to leave it sitting around the hotel room. So I had it locked up in the hotel safe."

"Of course," Frankie said. "That's what I'd do."

"Yeah. Except that the safe was robbed during the night."

"Robbed? They got the money? Why the fuck didn't you tell me?" Abruptly, his expression changed, becoming shrewd and calculating. "Wait a minute. You made the buy." He stared at Brent, disbelief in his flat, black eyes. "Didn't you?"

"Yeah. That part went off okay."

Frankie relaxed, just a little. "So how, if the safe was robbed?"

"I didn't put the real money in the safe. I put in a fake package, just in case."

Frankie stared at him a moment, then slapped his hands down on the desk. "Damn! They ripped off a fake package! Damn! Damn!" Then, with another of his mercurial changes, he stopped laughing and stared at Brent. "How did they know? How did they know you had the money in the first place?"

"Good question."

Frankie thought a moment. "Only three people knew about the money. You, Jaime and the dealer."

"The dealer had to work for somebody. He'd know, too."

"Yes. I'll talk to Quin—" He quickly corrected himself. "—to Corillo. Maybe his man is trying to go into business for himself."

"Yeah. Well, somebody was. I don't think it was a coincident the safe was robbed just when I put your money in."

Frankie nodded. "So? Where did you have the money?"

"Secret," Brent grinned. "I may have to use it again."

Frankie's eyes narrowed to slits. Then he laughed. "Okay, *amigo.* Whatever works." His eyes shifted and he lost his smile. "I'll look into this."

Brent hoped the seed of doubt was one that would bear Frankie a bitter fruit. Hopefully, he'd demand that Ortega show him the dope as proof of the buy. He would have to tell Hendrix to keep an eye on Frankie as well as Ortega.

A new thought occurred to Brent—one that stirred emotions. "What about..." He paused, trying to couch the question in terms that wouldn't antagonize Frankie. "What about Maria? If I'm out of the organization, is it okay if I see her?"

Frankie looked at Brent sharply, as though it was just occurring to him that there might be more to Brent's interest in his daughter than pure nepotism. "No. That stays the same."

"But if I'm out—"

"You know about the organization. That's enough."

The tone in his voice cut off any protest. And in a way, Brent was glad he had an excuse to keep away from Maria. She knew already that Frankie had issued orders for them not to see each other. She might not understand the reason, but she couldn't put the blame on Brent for ignoring her, even if she did think he was a coward for not defying Frankie.

Brent glanced at his watch. "Frankie, I've got to go. People coming in."

Frankie got up and reached for a fresh cigar. "No more instructing," he said. "Soon as I can get somebody else, you concentrate on yourself." He walked with Brent to the door. "I'll have your share of the purse in a day or two. Plus the dope money. My friend, you'll be a very rich man."

Walking down the hall to the elevator, Brent wondered what Frankie considered rich. As Brent's manager, Frankie had taken care of the details about the fight, so Brent didn't know for sure how much was involved. But it had to be in the hundreds of thousands. Duncan, of course, would get the lion's share even though he'd lost. But that would still leave a big chunk for Frankie. And the next fight would certainly be even bigger. His share could well be a million or more.

He had to wrench his mind away from such dreaming. There'd be no other fights. Not for him. There'd be no millions of dollars. There'd be no championship.

Still, it might not be too late to change his mind. It might not be too late to tell Hendrix it was all a mistake.

He walked faster. Why did that thought keep nagging him? He had to get this whole affair ended before it tore him apart. He had to cleave hard to the thought that even having a chance at being world champion had always been a chimera.

He didn't like to use one of the pay-phones in the gym, but he didn't trust himself to delay any longer. When he got through to Hendrix, he kept his voice low, his eyes darting to make sure no one was within earshot as he explained what he'd learned.

"I think Ortega brings the junk in those Samsonite bags of his."

"Twenty kilos. That's forty-four pounds."

"It's possible. Ten kilos in each bag. Ortega wouldn't even feel it."

"Yeah, I guess it's possible."

"If he went straight home last night, his bags must still be there. So he's got to drop them off somewhere—probably when he comes to the gym."

"Could be. Any idea when he'll be coming in?"

"No. But it shouldn't be too long. That junk must be burning a hole in his bags."

"If he's got it."

"That's right. If he's got it."

"Okay. We're keeping an eye on him. I'll pass it along."

"You might also keep an eye on Frankie. I don't think he trusts Ortega. He might want to do a little personal checking."

"We're already doing that."

"Oh. Okay. If anything changes, I'll give you a call."

"Call me anyway. If anything breaks on this end, I've got no way to get in touch with you."

"Right. I'll keep in touch."

Brent hung up and went into the gym. He was immediately besieged by fighters offering congratulations. The adulation in their eyes was unnerving. He wondered if it would still be there when his true identity was revealed. The fact he was DEA should have nothing to do with his work in the ring. Yet, he knew it would. Everything he'd done would be suspect. They'd probably believe the fights had all been arranged; the outcome planned to make his cover look good.

It was a lie, of course. Nothing had been arranged. But they wouldn't believe it. Nobody would. So any chance he might be able to resign from the DEA and pursue the title on his own would vanish with Frankie's bust.

The knowledge added to his depression, and when he began a light workout, he went through the routines mechanically, his mind bitter with hopelessness.

To shift his thoughts away from himself, he concentrated on Frankie. If Ortega had the dope, and if he took it to Frankie's secret lab, that still wouldn't help nail Frankie. If he was smart, he'd have no apparent connection with the lab. So all they'd net would be a bunch of peons and a few kilos of heroin.

Somehow, they had to get Frankie and the junk together. Anything less would be a total waste of the whole operation because Frankie would then know he was under investigation. He'd simply change his M.O. and keep right on dealing.

A short time later, Ortega came into the gym. He seemed to be in a particularly good mood. Brent actually saw him smile. And when Ortega smiled, something had to be wrong.

At lunch time, Brent drove straight to a pay-phone outside a nearby Thrifty Drug. He called the DEA and ask for Hendrix.

"I've been waiting for you," Hendrix said as soon as he recognized Brent's voice. "What the shit is going on?"

"What'da you mean? You lost him?"

"No, we didn't lose him. But something's screwy as hell. He came out of his place with the two Samsonite bags. But he didn't stop anywhere. He drove straight to the gym. No stops. The bags are still in his car trunk."

Brent held the phone to his ear, his breathing stopped, unable to comprehend. Maybe he'd been wrong. Maybe the junk wasn't in Ortega's bags. Which meant they were back to square one.

Brent was torn between relief and disgust. Without the dope, they couldn't bring down Frankie, which meant he would have to stay undercover. In fact, he could still claim that Frankie was clean.

At the same time he was disgusted with himself for being stupid. How could he have been so wrong? Ortega had to have the heroin. He just had to.

He started to say, "I could've sworn—"

His sentence was cut off by Hendrix. "That isn't all. We got an anonymous call. Some guy said that ten kilos of heroin were going be in Frankie's gym. He wants us to raid the place tonight."

"In the gym?" Brent tried to focus his confused thoughts. Frankie would never allow dope in the gym.

"What do you think? Was the call good or not?"

"God, I don't know. Maybe somebody's trying to set Frankie up—" Brent stopped, and his hand shook as he realized the truth. "Ortega."

"Ortega? What about him?"

Brent thought it through aloud. "He's been pissed off about me since day one. I think he'd like to take over Frankie's organization. He uses ten kilos for the setup, and keeps ten for himself."

"Sure. With Frankie out of the way, he could take over."

"How's he going to keep himself in the clear? He's in as deep as Frankie."

"We're not supposed to know that," Hendrix said. "You're the only one who can definitely tie him in. And he doesn't know you're DEA. It'd be your word against his. All he has to do is be someplace else when we make the raid. As far as we know, he's nothing but an instructor. Legitimate."

"Legitimate. Yeah. He's gonna get one sweet surprise when I testify."

"If the call was from him? And if it's on the level. Those are big ifs."

"Maybe I can check it out. What time are you supposed to make the bust."

"Nine o'clock. On the dot."

"That checks. We close tonight at eight. All he has to do is make sure Frankie and the dope are both here, and he isn't."

"And that the junk is where we can find it."

"If it's in those Samsonites, he'll have to take it out. They'd tie the dope to him."

"Can you keep an eye on him?"

"I can try. He'll have to get the junk stashed, probably in Frankie's office, and get himself out of the gym before you guys make the bust."

"Okay. We'll make the bust unless you call it off."

Brent groaned inwardly. Why did it always come down to his decision? He'd hoped that by this time it would be out of his hands and there'd be no more temptation to whipsaw his resolve. "Okay," he said tonelessly. "If I don't call, it's on."

"One thing," Hendrix said. "Keep your head down when you're watching Ortega. If he sees you, he'll have to kill you to keep himself in the clear."

"I'll keep that in mind," Brent said dryly.

"And if you're there when we make the bust, keep the hell out of the way. Nobody'll know you except Mark and me."

"Oh, I'll be there. Ortega will want to make sure of that, too."

When he got back to the gym it was almost the end of his shift. Normally, Ortega would be mad as hell at the length of time he'd taken on his break, but this time Ortega merely looked at him and snarled, "You ain't champion yet, Thomas. Until you are, get your ass back here on time."

Brent gave him a smile, which he was sure would irritate Ortega, and went back to work.

Time went by swiftly. News of his victories had brought several new fighters to the gym and these, added to the regulars, keep Brent unusually busy. But what was most disconcerting were the watchers. He was constantly surrounded by people watching every move he made, noting every word he uttered. At first, the adulation was flattering, but in time, it became annoying.

Just before six o'clock, Ortega came over to see him. "Excuse me, Champ. If you can tear yourself away, Frankie wants to see you."

Brent looked at the crowd of fighters working out. "Now?"

"No. At nine. You'd better be a little early."

Brent felt a chill of satisfaction. He'd guessed right. Ortega was laying the ground work to get him and Frankie together at the time of the DEA raid. "Okay. I can make that."

Brent watched Ortega walk away. The satisfaction of knowing he was right about Ortega was tempered with a deep sadness. The wheels were in motion that would destroy all the good things in Brent's life. It was now out of his hands. Almost. It wasn't too late to call Hendrix and call off the bust.

Except it was too late.

He couldn't reverse what he was. Somewhere along the vector of his life, he had assimilated a set of values that were set into his head like invisible bars. Even if somehow he could break free, if somehow he could override the voices of the past, his life would be so charged with guilt that it would be a living hell. He was trapped. Trapped by what he was.

For him, and for Frankie, it would all come crashing down at nine o'clock.

Chapter Thirty-Two

BRENT DIDN'T GO to dinner. He had to keep an eye on Ortega. At some point before nine, Ortega would have to pick up the heroin and bring it inside the gym.

By eight o'clock, Ortega still hadn't made his move. A few minutes after eight, when everyone had left, Brent went to Ortega who was putting away equipment.

"I'm going to get something to eat," he said. "Be right back."

Ortega nodded. "Yeah. Fine. Just be damn sure you meet Frankie at nine."

"Yeah, I will."

"Don't be late. Frankie don't like it if you're late."

And neither would you, Brent thought. "Yeah, okay," he said. "Don't worry."

Brent used his key to leave the gym through the lobby door and drove his car out of the lot. He parked it out of sight on the street and walked back to the gym. Letting himself in the front door, he left it unlocked. He hurried back down the hall and peered through the small windows in the hall doors into the darkened gym. He saw Ortega turn off the main lights, leaving only the security lights on, and exit through the large equipment doors that led to the parking lot, leaving the doors ajar.

Brent pushed through the doors into the gym and found a place in the boxing area where he could conceal himself in the shadows.

After a moment, Ortega came back carrying one of his two Samsonite bags. Brent smiled grimly. It was going down just as he'd figured. Ortega was planning a rip-off.

He watched Ortega carry the bag into the equipment room and click on the light. A moment later, Ortega reappeared carrying four of the plastic-wrapped, one-kilo packages of heroin. He crossed the darkened gym and went out through the gym doors into the hall. After a moment, Brent heard the elevator start.

Leaving his cover, Brent hurried to the equipment room. The Samsonite bag had been opened and a false bottom removed. Six plastic-wrapped packages remained in the bag. He'd been right. Ortega was ripping Frankie off for the other ten.

He had to see where Ortega was taking the junk.

Leaving the equipment room, Brent hurried to a new place of

concealment near the gym doors. When Ortega returned empty-handed and went into the equipment room, Brent eased out the gym doors into the hallway where he hid behind the drinking fountain near the door to the lobby. Most likely, Ortega was putting the junk in Frankie's outer office. He was taking a hell of a chance.

If Frankie came out of his office and caught him with his hands full of dope, it would be the end for Ortega. Any explanation he could manufacture would be punctuated by Frankie's .38 caliber bullet.

OUTSIDE, THE DEA raid party was beginning to move into position. In their cars, Hendrix and Duval called the surveillance team who'd been watching Ortega. "Fourteen-six. We're coming up. What have you got?"

"This is six. Your guy came out of the gym a while ago. He got a bag out of his car and went inside. He's still there."

"What about Frankie? Is he still there?"

"Yeah. His office light is on. His car's still here."

"Okay. Ortega should be coming out soon. When he does, stay with him."

"Okay. Ten-four."

"Everybody stay cool," Hendrix radioed. "We'll check out the situation."

"Ten-four," Inspector Hodges said, speaking for the group.

Hendrix cruised past the gym parking lot. There were two cars in the lot: Ortega's Camaro and Frankie's Cadillac. Marc Duval was about to report the situation when a red Porche entered the lot and stopped near Frankie's Cadillac.

"Christ," Hendrix muttered. "Who the shit is that?"

Duval picked up the radio mic. "This is two. We've got a situation here. Another car just pulled in the lot. Stand by."

Cruising slowly past the lot, Hendrix and Duval watched the door of the Porche open. A young woman got out and hurried toward the gym's front entrance.

"Oh, shit," Hendrix breathed. "That's Frankie's daughter. What the fuck is she doing here?"

The radio crackled and Hodges voice came through, "That car went in the lot. What the hell is going on?"

Using the radio, Duval said, "It's Frankie's daughter. She went inside."

"His daughter?" Hodges snapped. "What the hell is she doing here?"

"Beats me," Duval replied. "Our information is she isn't part of the organization."

"Well, it changes nothing," Hodges said. "They can sort that out in court. Everybody take your positions. Slow and easy. We don't want to tip Frankie off. Let's go."

Hendrix parked out of sight of anyone coming out of the building. He and Duval got out and checked their weapons. Hendrix carried his 9-mm automatic pistol. In addition to his holstered pistol, Duval carried a 12-gauge shotgun.

They eased toward the front door of the building, keeping to the shadows as much as possible. They were joined by Supervisor Hodges and the other Group 4 agents. On their left and right, they could see other agents moving into position.

Near the front doors of the gym, they crouched in the shadow of bushes and waited. Hodges checked his watch. "Seven minutes." He used his radio to call. "This is Fourteen-five. Hold your places. Wait for my signal."

"Seven minutes," Hendrix muttered. "My legs are gonna be dead."

"I hope to hell that front door is unlocked," Duval whispered.

"Should be. Brent said he'd leave it unlocked."

"Yeah, but Frankie's daughter went in. Maybe she locked it behind her."

"God, I hope not. I hate to break through glass."

IN THE HALLWAY, concealed by the water cooler, Brent waited for Ortega. He tensed. A sound. But not Ortega. Behind him. What the hell? In the dim hall night light, it was hard to see the face of his watch, but it looked like seven minutes to nine.

Seven minutes. Had somebody jumped the gun? Shit! They could ruin it all.

Continuing to crouch beside the cooler, he looked toward the door leading to the lobby. Abruptly, the door opened and Maria came in. Brent's heart leaped with a shock of alarm. Dear God! Why was she here? She wasn't part of this. He had to get her out of the building. She must not be caught with Frankie and the dope.

Then another thought stunned him. Any second now Ortega would be coming from the gym. If she accidentally bumped into him carrying dope, he'd have to shut her up.

But how could he warn her without blowing his cover? Shit! She'd know soon enough!

As she hurried past on her way to the elevator, he stood up and whispered, "Maria."

She turned, startled, her eyes wide, her body ready for flight. Then she recognized him and her face changed to a look of puzzled disbelief.

"Brent?"

"My God! What are you doing here?"

"I came to see Daddy. About us. I can't stand—"

She'd stopped near the doors to the gym—the doors where Ortega could appear at any instant. "Come here," he interrupted. "Quick."

She came to meet him, but hesitantly. Too slow. "Hurry," he said. "Damn it, hurry."

But she didn't hurry. Instead, she stopped before she reached him, suspicion in her eyes. "What are you doing here? Why are you hiding?"

He stepped away from the wall, going to meet her. "*Shhh*. Keep your voice down." Then he was beside her and he took hold of her arm and pulled her toward the shadows. "Over here. Quick."

She jerked her arm out of his grip and backed a step. "What are you doing? What is this?"

"Keep your voice down. I'll expl—"

Too late. The doors to the gym opened as Ortega shouldered his way through, holding four of the plastic-wrapped kilos. He took two steps toward the elevator before he became aware of Maria standing in the dim light. He stopped, his eyes wide. "Maria?"

She took a step toward him. "Jaime, what the hell is going on?"

"Maria," Brent said. "No." He reached for her. Dear God! She was already moving toward Ortega.

Ortega's eyes flicked toward Brent. He stiffened and one of the kilos slipped from his hands and fell to the carpet with a thud. He backed a step and Maria picked up the bag.

"What is this?" She looked at the bag more carefully and Brent saw her jerk as though she'd been pierced with a lance. "Oh, my God," she breathed.

Brent started toward Ortega, acutely conscious that if Ortega had a weapon, the hall had become a very bad place for him and Maria. "Take it easy, Ortega," he said.

Ortega's face twisted with a look that was charged with terror and anger. He had to believe Brent had come back from dinner early and would tell Frankie what he'd seen, meaning he was as good as dead.

As realization hit him, Ortega's face twisted and his eyes drew into a look of cunning. There were only two witnesses—and both were within reach.

Dropping the remaining packages, Ortega's hand lashed out and grabbed Maria by the hair. As he jerked her back against him, the package she was clutching slipped from her hands, and Ortega circled her neck from behind with his powerful left forearm. He reached his right arm behind her head, clutching his right bicep with his left hand to get leverage to break her neck.

Brent screamed in fear and rage and lunged forward. Oh, God! Too far!

But Maria twisted like a snake, turning inside Ortega's grip. She brought her knee up hard. She missed Ortega's groin, but her kneecap smashed into the thick muscle inside his thigh and Ortega grunted in pain. Instantly, Maria heaved upward on his circling arms with both hands. The move caught Ortega by surprise and she twisted away.

Ortega struck! His fist smashed against the side of her head, driving her against the wall with jarring impact, and she crumpled like a deflated doll.

Then Brent was on Ortega, reaching for his throat. He didn't want to hit. He wanted to feel Ortega's throat under his hands. He wanted Ortega to gasp for breath; he wanted his eyes to bulge with fear as he slowly died.

Ortega, reacting with the speed of a street fighter, brought his arms up levering Brent's arms wide. Ortega followed through, driving the edge of a rigid palm at Brent's throat.

Only Brent's finely-honed reflexes kept Ortega's blow from crushing his esophagus. But the edge of Ortega's hand caught him on the side of the neck with stunning force, and Brent felt as though his entire face was paralyzed.

He staggered back, gasping, and Ortega leaped at him like a panther, the edge of a rigid palm swinging in a powerful backhand blow at the bridge of Brent's nose.

Brent ducked and Ortega's blow caught him on the temple, exploding in his head like the blast of a shotgun and jagged red lightning flashed his vision.

Brent slumped to his knees, and Ortega clinched his fists together and smashed them into Brent's spine. Breath erupted from Brent's throat and darkness enveloped his brain, thickening with each of Ortega's heavy blows.

Maria! God, he couldn't let Ortega kill him. He had to save her!

Desperately, he reached out and his fingers taloned around Ortega's ankles. He yanked with all his remaining strength. He felt the floor shudder as Ortega hit with a bone-jarring crash.

Brent pushed to his feet, sucking air, and light began to pierce the blackness in his eyes. Dimly, he saw Ortega roll over. Holding the back of his head, Ortega pushed to his feet, his eyes wild with fear and hate.

Brent backed away. Time. He needed time for his head to clear.

But Ortega launched at him, driving his foot up at Brent's head in a vicious karate kick.

Brent scarcely saw the kick. It was as though he was looking through a curtain that made everything appear in slow motion. He reached out, his hands moving with all the speed of a sloth. To his surprise, his hand caught Ortega's foot. He twisted and thrust upward in the direction of the kick and Ortega went over backward, again hitting the floor hard.

This time when Ortega got up, he was wary, backing up a step.

Brent sucked in air. The brief seconds had cleared his head and he was able to focus his eyes. He had to stop Ortega before the body-builder's powerful arms tore him apart.

Attack! The best defense was an attack.

He moved in on Ortega, ready for the kick he knew would come.

There! Brent ducked, moving inside.

A feint!

Ortega had stopped the kick in mid-air. *Bam!* He smashed Brent in the side of the head with his fist.

But Ortega was off balance and there was little power behind the blow.

Brent drove up under Ortega's chin with his shoulder, sending Ortega flailing back against the gym's double doors, slamming them open with a crash.

Brent charged into the gym, hoping that he could catch Ortega before he recovered his balance.

Ortega was waiting—crouched and ready!

Ortega had been unable to use his karate effectively in the close confines of the hallway. But now he whirled, launching a powerful kick at Brent's head. Brent shoved the half-open door in front of him, and Ortega's kick tore it from its hinges.

Brent came in low before Ortega could regain his balance, rammed up under Ortega and cartwheeled him face down on the floor.

Now!

Brent dropped, piledriving his knees into Ortega's back, exploding breath from Ortega's lungs. Brent yanked Ortega's left arm up behind his back in a hammerlock. He wrapped his other arm around Ortega's neck and squeezed.

Ortega gritted a curse and surged to his feet, dragging Brent with him.

Brent held on, applying pressure to Ortega's throat and Ortega flailed with his free arm, fighting for air.

Suddenly, Ortega smashed his head back again and again, battering at Brent's face!

Brent lowered his head, taking the blows on his forehead. But his grip loosened and Ortega got his free hand behind Brent's neck and snapped forward and down, catapulting Brent over his back.

Brent slammed into a rack holding barbells and weights and the rack fell with a crash that shook the building. He landed on his back on one of the press benches, his senses reeling. Before he could recover, Ortega lifted a two hundred pound bar bell and slammed it down toward Brent's throat.

Brent rolled aside and the bar bell shattered the bench with a crack like a cannon shot.

Ortega snarled and lifted the bar bell again, driving it down toward Brent's head. Desperately, Brent's hands came up. He grabbed the bar, stopping it inches from his head. Ortega leaned forward, putting his weight on the two hundred-pound bar, and for a moment they were balanced, their muscles straining, their eyes locked in violent hate. Then, slowly, Brent began forcing the terrible weight up, his face contorted with agony.

Now!

He swung his arms back and released his grip, at the same time bringing his knee up between Ortega's legs. Ortega, pulled by the weight and pushed by Brent's leg, went over Brent's head as the weight smashed to the floor.

Brent struggled to his feet, gasping for breath. He tried to move around the shattered bench to reach Ortega before he could recover. Too slow. Ortega was on his feet, staggering back, a twelve-pound dumbbell clutched in his right hand.

He swung the dumbbell like a club at Brent's head.

Brent twisted and the heavy dumbbell hit him on the left shoulder. Pain stabbed through his body and his arm went numb.

Ortega charged, the dumbbell swinging.

Brent retreated, his left arm dangling. If Ortega hit him again, it'd be over.

Ortega, sensing the kill, swung wildly, his eyes brilliant with hate, desperate to smash Brent's skull.

Brent, timing one of Ortega's wild swings, came in under it. *Bam!* He drove his right fist into Ortega's solar plexus. Again. *Bam!*

Now the nose! *Bam!* Brent felt cartilage shattering under his fist. Ortega's eyes rolled. He dropped the dumbbell as he fell to his knees, gagging, his eyes glazed with pain.

Suddenly, the gym lights blazed and a voice said, "What the shit is this?"

Brent turned. Frankie! He was standing just inside the broken door, clutching a revolver in one hand and a kilo of heroin in the other.

"What's going on?" he snarled.

Brent jerked his head toward Ortega. "Ortega! He was ripping you off."

Ortega was on his knees, blood from his broken nose running down his face and chest. "Him," he snarled. "It was him! Kill him! Kill him!"

Frankie stared at Brent and took a step forward. The muzzle of the gun moved. Pain tore the word from his chest. "Brent?"

Brent shook his head. "It's a lie, Frankie. It was him. He was ripping you off."

Frankie's eyes slid to stare at Ortega, his face twisted with sudden fury. The muzzle of the gun followed his gaze, centering on Ortega's head.

Ortega paled and he snarled, "No. It was him!"

Frankie help up the plastic bag. "This was yours."

"He took it!"

The gun wavered uncertainly, Frankie's finger tensing on the trigger, his eyes darted from Brent to Ortega.

"Maria," Brent said. "Ask Maria."

"Maria?"

Frankie must not have seen his daughter in the darkness of the hallway. "She's in the hall," Brent said. "Ortega hit her."

Frankie started to turn toward he door, and Ortega lunged at Brent, sending him crashing into Frankie. The gun exploded with a deafening roar and Brent felt a hammer blow in his chest and a bright, burning pain.

My God, I'm shot!

The thought that flashed through his mind as he slumped to the floor was wonder at what it would be like to be dead.

But for some unfathomable reason his eyes remained open, his mind clear. He was able to watch in detached amazement as Ortega clutched at Frankie, trying to wrestle the gun away. There were two more muffled explosions just as Maria staggered through the doorway.

Outside, Hendrix had surged to his feet when he heard the first shot. "What the hell!"

"It came from inside," Duval said. "Let's go."

Hendrix yanked the door open and leaped into the lobby followed by Duval and the other agents. He raced across the lobby just as two more shots sounded. Finding the door leading to the hallway, he yanked at the handle. Locked!

"Shit," he exclaimed. "Duval, there's got to be a button."

Duval leaped over the reception counter. "Shit. There's buttons all over hell."

"Push them all!"

Frantically Duval pushed buttons while Hendrix yanked on the door handle. Suddenly, there was a buzz and the door came open so quickly Hendrix staggered back. Regaining his balance he charged into the hallway with Duval and the others at his heels.

He ran ahead toward light spilling into the hallway through the shattered gym doors, his 9-mm clutched in his hand.

Maria Rodriquez stood just inside the doorway, her hand to her mouth, her eyes wide and staring. Hendrix shoved her aside and went through the doorway at a crouch, his gun leading the way. He could feel Duval's hand on his back just like always.

Like the wink of a camera shutter, his eyes clicked a picture of Brent Thomas on his back on the floor, blood staining his shirt. Frankie was lying face down. What surprised Hendrix was that he didn't think that Fat Frankie was capable of lying face down. A man he recognized as Jaime Ortega pointed a revolver at him. He saw fire come out of the pistol's muzzle just as he brought his own gun in line.

He heard the report from Ortega's gun at the same time that a sledge hammer hit him in the head.

Boom! The sound of Duval's shotgun almost ruptured his eardrum and he saw Ortega's shirt shred. Now there was a real hole!

Then everything went black. The last thing he heard was Arty and Sandy's automatics spitting with that ineffectual-sounding 9-mm pop.

THE SILENCE WAS so abrupt Brent could clearly hear his ears ringing from the shotgun blast. His nostrils wrinkled from the ugly smell of burned cordite and the metallic odor of fresh blood. He stared at Hendrix who was lying on his side almost as though he was sleeping. But a trickle of blood poured from a neat, round hole on the left side of his forehead. Ortega! The son-of-a-bitch had been a hell of a good shot.

His eyes swung as though pulled by a string toward the other agents. They were staring down at Hendrix as though they couldn't believe—or didn't want to believe—what they saw.

Hodges broke the tableau. He reached down and picked up a plastic-wrapped package. "Here it is." Relief was in his voice. If they hadn't found any dope, they'd be in a pot full of shit. "Powder on the table," he said. "Powder on the table."

Duval watched a thin trail of Hendrix's blood seek out a pool of Ortega's. The two came together forming a single, silent bond.

"Yeah," he whispered. "Powder on the table."

Chapter Thirty-Three

TWO DAYS LATER, Brent sat uncomfortably in a chair in the Group 4 bay. His left arm was folded across his heavily bandaged chest and secured so it was immobile. Everyone had told him for what seemed like the thousandth time how lucky he was that the blow from the dumbbell had broken no bones and Ortega's bullet had struck him at an angle and glanced off a rib, plowing around beneath his skin and exiting under his armpit. The rib was cracked and he'd lost enough blood to make him a little weak for a few days, but there was no permanent damage. After two days in the hospital he'd insisted on coming to see Duval.

Duval sat at his desk, staring listlessly at the desk of his partner. Brent realized Duval was in a kind of shock. He was obviously trying to work up the courage to clean out Hendrix's personal effects. Sandy and Arty had volunteered to do it for him, but he'd refused their help. Hendrix had been his partner; it was his job to clean up his desk.

"I was too fuckin' slow," he muttered. "All I had to do was pull the damn trigger. I had him cold."

"It wouldn't have helped," Brent said. "Ortega got off his shot too fast. There wasn't half a second between the time you guys came through the door and he fired."

Duval looked at him uncomprehendingly. "Half a second?" He shook his head. "I can't believe it."

Brent turned away, unable to look at Duval's face any longer. But Duval couldn't hurt any more than he did. Duval had lost a partner and a friend; he had lost the girl he loved. "I wonder if it was worth it," he murmured.

Duval's head lifted, and he stared at Brent, the dark circles under his eyes giving him a haggard drawn look. "Worth it?"

Brent's voice sounded as dull in his ears as Duval's stare as he said, "People dying. For what? The idiots out there keep right on buying the damn junk. They don't give a damn. Why should we?"

Duval's eyes came into focus with a maniacal gleam. "There are some things you don't give up. Jim Hendrix wouldn't give this God damned world to the fucking goons, no matter how many ignorant bastards are out there helping them. Worth it? How the hell should I know?" He put his hand to his face for a moment as though to press back the pain. "No," he said softly. "The bastards don't get him for nothing. They'll pay. I'll see to that."

He turned his back on Brent and resolutely began putting Hendrix's affects in a paper sack. The only time he faltered was when he picked up a picture of Hendrix with his wife and two children. He shoved the picture in the sack.

When he finished, he carefully folded over the top of the bag and stapled it shut, the sound of the stapler like miniature exclamation points in the quiet room. Clutching the package in both hands as though it contained all the mortal remains of his partner, he walked out.

Silently, the other agents watched him go. When they turned back to their paper work, they didn't talk to one another.

Brent sat for a moment gazing at Hendrix's bare desk. How odd that all evidence of a person's existence could vanish so completely in such a short time. If anything happened to him, it would take an even shorter time to wipe away all evidence of his existence. At least Hendrix had left a wife and children. He didn't even have that.

He closed his eyes, remembering. He had given up two chances at immortality—marrying Maria and becoming heavy-weight champion of the world.

Now he had to make another decision. Did he want to continue with the DEA? It could very well mean going undercover again. More lies and more lives ruined. Could he face that again? And if he did, would he become so inured to misery, so inured to lying that it would have no effect on him?

The badge he wore for the first time hung from his jacket pocket with the heavy weight of responsibility. But it was also lightened by the buoyancy of pride. Men—good men—like Hendrix had died for what that badge stood for. There were, of course, those who would call them fools.

As long as he wore the badge, he would be a man apart. Like every agent, he'd continually be torn by the nagging thoughts. Was it worth it—the long, hard hours?—the deceit?—the stress of worrying about being found out?—of going through one door after another, knowing there might be some spaced-out freak on the other side waiting to kill him?—the many hours away from his family?—trying to do a job-many people didn't want done?

And the alternatives? What if there were no Hendrixes and Duvals? It was the fools like them and the other agents who kept the wolves from the flock.

He straightened painfully and stood up. He trailed his hand across the top of Hendrix's desk as he went by. His jaw quivered. Already there was a fine patina of dust.

"What hospital is Frankie in?" he asked Sandy.

Sandy looked at him, his lips thin. "Why? You're not going to see the son-of-a-bitch?"

Brent's angry retort vanished before it came. "Yes," he said softly. "I hear he's dying."

The glare left Sandy's eyes. "Yeah. Okay. He's at County General. Prison ward. I'll have Zylo clear you in."

As he turned to go, Brent looked around the room. It was hard to believe that in a day—a year maybe—some of these men might be dead. Maybe all of them. Maybe, he corrected, all of us.

AT THE MASSIVE County General Hospital, Brent parked the Caprice in an area reserved for hospital staff. He didn't give a damn if they did tow it away. The government owed him a fucking parking space.

Inside he was directed to the prison ward where as soon as he identified himself, he was cleared by the uniformed guards of the sheriff's office. After checking his gun, a pretty nurse led him through a ward lined with cots, each with a patient. In a corridor that separated individual rooms, she stopped in front of one and said, "He probably won't know you. He's heavily sedated."

"Okay."

She reached to push the door open and Brent asked, "Is he going to make it?"

The nurse's eyes flickered to Brent's badge. If he'd been a family member her answer might have been different, but she shook her head slightly. "Short of a miracle, no."

She pushed the door open. Before Brent entered, he slipped his badge case inside his jacket pocket. The nurse's eyes told him she understood.

Frankie lay in a hospital bed with his eyes closed, breathing fast and shallow. An oxygen tube was under his nose. An IV tube ran to a needle in his left arm. Maria stood beside the bed staring down at her father. Carmen sat in a chair next to the bed. Her once-gorgeous eyes were red, sunken, and dark. Her once-beautiful face had grown old and gray, sagging in lines of age and sorrow. A priest stood at the end of the bed, his head bowed, intoning phrases in Latin.

When Maria saw Brent, her lips pulled back and she snarled, "Why are you here?"

Brent couldn't answer that clearly, even to himself. "I want to see Frankie."

"Get out!" Her voice was low, cutting. "We don't want you here."

Brent stared at her. They were the words he'd dreaded for weeks. And he'd been right. They pierced him like poisoned darts. But he accepted them with prepared stoicism. "Frankie would," he said.

Maria's lips clamped shut and she walked past him out the door, her back rigid, taking care not to touch him as she passed.

Brent ran his hand over his face. It felt like the face of a stranger.

Carmen slowly stood up, her fists clinched. "Murderer! You lying, murdering bastard!" The venom in her voice caused the priest to look up, his concentration broken.

"Please believe me," Brent said. "I didn't want this to happen."

Her eyes blazed with incandescent fury as she spat, "I hope you rot in hell! Forever!"

The priest turned to look at Brent, and made the sign of the cross as though to ward off the curse.

"I'd like to talk to Frankie," Brent said, knowing it was a useless request.

"No!" Her fingers, instead of forming into fists, flexed like the claws of a tiger, and for a moment, Brent thought she was going to spring at him. Her lips drew back baring feral teeth. "Get out."

Brent's breath came out in a sigh. "Okay." He took one last look at Frankie. He was surprised at how small he looked in the hospital bed. It was as though all his bulk was draining away with his life. It wasn't the picture of Frankie he wanted to remember. He turned to go.

"Brent." It was more a whisper than a word. Both Brent and Carmen looked at Frankie. His eyes were open.

Brent took a step toward him. "Hello, Frankie."

Carmen leaned over the bed. "Oh, my God. *Franquito!* Don't leave me!" Her eyes swung toward the priest for support.

"It's all right," Frankie whispered. "Let me talk to Brent."

"But, *Franquito—*"

Frankie's hand spasmed on the white bed cover. "*Vaya,*" he said as loudly as he could. "*Llevemos un momenta.*"

Carmen slowly straightened as though she'd been slapped, tears washing her hollow cheeks. When she looked at Brent, the sorrow in her eyes became suppressed rage and she stalked from the room. The priest hesitated, then followed, gently closing the door.

Brent moved to Frankie's side. "Frankie," he said. "I'm sorry...about this."

Frankie made an attempt to smile. "I know, *amigo.*" His eyes focused on Brent's bandages. "You got hurt?"

"Not bad. I'll be okay. They tell me you're doing okay."

Frankie's head moved in a miniscule shake. "No. I don't have long."

"Frankie, I never meant for you to get hurt."

"I know, *amigo.*"

"It was a job. That's all it was."

"I believe you." Frankie's voice was a mere zephyr of sound, barely audible. "I'm sorry about Jim."

Brent was glad Frankie knew about Hendrix. It took much of the onus from Frankie's death, making it easier to talk to him. "Yes," he said. "We all are."

"Brent." Brent leaned closer and Frankie's eyes probed his face. "I can forgive the deceit. That's part of your job. I understand that." Frankie paused, fighting for breath. "But you and Maria... The pain you've caused her, I can never forgive."

Brent stared into Frankie's eyes in disbelief. Frankie was accepting no responsibility for anything. He was the one who'd caused the pain. He'd started it the day he started dealing. It was all his fault. All of it!

But why tell that to a dying man? He'd soon be explaining to God.

"Go now," Frankie gasped. "Send in the priest. I want him here when I go."

When Brent looked at him, it wasn't Frankie he saw. It was Hendrix and Ortega lying in their own blood. It wasn't Frankie fighting for breath. It was a baby in Mexico. He put his mouth close to Frankie's ear. "The priest won't do you a damn bit of good, Frankie. God knows about the babies."

Frankie convulsed and his eyes rolled. His hands were clutching at the bed cover as though he was trying to keep from slipping into hell.

Brent held the door open for the priest. "He wants you."

Carmen rushed past him, followed by the priest. Brent closed the door gently.

Maria was standing in the corridor with her shoulder against the wall as though she'd fall without its support. Her handkerchief was a sodden mass.

Brent stopped as anger drained from him. Despair swelled and rolled inside him. The pain was so strong he wondered if it would ever go away.

"Maria." She didn't look up. "I'm sorry. I'm sorry I couldn't tell you. I wanted to but..." He took a long shuddering breath. "But there was one thing that wasn't a lie. I love you. I always will."

He was walking past her when she said, "How could you do it? That's what I don't understand."

He stopped. Her eyes were luminous with tears. But the rage was gone and he felt a ray of hope break through the darkness of despair.

"How could I do it? When I started, I didn't know you. When I did, it was too late."

"But the lies. How could you lie like that?"

"I don't know. How could Frankie and your mother lie to you for so many years?" She was silent and he continued. "I guess when we met, it was already too late."

Her eyes slowly closed in anguish and tears gathered on her lashes like mist. "I know. But...it hurts so much. All the lies. I feel like my whole life is a lie." She pushed away from the wall. "I have to help my mother. She'll need me now."

She moved to go and he touched her shoulder. She stopped, her back to him, her shoulders slumping.

"I still love you," he said. "That will never change."

"I know," she whispered. "I love you, too."

An unbelievable happiness drove through Brent's pain.

She turned her head to look at him, her eyes laden with grief. "But I hate what you did. I don't even know you."

And now, she never would. Her memory of him would always be of a liar—of the man who'd caused the death of her father. Brent put his hand over his eyes. He couldn't look at her, not with that hurt in her eyes.

"I have to go," she said and walked away.

"Maria." He put all the hope in his heart into his voice. "Can I call you?"

She stopped, but didn't turn. "You must give me time," she said wearily. "A long, long time."

She walked away down the long, polished hall.

Brent took the elevator to the ground floor and walked out into the California sunshine. He drove out of the hospital lot, driving aimlessly, not caring where he went. He didn't want to think, to remember. He found himself driving past a high school, and he stopped to let a group of laughing teenagers cross the street.

On the other side of the street, standing in the shade of a huge, ancient pepper tree, two young men were dealing what looked like crack-cocaine to a group of school kids. They didn't even bother to hide.

Brent drove away, tears running down his cheeks.

~ * ~

Robert L. Hecker

ROBERT L. HECKER was born in Provo, Utah but grew up in Long Beach, CA., graduating from high school just as the U.S. entered WWII. Joining the Air Force, he flew thirty missions over Europe where he was awarded the Distinguished Flying Cross and five Air Medals. After the war, he began writing radio and TV dramas, then moved on to writing and producing more than 500 documentary, educational and marketing films on subjects ranging from military and astronaut training, nuclear physics, aeronautics, the education of Eskimos and Native Americans, psychology, lasers, radars, satellites and submarines. He is currently writing several movie screenplays as well as other novels.